THE
RED
THREAD

Book Five of The Chronicles of Eirie

PRUE BATTEN

AUTHORS NOTE.

Readers may remember that I wrote a four book fantasy series called *The Chronicles of Eirie* beginning in 2008. The first pair of books are intimately connected, being Parts One and Two of Adelina the Traveller's extraordinary experiences in Eirie, a world of my creation. Books Three and Four are standalones but involve characters that readers would have come to know within the world of Eirie.

In this new book, there is no real need to have read the previous Chronicles but if a reader wants to familiarise themselves with the Han, one of the provinces in the world of Eirie, then I suggest they read *The Shifu Cloth*.

I had always wanted to return to Eirie to write another fantasy. Notably to the Han because thanks to my father, I have an interest in Asian culture on which both this book and *The Shifu Cloth* are loosely based.

Serendipitously, a legend popped up one day in my reading. Simply, it read thus:

'An invisible red thread connects those who are destined to meet regardless of time, place or circumstance. The red thread may stretch or tangle but it will never break.'

In Asian culture, it's believed there is an unseen red thread that connects those who are destined to meet and fall in love. In China, Yue Lao, the God of Fate, is the deity who decides to whom the red threads will be attached. The people joined by the thread will always connect, in spite of anything that might happen.

The idea of a thread weaving through the story as an emblem of Fate was a gift to me as a writer, and whilst I manipulated the legend slightly, my characters threads wove and knotted and finally led to them to a point of no return – a situation predicted by Yue Lao when he appeared to each of them on their journey.

CONTENTS

CHARACTERS:

The Han

Ming Xao – Emperor of the Han

Chi Nü – Celestial Goddess of Weaving

Kitsune – Terrestrial Fox Goddess, sometimes called Fox Lady

Lien – daughter of the Shue House, the First House of Silk, and betrothed of the emperor.

Heng – maidservant to Lien.

Sun Sen – First Minister, Lord High Chamberlain of the Han Imperial Court

Yue Lao – Terrestrial God of Fate

Chimei – a vicious God, sometimes called the God of the Mountains

Huapigui – the spirit of a hungry woman who kills. Perhaps a shapeshifter

Vetala: a Raji blood-drinking spirit

Pymm

Iolanthe – a Pymm siofra

Flavia – a Pymm siofra and sister to Iolanthe

Amaranthe – a Pymm siofra and
sister to Iolanthe and Flavia

Veniche

Gallivant – a hob

Maximilian – Gallivant's eldritch mastiff

Trevallyn

Maeve Swanmaid – an eldritch swan-being – a shapeshifter

Seraphina – wise woman and healer, eldritch

Hester – housekeeper and gentlewoman
in Seraphina's house. Eldritch

THE PROLOGUE

'She weds him tonight,' said Chimei of the Han, 'She will be in the palace and will be able to find the map.'

Kitsune looked the God over – a man with cruel eyes and a swagger when he walked. 'Or else?' she asked, knowing full well that this time, it was no idle thing the Spirits toyed with.

She remembered a mortal man once who had diced with an Other, Huapigui by name, a shapeshifter. It was a mere dalliance of emotions. The poor mortal hadn't realised. He simply fell in love with a beautiful woman who appeared regularly when he took his goats to pasture on the mountain slopes.

Huapigui had undressed, displaying comely attributes, skin like satin and beguiling dark eyes fringed with thick lashes. She beckoned and they made love. Although love would not be how Kitsune would describe the emotion emanating from the Other as she reached for the heights of pleasure. Huapigui left the mortal almost immediately.

Done.

Bored.

Onward.

The mortal though, mind-struck, searched for her despite that his goats had become thin and begun to die. Single minded, he craved her like a drug, and finding her bathing alone by a river, he crept upon her, caught her and raped her under a Han willow, where the light was shadowed and the place seductive.

But nothing is secret from Others. They swore revenge for their sister.

They twisted the man's mind to a rag, sending him mindlessly searching for the woman he claimed loved him but whom he could never find. He trod league upon league beyond the walls of the Han and into the high Longma mountain range where if he looked down, he could have seen the rocky Mikal Desert of the Raj.

But the cold ate parts of his nose, his feet and hands. The haunting naked image of his consort gave him a forever-burning energy to place one foot in front of the other. He dwindled to rattling bones, his eyes dry and almost frozen, and he fell, still feeling such lust for the Other he had abused.

She came to him as he lay there and with the worst charm of all, she killed him, his body shattering like glass, the cullet becoming dust and the dust flying down the mountain range to the Mikal Desert.

Camel trains say that when the wind blows, one can hear the howls of pain as the mortal bones shattered.

The Gods could be cruel…

'Kitsune, don't play games,' another said, Vetala from the Raj, his head wrapped in a turban of vermilion silk. It was rare to see him dressed in bright silks as he preferred the colours of the night, hunting fresh-blooded prey. 'Throughout the Han, the Raj and the rest of Eirie – every Other realm is under threat because of the existence of that map.'

'What nonsense! You know you can move a gate when-ever you wish! So why is this map so important?' She looked around the crowd of Immortals and could almost smell the desire for a hunt. 'You all play games at mortal expense, your egos blown out, because Ming Xao, young Emperor of the Han, explored Eirie with diligence and subterfuge and in three years, discovered hidden gateways to our lives. How lazy and fatuous we have all become!' Kitsune paced back and forth, languid white furs trailing behind her. 'Sad. Or is it? Think. Even if mortals have knowledge of the secret entries to our worlds, what can they do if they use them? They have no powers; they have no enchantments. They would be babes to your slaughter,' she spun round, 'and I use that phrase very lightly.'

'Enough!' Chimei thundered, slamming his fist against his palm. 'No mortal, Kitsune, has the right to such knowledge as he possesses. No one! Despite that we can move gates at will. There are lessons to be learned here! This girl will do our bidding. We cannot enter the Palace grounds because some Spirit,' he eyed Kitsune as if he blamed her, 'has put around a barring enchantment. But it is weakening as we speak. If by moonset either the Emperor, or the new empress does not hand over the map, then there will be consequences.'

'You will use *her* as a lever?' Kitsune began.

'She is expendable. We will use her as we want. As for his life, it is forfeit already. Perhaps even the life of the entire Han, even the entire world of Eirie!'

'You would unleash such hardship on a world that has no knowledge of this map, all because one person transgressed?' Kitsune snarled, her lips drawing back from white teeth. Her amber eyes slitted. 'Fools! You will upset the balance. Your existence, once mortals are threatened with death, becomes meaningless. No one to tag, chase, tease, wound. Their existence gives dimension to yours,' she derided, and then, even more acidly, 'Think on it as you overreact!'

Chimei flew across the glade, grasping at her throat, squeezing, but with a flick of her furs, Kitsune vanished and then reappeared behind him, becoming her beautiful white clad self again. She liked mortals, dammit! She and the Emperor's last Almost-Wife had grown to respect one another. For beings with no enchantment at their fingertips, they were innately resourceful.

She thought quickly and then walked back toward Chimei. He towered over her, filled with ire. Above him, thunderclouds began to roll across the Heavens and the air of magick crackled.

'I shall be your conduit,' she said. 'Lien of the First House of Silk will do my bidding.' Kitsune was magnificent in her furs as she swept an ice-cold gaze around the gathered crowd. 'If any of you step in and threaten the Emperor or his Would-be Bride, then you shall feel my wrath!' In contrast to the vicious chill of her expression, her words scorched the earth in front of them.

'Why should we entrust you with this?' Vetala laughed, razor-like claws sliding down spines as he spoke. 'What have you ever done that would make us think you capable?' The crowd sniggered and Kitsune's blood pounded in her ears.

But she remained calm, a magnificent enigma that none could really claim to know. A loner, not a part of their company. 'Because I can wheedle life blood from a river stone,' she shrugged. 'And I have a way with mortals…'

A snakelike murmur hissed from the glossed and silked gathering and a vote was called. Three quarters of the company agreed unwillingly, the remaining quarter sat silent and angry, a freezing air wrapped around them.

'The job is yours, Kitsune,' Chimei snarled. 'But hark to me. From a small village in the far reaches of the Han, a message has already been sent which will help the Emperor make up his mind. By midnight this night, the Emperor or his bride must hand you the map. If they do not, then their lives are forfeit, along with anyone else whom *we* deem guilty of a crime against Others.'

A wind blew through the glade and all vanished except for the Fox Lady and she stood for only a moment, before she too disappeared to find a place where she could watch Lien of the First House of Silk and gauge the right time to tie her to an ethereal obligation.

***

As the Others left that fateful glade like a sweet-smelling but deeply poisonous mist, and after Kitsune, the Fox Lady, had disappeared like a white bird bent on swift migration, Chi Nü, the Goddess of Weaving, slipped from her hiding place amongst fallen trees and finely woven spiderwebs.

Her heart hammered and she could have wept if she had time, for she had even stronger ties to mortals than Kitsune and now she feared for their lives…

CHAPTER ONE
Ming Xao

'Ming Xao,' a tight voice sounded behind him – his friend of longtime journeys. 'You play with fire. I have warned you!'

Ah, she had.

But in those days he had not listened to her, this quiet and beautiful Goddess of Weaving. Named Chi Nü, she had cautioned him not to draw *this* map with its forbidden information. He smoothed the long doubtful parchment with his palm. The ink had dried and so he laid down the brush over a small white porcelain dish.

The map stretched along the table like a delicate river and in a quick glance, the spidery black lines were like so many wavelets. If one had no knowledge, the map represented daily life across the world of Eirie – all the provinces that Ming Xao had visited in his travels. The images of trees, mountains, lakes, cliffs, seas and people told the story of a world's existence. Precious, strange and one man's view – one man's view of the most dangerous gateways in the whole universe.

In the long time past, Chi Nü and Ming Xao had travelled far together outside of the Han. The woman had revealed to him that she was the Goddess of Weaving struck blind by her Celestial peers. By *Their* unkind calculations, she had spent too much time watching mortals and never enough time weaving celestial robes which was her job. Thus, she was blinded and banished to the world of the mortal until someone would help her find the bridge of *shifu* cloth that might take her home. Only such an action would break the curse and restore her sight. She had met the half-mortal Nicholas, a man of great kindness and care, and he gave her his life, guiding her over the *shifu* bridge to the Heavens from which he could never return.

Chi Nü had always remained Ming Xao's friend. Helping and counselling, moving with him as he ascended his imperial throne. He valued her counsel, her Divine wisdom and he listened. Always.

Except this once.

He turned toward the flawlessly beautiful woman.

'Yes,' he agreed. 'You did caution me. But what I have discovered, what portals opened for *me*, *must* be on record. It may be that one day, someone in the mortal world needs to save their loved one from the clutches of Others. How shall they do that if they do not know where to go?'

Chi Nü shook her head. 'My heart might agree with you. But you have transgressed in the worst way. Do you think They do not know what you have done? They're omniscient. They know when you vacate your bowels, for Heavens' sake. But in any case, Ming Xao, your map is redundant. One step ahead always, Others will just move the gates.' She bit her lip. 'You *know* how murderous Immortals can be when you raise their ire and you have done that successfully. Please listen to me! One can rarely barter unless it is with a life...' She moved beside the table, her silken robes whispering like so many premonitions. Her robes were the colour of peaches, of the newborn sun as it rose from a hazy horizon. Darker peach buds and spring green leaves patterned the fabric and as she bent over the scroll, her pink jade earrings gyrated, trembling with her movement. She reached out to touch the scroll and beneath her hand, figures on the map moved.

She pulled back with a gasp as the figures took furtive but intentioned steps toward illustrated landmarks. The painted figures in the painted landscape were as alive as if she and Ming Xao looked at a world in miniature – a secret world that girded Eirie like a dark reflection.

'How did you do this?' Her voice was breathless, horrified as she watched the figures move to their own tune.

'The ink...'

'From where...' There was an edge of fear in her voice, one he had not heard since she placed her foot on the *shifu* bridge with Nicholas, so long ago.

'From far beyond the Han.' He watched recognition spark in her eyes. It was like moonlight on night-black waters and he wondered how long it would take for her to make connections. The young emperor of the Han had oft wondered if he tempted Fate by the very act of painting this scroll. But he had done it nevertheless because something about the unfairness of existence had guided his hand.

'Chi Nü,' he said in response to her drawn-in breath. 'In my short life, I have watched people I know and love oft betrayed by Others. Of course, some have also been *saved* by Others, but it is always "in the lap of the Gods", like a game on a board. And I ask why should mortals be any less equal than Others? Why should they be playthings? What gives all of *you* the right to have *us* live in fear? To be afraid that one day we might accidentally step through a door, ride the seventh wave, push aside a silken veil and stumble into a forbidden world from which there is no escape? Finding our lives are forfeit because we have taken a wrong path? We live in a heightened state of anxiety all of our lives and this,' he said as he walked around the table, surveying the beautifully hand drawn map, 'is my way of redressing the balance.'

'A balance that is uneasy and swings and tips in the slightest whisper of a breeze,' argued Chi Nü. 'A breeze filled with innuendo.'

Yes. In the back of his mind, he knew this, but it was too late. He had done it.

'Chi Nü,' he asked, aware that the goddess knew something more. 'Are They coming for me?' The Celestial's eyes brimmed as she nodded her head, and he knew then. Knew that Time had run out. His heart sank to his silken slippers. One moment of wrongful ego and he had perhaps created catastrophe. 'How long?'

'Not long, perhaps when the water clock strikes the hour and the Rooster becomes the Dog. But what of your bride? Your Soon-to be Wife? She is in as much danger as yourself, Ming Xao. The Others will threaten your whole family in order to punish you...'

'My family? I *have* no family. They have all joined the Ancestors!'

'But you have a Would-be-Wife, a Would-be-Empress as of this evening.'

In the cloying silence, Ming Xao thought of the woman who would be his wife. His Would-be-Empress would be transported from The First House of Silk to the Palace, wrapped in the yellow silk that was a bride's costume, her marriage sash tied wide around her middle, telling its woven story.

His Soon-to-be Wife would have stitched images from her birth to this very moment on the sash, an *obi* that would be added to on every important occasion to the very end when her funerary rites began.

Funerary rites that could begin tonight. An irony surely, that the stitching should only show her life to the moment of her passage into his palace...

***

He had seen her once in the Park of the Singing Birds.

He had asked First Minister, his chamberlain, to find out where she would be because he wanted to make sure. Wanted to know that she was the one and not just a woman chosen by seers and diviners.

He stood by the side of the massive Han Elm, the Father Tree, famous for its size and breadth and for the heavy boughs that provided shade for those who wanted to sit away from the sun. He had covered his head in a bamboo dǒulì and sat with a bamboo cage and a singing linnet, watching as Lien of the First House of Silk walked, with her maid two steps behind.

She wore a robe the colour of ice-shadows, her hair hanging in a shining black horse-tail, and she walked with her face to the light as if she wanted to soak the sun into her marrow. Ming Xao's little bird began to sing in answer to others within the park and she glanced across from the path as he sat watching from under the Father Tree.

'He has a sweet song, Honoured Sir.'

He liked her mellow voice and her smile as she spoke to him.

'Your bird bests the others with his melody,' she continued.

'He looks for a mate, I think,' Ming Xao replied. 'He is lonely.'

'I see,' she laughed, not realising that she spoke to her emperor. 'And has he found any to his taste yet?'

'I think he wishes for a partner with curiosity and a desire for freedom. It is all he has ever wanted, after all.'

'Has he? You know your bird well, Honoured Sir.'

Ming Xao noticed the maid pulling gently at her mistress's ice-blue sleeve, as if she knew of the impropriety of an unmarried young woman engaging with a stranger in the park.

Lien shook her off. 'I can empathise with the bird,' she offered wistfully. 'There would be nothing like freedom to satisfy curiosity.'

Ming Xao looked at Lien and their eyes met. An understanding. And still she did not recognise him...

He slid the catch back on the door of the bamboo cage and she sucked in a breath as he reached in a finger onto which his little linnet could jump. Carefully he withdrew his hand and then held it up to the Father Tree. The linnet stretched its wings once, twice, and then with a musical chirrup, set off upward into the foliage and away and Lien, clasped her hands together.

'I commend you, Honoured Sir.' Her eyes sparkled. 'And I envy your bird.'

'As do I,' he replied.

***

'Then I cannot marry her. I must not have a family.'

'It matters little. They will use her as a hostage. She and others.'

'Shall They threaten the Han *as well*?'

She frowned. 'Their anger is profound, my friend.' Chi Nü paced, her face pleated. 'If you had not used the eldritch ink, I could have destroyed the map and you might almost be free, but such ink may be beyond destruction. From whom did you purchase it?'

He dared not look at her as he answered. A flush of guilt thudded through him but he owed her an answer. 'I did not purchase it.'

'You found it then?'

'No…'

'You *stole* it? You *stole* it!' There was no denying the fury building in the goddess who had been his friend.

So still turned from her, he nodded his head. Guilt pressed upon him on so many levels and it surprised him because not once in the creation of the map had the feeling stirred. With each calibrated stroke of his brush, he had thought he was doing the right thing.

'You *stole* from Jasper's house and thus you stole from Nicholas, *my Nico!* You dared to take what was Nicolas's legacy? How *could* you?' Her voice was chill enough for him to shiver and he was reminded of a winter breeze drifting down from the mountains, bringing snow and ice in its wake.

He touched the illustration of ocean water near a cliff, and a wave formed, then another, and another, seven in all, and as the seventh wave brushed the cliff, a fissure appeared, enlarging until a small boat drifted into its darkness. He frowned, saying honestly, 'You make me question what I have done. For the first time, there is a moment where I can see I may have committed an error...'

'*May? May?*' The Goddess of Weaving grabbed a jade seal and threw it across the room where it bounced off a thick silk panel. She began to pace again, her robe folds boiling around her, an anger that he had never seen before pouring forth like bile. 'Heavens and Gods, Ming Xao! You have betrayed your people! I always thought you were prescient, cautious.' She spun around, stabbing her finger at him. 'I am so aghast! You must go to the one person who can destroy the map because this is something beyond my experience, Gods curse it! My job will be to try and placate the Others before great harm befalls you and any dynasty you might wish to beget. By the stars! You are an educated man, a kind and humble leader. How could you have been so foolish? You didn't *listen* to me. It was bad enough that you painted the map! But enchanted ink? You, Ming Xao, are a fool! And I never thought you to be so!' Her words hung heavy, like winter storm clouds.

He turned his back on her and washed his brush, playing for time, patting the tip dry, his fingers shaking. 'But Chi Nü,' he threw the words over his shoulder, knowing nothing he said now would make any difference. 'Surely mortals must have rights. This was meant to even the balance. Do Others never think on what curses they throw our way? Every day is like walking a path between fields of quicksand.'

'Then heed me!' she begged. 'The cost of your foolishness will be higher than you could possibly imagine.'

Outside, the bugle cry of a white crane sounded, the bird that was friend and companion to the emperor. Ming Xao took a small bag from the table and slid the door open, stepping down to a bamboo landing where the crane waited. Digging into the little sack, he held out his palm on which lay some seeds that the crane pecked. The bird remained still as he untied a small silk roll attached to a long, elegant leg. He presented another handful of seed to the bird which it took politely, to then stand, plucking at its plumage.

Ming Xao unrolled the note. He scanned the words, his heart sounding in his ears like thunder. Then he crushed the roll and sank it into the mud and reeds surrounding the small pontoon.

He walked back into the library and Chi Nü faced him, a vision of such terrible beauty that at any other time he would have marveled and been breathless.

'You *know* what They have done, don't you?' he hissed at her.

Chi Nü answered swiftly, defiant and angry. 'I *asked* you, I *begged* you, not to make a record of what you discovered. If They are beginning to fight you, it is on your head…'

Rage flooded his veins – rage at the cruelty of the Others, at his friend, Chi Nü. But more than anything, impotent fury at himself that he did not think harder, further. That he did not use the wisdom for which he was loved by his people.

For a moment he was breathless, heart thumping, body almost trembling. Finally, he sneered at the Goddess. 'Then let them hurt *me*, not my people! By the stars, if it is possible to hate Celestials, to hate all Others, then I have reached that point! To hurt my people because of *your* vainglory and insecurity!'

'*Your* vainglory, Ming Xao!'

He growled, a rising roar. 'Damn you all to Hell! *Destroy* the map? I want to take an army and destroy the Other world, crush it beneath my boots like so much dust.' He slammed his fist down on the table and a *netsuke* of a fox fell to the floor and smashed, tiny shards of ivory skittering to his toes. The weights holding either end of the scroll jumped, and the map rolled upon itself. 'How much better our world would be without you all!'

Chi Nü slapped flat palms together and the air vibrated as if lightning had struck. Her wrath surrounded him like a noxious cloud. He had *never* heard her defend her kind. She had always protected those amongst his world who were the playthings of Others. And now?

'Foolish mortal!' she spat. 'You think you could win against the power of Others? What enchantment do *you* have that could kill those of my kind? We are indestructible! You played with fire and now your people will be burned! And it is your fault!'

In the Emperor's mind, he saw a little mountain village perched like a bird's nest on a great rocky cast surrounded by even taller mountains, deep dark ravines and tumbling mountain streams. A plume of smoke filled the sky as those who lived burned those who had died. With heavy hearts, the village elders decreed the gates shut against the world so that the terrible plague that had come upon them did not spread down the mountain tracks to the great palace city of the Han. Such was the message from First Minister that the crane conveyed. Tears pricked his eyes. Such innocents in that village – old and young and any in between. He could as easily have taken a sword to them all himself. Instead, he committed them to isolation and lingering death.

'*You* told Them what I had done,' he yelled pointing at her, his finger jabbing the air. '*You* betrayed me. You of all Others...'

'It was *not* me!' This goddess had always been so gentle, so calm. Such rage… and all because of him.

'Then who? If not you, then who of your kind knew. I told no one.'

'It could be as simple as a bird in your trees. Even a cricket crawling across your library floor. There are plenty of living creatures who are loyal to evil Others. But it is no matter because the damage is done, *created by you!*'

Chi Nü took a deep breath as if to steady herself and calm the air between them. Her voice softened. 'Ming Xao, what matters now is what you do next. The hours flow on with each drop of the water clock and the Hour of the Dog approaches, wild and angry. I can protect the library for a short while and I have placed protections around the palace for a slightly longer while. But Others will breech those defences. You have no option but to leave with the map, return to where you stole the ink and beg for the map to be destroyed.'

Ming Xao hated that she was right, hated himself. 'Beg who, exactly. Jasper is dead, his legacies were meant to be Nicholas' but Nico is now with the Gods. Who do I ask?'

'There is a new healer. Her name is Seraphina, and she came one day, an enigma, and never left. She is exactly as Jasper once was – wise, compassionate and with a healing touch that defies belief. As to her abilities, she will not fail you. Of that I'm sure.'

'And me? The map might be destroyed but I will still have the knowledge. Will they kill me as well, even after the map is no longer?'

'That is in the lap of the Gods. And something that per-haps the Wise Woman can deal with. We must hope so.' Her voice betrayed no hope. 'Ming, I suspect your Soon-to-be Wife will be a pawn in this misbegotten game. In fact, I'm sure she already is. Whether you marry her now may be immaterial. They will need to have a hold on you, and she will be their hostage. She and the people in that mountain village. The Gods will play on your heart and trample it.'

Ming Xao felt a creeping cold – the chill of bitter realisation. 'But if I take her with me to this woman, and we secure her protection?'

'You cannot wait for your bride. You will have to trust that I may be able to help her when she arrives at the palace. At the very least I will try. Go on your own, it will be faster. I will contrive for her to follow.'

'Could she catch up with me, do you think?'

'She could if she knew where you went, but you cannot leave any instructions.'

'Give me a little time, Chi Nü. I swear I will leave before the Hour of the Dog.'

Chi Nü closed her eyes briefly – a sign of relief, he wondered? 'Do what you must.' She reached for his hand, holding it in her own slim fingers. Her touch was feather-light, like a whisper. 'I must go if I am to help you both. I will not see you again, but I wish you well. Take no risks, my dear friend.'

As the wind-chimes rang from the willows she was gone, and Ming Xao breathed as if it was his last.

Take no risks?

He laughed bitterly. He had never thought he was a vainglorious man but now, with people threatened with death, he had to face the truth of his ego and it galled him.

He began rolling the map tightly, walking along the length of the table as the drawn world was swallowed in the roll. Wrapping it in a black cord, he dipped a brush in some black wax that melted beneath a small flame and dropped a bead onto the knot so that it would not slide undone. He blew hard on the wax, waving the roll in the air and then placed it into a small leather cylinder, pushing the stopper tight shut. Upending the cylinder, he held it so the tip dangled over the glutinous wax. The rim was thus sealed, he blew out the small flame and bit his lip.

How could he let the Would-be Empress know what she must do? How would she know to come to his library? He had to trust to his chamberlain, to his own imperial Ancestors and to the Fates. It was all he had.

The nightingale floor sang outside. If it were those who wanted him and what he had, surely they could avoid the chirrups of the floorboards. Perhaps it is the crane walking back and forth, he thought. Perhaps the crane deceived him. But no, he had raised the crane from an injured nestling and they were soul friends, she was his spirit animal. He knew he could trust her.

He tapped the wax to see if it was hard enough and then placed the cylinder in the deep pocket at the side of his tunic, along with a pointed, sheathed dagger and a small leather purse of gold and silver coins.

Kicking his silk slippers off, he pulled on some padded boots and wrapped himself in a heavily quilted coat. He thought of his bride, that curious and unusual woman called Lien, and he wished he had wed her in time, and that he could take her to this woman called Seraphina in the Ymp Tree Orchard, where she would be safe until his misguided error was righted.

For it *was* misguided, and even though he thought it had seemed a righteous thing to do for the world of Men, he had never thought Others could be cruel enough, nor so afraid of losing Their omnipotence that They would kill a whole village, an emperor, the emperor's family, an entire province.

By the stars! Such weak naïvete on his part!

Atonement would be hard, wellnigh impossible. But an idea flashed into his mind and quickly, because there was nothing else, he began to work.

He prayed that Chi Nü's enchantment around his library would last long enough for him to put a seemingly innocent puzzle together. He found a small cabinet and within each of three drawers, he placed strips of parchment on which he had written poems at different times in the map's creation when life had been easier, and he had lived in a fool's paradise. They were charms, the magick created by the ink that he had thought special enough to steal. For a mortal to utter them would speed them to the place the charm invoked. Lien could conceivably reach Seraphina before her pursuers captured her. He jammed a lock onto the cabinet's brass door and closed his palm over its plain key, hoping that Lien, if she should come to his library, if the Fates would let her, would find this cabinet.

But how so?

He laid out his brushes and pens on the table, systematically and with precision, and then blew out the lamp. He crept to the side of the library where shadows were thick and darkness prevailed, opening the doors of the large wall closet and walking inside amongst hanging jackets, stacked journals and rolled parchments. His heart smashed at his chest as he placed the key in the hem of a black padded silk jacket that was folded neatly on the floor, laying the little casket on the top. Everything fastidious, nothing out of the ordinary.

He pushed through the hanging robes to the rear wall of the closet, a back panel that had a painting of a mountain, of pines and cedars, of water falling, of clouds on high and mist rising. He had painted it with the ink from Jasper – an enchanted thing, perhaps created just for this day.

He sent his blessings and love to his people, asking for their forgiveness as he prayed to his Ancestors, begging those revered Ancients for their help and took a step into the painted scene.

The roar of a river down deep in the gorge reached his ears, the rising mist drifting to settle on his hair, beading the black quilting of his coat. As he moved to the path and the bridge that had appeared across the gorge, he hoped there were some who watched out for him. There must be, for the Bridge that Never Was would never have appeared. He offered his undying gratitude to any beneficent being who would listen, asking that the painted scene in which he now stood would fade behind him until it was needed again.

He stepped onto the rope-tied planks...

CHAPTER TWO

Lien

Lien sat beneath the elm tree.

In summer its dancing leaves and fractured shadows charmed her, and she was sure Terrestrial spirits hovered there. Why wouldn't they? It was such a charmed space. She never feared them – perhaps she should, but as she looked up through the filigree shade, it all seemed so benign. She pushed her needle back and forth, making sure the silk filament moved smoothly, no knots, or else Old One, her grandmother, would be displeased.

In the peaceful garden, it was possible to hear the thread whispering through the silk. She and the silk talked to each other – secret chatter. Lien spoke of her dreams and the silk filament answered back with acknowledgement. If it disagreed, for sure it would knot or break. No matter that others might think she was mad – such times made her content. For the moment.

The last stitch of vermilion finished the point of the carp's tail and she carefully laced the remaining silk back into the reverse side. She was skilled at double-sided embroidery where a mirror image of silken perfection appeared as the fabric was flipped over. Old One expected the skill to be handed down, daughter to daughter. Was it not after all, what gave her family First House of Silk status?

In the tree above, there was an agitated fluttering and she

looked up, sucking in her breath as her stiletto-sharp ivory needle pierced her finger with her inattention.

A bead of blood sat atop her skin – imperial red – and then dripped onto the white silk fabric, pooling and spreading. Another bead appeared and before she could suck her finger, there was a soft touch like kitten's fur, the leaves of the elm shivering with concern. Then it was gone. A quick bark beyond the Middle Court and then silence.

Lien spat onto the corner of a kerchief, dabbing at the bloodstain, wondering what had rushed by her to set her skin tingling and her stomach writhing.

Maybe something as normal as a bird, perhaps.

Or a white tamarind monkey escaped from the Imperial gardens...

Whatever – it was fast and gone in an instant so that she could guess at nothing at all for surety. With infinite care, she patted the stain and as she breathed and her unsteady heart settled, the bloodspot faded. Pure alchemy.

She would not like to say so but there was something in the air and it surprised her, for Old Ancestors had built the house to protect against evil spirits. Upturned corners of rooves, screens across entrances, dragon carvings, stone lion dogs. Even nightingale floors. Traditional protection, like every other house in the First House quarter of the Han – common practice which seemed to work.

She examined her finger, pressing near the pinprick to see if more blood was forthcoming and relieved that it had stopped, she slipped the ivory needle through the fabric, and placed her embroidery into a silken bag, pulling the drawstring tight. With the carp finished, she had no wish to begin a new part of the work, not when she would swear a spirit had brushed past her.

She stood, her robes falling about her, and walked along a gravel path where shrubs had been clipped into such submission that they almost kowtowed at her feet. The fragrant air of Small Garden parted and then drifted back around; the clatter and bash of the kitchens and the shrill chatter of the cook bringing such relief, such a sense that all was right with the world.

And yet…

Looking back toward the walls of the Middle Court with its elegant moon gate, something pulled at her, something as delicate as a cobweb. And like that thread, it was strong. Perhaps too strong. It pulled at her with the strength of the ropes on the Bridge that Never Was, the legend that Old one had talked of. She shivered, wrapping the silk folds tight around her body.

'Lien,' Old One called from the verandah of the living quarters. 'You have been too long in the garden. You have surely not forgotten your duty, today of all days?'

She hadn't. How could she? Not when it would mean a change in her life beyond recognition. Her garden and stitching time had merely been an escape from the inevitable.

'No, Grandmother. Has it not been all this house has talked of for weeks?'

As if its fortunes would rise higher than the sun…

'Do not be glib, my blossom. This is to your advantage as much as the House of Shue. Show me your embroidery.'

As Lien pulled the silk from her bag, she sighed. Her advantage? To become the betrothed of a man who was supposed to have become the emperor but who had absconded on a self-indulgent journey of exploration for three years with his previous betrothed? Did she want an egotist for a husband? If she was honest with herself, she wanted no husband at all – imperial or otherwise.

But on one point she envied the Emperor, because she desperately wanted to see beyond the Han for herself and he had done that. She wanted to see beyond the constraints of

First House life, see the Raj and Pymm and the rest of Eirie. Different people, strange lifestyles…

'Lien – are you listening?' Old One sat back, her grey silk robes settling in whispering folds, her tiny feet in their embroidered slippers appearing beneath the pooling cloth. Lien respected her, loved sitting by her and listening to legends and folktales – stories of the good Celestial Spirits who watched over the mortals of the Han, looking after their interests against the evil dragon spirits. She reached for Old One's knobbed fingers and smoothed them.

'Yes, Grandmother, I am listening. Always. You are my light in darkness.'

'Darkness? You are such a dramatic little thing. Your light from now on will be the light that shines upon the whole of the Han. No, do not…' She grasped Lien's hands as she tried to pull away. 'Do not be afraid. His Imperial Highness, Ming Xao, is reputed to be a kind man and will make a gentle husband…'

'I am not afraid…'

'But not confident.'

'Grandmother, be honest. Were you, when you became a bride?'

Old One sat back, laughing. 'Oh, indeed yes. Your honoured grandfather was a much-desired man amongst First House maidens and I was lucky enough to be the one who wedded him. We lived a long and fruitful life of love and respect before he took his place with the Ancestors.'

'But you knew my honoured grandfather beforehand. Your families were close. I do not know the Emperor.'

'Oh yes,' Old One's face softened, and her gaze drifted to some far-off place. 'I knew your grandfather…' But then her wits sharpened, and she clapped her twisted hands together. 'But it is no matter. You have been chosen as the Bride-Empress and you should be proud. It is settled.'

'But Grandmother, another was chosen once before me,

and she and he ran away together before the ceremony. Then, if you remember, he returned alone. How do we know something foul did not befall the Lady Ibo at his behest? He may be an evil man.'

'An evil man does not do what he has done since he returned. We no longer seek slaves from beyond the Han. We have excellent trade with the outside world and are more prosperous than we were before.' She looked down at her tiny feet and grimaced with the pain of the folded bones. 'He has banished foot-binding, thank the stars. Whilst I might be old, my blossom, I do not hanker for what was cruel in our past. He has loosened our fetters in a short time, and I commend him for it. And not only that, it is rumoured he returned the Lady Ibo to her home and her people. She had been abducted as a slave to the Han. Have they not told you this?'

'No one has told me anything beyond how lucky I shall be. How honoured…'

Old One smoothed her fingers over the ebony silk of Lien's hair. 'I have heard that he has grown into a strong man, much taller now and with a pleasant countenance.'

Lien said nothing.

She had been amongst the guests at the Koi House when the Imperial Son, Ming Xao, had come to collect his bride three years ago. Lien was younger but not too young to be interested in the progression of the Imperial Family through the First Merchant's house. The Lady Ibo, a former slave reputed to be of high standing in her own province, waited for the Imperial Son to greet her. She was gracious, obviously beautiful – but strung as taut as a wire.

Ming Xao had stepped from the litter – a man of middle height, thin and ascetic and despite his glossy black hair pulled tightly into a knot at his nape and despite the exquisite embroidery and tailoring of his robes, he seemed old beyond his years.

He looked at the Lady Ibo through thick spectacles, really studied her, and soon they were talking intently whilst the Koi household moved ahead with the Emperor and Empress. An earnest discussion between the two younger people – one that produced no smiles.

The next day they vanished.

No one knew where.

Only that there was a trail of blood behind. At the Bridge that Never Was, a man was killed, and others were injured at the border gates near the mountains. The Han shut its face to the world. Gates were barred and the Han fell to mourning. The Old Emperor faded with grief and died, and the Old Empress ruled as Consort, but her heart grieved for the loss of her venerable husband and for the perfidy of her only son and she cared not that the country sat immobile for almost three turns of the year wheel. Lien often used to think that if they all sat any quieter, any more immobile, they would have been covered in cobweb filaments; to die a suffocating death of never knowing and never seeing.

But then Ming Xao returned from wherever he had been. He had grown straighter, broader, taller, they said, and the Empress willingly handed over the governance of the Han to her enlightened and handsome son. She slipped away to join the Ancestors one day not long after, and thereupon the Han changed – becoming outward looking, everything of intrinsic value being in demand in the other provinces beyond the walls. Many benefited but none more than the First House district, and even more, the merchants and silk houses.

Which is why Lien worked hard at her embroidery within the First House of Silk and why she chattered to Old One and why she asked questions of anyone she knew who might just take the risk and talk back. Slowly she realised she wanted to see beyond the huge wall that wrapped around the Han. Sometimes she felt they lived like silkworms in cocoons and that all she had to do was find the filament at the edge of that cocoon and her prison would unroll.

She loved the racks in the silk sheds. Where the silk-worms fed on mulberry leaves and grew the lovely thread for which her family was recognised. It was a quiet, dusky world filled with burgeoning wonder laid out on bamboo slats and at the start of every week, she lit incense sticks to the Celestial Spirits, asking them to protect the little moths she so loved for their industrious but short lives.

Between the Visitors' Court, the Middle Court and Small Garden, she made a life for herself. An ordered existence to be sure, a safe existence. But not enough for someone as curious as she. She wanted more.

As Lien watched Old One smooth her work, her finger tingled as if half of it lay in another world. And whilst she listened with half an ear to Old One opining on the Emperor's qualities, all she could think of was the touch of something eldritch in the garden.

She sat in her chamber whilst her hair was perfumed, combed, piled and pleated and as the maidservant, Heng, began to place the silk blossoms across her head and to wiggle jade and ivory pins into the ebony arrangement, she looked at herself in the mirror. A waxed statue stared back. One whose face was tinted ivory and whose lips had been strangely shaped. One whose hair tilted skyward like some awkward pagoda and which shimmered with too much ornamentation.

'Why did they name you Heng,' she asked, more to divert herself from the fast-approaching hour.

The maidservant looked up from her task and frowned a little. 'I believe my mother said I had white skin that looked like moonshine.' She coloured, a faint stain spreading up her pale neck and over her cheeks.

'You do have pale skin. Many would envy you.'

The servant proceeded to push in more pins to Lien's elaborate hairstyle and shocked at herself, Lien growled and brushed at her servant's hand.

'Stop!' she cried. 'Stop now!'

'But my lady…'

'Leave it. Get me a bowl of rosewater and a fresh towel and then leave me.'

The maidservant looked aghast.

'Now!'

The tall woman bowed and backed from the room, sliding the door across. Her feet pattered away along the gravel paths of the forecourt and Lien had no doubt her mother and Old One would be told of her behaviour. In moments, the nightingale floor of the verandah would squeak like a murdered bird as they all came to remonstrate with her. Instead, her chamber door slid open, the maidservant edging in with a porcelain bowl of gently warmed water and a towel and Lien wondered how she managed to negotiate the nightingale floor so easily.

'Who did you tell?' she asked.

'No one, my lady…'

'Truly?'

'Yes, my lady. *I* will be at fault if anything goes wrong and I will not arouse the ire of your honoured mother and the venerable Old One.' She laid the bowl down and bowed over folded hands.

'So, you kept quiet to protect yourself, Heng?'

'Yes, my lady…'

Lien laughed – a sound more tinged with a sigh than merriment. 'But Heng, your duty is surely to the First House of Silk. Not to me and certainly not to yourself.' She began pulling at the pins and blossoms in her hair.

'I know, my lady, but…' She stopped. She was as skinny as a kite string and quite plain, her hair wisping about her face, but whilst physically she had nothing to recommend her apart from her pale silk skin, her touch had always been feather-like and often Lien had barely to think of something and the object of her desire would be at her fingertips. Occasionally Lien wondered if she was a spirit but mostly, she took her servant for granted.

Now she studied her more closely.

The maidservant's eyes were shadowed, and Lien wished she had been observant. She suspected the woman had quiet depths.

'But?' she prompted.

Heng huffed out a breath. 'Because … because I like you, my lady. You have never been unkind.'

Lien began to pull at the pleats in her hair. 'I have never been anything. You have wafted around me like a Celestial Spirit.'

'Let me do that.' Heng unrolled one of the hairpleats, smoothing it out with her fingers. 'If you have barely noticed my presence, it means I am doing my work correctly. To arouse your displeasure, to disturb you in any way … it is not right.' She unrolled the last pleat and almost whispered. 'Besides … I can dream through you.' She blushed, grimacing, and her oval face tightened like a mask. She took up a brush and pulled it through the silken length that lay across Lien's shoulders. 'There now – I have broken every rule of servitude.'

Lien's hair shone like a piece of polished ebony and she had a quick thought. 'Sweep it up into a high tail on my head, so that it swings as I walk.'

Heng's eyes widened, and she opened her mouth to speak but in moments Lien's glossy waterfall hung down, a blossom lodged where the hair was tied.

Lien began to wash her face, removing the cosmetics with which she had been painted. From behind the towel, she asked, 'Dream of what, Heng?'

'Life beyond...' The answer came readily but her gaze remained low as she passed over a porcelain jar of almond cream.

'Beyond the First House of Silk?' But she knew the answer before Heng dipped her head and shrugged her shoulders. 'Oh!' She turned and gripped Heng's hand. 'Beyond the Wall! You too! I wish I had known.' She smiled at her servant, clutching at her. 'You see things my way.'

Agitated voices sounded from the Middle Court and then the nightingale floor squeaked in alarm. 'Lien, you should be ready.' Her father growled from the other side of the paper screen. 'Your mother has already left for the palace with Old One.'

'Nearly, Father. I am almost done.' She smoothed on the face cream so that her skin bloomed like a magnolia petal and with a light finger she dabbed colour on her lips. Heng enfolded her in a soft silk chemise, but as she took the stiff yellow marriage robe that seemed to stand on its own, Lien shook her head.

'No, give me the softer yellow robe, that one...' she pointed to a smooth damask silk garment of multitudinous draping folds that lay across her bed and which Heng now held for her to enwrap herself. 'And the red *obi*...' She wound the beautifully worked cummerbund around her waist twice. It was a wide riband that wrapped from beneath her bosom to her waist and it told a story from her birth to her imminent marriage – a journey along a road lined with pagodas and willows, with hump-backed bridges, cranes and tumbling streams – a story that would be added to as she lived and then folded and burned when she died. Lien felt as if it stopped her breath, as if it was ending her life now and she hated it, watching as Heng's fingers knotted it.

Heng slid the silver and white jade dragon ring onto Lien's finger and Lien stepped into red slippers embroidered with yellow and gold dragons.

Imperial red and yellow. All alone with dragons for company...

'Heng,' she said with urgency. 'Take off your robe and pull on my sea-green one. Quickly now, brush your hair into a tail like mine and place a blossom in it like mine. Good. Are your hands clean? Your teeth? You have good slippers? Come now. Father grows impatient. Do you not hear the nightingale floor caterwauling?'

Lien slid aside the paper screen and her father turned. She wished she could see sadness in his eyes, recognition that he was losing his only daughter, his only child, but there was only satisfaction reflected back.

I am the means to position and more wealth than even you could dream. I wish I had been a male child!

Heng picked up the trailing folds of Lien's robes as she stood on the steps of the verandah, and Lien could not see the lustrous damask silk, only the dragging wreckage of her own dreams. 'Father, I need Heng to come with me. It is only right that the First House of Silk hands me to my future husband with a servant who knows my every need.'

Master Shue passed his gaze over Heng, noting the excellent robe and neat hair. 'As you wish...' But then he noticed Lien's own face and flicked at her hair. 'Lien, you are not prepared...'

'Honoured Father. I wish no insult to our house, but I would meet the Emperor unmasked and honest. If my honourable future husband is the progressive man I believe him to be, I think he will more than appreciate the gesture and the Shue house will receive plaudits accordingly.'

Master Shue remained unconvinced and so she pressed harder. 'Father, he has removed foot-binding and lowered taxes, he has made a point of honouring those who have been less fortunate with compassion and honesty. I believe I am doing the right thing to meet such a man.'

Her father frowned and then grunted. 'Perhaps you are

right. But it's as well Old One cannot see you as you leave.'

Outside the Shue compound, the Voice, the harbinger of all things imperial could be heard calling her name, and a rustling sound, like the wind through river reeds, swept along the street as observers kneeled, ready to honour her passage.

'Come, Lien. It is time.' Her father took her hand and led her to the silk litter, helping her to sit amongst the cushions as Heng folded the trailing yellow silk in around her feet.

'I will follow, mistress,' she whispered.

'Heng, I apologise. I didn't ask you…'

'You didn't have to. I think this is the beginning of my dreams,' Heng replied quietly, placing the final fold inside.

Lien took a last look down the sweep of the paths, into the branches of the elm. She gasped as amber eyes gazed back, her finger feeling as if the tip had been sawn away.

CHAPTER THREE

Ming Xao

The bridge quivered as he stepped across. Despite that it was night, he tried to place each foot down with confidence because the bridge would know who was scared and who was not.

At either end of the eldritch structure, carved temple dogs hunkered down and flambeaus burned – but the flame only illuminated a few planks at the entry and exit, the rest lay in an enchanted and profound darkness because night had come early it seemed and there was no moon, nothing to light his way.

A small vibration rippled beneath his feet and set his nerves even more on edge as the suspension took his weight. The ropes creaked. Even above the roar so far below, he could hear the massive hawsers stretching. The mist settled over him like a net and he was glad he had sealed the map carefully in the cylinder within his pocket. He looked straight ahead, focusing on the exit to the bridge and praying, always praying, to his Ancestors and to kind spirits, Terrestrial or Celestial, and to the Great Mother Cheng Mo, to aid and abet him.

He felt as if he was running away to leave his people to a deadly future and when the thought twisted through him, he prayed that Chi Nü would argue strongly for him. Even so, he wished he had a counterthreat against the Others, something he could use to protect the Han. But such a wish was pointless. They always held the upper hand. Always.

Which was why he scurried like a rat over the Bridge that Never Was. For a moment he wondered if this darkness, here right now, was contrived by the benevolent spirits to whom he had prayed. Perhaps there was a little hope?

He paid no attention to the dark, damp heights, to the swinging and trembling of the bridge, to the clamour of the gorge waters below. *Murderer! Slaughterer of innocents!* So the waters roared at him, and he felt branded, as if with a hot iron. He shouted into the night air, a cry of anguish as he went beyond the shadows to the flame-lit last few planks, sliding his hands along the ropes, gripping hard so that the fibre burned into him. He wanted to feel physical pain – it blocked whatever blame whispered into his ears.

He reached the other side of the gorge, bending to pick up an unlit torch from the pile laid there, holding it to the flambeau, the light rising up, illuminating his shrubby surrounds. The Bridge That Never Was began to fade and for one brief moment he wondered if it had appeared because he *was* a man trying to do the right thing, a man who needed help. The legend said it only appeared for those in need…

'Do not be too unkind to yourself, Ming Xao…' a creaky voice murmured from the dark as he watched the disappearing bridge.

He spun round, on edge, expecting nothing but trouble and a small, bent ancient smiled up at him. The man's face was so lined it was almost impossible to discern any expression and he could have been five hundred years old but for the clarity of his eyes. Knowing eyes that sparkled. At any other time, Ming might have said kind eyes. But in his predicament, kindness was something he thought might be lacking.

The old man tapped a finger on the side of his nose and continued. 'Some things like the bridge are illusory. Indeed, perhaps what you *imagine* might be happening in the mountain village is also an illusion.'

'What do you say?' Ming was hardly polite. Now was not the time to debate semantics with some old man.

'Greetings, Ming Xao. I bow to Your Imperial Highness.' The little man bent himself even lower and then looked up. 'I am Yue Lao. I am a Terrestrial spirit…'

Ming Xao gasped, hastily returning the obeisance. 'You're the Spirit of Fate…'

'Indeed. It is reassuring that the Emperor knows these things. Do you believe me when I say that the threat against you could just be an illusion?'

'But…'

'Think of dreams and nightmares, Excellency. They are figments of our mind, are they not?'

'Yes, but in this case…'

'The Celestial Spirits think to frighten you. It seems they are succeeding.'

'Are you saying that if I don't react to their threats then all will be well?'

'Ah…' Yue Lao moved to a flat boulder. 'Do you mind if I sit in your august presence? My legs are not what they were, and I get very tired. Fate is a heavy load.'

'Of course. In any case, Yue Lao, you are a Terrestrial spirit and I should be deferring to *you*.'

'I think you are, Ming Xao. You are *listening* to what I have to say. I shall go on. The Celestials know you have a great map, a map of the entrances to the Other world. They do not want anyone to have that map because it creates an imbalance and offends Them.'

'You mean it creates balance and that mortals have a fighting chance at life.'

'That might be how you see it, but Others do not. They see the end of life as *they* know it. The life that has been infinite into the past, doing just what They want, and, which should be infinite into the long-time future.'

'And mortals must continue to exist in fear for a wrong step. I would say imbalance describes it perfectly.' Ming sighed. 'So you too think the map should be destroyed.'

'In a word? Yes. Despite that Others can move the gates anywhere they like, whenever. The thing is, Emperor, you must be seen to be making some kind of effort to right a situation.'

Ming Xao gave a dry laugh. 'But if the Celestials' threats are an illusion, what power do They really have over me?'

'I think you are being a little obtuse.' The old man's eyes slitted and he clasped his hands together. 'I said they *might* be an illusion, but perhaps because I am an ancient, I am not as clear as I should be.' He cleared his throat, balled his gnarled fists, laid them on his knees and pushed himself into a more upright sitting position. 'What I meant was *at the moment*. If they do not get what they want, Excellency, then there will be no illusions, there will be actualities.'

'So nothing changes. I run for my life to find the one person in Eirie who can destroy the map because I must be *seen* to be making an effort.'

The old man replied with some sadness, 'You have so inflamed Them that They *want* to hunt you. You have given Them the thing that is their lifeblood – a reason to hunt and even to kill.'

Ming's heart was thumping as Yue Lao spoke. That a little calligraphy should come to this!

He realised his face must have paled because the God of Fate put a gentle hand on his arm. 'I needed you to know,' the old man said, 'that at this point in time, Fate has *not* been cruel to your mountain folk. They live, they breathe.'

'Thanks to the Gods and the Great Mother!' Ming Xao looked to the dark heavens where no star glittered and no moon shone its beneficence upon the earth, and he was convinced that this aged Terrestrial had created night to shelter him at this moment. 'But for how long? You are a kind spirit, Yue Lao. Can't you argue with the Others that I am sorry and that I am doing the best I can? That I take responsibility for what I have done and will have the map destroyed?'

'I will try, but they don't like we Terrestrials particularly and it will have little effect.'

'Then I must go.' Ming Xao headed toward a faint path that led away from the bridge. 'I have no time. They will either catch me and kill me or they will kill my people. Vainglorious bastards!'

Yue Lao snorted. 'Yes, true. Vainglory is a *dreadful* sin.' He looked sideways at Ming Xao. 'Don't you think? Fate never smiles on the vainglorious. Remember that, Ming Xao. There will be moments when you might second-guess yourself and think that drawing your map was the right thing to do. Hubris will cause dreadful harm.'

Thus chastened, Ming Xao bowed before the spirit and went to leave. 'I thank you for your kindness, Yue Lao. It will not be forgotten.'

'Wait, Excellency. I will give you something.' The old man grunted as he stood, as if his limbs spoke to him of pain. 'I have it...' he felt in the left pocket of his robe. 'No, not there...' He scrabbled in the right pocket and withdrew something. Shuffling over, he said, 'Hold out your right hand.'

Ming Xao did as he was ordered, and Yue Lao pushed back the Emperor's heavy black sleeve. He laid a red thread across Ming Xao's wrist and looped it around the wristbone, knotting it off firmly. Looking up into Ming's face, he said, 'Remember that Fate is inexorable. What will be will be. Remember too that a red thread connects one to one's destiny. This,' he said as he gave the knot a final tug, 'cannot be undone until the right person, time and place happen upon you. You and Fate are now bound to each other more than ever.'

Ming chafed to leave. He had little time for enigmas and would rid himself of the thread soon enough.

As if he listened to Ming's thoughts, Yue Lao, said, 'Remember hubris, Excellency and if you want my advice, take the left path. It goes down to the river where you will find a punt.' Bowing low over hands that he had concealed in the deep cuffs of the midnight-sky robes, he faded into the shadows.

Ming hurried down the left path, holding his torch high. That he had listened and headed left meant he must have some faith in the Terrestrial. Something about the Ancient spelled kindness and for that he was grateful. Perhaps he had two spirits looking out for him after all – Chi Nü, a Celestial and Yue Lao, a Terrestrial.

But he was leaving the Han.

What use would they be to him in other provinces?

The path was narrow and steep and it switched back and turned. The roar of the river filled the air, and he wondered how a punt could matter in these rapids. He would surely be committing he and the map to a swift demise. But as he turned a corner on the heavily shielded path, he realised the noise had softened almost as if he had turned a bend away from the river.

The path was hung with branches of cedar and pine and the air was damply resinous. Beneath the massive trees, shrubs the height of a tall man created a tunnel so that he could barely hear anything – not even a breeze sighing through the branches. His footfall was cushioned by mosses and pine needles and an eery silence pervaded his progress, the flickering light from his torch stretching shadows, making them gyre around him. He shivered. Prescience could be a terrifying thing.

But he reached the bottom and despite the night, he could

see that the river had broadened into a dark, silent swathe, fast to be sure, but with no rapids, just a swirling current that pushed ever onward from the heights of the Han towards the red and pink cliffs of the Raj far far away. He sucked in a breath and held it, listening, expecting some banshee spirit to come spiralling out of the night gloom.

But there was nothing.

Just he, the river and his guttering torch.

As the flame began to die, he saw the punt. A small craft that could perhaps fit two aboard. It reminded him of his own punt, his lake, his library and the white crane, and he hoped to the Ancestors that she had been a true friend and loyal only to him.

The punt looked as aged as Yue Lao. Sturdy and safe? By the spirits, all he could do was trust what the Ancient had offered him and jump aboard. It would save hours of walking to the Great Wall, time when he could be halfway to the Wise Woman before the Others had sniffed his tracks. What frightened him was the knowledge that the Others would surely have all the portals guarded. For one fleeting moment, he wished he could disappear. Or at the very least bargain with them.

But bargain with what? They could kill his entire province on a whim if They wanted.

Unless…

No.

But…

No. One didn't bargain with Others unless one was a fool.

But…

The map lay curled in the canister in the deep pocket of his coat. Its value was unarguable. Could he not bargain for the safety of his people with it? The Others wanted it after all.

But there was Yue Lao's voice whispering 'Hubris, Ming Xao. It is every man's downfall.'

39

And he knew. In truth he had no power to bargain. He would hand the map over and They would punish him. Quite simple really. Death seemed so close that he grabbed the punt, pushed it into the current and jumped aboard, wishing against all hope that he could just vanish.

He looked for a pole but as the punt swung its nose into the current, he realised it was like his own on the lake, propelled by some unknown magick. The current took it in its grasp, and it half swirled for a moment but then settled, floating like a leaf in a stream, onward and as lightly.

He had often wondered how an enchanted punt existed behind the palace walls and why the waters were guarded by some unseen force. He had found a legend of an ice dragon in his library amongst the aged rolls that had been written many lifetimes ago. There was a picture of an impressive serpent rising out of the water, arching toward a small punt not unlike his own, and breathing frost and ice over the single occupant.

How was it that an enchanted being could exist on palace grounds so carefully guarded by carved temple dogs which represented calm and goodness, something alien to many of the Celestials? The palace had upturned corners on every roof, so that if invading spirits slid down them, their impetus catapulted them straight back into the Heavens. There were screens in front of entrances because everyone knew, or thought they knew, that spirits could only approach in a straight line. There were water features which created infinite harmony and yet a magick punt and an ice dragon existed within Ming Xao's lake domain.

He had never been threatened by the dragon. He had seen it swimming its sinuous path beneath the imperial punt but it only seemed to watch him, eyes burning with icy fire. Sometimes he thought it would take one little mistake to have it loop in front of the punt's bow and rise up.

But it never did. It was just pervasive, shadowing him to and from his sanctuary.

Sometimes he wondered if it was all to do with Fate. That the dragon and the punt waited until the hourglass had turned. But whose hourglass? Till now it had never been his. He wished he'd asked Yue Lao and he was sure he could hear the old man laugh above the sound of water against the sides of the punt. For let's be honest, little Ancient, Ming Xao thought, as I sit here now with no control over a punt that has its own will, and on a river whose swift current is deathly, am I not at the whim of Fate whose machinations You control?

He hated the way thoughts chased each other in circles, tightening his scalp so that it ached with tension. He pulled at the knot of hair on his nape, loosening the pins and wishing for a...

Knife!

He pushed into his pocket, dragging at the blade he had sheathed there. The punt rocked a little and he grabbed the side with his free hand. In the eastern sky, a faint lightening of the horizon indicated that dawn was not too far. He was glad. It would surely be easier to face one's enemies in the light than dark. Still his head pounded and so he grabbed at the knot at his nape with one hand and with the other, sliced through with the knife. The clump of hair came away easily and he hoped to whatever good gods there were that the Would-be-Empress would find his cabinet, the key, the poems. That to the Others if They came, there would be no trail, no clue.

He threw the hair over the side of the punt, caring little, and sheathed the knife, feeling the punt skew as if the water flowed round a bend. He thought he heard a deep sound from the cliff ahead and realised there was a massive crag, a cast, something common across the Han and which gave it its intrinsic and dramatic beauty. At the top, lights flickered like stars. The sound rolled out again, a chant, followed by a profound vibration – a bass horn perhaps or deepest voices as if from the bowels of the earth.

He recalled there was a monastery on the very edge of his domain – the Jhokang Monastery where a small group of monks and nuns prayed for the security and peace of the Han and all who lived within the province. The sound resonating around the sheer walls that bound the river was their pre-dawn meditation and he listened in wonder as he floated past, the chant loud and then as quickly soft. He wanted to halt the punt, to climb the hundreds of steps to the top of the crag and beg the monastics to intercede for his people.

But then what right did he have to beg anything from anyone? He alone had caused the wrong and he alone must right it.

The sound vanished as the punt flowed around another bend and dampness settled in the pearly dawn – over the cloth of his coat and on the floor of the punt where he knelt. He fancied he could hear the rumble of the meditation still, but it had changed tenor, a more constant sound, a roar. A mist rolled around him, a veil of moisture and then, his heart froze as he realised what the mist and the roar signified.

The punt rocked from side to side as the water buffeted it, the river narrowing to a gorge. Ahead, the mass of water was being forced into a narrow-necked exit – and beyond, a cascading waterfall from which he knew he had no hope of surviving. The roar bore no resemblance to the divine chant of moments before and he quickly threw a prayer back to the monastics and then holding tight to the sides, wondered why Yue Lao had directed him to the punt, to the river and certain death. Was this the way Terrestrials played the game? Just like Their Celestial cousins?

The mist became thicker and he thought how like a silken veil it was, noting the way the cliff sides blurred and almost folded as he lost sight of them. The punt slid remorselessly forward, and the roar became explosive as he envisaged the massive drop over the edge of the waterfall, the matchsticks that had been the punt, his own smashed body.

He closed his eyes tightly as the cliffs disappeared, the veil thickening with spray, the bow of the punt dipping. He begged for forgiveness from his Ancestors and from Chi Nü, asking Them to care for his people; and then the punt tipped sideways and into a terrifying drop that lasted only a heartbeat before the icy water snatched his breath away, his lungs almost in his mouth, his thick coat weighting him down. He sank knowing he was dying; holding his breath seemed pointless. He let go, watching the bubbles rise above him, seeing a golden light.

So I am gone, he thought. How painless…

But his legs bumped against something hard… He grabbed at it, holding on before pulling himself up and sucking in a breath. He wondered what hell or heaven he had come to and gazed as if through a sheer veil, men and women ignoring him, half immersing themselves in the water, offering flowers and spices to the mighty river and filling jugs to pour the sacred water over their bodies. They too chanted, but not with the resonance of Jhokang.

Beyond them were watermelon pink city walls with gates open to the wide dawn. Camels and donkeys, highly strung horses with curved ears and prancing hooves, all entered and exited through the gates.

Ahmadabad?

He should have known.

He should have realised.

Ahmadabad, the pink city of the Raj.

He knew the map like the lines on the palms of his hands. He had fallen through a gate. But where had the waterfall come from? He couldn't recall that on his previous journeys.

Was this how the Others would play then? To change

places and twist things. If that was so, it was obvious the map did not matter at all? And of what use were his clues to Lady Lien?

Yue Lao had alluded to this. He was quarry, he was hunted. So too, Lady Lien and they both needed to stay at least one step ahead. Their lives depended on it.

Hubris, said a voice and he realised that the waterfall was an illusion, that it was Fate that had saved him from drowning and that the veil he looked through had been *exactly* the way one entered and exited the Other world. He needed to push one step further to be in the land of mortals.

He climbed up onto the damp steps and a young man clad only in a loincloth and smelling of cumin and star anise bent to help him, 'You're very wet, sir, did you fall in? The steps are slippery after the rains. Have you hurt yourself? Can I help you?'

Ming Xao shook his head, thanked the man and headed for the gates.

It was time to vanish.

CHAPTER FOUR

Lien

The procession to the Palace seemed to take a lifetime and yet flashed by in the beat of a cricket's wings. She could see nothing but the silk of the litter drapes and the empty seat across from her. The air was scented with jasmine and rose and clung to her, her heartbeat rising as she choked.

Outside the swaying litter, the Voice preceded her, and she rammed her fingers into her ears.

Be calm. Think of the carp pool – fish swimming in lazy vermilion loops, their mouths puffing bubbles to the surface of the mirror-calm water. Think of the elm tree dangling its shaded branches over the water. Think of something soft…

Her mind veered off on a tangent. Away from suffocation as her eyes crunched harder together. Now she could see and hear nothing.

And yet…

'Open your eyes, Lien.'

Warily she relaxed her eyelids so that the surrounding darkness softened.

'Lien…' a soft voice caressed, gentling her as one would a nervous child.

She glanced up. A woman swathed in white fur sat opposite, elegant hands lying relaxed in her lap.

Lien gasped, reaching to open the curtains and call for help but the woman grasped her arm.

'Do not. They won't see me, and they will think you are

hysterical.' Amber eyes mesmerised and Lien subsided in a cloud of yellow silk.

'Kitsune...' she managed. She knew about Kitsune – that she was eldritch, that she was dangerous...

The woman gave a delighted laugh, a sound like the tinkling of icicles in the elm – pretty but chilling. 'Ineffably better than the Lady Ibo, your future husband's first Would-Be-Consort. She called me Fox Lady, but you at least call me by my name. I am hoping you and I might become good friends. The Lady Ibo and myself had a bond that was good for us both in the end. So might it be for you and I.'

'Why?'

Kitsune waved a hand with inconsequential grace, shrugging her shoulders. 'Why not? I am a Spirit, I can do anything I want. Even be your friend if I so choose and I think it might be that you need one or two where you are going.'

Lien shook her head, thinking this was some sort of night terror, perhaps she was ill and this was illusory. 'That's not what I mean. Why are you *here*?' She rapped the seat over which the yellow river of her silks cascaded.

Kitsune sat back. Every part of her was perfection – smooth pale skin, flawless lips, brows as if a calligrapher had brushed his finest ink into a perfect arch, eyes that sparkled. Too perfect, perhaps that same calligrapher had painted her whole being. And yet she sat opposite Lien, smiling.

A fox's smile, beware...

Something prescient tiptoed down Lien's spine.

'Indeed. Why *am* I here?' She sat forward again, her white furs brushing against Lien with a suggestion of tenderness. Her hand reached for Lien's clenched fist and opened it out, pressing each of the fingers until she reached the index finger.

Argh! She severs my finger!

Lien snatched her hand back, cradling it.

'It hurts,' said Kitsune, reaching for Lien's hand again and smoothing it. 'Doesn't it? Almost as if I had taken a dagger and sawn through the bone. And in a way, my dear, I have. Remember you pricked your finger with a needle? Remember the blood? That tiny droplet that sank into your work? Such a nuisance, wasn't it? Do you remember another drop welled and something flashed by and wiped it away before it damaged any more of that magnificent embroidery? Ah…' Her voice became a breath and a whisper. 'I see you do.'

'You? You took it away? Why?' Lien's heartbeat tripped over itself. She wanted to leap from the litter but sat immobile, like a rabbit in the flame of a torch.

'The Others require an acolyte, Lien. We need you to find something for Us.'

'But you are omnipotent. Why do you need me?'

'Because some cursed spirit has placed protection around the Palace, and it forces us back. But you, Lien, are mortal…'

Lien wondered how any Spirit could have entered the Palace to charm it. But then Kitsune had breached the Small Garden. How? And she, Lien, had her blood stolen. Was Kitsune good or evil? How would she know? She scrutinised her finger, still clasped in the Fox Lady's palm. Everything about the day held an unreality that frightened her. Her imminent marriage, an horrendous binding contract with the Spirit world. She was going mad, without doubt.

'You are not mad, Lien.'

'So you say,' Lien said, trying hard to be bold. 'How can I trust you?'

Outside, the Voice sounded louder and the litter stilled.

'Of course you can trust me, else I wouldn't have been your garden companion, would I? The protection around the House of Shue wouldn't have let me enter if I was an evil Other. But listen, I must be swift. In a few heartbeats, you begin your new life.'

A dark cloud edged Lien's consciousness and she vacillated on the edge of a faint, everything conspiring to overcome her, her freedom, her life – all gone.

'Silly woman,' Kitsune's voice came from a far distance. 'Here,' she wafted a hand beneath Lien's nose, an astringent essence curling and pricking her to a state of alert. 'You have strength, use it!' She threw herself back in her seat with a petulant sigh.

The Palace gates began to open and as the entrance widened, the sound of pebbles grated as the litter carriers crunched them. Lien searched Kitsune's impassive face. 'What would you have me do?'

The Fox Lady sniffed and pulled her white furs close. 'Somewhere in the Palace, a map exists. You must find it.'

The litter began to move again, the timbre of the Voice changing with the noise of the people outside. Less folding of the knees and the crackle and whisper of gossiping silk and more of the snapping to attention of martial ankles.

'A map? Of what? Who painted it?'

'A map of entrances and exits,' said Kitsune. 'As to your other question, We believe your Soon-to-be-Husband painted it.'

Fear bit into every part of Lien, her hands trembling. She had not been afraid to be married, but she had been angry and disappointed that her life would change, that her dreams and freedoms would be gone. But she knew enough of legend and folktale to know Others could never be refused. Even less so with a blood contract. Her head felt as crushed as an over-ripe apricot. 'The Emperor? I am to steal *from* him? I would be condemned in an instant if the officials found out.'

'But then, dear one, what do you think *Others* might do if you do not?' The Fox Lady's eyes narrowed to slits and for a moment, Lien wondered if those red lips might draw back over rapacious teeth. Kitsune leaned forward and once again cradled Lien's hand. 'Whilst I am feared by those I don't like, Lien, there is no need for you to be afraid of me. I have told the Others that I would talk with you, persuade you. I did it in order to spare you worse treatment. There are Others who are not as kind as myself and I will help you when I can. But *you* must help *me*, and like I said, you really don't have a choice.' She rubbed Lien's hand in mesmeric circles, the gentle stroke continuing, like a fox mother licking her cub. 'Ah,' she twitched the silk curtains. 'We are at your destiny, and I can go no further. Even now I feel the net about the grounds, and it is uncomfortable. Do what I ask and I will make sure that no Others touch you. Reward my faith in you.'

'But how will I find You? How…' Lien's hand grasped Kitsune's as the litter settled and the Voice called to the imperial courtiers that the Lady Lien had arrived.

'You must find a way to leave the grounds. I will know.' Barely a blink and Kitsune vanished. Not a sign that she had been, and Lien shivered, ripples of fear that shook her to the very core.

Heng's head poked through the curtains. 'My lady, we are h… Oh, by the stars you are pale. Pinch your cheeks and bite your lips – you don't want to appear as though this is a fate worse than death.' She bent and pulled the concertinaed folds of yellow silk into her arms.

But it is, Heng, and I will tell you…

'My lady? Come, they wait for you.'

Feeling as if her head and heart would burst and that her dreams might drift away like the dying sparks of the skyfire beloved of the Han, Lien placed one foot out of the litter.

Immediately there was silence around her. So thick and cloying that one could slice it into pieces like moulded sticky rice.

'The Lady Lien...' called the Voice and the words echoed down the Imperial Way to the Palace steps. A white crane flew up from the lake, a mournful cry accompanying its graceful ark. Lien knew without doubt that it presaged a death, an absence – surely the death of her old life.

She placed the other foot down, Heng laying the yellow folds carefully so that they would trail in a suitably breathtaking manner. The silence became filled with a rushing sound, like a sigh of wind through pine-trees, silks and satins whispering and shifting as the hundreds of Imperial staff, noble and common, kowtowed.

The light had slipped into soft dusk as she had progressed in the litter. It would have been light enough to see colour had she been in the mood to absorb her astonishing surroundings, but she froze, not conscious of anything but that the gates on her life had shut and locked and that she was about to be reincarnated into something she had no wish to be.

Heng gave Lien an inconspicuous nudge and she started, placing one foot in front of the other, beginning to walk onward past people who studied the ground and could only see her dragon emblazoned slippers. Behind her, she trailed a yellow river of silk and Heng followed, close enough for Lien to take comfort but not too close to touch the almost-imperial presence.

Lien tried to imagine she was walking along the path of Small Garden, with the singing birds in their bamboo cages, and crickets chirruping under the leaves of the camellias. But the sound of that one lone Voice, heralding her progress down the Way, shattered the image. She had a brief spark of anger – if the Emperor asked what she would like as a wedding gift, she would ask that the Voice be banned from her presence, from her earshot, from the Han!

The Palace entrance was guarded by snarling stone temple dogs but she ignored them, glancing back to check that Heng had care of the silk. It was unnecessary. Was Heng not her shadow? Did Heng not read her mind? Instead she saw acres of bent forms, all in rich blue or black silk, little black caps on heads, all with their faces in the dust of the mighty forecourt of the imperial surrounds. Surely such ridiculous behaviour could have been outlawed along with foot-binding! What honour did it imply? Nothing to her, that's for sure!

She liked feeling anger. It made it all easier to bear. It straightened her spine and tipped her head, gave her a confidence that she might not have otherwise had. And of course, there was faithful Heng at her back as well. *That* mattered! But still, she did not want to move forward between the lions. It would surely be the end…

There was an ancient Han saying that the longest walk began with the shortest step. Lien's first step under the carved stone arch was halting, unsure, her slipper almost stuck to the paving stones as if some evil maw held it. Heng gave her another push and she stood straighter, ignoring the crowds behind her, relieved that at last the Voice had silenced. She focused on a small man in the distance as she stepped down to the imperial forecourt. Behind her, she heard Heng's intake of breath as they both surveyed the further mass of people bent double. It was as though an artist had painted the scene and added a hundred bent backs and hundred more for realism and effect. Surely so many people did not live inside the Palace grounds!

She stared at the man in the distance who stood at the vast Palace entrance. His hands were neatly concealed within the huge azure cuffs of his black silk robes. The cuffs glinted like lapis in the last rays of the day's sun.

So, he is the Emperor? He certainly has grown no taller. I look forward to telling Old One that she is wrong…

She drew closer.

The man before her was so much older than she imagined. That was surprising. The man she had seen at the First

House of Merchants was younger than middle years, but this man's hair had thick streaks of grey and her heart sank. He looked older than her father! What had happened to the emperor in his time away to make him so elderly?

Reaching the Palace entrance, she climbed the wide steps, one and then another, seven in all – a fortuitous number – and she noticed that this little man did not look at her; that his head bowed as she approached. Her scalp tightened, and she was glad Heng had released her hair from that towering, ornate hairstyle. Otherwise for sure, her head would be splitting in every direction. As it was, her head thumped with each step, but it was bearable, leavened by her courage to get this day and the beginning of the future over and done.

Only she and Heng approached this man. Only she and Heng could see him. Every one of the hundreds of pairs of eyes in the Palace forecourt were staring at the ground, waiting for the sign that they could stand and observe the Would-Be-Empress enter the hallowed buildings.

'My lady,' the man said.

She gripped her fingers within her cuffs and bowed her head, saying nothing.

'My lady, I welcome you to the Palace...' he took a breath and there was a tremor in his voice. 'My Lord is indisposed. Please follow me.'

She almost turned to exchange glances with Heng but instead, 'Indis...'

'Please, my lady,' the man spoke so quietly she doubted his breath would have bent a fragile grass stalk. 'Do not speak. Just follow.'

She swallowed her confusion, stepping after the palace official into the cavernous interior of the Palace.

The place was deserted.

But then was not everyone bent to the ground outside? Of course it would be empty. She kept her attention on the narrow back of the elderly man as he picked up pace and hurried across the shining floors. Past red dragon entwined pillars. Onward past white silk gauze drapes that wafted in the suggestion of a breeze. She wished she could see the lake and the ebbing daylight, a glimpse of space and freedom. She and Heng passed through another massive set of doors, turning right into a plain antechamber where the official heaved the bronze trimmed doors shut and then led the two women across to paper doors which glowed with amber dusklight from outside. He pushed these apart and the three finally stood on a balcony completely shielded by swaying willow fronds.

Lien could not help herself. 'Indisposed? How so? No messages…'

'My lady,' the official briefly closed his eyes and for a moment, Lien saw a tangible weight sitting on his shoulders. 'He was well this morning, in anticipation of your arrival. He knew much about you, and I do not speak lightly when I say he has … had … high hopes.'

'Had?' she asked, a flicker of unease licking at the glowing coals of her nerves. 'He has changed his mind.' It was a statement and even she was surprised at the faint note of disappointment that hovered.

Did she care that he had changed his mind? Wasn't it what she had wanted all along?

'No, my lady. You are wrong. He had no change of heart. When I last saw him, he was enthusiastic.'

She was tired of word-games. 'And when exactly did you *last* see him? What has happened since then?'

'Please,' said the official. 'Will you sit?'

She thumped down with ill-grace and Heng frowned at her as she settled the yellow folds around her mistress. 'I am sitting, sir,' Lien could barely contain herself. 'And I am curious to know what ailment could possibly have consumed the Emperor so quickly that since you last saw him, he finds it impossible to meet me himself. It smacks of gross ill manners.' Heng sucked in her breath, reaching forward to pinch Lien's back but Lien didn't care. 'How severely is he indisposed?'

Silence.

She spoke quietly then. 'So indisposed that he is dead, perhaps?'

This time, Heng could not restrain herself. 'My lady!' she hissed.

The official waved his hand at Heng, suddenly the old uncle. ''Tis no matter. Your mistress is quite right to be disturbed. *I* am disturbed. He gazed beyond the willows as if he hoped answers would float across the lake to their sides. 'My lady, I don't believe he is dead, or at least, I hope he is not. You see, between midday today, which was when I last saw him, and now, he has vanished...'

Lien recalled a flash of white fur, a yip and threats of evil spirits. 'Vanished!'

'Please, Lady Lien, quietly. No one but myself knows.' He cast anxious looks about.

'This is surely history repeating. This happened before with his *first* Betrothed.'

'It did and I am... I can't...'

'You don't know what to do, do you?' Lien's mind ran fast. In one swift moment, all her prayers had been answered and she was free.

A lone duck, all teal, chestnut and curling tail quacked sadly and floated under the cantilevered balcony as the old man replied. 'You are right. This is a disaster for the Han. We have been settled and prosperous under his leadership. I don't know how to tell anyone...'

'You told *me*.'

He studied her then and she coloured a little at her forthrightness.

'Lady Lien, I can see he chose well. You have a strength.'

'I am not so sure,' she demurred. 'That aside, I feel for you, the weight of your predicament.

'Indeed', he sighed. 'It is unbearable.'

'Then you must tell the First Minister, sir, so that an interim government can be formed.'

'The First Minister knows, Lady Lien. You see I am he, First Minister Sun Sen, Lord High Chamberlain.' He bowed over his hands. 'To me, the government of the land falls until my lord returns.'

'*If* he returns,' Lien uttered under her breath.

A scandalised 'My lady!' puffed forth from behind her.

Silence hung, punctuated by frogs along the edge of the lake, the base burrs joined by the mezzo trills of the crickets. Birds had long since fallen quiet as the shadows lengthened and the island in the middle of the lake became a mere silhouette.

'You speak as you find, Lady Lien,' Sun Sen kept his face turned toward the island. Lien would have liked to measure his mood, but the dimming light and no lamps made it difficult. Behind her, she heard Heng move, then the strike of a tinder and a flare as the maidservant lit a lamp and carried it to a low table.

'If I seem rude,' Lien replied, 'then I must apologise. But I find myself shocked by your revelations. And confused about my future. I was brought here today as the Betrothed of the Emperor. Now that he is missing, I must surely ask myself, what is my place? May I return to my home?'

Sun Sen turned and in the flickering dance of the lamp flame, he appeared aged and beset. 'Sadly, my lady, you cannot return to your family. Papers have been signed. You are, by law, the Would-Be-Consort-in-Waiting.'

'But, First Minister, I think there is a time for honesty and that is surely now. What if the Emperor never returns? Do I sit in the Palace and gather cobwebs? There is surely a law of succession which might free me from my obligations.'

'The Emperor said the same...'

'So there is none?' Her voice lifted. Not shrill, but almost.

'Not yet.'

'So you are indeed the person who governs the Han.'

'As you say.'

'May I be even more honest?'

In the light of the flame, Sun's face softened. 'In a very short time, my lady, I have learned that you will be honest regardless of what I might say. Ah,' he sighed. 'I find I am ineffably tired. It has been a long afternoon.'

She squirmed on the bench, angry, rustling her trailing silk folds, almost as if the cloth was a fourth voice on the balcony. Not such a fool's thought, Lien mused. She represented the first House of Silk after all, and silk had its place. Did it chide her or guide her, she wondered? Heng smoothed out the river of gold and then took a seat on a chair against the wall. 'Behave yourself,' she whispered to her mistress.

'With the greatest respect,' Lien began quietly, 'I would say this to you – firstly, there must surely be a danger that you might be seen to be the person who surreptitiously arranged for the Emperor's disappearance before he could marry and create an heir. You are now in a position of great power.'

'This is true.' Sun replied without rancour. 'Except for the fact that I love the Emperor as if he is my own son. Which I might add, everyone knows.'

'They may know, but you know what kind of gossip grows with fertilisation...'

'Indeed.'

'My other point is that, again with respect, First Minister – you are old. What happens if the Emperor never returns? What happens if you...'

'If I die? Then the Second Minister takes my place.'

'And he is old?'

'Not as old as me.'

'Is he a worthy man?'

Sun's mouth flattened. 'Most think so.'

'But you do not? Might he have instigated the Emperor's disappearance?'

'He might, but I think not. Because the disappearance happened on the island.'

'Why are you so sure that he was not involved?'

'No one but the Emperor goes to the island, my lady. No one but the Emperor can find the way. Either by water or by the little bridge that appears. If one goes by boat, one can paddle and paddle and the island never gets any closer. And as for the bridge, it is of the same ilk as the Bridge that Never Was. It appears only to those who need it.'

'And you have never needed it? Even now?'

'Apparently not.'

Lien leaned back against her chair. This had become curiouser. Against her better judgement she was intrigued. Surely this was better than sitting in Small Garden and stitching carp! But then, there was also freedom, true freedom…

'How is it that enchantment can exist in the Palace grounds when it is surrounded by the strongest protection?'

Sun Sen looked out toward the little island, fireflies dancing through the air. The Palace surrounds were slowly being lit by flame and a hum of voices could be heard further away.

'The celebrations are beginning. And in answer to your question, I do not know. It seems that such enchantment existed only in the Emperor's presence.'

'Then I reply with two more questions. Firstly, is it not at all possible that an evil enchantment might have whisked him away? And secondly, the celebrations go ahead?'

'Simple answers? Yes. And yes. In respect of the latter, it gives me time to deal with what has happened and to formulate a plan. And remember, no one but you, your maidservant and myself know the Emperor has disappeared. There *is* one other thing. I sent word to my Emperor on the island earlier this day to say there is a rumour from far in the mountains of the Han, in Sie. It is rumoured a plague has broken out and the gates of the village have been shut to prevent any from entering or leaving. It is an isolated village, with barely any contact with those beyond...'

'You are concerned about how such an illness began?'

'I am. The village has had no outside visitors for more than three moons. Something is not right.'

Lien blew out her lips in what she was fully aware was neither ladylike nor the way a Would-Be-Consort should behave. She said what was in her head, aware that something was happening to turn the Han inside out. 'Are you saying this is an Other-contrived rumour? That Spirits are coercing His Imperial Highness?'

Behind Lien, Heng sucked in a breath but said nothing.

'I think I might be. Yes.' Sun stood and made his way to a side table on which sat pitchers, porcelain cups and lidded pots. 'May I offer you tea, my lady? I can heat the water quickly. For myself, I find I need something. And you, my dear,' he turned to Heng. 'You must surely want refreshment.' He took a slip, held it to the lamp flame and lit a small iron brazier before placing the waterpot atop. Taking a lidded celadon pot, he ladled the tea leaves in, sniffing the fragrance with what seemed to be relief, if not pleasure. As if completing the ritual gave him a reprieve.

Lien said nothing and allowed him to make tea whilst her own mind raced across all that she had heard. Part of her strained at bonds that remained tight and another part of her fussed with anxiety. She reminded herself of the unwilling commitment to the Fox Lady and she squeezed her hands until they hurt under the silk cuffs. A more logical stream of thought wondered if this entire moment, finding out that the Emperor had been spirited away, dovetailed completely with her own dilemma. The lamp flame flared, illuminating the room, and as the light settled again, shadows filling the corners, she knew that in order to be free of one, she had to examine and perhaps solve the other. The two were linked and like any convoluted knot, needed to be unravelled.

First Minister made the tea with a delicacy that surprised her, taking the hissing water from the flame and pouring it gently over the tea leaves. Wiping any drops from the smooth glaze of the pot, he turned it one way and then the other, each turn swishing the leaves as they steeped. He placed small porcelain cups in a measured row and poured the tea carefully, so meticulously measured that each cup held exactly the same amount. He took a green linen cloth and holding a cup with the cloth beneath, he passed it to Lien, doing the same with Heng's cup and then returning to his seat with his own.

For a moment, the three sat in a taut silence, sipping the aromatic tea, as it endeavoured to loosen tired muscles and relax stretched nerves. But Lien could drop her guard only so far and so she placed her empty cup on the low table in front of her.

'But why,' Lien broke the quiet, 'would Others find the need to pressure the Emperor to do anything?' She needed to know how much Sen Sen knew of the fateful map.

He looked at her sadly. 'I am not sure and all I can add is that I don't know…'

So he knows nothing…

'First Minister, what is on the island that so beguiled the Emperor?'

'He has a pavilion there. You cannot see it for it is shielded by a luxurious growth of trees. He has always been a very intense and studious man and it is that same intensity that took him away in the first instance, returning the Lady Ibo to her home and examining all that our world is, beyond these walls. Anything he found whilst away, he keeps in collections in a library which is within the pavilion.'

'What happened when he returned? I don't recall. There seemed to be no word from any of the Han gates…'

'That is because one night as we all slept, he arrived as silently as a Celestial. When we woke next morning, he stood in the Audience Chamber dressed plainly, but stronger, taller, very pleasing of face, as though he had grown into himself in his absence. He was a more mature version than we remembered. Our lives have been improved since that moment. We owe him much. Think on it – since the Emperor returned from his absence, there has been universal care for all, there is no hunger, no strife. Beyond the Wall, they crave our goods. We are a wealthy province, Lady Lien, and it is entirely due to his vision.' Sun Sen's expression when he looked at Lien was pleated with woe. 'We *must* find him, Lady Lien. We must.'

She took a breath, unbelieving of the spontaneous words about to leave her mouth, saying without thought. 'I think I can help you. I can give you time…

CHAPTER FIVE
Ming Xao

His heavy coat hung dipping and limp around him, so he shucked it off, feeling in the pocket for the canister, the dagger and purse as smoke rose along the *ghats*. The smell on the air was sickly sweet – filled with the scent of flowers, oils and spices but nothing could disguise the smell of death. He shuddered as he thought of the small mountainous village of Sie. By the Gods he hoped that Yue Lao was right, that there were no funeral pyres in the Han, that it was all a cruel illusion.

The Raji fires danced harshly bright in the twilit dawn, the flames orange against the soft pink and gold of the sky. Mourners stood respectfully, no breeze stirring their white robes, and from their circles, priestly *pujaris* in umber *dhotis*, wild hair twisted and threaded with ochre flowers, offered up prayers to the Gods for the safe journeys of the dead to the Heavens.

Further along the *ghats*, two fires burned solitary. No mourners, nor priests, no flowers or oils and it was to these that Ming now hastened. Beggars and paupers were pariahs in the Raj and thus they were burned alone. No one would soil themselves by venturing close and the emptiness around the fires suited Ming.

He had wondered if he carried a scent, where he could be tracked like prey by hounds and so gagging on the pungent smell of burning flesh, he balled his coat and threw it into the flames, followed by his quilted boots. They fell with a sizzling hiss and he felt no sadness, just relief that he could shed more and more of his identity. He ripped off his black silk tunic and used the dagger to cut wide strips which he joined with knots until he had enough to tie a mediocre turban around his shortened hair. With a strip that was left, he hiked up his baggy trousers and tied them so that they looked like a *dhoti*. Finally, he tucked the dagger, purse and canister into the waistband. He had hoped he looked like a *pujari*. But to make sure, he dipped his fingers in the river, grabbed some mud and drew two horizontal lines along his forehead and two more along his bare chest. It would have to be enough until he could find more clothes and a new appearance.

He swept his hand from his forehead to his waist in a calming gesture and turned toward the city gates as the remains of his Han life curled and crimped into ash and dust.

Kebab-sellers called out as the city swirled with frenetic business. Rice-sellers scooped cups of fragrance onto glossy pandanus and banana leaves. Others stirred spicy yellow curries in metal pans over flames that were fed with ox-dung. Ming's stomach churned with nerves and hunger, and he passed over a coin for some plain rice on a banana leaf.

The rice seller bowed his head and returned the coin, saying it was a blessing that a *pujari* ate from his stove. Ming pressed his palms together in thanks, smiled as he picked up the banana leaf and kept walking, adding the lie to the weight of guilt he carried on his back.

If he took one moment to think on his predicament, he wondered if he would just fold to the ground in a twisted bundle. He, who was supposed to be an emperor and who had successfully introduced his province to the wider world, had effectively signed the province's death warrant. Why did he do it? *Was* it vainglory? Was he so shallow, so arrogant, so blind? He knew he'd been stupid, but the rest?

It took monumental effort and prayer to push the thoughts away. He knew such thinking was doomed, that he had just to focus on reaching the Wise Woman's whole and undamaged. Surely all would then be well. But then maybe that too was naïve…

The warm rice smelled vaguely of lemons and cumin, and he savoured it as he walked, the glutinous mouthfuls settling a modicum of comfort in his belly. He looked for a fountain from where he could drink, walking on against the crush and smell of bodies, the noise of the marketplace assaulting him. The Han was so different – a strange place filled with gentility and codes of living. Even the poor were cherished and were scooped from the streets to be cared for in hospices until they died. He had made such care an imperial edict and the idea had been readily adopted, people aware that only good fortune could follow if they cared for others.

Even the marketplace in the imperial city was ordered. There was always excitement and happiness, and each stall holder had his regular place. There was a First Market, a Second Market and so forth throughout the days – positions changing monthly in an imperially devised selection. It was equitable and had proved successful. Only the First Merchant Houses made exceptional money. They sold to merchants outside the Han because Ming Xao knew that only the best must be offered to foreign traders if the Han was to survive and thus the First House hierarchy strengthened. With their wealth, they attracted government taxes which they paid if they were to remain First Houses. Such taxes supported the poor and paid for the provincial infrastructure and the province grew and prospered. Emperor Ming Xao had wrought masterful change.

He hoped that if he did not return, the Han would be

strong enough to survive. He wished he'd asked Yue Lao – the God of Fate must surely know something of the future of the province.

He saw a fountain playing against a wall near a sign that indicated a bazaar. He was glad he had learned the tongues of Eirie in his time away because the ability to converse with others had opened trade between the provinces like oil greasing squeaky doors. Even now, he spoke to the children splashing each other and they glanced at his mud stripes, made shy obeisance and let him scoop some water for himself. He gave the oldest a coin and told the boy to take the others and buy some sweet rasgulla and they ran off shouting, leaving him alone to remove his turban, wash his face and chest, and rub it hard with the balled-up black cloth. He smoothed back the shorter hair, wishing he had some oils to change his body odour, something to throw the hounds off his scent, scooping a handful of the constantly playing water, and then another. The sun was higher in the morning sky and time was as precious as life.

The bazaar opened out from the wide entrance – graceful stone arches supported cupolas and between the crowds, one could see delicate azure and crimson lotus tiles covering the walls. It was blessedly cool and Ming shivered as a breeze, the breath of something, touched his bare shoulder. He looked back – nothing there. Just a feeling that left his skin tingling.

Something … something… Hurry, hurry!

He pushed through the crowds until he faced a clothing stall where garments were folded and piled into multi-coloured heaps.

'I don't give credit,' the merchant said. 'A thousand sorries but I have a wife and five children to feed.'

'Don't apologise.' Ming dug into his purse and pulled

our two pieces of silver. 'I would like those,' he pointed at a clay-coloured *khurta* and *churidar*. They were untrimmed, workmanlike, and smelled of camphor for which he was grateful.

The merchant bit into the silver and his eyes widened. 'Yes, sir, of course, sir. Would sahib like to change at the back of my stall?'

'Thank you.' Ming edged around the trestle, passing over a further coin. 'For directions to a barber…'

Changed, his old clothing squashed at the back of the merchant's stall, his new attire scented with camphor, the small map canister, his knife and purse tucked into the waist and with feet shod in soft leather shoes with upturned toes that reminded him of palace roofs in the Han, he found the barber. He was deep in the marketplace, far from the entrance, and light fell from glass windows that surrounded the base of the cupolas. The whole space seemed as if it floated in light and at any other time, he would have wondered, examined, made notes and diagrams, but time was against him, so he pushed past brightly clothed men and women, the women's many gold bracelets jangling like dainty percussion instruments. It seemed so normal, almost intoxicating with exotica at every corner, so that when the cool breeze brushed by his ears again, bumps rose on his skin. This deep in the bazaar, there was no possible way a breeze could enter.

He swallowed on a dry-as-sand throat as he looked back, fear curling around his heart, but as before, there was nothing, and he sidled backward into the barber's stall, jumping as the barber tapped him on the shoulders, asking him what he wanted. 'Cut it right back,' Ming gestured to his hair. 'I want to look different, smell different. Do what you must.' He passed over more silver and the barber folded a warm towel that had been steaming over a brass kettle on a brazier.

'Completely different?'

'Yes, put henna through my hair.'

Without another word, the barber picked up sharp scissors and began to cut Ming's hair evenly. Snip-snap and raven black chunks fell onto the cloth the man had tied around him. When he had finished, he lathered Ming's head from a bowl smelling of rosemary, rinsing the hair that was left, pouring henna through, rinsing it, rubbing it dry, smoothing a handful of cedar oil through it, over Ming's face, massaging it in and then taking another cloth to buff his face and hair again.

'If sahib wants to be really different, I can direct you to a tattooist…'

'A tattooist?'

'Some like to change their faces, but they fear the permanence.'

'And…'

'Sahib, you could have henna tattoos. They will wear off in time.'

'On the face?'

'Wherever you want.'

The tattooist was not far on and Ming lay on a table as the man dipped a fine brush into henna. Ming asked for his eyes to be widened, to lose the Han face. He asked for a flying crane to be painted low on his chest and for Raji lotuses to be painted on his hands.

'I will have to remove the red thread at your wrist,' the tattooist said.

'No, paint around it. It must stay. It is a custom.' He would not explain its significance or the strange permanence of its properties. It was no one's business but his own and the less people knew of him the better.

As he felt the brush bristles prick over his chest, he hoped honouring the crane in such a way would bring him good fortune. She was his spirit animal, his soul friend in a time when he had few friends at all and they had grown together, bird and man. By the stars he hoped she lived now.

Eventually, almost too long Ming chafed, the sensation of brush strokes ceased, and the tattooist signalled for Ming to stand and observe himself in a mirror.

The reflection that looked back was not that of a Han man. It was a stranger, an outlier from the vast peaks of the LongMa mountains perhaps. The crane was glorious, her wings stretched in flight across the breadth of his chest, her long legs lying in the cleft of muscles in the flat of his belly. His eyes could have been any shape – so detailed was the henna lacework that outlined them, opening out to his temples, and the lotus on each hand spoke of resilience and rebirth.

He breathed in, smelling cedar and camphor and could do nothing but hope that cranes and lotuses would protect him. He paid and then hurried from the crowded market-place, as ordinary and unordinary as any of the disparate folk who peopled the Raj. Surely he must be safe.

He headed to the *ghats*, walking along a path that edged the pink city wall. Below him, men and boys fished in the closer reaches of the delta, some sat on boats in the water, throwing circular nets in looping graceful slow-moving arcs so that they landed flat on the river surface, sinking as the fisherfolk pulled them in. Flapping, sparkling fish were hauled into boats and even on the shore, men pulled catches off hook and line.

He needed a punt, the urge to get going almost choking him as he observed an old man sitting on the shore by a battered vessel. A large needle was fed back and forth through nets as the fellow's old boat guarded him with baleful eyes painted either side of the prow.

'Greetings, grandfather,' said Ming. 'I would buy your boat...'

The old man sucked a mashed betelnut between his gums and then spat the red juice to his side. 'My boat is my wife, my mistress – in another's hands she may be unhappy. And you know the saying,' he hoiked more betel juice. 'Unhappy wife, unhappy life.'

Ming dug into his purse, noticing how the supply of coins was depleting. He shuffled the silver around and found a solid gold coin inscribed with the imperial insignia of the crane. 'Will this make for a happier life?'

The old man reached out with fingers that were knotted, the nails broken and split. His eyes widened when he saw the crane. 'This is from far...' he drew out the word as if to explain the distance, 'beyond the headwaters.'

'Yes.'

The man spat the betelnut into his palm and with his few remaining teeth bit into the gold. 'It will do.' As he spoke, faint smoke from the ghats blew down the edge of the river and around the boat and the old man coughed and swatted. 'See? An evil wind.' He made the sign of the horns, shoved the coin into a slit in the side of his *dhoti* and threw the betelnut back into his mouth. 'It is a strange day filled with portent. A breeze blows and yet no sign of it ripples the water. Huh! Take the boat. I shall take your gold and stay in my home until the morrow when evil will have tired of itself and left us alone.' He piled his net into a basket, stood and with the basket on his bowed spine, left without a backward glance.

Ming wasted no time, threw his pointed shoes into the punt, waded into the water and pulled the boat out to where it floated. Jumping in, collapsing on the only seat, he grabbed up the battered and silvered oars and began to row to the middle of the river where he could catch the current. A small puddle of leaky water swilled at his feet as he felt the boat pulled into the channel and he watched the shore as the vessel moved round the headland.

In moments he had drifted beyond the city, the river broad and swift with an occasional ripple or miniature whirlpool. Nothing evil, he thought.

Except...

Something skirled at his neck, a puff of cold air and he looked to his stern, blood freezing.

Streaming toward him, grey and evil, were two clouds of smoke, growing, with the faces of death and destruction, mouths open so that an evil sigh issued forth. He paddled as though the hounds of the dead were behind. Perhaps they were, and he shrieked to Chi Nü, to Yue Lao and to the Ancestors.

'Help me...' but his words were spat away as a storm raged toward his bow from downriver, saturating him as it sped over his boat, meeting the smoke with a crash of thunder and jagged bolts of lightning. Still he rowed, watching the smoke and rain storm collide, realising that the smoke... or maybe the rain... was dissolving before his eyes.

The colours of the day – the umber, the grey, the metallic sheen of pelting rain, all ran together like paint that has had water spilled upon it and he shook his head, yelling to the heavens, knowing he had reached an Other gate, that he was sliding into... into...

Where?

His map had showed a portal on the river – he had been expecting it, but in his fear he had neglected to recite the necessary words – the little charm that would direct him to the Ymp Tree orchard and safety.

Where then?

He drifted in pearly mist, no sound of thunder, no lightning. Peaceful glistening waters that stretched away through the haze.

Here a pole defining the channel.

Another…

Another and then a boat with a boatsman aboard, and steering from a side-mounted tiller, a small sail set above him.

'Leeway!' called the man.

Ming heaved hard to port and gave the fellow space.

'Good day to you,' the sailor called, floating on, a tune breaking forth from a mellow voice.

More song, more channel markers, more vessels – punts, fishing boats, sailboats, and there! Gondolas!

A city appearing beyond the thinning fog!

The pearly ribbons of mist
slide back like a maiden's diaphanous veil
to seduce and bodily entwine…

He knew this place of elegance, of soft light and buildings coloured in earthy pinks and umbers, where streets were water and bridges joined buildings together like graceful tethers. The palatial structures were gems around the watery diadem that was the laguna, holding the city in sparkling radiance.

Veniche - the enigmatic lagoon province of Eirie smelling of fine foods, mould and fish. Loaded with wealth, silk, gold leafed interiors and little iron gates that led to eldritch squares of secrets and silence.

This place above all others was filled with dark and light and he knew that something as simple as a mirrored reflection could pull him into the Other world as easily as he breathed. If he was not already there…

But how? The portal in and out of the city was surely in a ballroom.

His heart froze as he realised the gates he had drawn were just four of many, that no matter where mortals trod, they would always run foul of others.

Damn it to burning Hell! Naïvete and ignorance!

Wits, he needed wits. Something he should have had before drawing the cursed map.

Cursed. He could not deny it.

He paddled the punt onward across the laguna toward the palazzos and then down the central canal amidst many gondolas and punts going about the watery business of Veniche. The canals smelled humid and musty and verdant green tidemarks stained the walls of the buildings. The water had less denseness than the river in the Raj, but even so, the constant boat traffic, the watery breezes, the fact that Veniche sat on a muddy delta – all conspired to discolour the laguna. Astonishing then to think that the light of the water dazzled the eyes and created an opalescent veil over the canals and palaces.

He had paddled more than half the Grand Canal and his muscles ached, his shoulders burning with muscle tension, hands blistered and sore. He hated that he had no plan, his mind as blank as a new piece of parchment. He needed to rest, to eat and to think.

There was a thin watery alley to his left and he directed his punt along its length, looking for a *fondamenta* onto which he could climb. But the buildings dropped sheer into the water and he paddled on, turning a corner, moving deeper into the interior of the floating city. A single landing stuck into the canal, one paving stone deep with a rusted iron ring mottled with verdigris hanging on the wall where paint flaked and bricks crumbled. He tied the boat and heaved himself onto the shallow platform, glad that a half-timbered gate was open and he stretched his shoulders, slipped on the Raji leather shoes and then moved silently past the entrance.

The gate was as dilapidated a state as the building, the timber warped, massive iron hinges hanging. Barely a dusting of faded black paint clung to the surface and a rusted grille was set in the upper half. His heartbeat lifted as he edged around the gate, expecting something, someone, to grab him and put a knife to his throat. But the patio was empty of life beyond a pair of fat doves who grumbled at him from deep in their throats. A walnut tree hung over the wall and in its shadow, a black cat sat observing Ming, its green eyes slitted, its tail flicking back and forth in a mean-tempered way. The patio was filled with half-grown weeds – barley grass, plantain, seawort and dandelions and such an air of emptiness that for once he felt safe. If only he had food and water, he could stay here, sleep perhaps, and then be fresh enough to formulate his next move when he had devised a plan.

He sank onto the paving stones and the doves flew up with a clack-flack of wings. The cat watched them go and settled back to observe Ming. Ming looked at the animal, eye to eye, but the cat demurred not once. Just swung its tail in a mesmerising pendulum-like way. Flick this way, flick that and Ming pushed his head back against the wall, allowing the sun to warm his bones, to soothe the headache that pounded at his temples.

Still the cat's tail flicked back and forth and Ming's eyes grew heavy, his tired body slumping. As his head dropped onto his chest, he was conscious of shadows as the sun moved, but was too tired and sore to care. A quick sleep – just a swift nap, it would not hurt in this empty, forgotten place.

And the cat's tail swung back and forth, back and...

CHAPTER SIX

Lien

First Minister looked at Lien, a perplexed bow to his thin eyebrows.

'It occurs to me that people think I am meeting the Emperor as we speak,' she said surprised at herself but recognising his perplexity. 'It also occurs to me that Heng may be about the same height as the Emperor, yes? And if she is not, she is taller than me. If she dresses in the Emperor's attire, and we are seen together from a far distance in the night and by the light of only one flame, people will think all is well. I would that Heng and myself go to the island. It will look as if the Emperor takes me there. We are then out of the way of Palace staff for a night and a day, and it gives you time to think…'

Sun Sen went to interrupt but she held up her hand. 'Yes, I know what you would say. I may be denied entry by whatever force keeps the island secure. On the other hand, I may not…' she shrugged a shoulder and then, 'In which case, I may be able to search…'

Besides, what are your options, First Minister.

But she didn't say that. He was an astute man.

'My only concern,' she concluded, 'is that once we are there, how do I send you a message? You say you are unable to broach the island.'

''Tis true. But the Emperor has a trained bird. It would fly to me with messages strapped to its leg.'

'And the bird will be there?'

'It is always there.'

'I will recognise it?'

'Yes. It is the white crane – the bird is the Emperor's coat-of-arms. Lady Lien, there are a number of problems. The first being whether you are allowed access to the island. What happens if you and your maidservant are denied? People will see and know that something is badly wrong. You will both return under the worst scrutiny. Many questions will be asked, and your way forward will not be a happy one.'

'But what alternative do you have?' Lien played with her cuffs as Sun Sen closed his eyes, rubbing at them with gnarled bony fingers. It was hard not to feel compassion for him – whilst she had her own problems, she knew how impossible it was to deal with Spirits. Either way, she felt as if she would be torn apart – by the Han people for what they began to suffer and by the Spirits with their selfish cruelty.

'None,' he admitted.

'Then can you collect some of the Emperor's clothes for us?'

He stood, opened his mouth but then thought better of what he might have to say, collected the three porcelain cups and placed them on the side table. 'I will be swift. Place the bar across the doors whilst I'm gone. I shall knock twice and twice again, when I return.'

As Heng slipped the bar across the door, Lien realised her maidservant was speaking.

'I am ugly then,' the woman said, so very quietly.

Lien swung round, jerking the silk folds away in a temper as they threatened to trip her. 'I beg your pardon?'

'You think I am tall and perhaps more man-looking than woman.'

'Heng, no...'

'Then why did you say I could dress as a man?'

'It is not meant as an insult. Look...' she dragged the trailing yellow silk over to where Heng stood and placed her shoulder next to Heng's side. 'You are a head height above me. It is not a bad thing. I am short and that is *not* a good thing. And I never said a word about your looks.'

'But to dress as a man?'

'Heng, please,' Lien took the maid's hands. They were soft from days and months of smoothing creams into Lien's body and face. 'There is so much I need to tell you. But it needs to wait until we are on that island, in the library pavilion. This is all just subterfuge to get us there. Can you trust me?' She squeezed Heng's hands. 'I cannot do any of this without you, nor do I want to, and I mean that with all my heart.'

Heng looked down at her mistress and Lien was struck by the woman's comely pale face now that it was revealed with her hair drawn back, the odd curling strand wafting in the night air and with the pleasing sea-green silk robe enhancing her complexion.

Sea-green? What do I know of the sea? This is Heng's and my chance...

'You said you wished to see what is beyond the Wall and I have a feeling, Heng. I feel it in here,' Lien tapped her head, 'and here...' She tapped her heart.

Heng huffed a breath. 'Then I must trust you. But if I may be so bold, Lady Lien, I would appreciate you asking me in the future.'

Lien's eyebrows lifted. Such brazenness from a servant! Her mother would have whipped the woman. But the maidservant just stared Lien down, strength and honesty in her expression and Lien grinned. 'I shall call you Heng-O from now on because you are surely a powerful Celestial!' She squeezed the servant's hands again. 'I will, I swear. I will always ask. Can you accept my apology? I do not take you for granted, I assure you.'

Two knocks sounded through the timber of the door and then two more and Heng lifted the bar, First Minister passing through with silk garments folded over his arms.

'I met no one. Everyone is at the banquet hall awaiting the emperor's arrival. And I have thought on that. I will go to the hall and announce that the Emperor takes his bride to the island. We will watch you and I pray to the Celestials that whatever intuition has prompted this will be right and proper. Assuming you are able to reach the island, I will then announce that the emperor intends staying at the pavilion but insists that all celebrate his union this night and that when he returns, he will have a marriage ceremony in front of the whole city. Beyond that, I am in your hands.'

Lien took the fine silk jacket, trousers and small red imperial cap from Sun Sen and passed them to Heng. 'The sooner we are away, the better. Chief Minister, perhaps you and I should turn our backs and give our friend privacy to change. I wish I had something easier to wear, these folds are an encumbrance.' As she walked to the railings of the balcony, she twisted them over her arm with a tug. Her nerves played with her, her stomach tossing and turning, her legs wobbling like almond jelly. She wished she could believe in her plan, but even she found it as flimsy as a cobweb.

'The Emperor keeps clothing on the island. I am sure you will find something.'

'You have no idea what the pavilion is like? What it contains?'

'Only what he has told me. He speaks of it with pride and joy. He often spent night and day there when not required for government and imperial duties.'

'Do we need to walk far to find the boat?'

'You will go by boat?'

'Yes. At least we might be seen floating across the water. If we wait on the shore for the bridge to appear and it doesn't, then we are discovered, are we not? The boat gives us time and a fighting chance.'

'Lady Lien, if the boat fails, you realise I cannot help you? Either way, boat or bridge, you may be discovered.'

The thought hadn't occurred to Lien at all, and her heart skipped a lifetime's beats as she examined what Sun Sen has said. That he absolved himself from any involvement in this plan. She realised that for the sake of the now rudderless Han, that Sun Sen must protect himself and his position at the helm of the country. She closed her eyes, hoping First Minister could not see fear writ large. 'I do. But then the boat will not fail. I am sure of it.'

Are you, Lien? What gives you such confidence when there should be none?

Suddenly her innermost voice had changed tack, voicing against her rather than with her. She pushed at the whispers and dragged deep to hoist her intuition back to where it belonged. 'And so, where is the boat?'

'Here,' Sun Sen leaned over the rail and she leaned with him to see a beautiful timber punt glowing in the light of a thousand stars. It swung lazily, almost flirting with them as they gazed at it, the bow ducking back and forth in the softest and most sweet-smelling night-breeze. To Lien, the craft looked willing. But perhaps that was mere enchantment. The water on which it floated was dark, reflecting their rippling faces and the stars, but beneath, a stirring of something else. She shivered.

'I am ready, Mistress.' Heng's voice startled them, and they swung round. The maidservant fitted the Emperor's clothes well and she had plaited her hair and rolled it into a neat bun at her nape, man-style, placing the imperial cap on top of her head.

'Heng, well done,' Lien turned to Sun Sen. 'Then now that we are ready, First Minister, shall we descend the steps? If you can help us into the boat, we shall paddle into the centre of the lake while you inform those in the hall that we go to the island.'

Heng's face had bleached white. 'We go in a boat? On water?'

'Yes...'

'Mistress, we might d...' She tripped over her tongue. 'Drown...'

'Many things might happen, Heng. But I am more like to die than you. In all these silks, I shall sink like a stone. Remember I mentioned there will be moments where you must trust me? This is one of those moments.' Lien gave her hand to Sun Sen and he led her to the side of the balcony where wide steps led down to the boat which nudged the landing. Sun Sen helped her in, and she eased herself to the stern, settling in a billow of yellow. Heng stepped in with gentle assistance and sat gingerly in the bow.

'More upright, my dear,' said the elderly official. 'Look as if you are confident and ... imperial.'

Heng straightened her spine, pinpointing Lien with an expression of anxiety and dislike.

'This plan, Lady Lien,' worried Sun Sen, 'is filled with flaws. I cannot believe that I am agreeing to it. But I leave you with hopes and blessings.' He untied a silken rope, coiled it and placed it in the bow, pushing at the little craft so that it slid backward through the willow fronds. 'We will watch from the shore. May the Celestials aid you in your passage.'

He climbed the steps and the flame on the balcony was extinguished. As the light dimmed, a small lamp affixed to the bow begin to glow and the maidservant's eyes opened wide, her gaze scraping back to Lien with horror and fascination.

'Have faith, my Heng.' Lien said. 'It is all we can do.'

The little craft rocked, and the maid's hands grasped the sides, her knuckles gleaming white in the flame.

They glided out into open water, Lien convinced that the night-breeze propelled them, Heng sat even more rigid, her shoulders as stiff as a yoke. In silhouette, Lien had no doubt she would look like a man, the flame shining on the red of the imperial hat and alighting on the gold weave through the silk fabric.

Flames etched along the shore as people hurried from the banquet hall to watch the distant boat slide through the darkness, the torches creating a flickering gold line of stitching edging the lakeside. A cheer sounded and in moments, skyfire began, lighting the water, reflecting sunbursts, showers of diamonds and silver, flaring rockets whistling to the stars. And synchronous with the illumination, the boat turned away, guided by an unseen hand, so that all that would be seen from the shore was a taller shape and a shorter shape in the imperial punt, heading to the island where no one but the Emperor had ever gone.

Lien could barely hope that her prayers had been answered, that some unseen force was taking them beyond mortal understanding. They floated across dark waters striped with metallic bursts and braids and above them, the crack, crash and thud of the skyfire filled the heavens.

'Mistress, it floats alone! Yi! Where does it take us?' Heng's face had paled to moon colours.

'Be calm, my friend. This is what I hoped…' Lien's voice manifested a calm she didn't feel. From her dry throat to breath which seemed dammed in her chest, to every jumping nerve and stretching muscle, she covered it all in a smooth lacquer of confidence. 'We are safe…'

Chi Nü, Spirit of weavers and cloth, of embroiderers – watch over us…

The flickering line along the shore disappeared as the punt drifted around a corner of the meandering lakeside, past shadows of trees and beyond the sparkling fire in the sky. If nothing else, Heng and Lien had perpetuated the lie of the Emperor and his Would-Be-Bride. Beyond that, the truth was that she had no plan at all. None.

'Mistress, the water is so dark…'

'Of course it's dark. It's night. In the day, you would be able to see the rocks on the bottom, the imperial carp and the lily pads floating like giant saucers. Have no fear.'

'But mistress, I swear something big swims beneath us...'

'You see nothing but shades of the dark, Heng. Please be calm.'

'Mistress, it loops back and fo...'

Heng shrieked as a shape broke out of the water, sinuous and glittering with gold and silver discs all over its body. It towered over their little craft, waves rocking them and water showering over their clothes. Heng screamed again, a sound drowned by a cascade of sunbursts as the final volley of skyfire broke across the sky from the further reaches of the imperial compound. Lien grabbed the sides of the punt, shouting to Heng to stay seated, to hold tight. 'Chi Nü,' she yelled to her spiritual guide. 'Have a care for us! Help!'

But too late.

The dragon opened its mouth, rows of needle-fine teeth gleaming in the light of the skyfire, a stream of ice-flamed breath flowing toward them, the dragon's tail whipping the lake surface into a maelstrom and the punt filling with more water. 'Stay seated, Heng!' Lien shouted, her teeth chattering as the dragon's breath surrounded them, her life's blood chilling. 'Hold to the sides!' Her screaming fixed in the air as her breath hardened, her eyes glazing over. Her last sight was ice forming over her maidservant like a shroud, spreading along the floor of the craft to the yellow silk folds of her wedding robe.

Suddenly there was nothing, not a sound, just a prism-filled casing of such coldness that she knew at once she was dying, and that innocent Heng had preceded her. A tear rolled down her cheek, but she also knew as she slipped away, that it too had frozen in a perfect drop against her flesh. She was glad she was dying, because she would not wish to see what an ice-dragon spirit would do with she and

Heng and she cursed the evil Others of her world and hated Kitsune for singling her out.

Pinging, the sounds of unearthly birds, or was it something else? Cracking, whispering with a crisp sibilance – and perhaps the resonance of breath weaving amongst the eldritch noise. She didn't know. In its own way, it was beautiful and if this was indeed the sound of death, she could do worse. She didn't even feel cold. But she couldn't see. Her eyes were weighted down by ice, and so she let herself sink, the ethereal sounds holding no pattern, nothing to tie her to life. She wished Chi Nü had heard her, she was Lien's very own spirit after all, but then she vaguely recalled that the Goddess of Weaving only ever came to the lands of mortal men on the seventh day of the seventh month and this, she was sure, was the seventh day of the sixth month. Wasn't it? She breathed in a last breath, wishing she could hold Heng's hand.

And then there was nothing.

A sharp sound, high-pitched like forest birds, pierced her dulled consciousness. Perhaps the ice moved. She found she could take one breath. Then another, the pressure on her chest easing. The weight on her eyes lessened and she lifted the lids, looking at a surface like isinglass, clear yet not and with the tint of azure and white in fissures that had formed. Beyond the cracks she could see nothing, nor move anything but her eyes and chest, as another breath entered and escaped. Where her small breaths brushed the ice, so it melted, a pocket forming, and she breathed again. She could feel an awful ache as her hands remained cramped and frozen to the side of the punt, but she could move her head now, not crushed by frozen layers. Her ruined silk folds were revealed swiftly as the ice thawed away, the same thing happening to Heng whose expression was ever more confused.

'Heng, all will be well. Stay still until the ice has thawed.'

'You do well to counsel her, Lien,' a soft voice said. 'It won't be long and she will be free of the freeze and then I can make sure you are both dry and warm.'

Lien was able to turn her head. She was shocked to see the punt was on the shore and that ahead was a winding path. She turned further and saw a woman with dark hair and gentle eyes standing on the lake's edge. The woman's robes were of gossamer-fine pearl silk, with borders of pale grey peonies and she was such perfection that Lien gasped, feeling the last of the ice melt.

'Chi Nü!'

'It is I,' the Celestial responded. 'I would not let you suffer.'

'But…'

'We must hurry, Lien. I have come in secret because there is much at stake. We have until the moon sinks and then I must be gone. Come, both of you.' She began to walk up the slope, calling behind her. 'Please, follow me quickly.'

Lien began to clamber toward the seat on which Heng sat unmoving, the maidservant's mouth ajar and wide fearful eyes staring after the Celestial. The trailing wet lengths of yellow silk impeded Lien's movement and she grew angry. Angry with herself, with her situation and with her stupidly inanimate maidservant. With one cold hand, she slapped Heng on the cheek and the woman gasped.

'Heng, I order you to attend me now,' she smacked the woman's shoulder. 'If you do not, I shall send you back over the lake alone.' Then she added maliciously, 'In the punt!'

Heng directed her haunted gaze to Lien, her face pale, but she grasped the dripping silk, and both women slipped and slid to the shore. 'Is she the Goddess of Weaving? Have we died? Did the dragon kill us? Mistress…'

'No, we are not dead. But we *will* die if we don't get warm. And yes, she is the Celestial so named. If you do not please her, she will turn you into a silkworm! Come on!' Lien's teeth chattered. Never in her life had she been so chilled. Not even when the winter winds blew off the Long Ma mountains surrounding the Han and when snow lay across the moon gates and weighted the branches of the elm so that they dangled across the iced-over koi pond. The servants would catch the koi and transfer them to a pond in Father's plant house, where tender growth and frail living things were nurtured until the thaw. No, never as chilled as from the ice dragon's breath, or from fear of what lay ahead.

It seemed the Spirits, good and bad, had begun to play their game and she and Heng were being spun across a chequerboard with little care.

They hurried after the Celestial who had disappeared round the bend of a finely chiselled path leading from the shore into a coppice of elegant trees. Elms, she thought, and birches and maples. Despite the darkness of night, small lanterns glowed in welcome, lighting their way and guiding them and for a moment it was possible to take a breath.

'Where do we go?' Heng panted as she stepped up the incline behind Lien.

'I don't know, but she went this way...'

Looking back, the lights of the Palace across the lake had vanished, the trees concealing everything – a precious island home separate from the court and its intricacies. Was this where the Emperor chose to hide himself? Away from the pressures of imperial leadership. Gossips had said that he took to his role with sadness in the back of his eyes. Was this the only place that he was truly happy? Lien could understand, if only because there was nothing worse than living a life one didn't want.

'Good! You are come.' Chi Nü stood at the doors of the pavilion where the trees fanned out to create a lantern lit space. Moss-covered mounds edged a rill that trickled from behind the pavilion and a small hump-backed bridge spanned the tinkling water, paper butterflies on bamboo rods fluttering at either end of the bridge in the sweet-smelling night breeze.

'This must surely be Celestial Paradise,' Heng whispered.

'For the last time, Heng, we're not dead,' Lien whispered back. 'This is the imperial pavilion over the lake. Exactly where we're supposed to be. Where have your wits gone?'

'Swallowed in ice by a dragon…'

There was an angry note to Heng's words and Lien had the grace to feel guilty. It was she after all who had persuaded Heng to attend her into danger.

'I apologise, Heng. It is a lot to absorb but we must try.' She took the damp folds from her maidservant, bundling them into her own arms, and then turned toward the beautiful woman who stood waiting. 'My lady Chi Nü,' she bowed before the Celestial. 'I thank you for rescuing us…'

'Come inside where it is warm. I would not have you catch an ague. You must be hale for what comes next.'

The words hammered like an anvil. Then this is not the end of it, she thought. She followed the Celestial through the wrought doors of the pavilion. But unlike the Palace which reeked of dragons and lion dogs, these welcomed with carved peonies and cherry blossoms, lotus flowers and poppy heads. Lien followed the straight-backed Celestial as she led the way. Nothing about her was at all intimidating – except perhaps her flawless beauty. Her robes, her flowing hair, her modulated voice – all conspired to calm and encourage those with whom she engaged. The comparison with Kitsune was pronounced because whilst Chi Nü was warmth and subtlety, the fox-spirit was glacial.

'There are clothes in the antechamber,' Chi Nü pointed. 'Leave your wet things behind, and they will be dealt with. There are linen towels to dry yourselves. When you are done, join me.' An apologetic half smile flitted across her face. 'Please be as quick as you can.' She opened a peony door and slipped through into amber light but the door was closed swiftly and they could see nothing more.

'Come then,' Lien said to Heng, walking through the door into the small chamber and beginning to rip at the sodden robes. 'I never want to see these again. Nor anything purporting to be for a marriage.'

The room was warmed by a brazier and lit by two flickering lanterns and sliding paper screens shielded the room from beyond. On two low stools, two piles of clothes lay folded neatly – all as black as the night beyond the screens. Unadorned felt boots sat beneath the stools. They had sturdy soles for walking, and Lien's heart sank low.

The two women towelled themselves, trying to rub warmth into pale, goose-bumped skin where cold had penetrated their marrow.

Heng searched through the clothes. 'Mistress, there is no *hanfu*...'

She referred to the strip of clothing that tied to flatten a woman's chest and Lien replied dryly. 'That's because it seems we dress in men's clothes,' she held up a pair of knee length *dubi* undertrousers. 'Put your damp *hanfu* back on. It will dry quickly if we are warm.' Lien dressed fast, pulling on layer after layer until all that remained as she buttoned the simple frogs of her thick jacket, was a three-quarter length heavily quilted coat.

So thick. Where are we going?

'Mistress, you should not be doing all this. If we were at home, I would be flogged for allowing you to do something as unseemly as clothing yourself when it is my job.'

'Nothing about any of this is seemly,' Lien replied. 'And I suspect that from now on, you won't tend me at all, unless it is to care for the bonds of companionship between us.'

Heng had almost settled back into her phlegmatic ways. 'A servant is a servant. You know this. A companion for one such as yourself is chosen from the upper ranks and I am baseborn.'

'Status has no meaning now, Heng. Whatever I've dragged you into, it has levelled us quicker than death. I'm sorry – not a good analogy and I wish I could explain better, but I suspect we must leave that to the Lady Chi Nü.' Lien grabbed the maidservant's hands, registering how cold they were. 'If this is too much for your sensibilities, I am sure our Celestial guide will transport you back to your home safely. But for myself, I think I am forced to follow a different path.'

Heng buttoned her jacket closed and began to comb the knots from her hair, plaiting it and looping it. She moved to comb out Lien's, dexterous and quick as she smoothed the hair, slipping it into a tail and then knotting it at Lien's nape. 'I have no home, mistress. Your home was my home and if your home is yours no longer, then it's not mine either.'

Lien turned to face Heng and squeezed her hands. 'You are more loyal than I deserve but I am heartened by it, and I think between you and I we might be strong enough to deal with what comes our way.'

But she demurred to mention that a task had been forced upon them by Kitsune, the fox-spirit – a potentially deadly task. Or that by saving them from the ice-dragon, Chi Nü, the heavenly Celestial, probably now had them in *her* debt and when a life debt was called in by a Celestial, one could have little hope of denial. She felt as if she were tied between two horses, a brutal punishment from the old regime where one was ripped in half by the animals galloping in opposite directions. No, she would not tell Heng anything just yet...

'Are we ready, do you think?' she asked as she picked up her coat. 'I think we have been long enough. Be brave, my good friend.' She gave Heng a kiss on the cheek and led the way to the peony doors and the warmth of soft amber light.

Chi Nü turned as they entered. The chamber was long and wide and lined with shelves and cupboards, large chests and small and there were avalanches of scrolls and neatly shelved books. The room smelled of vellum and parchment, of leather and linen. Of camphorwood and pine and the most recent smell, just a wisp of a fragrance of sandalwood, indicated a man's recent presence.

He has been here…

Lien turned her head this way and that, absorbing her surroundings, noticing a simple bed with a sleeping roll lying folded at the end – precision and orderliness as if a servant followed the emperor around, tidying as things were used and discarded.

But then no servant comes here – thus I can presume the Emperor is fastidious…

'Please be seated.' Chi Nü indicated three chairs around an unlit brazier, and even as Lien moved forward, Heng behind her, the brazier sprang into warm life, a skein of smoke spiralling to the simple gabled ceiling. Both women sat and Chi Nü followed, lowering herself with the grace of a courtesan, her robes sighing around her.

'You are warmer?' she asked. 'Would you like tea?'

Lien shook her head. 'Thank you, no. What I would like is to know why we were attacked by a dragon-spirit and why you saved us.'

'My lady!' hissed Heng.

'I mean no disrespect,' Lien continued. 'But something happened to me earlier today and along with what Sun Sen has informed me, and with the terror of the attack on the lake, I feel all events are interlinked. Please…'

Chi Nü held up a hand to forestall any further words from Lien. 'Let me speak. I shall tell you all. But please, let me make tea…'

Lien ground her teeth but nodded, champing at wasted time. In the event, no moment was wasted as the Celestial Spirit wafted her hand across a small table in front of them and a white porcelain waterpot filled with steaming contents, three celadon cups, and a celadon teapot with aromatic green tea appeared. The Goddess of Weaving passed each woman a cup and began.

'Today you were coerced by Kitsune, were you not?'

Heng turned swiftly to her mistress. 'My lady, you did not say...'

But Lien merely frowned. 'How did you know?'

Chi Nü shook her head. 'I know everything. She asked you to search for a map, did she not? And whilst she did not threaten you directly, the threat was there, was it not? And lately, you have heard two things from Sun Sen. Firstly that Ming Xao has vanished and secondly that the village of Sie, in the high mountains, may have been decimated with a pestilence that is not mortal. Please,' she gestured with her hand as Lien drew in a breath to ask a question. 'Let me speak and then you may ask what you wish to know. The point, dear Lien, is that these events are all connected to Others. And they are connected by a common thread which is a map. The map was incautiously drawn by your emperor, to indicate unique locations he discovered in his time away from the Han. To be frank with you, the map shows all the entrances across this entire world, not just the Han, through which any may pass into Other worlds.'

Chi Nü sat perfectly still, raising her tea to her lips in one seamless gesture, and then she continued. 'Immortals across Eirie are incandescent with rage. They want the map destroyed and Ming Xao's knowledge with it. It may be why the ice-dragon attacked you. That one of the Others is so filled with rage, it was ordered. And no doubt you would ask if They would kill the Emperor? In answer, it is a possibility. But he is my good friend, and I will not allow this to happen. Thus, he is gone to the only Other in Eirie who can destroy the map and perhaps assist him to escape death as well. You, my dear, are also in grave danger by the very act of being his betrothed because They will use you as a hostage either dead or alive to achieve their aims. So now you understand the ice-dragon perhaps.' She stopped for breath and Lien tried to digest what had been said. Heng, of course, had silenced completely, her cup shaking in her hands.

'I would see you escape to the same woman toward whom Ming Xao hastens,' Chi Nü continued. 'I have secured this pavilion for long enough for me to talk with you, but They *will* find a way in. They have already tried once this night, but I was able to strengthen the force which surrounds the island to enable Ming Xao to leave. However it will not last. By moonset, I can no longer defend the place and They will be on your scent.'

'Which way did he go? How do we follow?' Lien felt as if there were two of her. Deep in her heart she quaked with fear. She had read stories of Spirit anger. But on a rational level, she now knew she must ask for answers and with speed. Beside her, she heard Heng's cup jostle the teapot as she placed it back on the tray. Glancing at the maidservant's trembling fingers, Lien reached over and grasped the woman's hand and held it in her own, squeezing gently.

'I do not know how he left here...' Chi Nü frowned, a furrow appearing between her brows, 'And it disturbs me, because I am an Other and I should know! If I am to help you, we must find *how* he left because it may help you. I am sure if it were by enchantment, I would feel something, but there is nothing and yet there *is* no other way. It only serves to make me nervous because I believe Ming Xao to possess more than just an enchanted map. How this is so, I am at a loss, but it makes your escape even *more* fraught.'

Lien placed her cup down on the tray, having no care for its fragility, and pushed herself up angrily from her seat. 'This is abominable! My friend and myself are pawns in some death hunt by Others and through no fault of our own, beyond some stupid wish by my family house to have me marry into the Imperial Dynasty. Add to that a man to whom all show such respect and devotion, but who is unwise? Not just unwise but brainless? Even egotistical if he thought he could get away with deceiving Others! Is that what being an emperor does? Makes one lose sight of the wider picture? To lose caution?' She paced around a long table on which lay a stoppered pot, a brush, writing requirements and a white porcelain dish, whilst Heng watched her with wide eyes alive with fright.

'I cannot gainsay anything you have said,' Chi Nü replied. 'But I need you to move your anger aside. You need to search this room, Lien, from top to bottom. There is something here, some powerful enchantment for those who rightly must find it. How it has been done is beyond my experience – an enchantment that I can't detect – it is odd.' She shook her head and stood. 'I must leave you. I must make the warding-off spell around the pavilion as strong as I can. Ming Xao may have found enchantments on his journeys that defy even those of my kind. Oh, it is such a two-edged sword! This strange enchantment is your best chance of escape, and yet when They enter here and discover some sort of magick that prevents them from finding which way you and the Emperor escaped, I will be hard put to prevent them from calling out war upon your kind. Ming Xao has been so unwise…'

'He has been a fool!' Lien hissed. 'I must get a message to Sun Sen and let him know…'

'No! You must tell no one.'

'Then how will our disappearance be explained?' Lien swept out her arm to include Heng. 'Or the Emperor's disappearance? Or a pestilence and any other misfortune that falls upon the Han because of what an idiot has done? Sun Sen is a kind man who must step in and lead whilst this stupid game plays out. He deserves to know something.'

Chi Nü stood. 'Then I will fabricate something after you are gone. In the meantime, search, good Lien and Heng. Search as you have never searched before. Somewhere in this room there is a means to escape and only you can find it. I will make magick outside, but the moon will be sinking soon, and you must be gone by then, as will I. Then there will be nothing to help you beyond your own wits.' She pulled a screen and slipped out onto the nightingale floors and left a vacuum that rapidly filled with horror and fear.

For a mere breath, the two women stared after her and then Lien grabbed Heng. 'We check all the walls, the cabinets in front of them. If he did not depart through the doors, then he departed *somewhere* in here. You start at that end, and I will start at this. Go!'

Heng said nothing, just moved to the far wall and began to open and close drawers and doors, being assiduous as befits a conscientious servant. Lien heard scraps of her speech drifting on the quiet night air and frowned.

'Unfair ... our lives ... Damn the Spirits to the never-ending days and nights of Hell. We cannot die!'

No, Heng, we will not! We will find the exit-point...

Lien pulled at the silken cords hanging from the chaste iron handles of a large cabinet. The doors opened soundlessly, and she pushed at the neatly shelved scrolls, feeling behind them. Then to the floor of the cabinet, but there were just books, carefully bound with linen thread. Nothing to show.

She moved on to open shelves, but the walls behind were smooth and impregnable. She even pushed at the delicate mouldings on panels but there was nothing. Heng moved methodically, still muttering under her breath, but the cadence had changed and Lien realised she was praying.

'May all beings be free from fear. May all beings be filled with the spirit of tranquillity and serenity. May all beings threatened by evil spirits be protected by the powers of beneficent Celestials...'

She spoke the same words, over and over, so that the mantra underlined each movement she made.

'Anything?' Lien asked, knowing there was nothing. There was no reply beyond,

'May all beings be free from fear. May all beings be filled with the spirit of tranquillity and serenity. May all beings threatened by evil spirits be protected by the powers of beneficent Celestials…'

Lien moved systematically around two walls, before walking to the table to stand gazing at what lay there. Fresh ink in a stoppered bottle, a small ceramic bowl, three fine calligraphy brushes, a pile of parchment, and some silk cord. She dragged her finger along the smooth rosewood of the table surface stopping at each calligraphy tool, frowning as if something tapped in the far reaches of her mind. There were a few drops of ink in a bowl, barely any but enough to know that it had been used recently. The parchment lay neatly, its deckled head toward a wall, and a longitudinal skein of silk cord lying on top. The brushes, a plain bamboo-handled one with a silk tassel at the end, a white porcelain-handled one and a mottled red sandalwood pen shaped with immense grace lay neatly aligned. The heads were goat hair, honed to a fine edge, but damp with recent washing. The heads all pointed in the same direction and Lien sucked in a quick breath.

The parchment's deckle, the vertical angle of the silk skein, the brush heads – all pointed toward the wall to which Heng had begun to move.

'Quick!' Lien rushed past her. 'It's here. I'm sure…'

Before her a tall closet reached almost to the ceiling. The dappled lights of lamps and the brazier caught upon mother of pearl inlaid upon deep jet lacquer. The clever decoration detailed an old man's journey across rivers and streams, mountains and tracks.

Not so far from the truth then…

Lien pulled at the red silk that decorated the plain handles and the doors swung open and Heng stood at her mistress's side as Lien examined the neat shelves on which lay slim journals – the Emperor's. She opened one and read his calligraphy – descriptions of a sea journey and she wished she had time. Instead, she slammed the book shut and kneeled where clothes were neatly folded on the floor of the closet. On top of these, lay a carved casket with heavy brass hinges and a brass lock. She knew the kind. Inside would be a few little drawers, maybe even a secret drawer that would spring open with a hidden catch. But the casket was locked and there was no key.

'A key! There *has* to be a key. Feel the pockets of the robes, Heng. Feel the hems…'

They both examined all the hanging robes and padded jackets but there was nothing. Except…

Underneath the casket, a plain black jacket lay folded, and Lien pulled it out, placing it across her knees and feeling deep into the concealed pockets and along the neatly sewn hems. In moments, from deep within the folded and welted edge, she had a brass key in her fingers and her hand shook as she inserted it into the lock and turned it. A small click and the lock fell open, the little doors were pulled apart, and drawers were revealed.

Lien and Heng looked at each other.

Lien was not sure that they were any closer to finding a secret exit from the pavilion, but she eased the first drawer open. It slid smoothly, its flat brass handle just fitting Lien's finger through its loop. Inside, and resting on midnight silk was a piece of parchment, she unrolled it and read the characters detailing a haiku down the side. Inside the next drawer was another miniscule roll – with a different poem. Likewise, the third drawer. The fourth drawer contained nothing.

Lien's spirits sank. None of these poems meant a thing.

Chi Nü's feet walked back and forth on the nightingale floor of the verandah and it spoke quietly of things enchanted and mystical. 'The moon is sinking,' she whispered through the screen. 'I have cast as much magick as I can but when the moon is gone, my enchantments and myself will be gone as well. Be quick, good Lien.'

'Mistress,' Heng's hand pressed against her heart. 'Please…'

'This can't be all, Heng. It can't be! Why hide the key to *this* casket? The writings must be connected.' She felt along the top of the small cabinet and then round the edges but nothing revealed itself – no catch for a compartment. She dragged in a breath, trying to expand a chest that had shrunk to the size of a peach-stone and which hurt when she sighed and she examined the small scrolls again. 'I wonder,' she said, 'if they are clues. They have to be, Heng, because there is nothing else. I think they're locations, and I refuse to believe it's just a mere happenstance that this particular casket lies in this particular closet with a key hidden in the hem of a jacket. The Emperor knew someone would come searching – someone who needed direction. Our exit *has* to be close.'

Lien sat on the floor of the closet, pushing at the many long robes that hung above her head and which dragged at her hair so that she swung an arm in temper. As she did, one robe pulled back, and she caught a glimpse of a painted backdrop. A scene of trees, a ravine, rocks.

The hissing and angry sound of water tumbling into rapids.

Sound?

She grabbed the hanging robes, tearing them back so that she could see more clearly. The scene vacillated, wavering and wafting with a dissolving clarity as if it wasn't sure it wanted to be seen. Lien sat on the precipitous edge of a gorge, as real as the chilled hair standing on her arms.

'Mistress!' Heng's lexicon had grown no larger with the revelation of the scene and she stood ashen of face with eyes wide.

'It's an exit, Heng. We must go. Our coats! Quickly!'

But Chi Nü slid one of the paper panels open and immediately, in her presence, the scene vanished.

'It was here! I stood on the edge of a gorge!' Lien cried. 'And now it's vanished!'

Chi Nü slid the panel shut, staying on the verandah. 'And now?' she called.

The two women turned to the misty gorge with its roaring waters. 'Here!' To Lien's own ears, her voice sounded warped with nerves.

'Stars above! The Emperor has more magick at his fingertips than I would have wished! By the Heavens may it play in his favour. Go now, my good women. Immediately. And may Fate smile upon you. Your time is here, as the moon is almost at rest. Take care…'

Her voice vanished as the first cock of the morning called from the imperial compound across the lake.

'Mistress, we cannot leave…'

'Of course, we can! We said we wanted to see beyond the Han and now we must!' Anxiety gnawed at her belly, but she would never admit to her maidservant that she had no confidence at all in what they were about to attempt. How could she say to her loyal companion that this whole journey was a moment of reckoning where they might live or die? She softened her voice and continued. 'We must go, Heng. We must help the Emperor and we must flee to survive.' She shrugged her padded coat into a more comfortable position then grabbed Heng by the hand, stepped off the floor of the closet and onto the ground at the edge of the gorge.

As Heng joined her they both turned back, but the closet walls had vanished. So too the floor and doors. Dark shadows of leaf and tree surrounded them, and a silky white mist rose from the angry waters far below.

CHAPTER SEVEN

Ming Xao

Sleep of the dead perhaps.

Every part of his body had softened like honey and his head, pounding before, felt lighter. But he kept his eyes closed, pulling at the dream that had begun to fade as his senses returned.

The woman had the soft ebony lustre to her hair that Lady Lien possessed when he had met her in the Park of Singing Birds. She smelled of roses like Lien. Her robes were shades of celadon and wrapped round her was an obi … *the obi*. The one that told her history. He took one end in his fingers and she twirled away, smiling as it unwound, and he read the embroidered design of her life. Her babyhood, her childhood where she crossed small, arched bridges and played under willows, and more lately where she sat in a garden, stitching on her lap whilst koi swam in a calm pool beneath an elm. Then further on, her passage to the palace in yellow silk, her journey across the lake with an ice dragon rearing up.

At that he sucked in his breath and grabbed more of the obi to read. She meanwhile stood in shadows whilst he scanned the meticulous stitching. She stood on the edge of a gorge and then walked hand over hand across the cobwebs of the swinging bridge with another woman. Down a steep zigzag path to a punt and a wide swathe of river.

He knew the punt, the river and the gorge and when

he held his breath to see what stitches followed there was nothing. Just a loose thread trailing off and the woman in the shadows laughing meanly. She began to change, features sliding, hair waving.

He opened his eyes and jumped up, grabbing his knife from his waistband and crouched before this woman who stood before him with sharp teeth, an angular nose, her hair hanging like lank weed down to drooping breasts, her celadon gown replaced by grey rippling robes. The obi had vanished, and fear tangled with hatred as he stared at her, this witch, this demon whom he knew was the shapeshifter they called Stegge. Bringer of harm and panic, a creature who might feed on his fear like a *vampyra* on blood.

She advanced upon him, sniffing like a dog, closing her eyes with lust for the alarm that sweated from his pores. He backed away, his knife hand clenched, the knife point aimed at her.

'You think to kill me, Ming Xao? You who we all seek to kill ourselves? You jest!' She flew round behind him, and he felt her tongue slide across his neck. He scuffed away the sensation and swung on the balls of his feet to face her. 'How fortuitous that you chose my courtyard in which to rest. I lay there on the wall watching you and it was so easy to send you to sleep. Just my tail switching back and forth...'

The cat!

'Ha! You may be a mapmaker, but your wits are dull. Has no one told you to beware black cats?'

She advanced once more, her eyes, amber and pinpoint, fixed him with a feline glare and his breath shucked in and out, his heart racing. He knew each beat radiated more fear and such panic excited and enticed her like meat to a starving dog.

He retreated, his knife still held in front. He felt the stirrings of fury pulsing with his heartbeat, and he was damned if he would give in. He stopped, stood tall and was glad to see that he towered over her diminutive form. She stopped moving forward and side-eyed him.

'Think you to fight me, mortal.'

To answer her was a waste of his time and breath. Better that he maintained silence. He discerned the faintest furrow between her fine brows when he said nothing.

She advanced again until he could smell her – the scent of feral cat. Not an odour he ever liked. He preferred dogs. They were now an arm's length from each other and still he said nothing.

'You don't speak, you don't fight. I cannot see you as a worthy adversary. Still, They want your map and I shall get it for them and reap rewards. Ha! Stegge, the protector of the Other World,' she preened.

Ming thought he heard a noise behind him, something brushing through the long grass, perhaps it was the beginnings of a lagoon breeze.

But no!

There, again!

Stegge, meanwhile, had been hissing on and hadn't noticed.

'I *feed* on the frightened.' She dragged out the word 'feed', her tone lowering as she spoke. 'I like to breathe fear deep inside me. Can I breathe yours?'

But as she moved in to reach for his face, the brushing of grass became a crackle and a massive grey dog leaped in front of Ming, seedheads falling from his back, his spine rigid, bristling with fight. He stood with eyes locked on Stegge, his lips drawing back to reveal wolf-like fangs. He advanced one pad at a time and the shapeshifter retreated.

Her eyes had slitted, and her own hair lifted in fight response.

The dog could easily have leaped upon her, but he just padded intently towards her, a deep growl coming from slavering lips, the teeth flashing in the sun that now beat down into the courtyard.

With a yowl, Stegge changed to a cat and leaped in an ebony streak for the wall as the enormous dog jumped up, heavy paws against the stone, furious barking issuing through sharp teeth. With each bark, it sucked in breath noisily. If it could reach the cat, it would have dragged it down and dismembered it in moments.

Instead, the cat humped its back, its black hair vertical, tail upright, ears flat against its head and the amber eyes on fire with anger. In a heartbeat, it had vanished. The dog's barking quieted but each inward breath filled with snarling belligerence. Ming wondered if he moved, whether the mastiff would turn its dangerous attention to him and so he kept still.

A voice called from behind him. 'Max! Maximilian! Down! Come!'

The dog turned, its face loosening to a soppy dribbling mass. It brushed past Ming at waist height, knocking him roughly, and he turned to see a slim young man, buttercup blond hair wisped and urchin-like round his face, rubbing the dog's ears.

'*Hola*, sir. You are safe now.' The fellow rested his hand on the massive dog's back as though the dog were a table or chair to lean against. 'Maximilian is such a good boy,' he cooed. 'Aren't you, my handsome creature?' He ruffled the dog's ears and the dog grinned at him, all aggression gone in a bucket load of dribble which fell in a silver trail from the canine lips. 'Oh,' the elegantly clad young man added. 'I should have asked. Did Stegge hurt you?'

'No. I am well. Thanks to your… your dog.'

'Think nothing of it. I have to say that the cat was one of Stegge's better shape-changing iterations. Anyway, It's Max's job to keep you safe. Max's and mine.'

'I beg your pardon?'

'We are to stay with you until you reach the Ymp Tree Orchard and the Wise Woman. We have our orders.'

'From whom? And who are you?'

'Sink me, do you not remember me from so long ago? Surely you do.' He seemed regretful, almost hurt, but bowed low over a rippling hand, his left leg extended in a very white stocking and a fine brown leather laced ankle boot. 'I am Gallivant the hob. Not perfect at magick, you understand, but I have my ways.' He smiled an impish smile. '*Now* do you remember me? Tuh! I thought I was the stuff of legend!' He frowned. 'I take it you *do* know what a hob is? They tell me you know rather too much about the Other world.'

With eyebrows shooting up his forehead, Ming tried to regain sense and sensibility. He did remember the hob – a frothing, busy individual who had appeared in the journey with the *shifu* cloth, when he had run from the Han years ago. 'I do remember you as it happens and of course I know what a hob is! I think you'll find all mortals know a lot about Others. They need to so that they can live amongst the perversions cast their way!'

Gallivant, undeterred, replied in a soft voice. 'But not I think, where the entrances and exits are to the Other World.'

Ming said nothing.

'Ah. A difficult subject. Then we shall leave it for the moment. Are you hungry? I will take you somewhere where you can bathe, change, eat, sleep – whatever you like and be perfectly safe.'

Ming shook his head. 'I think not. I can find my own way. But thank you and especially thanks to your dog.' He went to walk to the gate on the other side of the courtyard.

'Ming Xao,' Gallivant spoke with determination. 'I understand that you might not trust me, that I dupe you. But I swear I do not.' The hob hopped around to stand in front of Ming, the dog beside him. 'I truly am here to help as I was asked…'

'But Master Gallivant, *I* did not ask.'

'That is true. But *I* was asked and *I* said yes.'

'By whom?'

'Does the name Adelina mean anything to you?'

Ming nodded. He knew of the Traveller, stitcher extraordinaire who developed the most intimate relationship with Others and who had told her story in tiny books secreted beneath heavy padded embroidery on a breathtaking and terrifying gown. 'Adelina the embroiderer? The infamous gown that is in the Museo in this city?' He frowned. 'Mother to the lovely Ibo who was my betrothed?'

'Exactly so,' Gallivant smoothed a hand over the mastiff's head. 'Adelina is my dearest most loved friend. She knows what you have done and what you are trying to do...'

'How does she know?'

'She heard it from a djinn called Balraj who heard it from Chi Nü.' He laid a finger against his nose, tapping it, his hazel eyes sparkling, his hair like new-minted gelt. 'Some of we Others stick together, you know.'

'And I am supposed to be reassured, Master Gallivant?'

'Please, it's just Gallivant, and no, I can see what you mean. But some of us, believe it or not are quite kind, and in this instance, my dearest Adelina, a mortal, asked me to look out for you, because Chi Nü had expressed such concern to Balraj. Balraj, being what he is, manifests wherever he likes and he and Adelina are good...' he stopped and then grinned. 'But why are we standing here? Could you not trust Max and I enough to see you safe where perhaps we can talk in comfort?'

Ming felt exhaustion dragging at his wits. His instinct had been to cut and run but the fellow's story rang with a naïve plausibility. There was no doubt he was tired, hungry, and dressed wrongly for the rest of his journey. Perhaps the hob *could* help...

'I do this unwillingly, hob. Your story needs more depth, I think, for me to believe that you act in my best interests. But then I owe you for saving my life so I will come with you. How far?'

'Not far. Out the gate, along the *fondamenta* and into a small palazzo that belongs to the very person you seek.'

'The Wise Woman! She is here?'

'No, sadly. But come, we will eat, drink and talk and then you can make choices about your future. Does it suit you?'

Ming nodded and followed behind the hob and his mastiff as they pushed through the wood and iron gate and turned along the *fondamenta*. There was no one around which surprised him, only his and the hob's footfalls echoing between the walls of the graceful buildings.

Gallivant waved a hand around. 'It is *reposo*. Everyone rests in the middle of the day –we get to move without interference. Almost in secret – *segreta*. Ah,' he paused outside a narrow umber-coloured building with a heavy studded iron door. He took a key from the capacious pocket of his silk tailcoat, slipped it in the large lock and turned it. There was barely a click and then he twisted the enormous handle and the door opened soundlessly to a long corridor. 'This is actually the rear entrance. Come...' He closed the door behind them, locked it, and slipped a heavy bar across. 'Follow me. Here Maxi!' He whistled and strode off light-footed, with the great grey dog on his heels. His confident manner calmed Ming and for once he felt as if the events of the last night and day were stuff of his imagination – as the God of Fate had said, 'an illusion'. But then the canister at his waistband pressed into his skin and he knew that it was an 'if only' thought.

They passed through a carved wooden door into an elegant front hall. A stair with a wrought handrail curved to a landing and a creamy marble floor, veined like a woman's breasts, stretched before them, unadorned and satin-like. The walls were frescoed with scenes of pastoral idylls in soft colours and above everything, a pretty dome sat like a crown, with clerestory windows below it, casting down beams of light. Eldritch? Without doubt, thought Ming, but the house echoes with a profound emptiness.

'There is no one here?' he asked.

'No. Deliberate, I believe. The Wise Woman, Seraphina, gave me the key and suggested we keep low until your next move is made. Come…' Gallivant leaped up the stairs with far more energy than Ming felt as he followed, wondering how these Others were so aware of his movements – a point-less thought when all was said and done.

All I can do is keep moving, keep ahead of them…

They climbed to the landing and Gallivant walked along the squeaking parquet floor to the end of the hall from which rooms opened. The floor reminded Ming of the nightingale floor and a flood of thoughts followed – his people, his palace, his province. His bride…

'So! Bedroom,' said Gallivant dancing along the hall. 'Bedroom, bedroom, and…'

Ming passed a green room, a pink blossom room, a purely white room and then a dark room with heavy drapes and into which Gallivant had turned.

'Bear with me whilst I light a candle…' the hob struck a tinder, held it to a small candelabra and the chamber bloomed seductively in the flickering light.

Shelf upon shelf of books. As high as the ceiling, over the door and on every wall. A ladder, more books.

'A library…' Ming whispered, unable to hide the awe.

'Jasper's occasional study when he was alive. There is a chaise in the corner there,' Gallivant pointed, 'and blankets, but we cannot light the fire and this light is all we must use for fear of letting anyone know there is someone within. Do you think it will suit?' Without waiting for an answer, he continued. 'You can bathe along the corridor whilst I find some clothes. I shall leave you to freshen. Come, Max.'

He left like a swift breeze, the dog padding obediently

behind, as Ming turned in a slow circle to examine the room. The drapes were heavy damask – black and grey, he thought. The furniture was elegant without being showy, shades of steel and iron-grey brocades covered seats and cushions. The chaise was well-padded in mellow honey velvet with sparkling white linen bed pillows and a neat stack of honey-coloured blankets. A tellurion sparkled shyly in a corner, the globes of the heavens rotating in a never-ending celestial waltz. The tables were golden walnut and piled high with books and at one end, a long desk had the creamy trail of a map laid out along its length.

Ming thought he might be in the library of the Celestials, so beautiful was the room and if he hadn't been so tired, he would have examined book after book, climbing the ladder to see what the immortal Jasper had found pointless enough to leave in Veniche, where the shelves might only gather dust.

Jasper – renowned for such wisdom and knowledge. I wish I had met him while he lived.

Meanwhile, the books sat in serried rows – some pushed back a little further than others. Some with parchment covers and beautiful chaste spines – calligraphy that curled in the language of Trevallyn. Other books were leather covered, the titles picked out in gold leaf that sparkled shyly.

Later, he thought. Gather myself, wash, eat, and then per-haps just a quick look at some books before sleep. He turned back to the corridor and found the bathing room. A bath stood filled with warm scented water, steam curling upward. Bathing paraphernalia lay stacked on a long bench – almost as if mesmered just for a man's use. Nothing at all to serve a woman, even the fragrance was of cedar and lemons.

He shut the door, shucked off his pointed shoes, stripped off his *kurta* and *dhoti,* and laid the canister, purse and knife carefully on an oak stool away from the bath where they were safe from moisture. He stepped into the welcoming water, sank down, breathing out, letting his muscles loosen, feeling the water lick at his shorter hair. He plunged his head under, scrubbed at his scalp and then took a cloth to rub at the henna around his eyes.

The crane on his midriff was another thing. He touched it, traced the wings, forbearing to rub at the henna artwork. A wave of such painful nostalgia, even heart-hurt, swept through him. This, he thought, this image of his spirit animal was a reminder of what he must do. It was also a whiplash reminder of his hubris. *He* had created peril, no one else, and he must fix it or pay the price.

The water stayed warm as he stretched his limbs, trying to ease the tension. He dared close his eyes, just for a moment, and thoughts vanished into a soft darkness. He wondered if it was some kind of enchantment, a bath that mesmered, and decided that in this house, a moment to just give way must surely be safe…

'Sink me!' The door flew back and Gallivant stood in the light of a single candle. 'I thought you had drowned you've been so long!'

Ming's eyes were as heavy as if he had taken the poppy. 'How long?'

'An hour. In the beginning I left you alone but finally I could take it no longer – ooh, what a lovely tattoo!'

Ming had stood and wrapped a towel around his hips, the hob unabashed at his nakedness. 'It is my spirit animal,' he said.

'Beautiful,' Gallivant replied scrutinising Ming's naked chest and muscled belly until Ming dropped his head, embarrassed. 'I must say you have changed since you were with Isabella, Ming. You've grown taller, broader…' His eyes lingered on the tattoo and then, 'Clothes are in the study. Dress yourself and I will bring food on a tray for us both and we can talk.'

Talk? thought Ming. I want to think, maybe sleep…

Gallivant left and Ming heard his footsteps bounce along the corridor and down the stairs and so he hurried to the study and found a pile of clothes on the chaise. Underclothes, a lawn shirt, creamy coloured britches, white stockings, brown leather boots as soft as velvet. And finally, a black tailcoat with deep pockets into which he slipped the knife, purse and the canister. Something fell to the floor with a muffled thud and looking down he saw an ivory comb with a black ribbon wound round and so he combed his jaw length hair and tied it into a tail. It would serve.

The clothes and boots fit like gloves, and he was unsurprised. All was magick in this place. He tried to decide if it made him feel ill at ease and then gave up to the sensation of comfort and relief – a moment where he might forget about what damage he had wrought.

Forget, Ming Xao? How could you? Chi Nü's words chided him, slipping in easily from shadowed corners.

No – he couldn't forget. Events might appear illusory but there were people's lives at play. And what about his Would-be-Bride, Lien? Where was she as he walked along this palatial corridor to eat and rest in safety? Had she reached the island, found the clues he had left? Was she somewhere that could offer her safety and solace until the map was destroyed?

His guilt churned within his guts, an acid burn that he knew no amount of tender care from a hob would ameliorate until he saw the damage he had created burning under a spell from hands of the Wise Woman whom Gallivant had called Seraphina.

They ate simply– fish pie with fresh steaming bread and a little pile of greens which had a wildness about them. A platter of cheese and oval black grapes which burst with sweetness against his teeth and tongue. He had not planned to drink anything but water, but the wine offered, a golden nectar that smelled of oak and apricots loosened his muscles, took the edge off his headache, and eased the tension that threaded through his spine like sharp wire.

Gallivant sat back, peeling a peach with a small mother-of-pearl handled knife, a thick damask napkin over his knee to catch any drips.

'So,' he said. 'Better?'

'Thank you, yes. I've not had the inclination to eat. Or the time.'

'Yes. Time.' Gallivant laid the peeled peach on a plate and cut slices off, offering the plate to Ming who shook his head. 'Methinks you've not got a lot.' Gallivant swallowed a slice. 'Of time, I mean.'

'No...'

'Sleep, then leave?'

Ming nodded and yawned.

'Good. Then Max and I will attend you to Trevallyn.'

'There is no need. I know where the Veniche gate is. I can find my own way.'

'I dare say you can, to a point. But your fancy dagger is not going to protect you from Others, Ming. You might need a little help. Max will provide the brawn and I will provide the brain. The magick brain. I do have a few little skills.'

'I thank you but...'

'But, but, but. There's always a but, isn't there, with you mortals? The stitcher was the same and strong-willed with it and I am guessing you are as well. *Such* a mortal thing,' he sighed. 'Sink me, dear man, I'm not planning on an early demise by attaching myself to you. I just have a way.' He brushed a hand through his golden wisps. 'All hobs do. We can confuse, addle, cause a little chaos. It all helps, you know.'

Ming was too tired to argue. 'I agree then, if it makes you happy. But I need to get to Trevallyn and soonest.'

'Of course. There's just one thing.'

Ming felt the headache knocking against his scalp again. '*What* one thing?' he asked, sounding testy even to his own ears.

'Seraphina is someone we value. She took the role that Jasper the Healer left behind when he met his bane. None of us know of her history, just that she fitted like a hand in a glove. Therefore, I ask that you respect her…'

'Of course.' Ming's cheeks burned.

'I don't mean to treat you like a callow youth but I thought I needed to remind you that by doing what you did in the past, stealing the enchanted ink, you showed little respect for those with whom you shared much, with the consequence that you are now heading to Seraphina's home with something that could blow the world apart.'

Ming replied tiredly. 'Master Gallivant, if I could turn back time I would. Also, I come from a culture which respects its elders and ancestors. I don't plan to upset or disrespect the lady in any way, I can assure you. There is too much at stake.'

'And yet,' Gallivant stood up, waved his hand and the remains of the repast disappeared as if it had never been, as he pinioned Ming Xao with extraordinary hazel eyes that had darkened to mud. 'You abused kindness and hospitality and stole from the house that welcomed you at the time.'

At which Ming was winded and could make no reply.

It was an awful truth.

CHAPTER EIGHT

Lien

'I can't.' Heng's words whispered and hovered in the mist that rose from the gorge far below, her face as bleached as the moon. 'Mistress... look! There is nothing there!'

Indeed, as Lien gazed across the chasm, it seemed nothing but thin, moist air, the other side drifting in and out of vision as the mists rose and dispersed. The rapids roared as the waves smashed and broke, fell back and crashed again while the river the Han called the Golden Path made headway to disappear around a further bend. Onward until it reached the Raj where it changed names and watered the dry edges of the Amritsands.

Lien shifted with worry, convinced that behind her in the fusty shadows, Others watched and waited.

Her breath sucked in as the mist shifted again and giant stone pillars stood in front of her within carved timber frames. The carvings seemed to roar as loud as the river below and she realised as the vapours thinned briefly, that they were renditions of temple dogs and she took heart. She moved forward.

'Mistress!' Heng grabbed at her sleeve. 'Have a care!'

'But Heng, look!'

A few feet out into the ravine, a bridge had appeared. Narrow, one shoulder wide, with twisted-hemp hawsers arcing back to the stone pillars. The whole thing was laced like a spider's web for that few feet.

Beyond though, there was nothing.

And yet the bridge hangs suspended as if invisible hands hold it. There's magick here.

'Heng, we must step onto it. Keep looking straight ahead. As long as we walk, the bridge will be beneath our feet because we need it to be.'

'I can't...'

'You can.' She turned and faced Heng. 'You have done things that are beyond brave since we left the House of Silk. The bravest, I think, is to be my voice of reason. I must repay that in the only way I can. I will lead us, yes? You can hold my hand. I ask you to trust as you have never trusted before. Please...' She almost begged her maidservant, knowing what she was asking of her. Knowing also that she didn't want to carry out this journey – *this escape, she thought, let us be honest* – without Heng next to her.

Heng's face was as pale as parchment, ivory like moonsheen, but she said nothing, just shook her head, breathed deep and then held out her hand. Lien took the trembling fingers in her own, kissed them and smiled. Concealing the dread, stilling her vacillating heart as she took her first step onto the bridge, leading Heng behind her.

'Look up, Heng, look at the Heavens. Keep your eyes raised. Look at the dawn colours – how the clouds break and the sun rises to shine through in great golden stripes. It is a sign from the Great Mother.' She had reached the end of what had laid before her but as with heart in throat, she placed her foot down in a step of nothingness and abiding trust, the next length of bridge revealed itself. Behind her, she could hear Heng, 'May my noble Ancestors protect me in my hour of need, may Chi Nü support me. May the Great Mother, Cheng Mo, take my soul in Her hands.' She would repeat the cycle of prayer with every second footstep and her hand gripped Lien's with such force that Lien's fingers began to numb.

But nothing mattered as footstep upon footstep, the delicate suspension bridge, built with a spider's skill across the great chasm, revealed itself. The mist shrouded them, settling on their hair and clothes and still they walked. Slowly, carefully, but with determination.

Not once did Lien look back. To do so she felt would break the enchantment of the bridge and she stepped on until she could see the sister cairns and the carved timbers and realised they were almost on the other side.

'Heng, we are almost there…'

Three steps…

Two steps…

One step.

She dragged Heng off the bridge and the maidservant collapsed to her knees, her face in her hands as she murmured thanks to Cheng Mo.

Lien closed her eyes and breathed as deep as she had ever done, and then turned to look behind her over the ravine.

There was no crossing.

The Bridge that Never Was had lived up to its name and vanished. The pillars, the carved temple dogs, the spiderweb weaving – all gone.

'Heng…' she whispered, shocked, dragging her maidservant upright. 'It's gone…'

Heng turned round, allowing her hands to slip from her eyes. 'Ah,' she cried. 'I don't like this, mistress. We are in a realm we can't control.'

'Indeed, and I would lie to you if I didn't say I'm afraid.' But she took Heng's hands and held them tightly in a gesture she hoped the maidservant would see as solidarity. 'But think on it – Chi Nü advised us, the bridge appeared for us. There must be more folk from within the Other realm who are kind and will see us safe.'

'Quite right, Lien of the First House of Silk. You are wise and steadfast and there are those who will honour that.'

Both women jumped at the sound of an old man's creaking voice. They looked to the shadowy pines and cedars, and an Ancient shuffled toward them, bent and holding a staff. Fine white hair lay silkily on his shoulders, and an apology for a beard and moustache hung to his chest. His face had the creases of a thousand years, and his aged hands were gnarled and knotted.

But his eyes!

His eyes sparkled with wisdom and life, as clear and honest as a child's. 'Don't be afraid, ladies. I am Yue Lao.'

Heng collapsed to her knees again.

'Dear Heng, calm yourself,' Yue Lao said. 'Have no fear of me, dear lady, for I am your friend in dire times.'

Lien pulled Heng to her feet but she grasped Lien's hand, unable to stem her trembles.

'The Spirit of Fate...' Lien said, bowing. 'An honour, Revered One.'

Was this a trap? Were they caught in a net? The thoughts chased themselves around her head as she lifted her gaze from the ground.

'I'm glad you should think,' the Ancient observed, 'that it is an honour. Some are not so polite. My life and Fate have been linked for so long, I get tired thinking about it. May I sit?'

'You ask *us*?' Lien replied. 'We should be kowtowing to you.'

'I don't like kowtowing. It implies fear and power and I have no wish for you to fear me at all. Besides, I know you hated everyone kowtowing to you in your wedding procession, did you not?'

Lien gasped, remembering the hateful journey 'How did you know?'

'I know everything,' Yue Lao sighed. 'It is a heavy weight

to bear. But in any case, it hardly matters, Lien. You must flee for fear of being caught by Others and used as a hostage, because the moment you became betrothed to the Emperor, you became indelibly linked to his actions. Goodness,' the Ancient continued. 'The problems some paper, a brush and ink and a mortal's misguided actions are causing! Right!' he clapped his hands in a gesture of someone far younger, the sound sharp in the glade. 'Let us make a swift plan. Come come!' He waved a hand and a brazier appeared, casting mottled light and warmth in the early dawn chill. In front of the three, steaming cups of tea appeared with a finely moulded platter of honey pastries. 'Please, help yourself,' he said as he reached for a pastry and placed it in his mouth.

But Lien delayed. Was there not a dictum that if one ate Other food, one was condemned to stay in the Other realm forever?

'So they say,' Yue Lao said and she kicked herself for not realising how much of her mind he could read. 'But you are not *in* the Other realm and if you are hungry and food is offered, is it not rude to refuse the kindness? I realise you may not trust me, but please, in the name of Chi Nü who is my dearest friend, believe that I only mean to help, and that the food is as ordinary as any mortal food can be. Eat and drink while I speak.'

Lien and Heng reached tentatively for the aromatic tea. The ivory-coloured cups reflected the flames of the brazier, their fingers shadowed through the translucent porcelain. Delicate green leaves floated inside the bowls, sending out a fragrance at once cleansing and calming. They sipped, expecting the worst, but nothing happened except that a warmth spread through their bodies and Yue Lao's eyes sparkled, one hairy grey and white eyebrow lifting and his mouth tilting with amused irony.

'Good. You will be refreshed. Tea and something sweet always lifts the spirits, I feel.' He chuckled at his own little joke and then placed his cup down carefully, his manner at once serious. 'Ladies, you must leave in a moment. There is a punt… you groan, Heng? You do not like watercraft? Rest assured that you will be safe.' He smiled kindly at Heng, like a wise old grandfather. 'On this you must trust me. Now, the punt is down that path,' he pointed. 'It is filled with everything you might need for your journey as I think you might be a lot less prepared than the Emperor. He at least has experience with Others.'

'You have *seen* the Emperor?' Lien gasped.

'Yes. And he and I talked, and I sent him in the exact direction I am sending you. You will meet, of that I am sure. Just when though, is, I hate to say, in the lap of the Gods.'

'I see.' Lien tried hard to stem temper. 'So we might run but where we go, how safe we are and when we will reach the Ymp Tree Orchard is still within the power of the Gods to control.'

'Gods, Others, Immortals. Call them what you will.' He sighed. 'And on that, I must tell you of such Others that will make your hair curl.'

Lien growled. 'Why? It's enough that we run, surely!'

Yue Lao grimaced and rubbed his knee with a circular motion, as if in pain. 'You need to know, to have a care…'

'But we don't have time for this…'

'You do, my dear. It is important. You may be approached by Others of whom you know nothing as you journey to the wise woman they call Seraphina, and you need to survive. In the mists of time, during the Wars of Chaos,' Yue Lao rubbed at his eyes, 'Immortals fought one against the other for dominance and one such, a Charm-Master of exceptional knowledge, created a number of fatal spells which became known as the Cantrips of Unlife. He used what they call the Earth spell to quell those he saw as enemies. The damage was far-reaching. Every single walking creature, two legged or four, six or eight, everything within leagues, whether on the battlefield or no, mortal or Immortal, died in unparalleled agony. There was a sea of dead with not a drop of blood spilled. Just acre upon acre of twisted wrecks, and for hundreds of years nothing has grown where the dead lay and our world of Eirie quaked at the power that the terrible charm evoked. Even now the Vale of Kush is a desolate place. And so Other Elders looked at what had been done and thought such destruction was contemptible.'

'How civilised of them,' Lien said, unable able to hide her caustic tone. 'To be honest, it's reassuring to know that Others actually fear *something*. And yet They have learned nothing!' But it was hard to be cynical with an old man who was kind and grandfatherly.

'Believe it or not,' he continued, ignoring her cynicism, 'there are conclaves where Others discuss Their place and how best never ever to let a War of Chaos occur again because it is obvious, if such a situation was to unleash, there would be nothing left of the Eirish world – mortal *or* Other.' Yue Lao paused and the image of a shattered world lay at their feet. He looked at each woman and spoke slowly. 'It was at one such conclave where a mortal-drawn map of portals was mentioned and it was decided by each province's fey representative, that for eternal balance to exist, the map must be destroyed, and the maker punished.'

'Huh,' Lien could not contain herself. 'Balance for whom? Certainly not for mortals. We live in fear of Others, of falling into their world… *your* world, and suffering the consequences.' She eyed off the Ancient. 'Everything is by *your* rules.'

Heng hissed from behind Lien, in much the same way she had when Lien had been speaking to Sun Sen so Lien took a calming breath.

'I mean no disrespect, honoured one, I realise that you are Gods and we are… mere mortals, but it seems to me, the one thing that is forgotten in these conclaves, is that mortals *suffer* and that one man, a mortal, tried hard to redress the balance, to make it more even. Whatever you all might think, he is not guilty of malfeasance.'

'And you may be right,' Yue Lao agreed. 'There are those of us who despise the cruelties that befall mortals when they stumble into our world, what happens to mortals when they become bait.'

'So in fact, there *is* no balance,' Lien said. She wished she could make all these Gods see the damage they did, the anxieties they engendered and just leave the mortals to their own devices. 'No balance as we mortals know it,' she continued, 'and Others seem happy for that imbalance to continue.'

Yue Lao looked down at the empty cups. And then, 'Well yes, when you put it like that. But it is the way of it. In any case, I suspect we talk semantics. But what I want is for you to be wary of every single being you meet – even animals. Assume that each is Other and evil with it. Remember everything you were taught – don't eat offered food, don't give your name…' He sighed, his words heavy. 'I think it must be time for you to depart if you have any hope of catching the Emperor and getting to safety.'

Lien felt no better with the knowledge that Yue Lao had passed on. She raged at the complete unfairness of life in the world of Eirie, at the imbalance between worlds, of the divide between Others who had, and mortals who did not.

'I know what you are feeling, Lady Lien, and wish I could dissipate your unease, but it is the way of our life and there is little to be done.'

Lien bowed before the Ancient. 'You read my mind, Revered One. I apologise for my thoughts. I *am* grateful… *we* are grateful for your kindness and for the time you have spent with us. But just one thing…' She clenched her fists as if to give herself some kind of moral strength. 'I suspect that you have an idea of what Fate holds for us. May I…'

But Yue Lao held up a gnarled hand. 'I cannot tell you,

my dear. Whilst I know what Fate holds for you, I would never reveal it.' He frowned as if pushing against something. His better judgement, Lien wondered?

'Let me say this,' he continued carefully. 'It is not your Fate to die on this river journey away from the Han. That is all I can say. And I would tie this red thread, the thread of Fate around your wrist…' He took Lien's right wrist. 'You will never be able to remove this. It will untie itself when you meet your Fate. That is the way of it. As for you, Lady Heng, you have an extraordinary Fate. I had not realised.' He looked at her, his many wrinkles reshaping into puzzlement. 'I think you are better named Heng-O after the Moon Goddess, the lovely Lady Moon…' But then he shrugged his shoulders. 'But I digress. As to Fate, I cannot say more. But listen to what your soul whispers to you, dear Heng, and act upon it. You are so much stronger than you realise. Give me your wrist…'

He tied red thread on Heng's wrist as Lien watched, chafing to leave, to get on their way. Every moment counted.

'Go now, ladies. Fortune and Fate await. Yes, that's right – down that path.' He pointed to the cedar and pine shrouded track.

'Thank you, Revered One. We are in your debt,' Lien said as she and Heng bowed low over their hands.

'Yes, yes. That's as may be. Begone now and may the Great Mother watch over you.'

The women hurried away, only looking back as they took their first step on the descent. But Lien wasn't surprised to see that any sign of the Ancient, the brazier and the cups had dissipated. She began to think that Others played with the world of illusion the way mortals played *mahjong*. Click clack and another game was done.

'I wonder if Others get bored with what they do?' she

said as they stepped carefully down the winding dirt track, ducking under tree branches as the roaring of the gorge became less. She recalled the darkly serious face of Kitsune and a shiver coursed up her spine. The Fox Spirit scared her, an invisible yet tangible threat that she would harm Lien if Lien didn't do her bidding. That pain in her finger which she hadn't felt since they stepped onto the emperor's island.

Curious…

'For us,' she continued, 'life is an unknown. Every day, even a planned one, can turn on itself and be something else entirely. But for them, they know what they want to do, they know exactly the outcome and they do it anyway. Heng, are you listening?' She turned back to look at her maidservant.

Heng's expression was serious and drawn and she still retained the moonlike pallor.

Lien stopped. 'Heng, are you unwell? Do you wish to stop? Please tell me…'

But Heng shook her head. 'I am… I am discombobulated. I just need silence, mistress. I need to digest all that has happened. Too much in a short space of time.' She bowed over folded hands. 'Please. Forgive me.'

Lien touched the woman's wrist, her fingers brushing the red thread. 'Then I shall be quiet. I understand what you say. I find myself as confused as a tangle of silk strands. But Heng, we will get through this, I swear. And please, my dear friend, because you *are* that, don't call me mistress. We are equals.'

Heng gave a wan smile and so Lien walked on, down the switchback trail where light fell in gold stripes through the branches of the huge resinous trees and the roar of water was subsumed by forest silence and the occasional call of a thrush. The weight of guilt that she had begged Heng to come with her hung heavy.

They turned a long bend, with no sight nor sound of the river, the descent over root and rock precarious and slow.

Lien's mind dipped and darted like a swallow chasing insects.

She hated running away because they *were* running. From an unseen, unknown enemy. She cast a quick glance around because Others could be anywhere, watching, waiting. That tingle, that fizzing on the skin that had happened in the presence of Kitsune, of Chi Nü and Yue Lao stayed with her now like an ever-present charge from a thunderstorm, but she decided it was anxiety. Best to ignore it and plan.

Heng was sunk deep in her own thoughts, and she left her alone, understanding the vast changes the simple maid-servant had observed in such a small space of time. Not that Lien felt any different. As she had said to Heng, they had been equalised the moment Sun Sen spoke to them. They were two women fleeing for their lives.

She could think of nothing they could do to ameliorate their position. They were at the mercy of the Emperor's mistaken actions, of the whims of Others who might stand in their way and, as she walked ever downward on this narrow path, of the unknown.

The trees had remained thick and shadowed, the resinous tang from the pines heavy on the air. There was little bird call, although once she heard a kite high above, but when she gazed skyward, the trees were too big and she could barely see the heavens. The path was root-strewn and one needed to keep one's eyes on the ground for fear of tripping

They wound round and down and presently, she could smell water but with no sound of rapid flow and wave crashing over rock.

'Heng, the river is close...' she called over her shoulder, but the servant remained quiet.

Why did the Ancient call her Heng-O, Lien wondered. Because the strange thing was that she had thought Heng looked as pale as the moon before they had left through the closet and had even called her Heng-O. She thought of the legend detailing the story of the Moon Goddess. It had been one of Lien's favourites as a child, but Heng had led a different life, a harder one, where children had no leisure to sit with Old One and listen to stories. Lien thought of her grandmother now, her calming words as Lien expressed fear of the oncoming marriage.

Ah, Grandmother, if you only knew what is happening, she thought. Would you have pushed me so confidently? And Father. What of you? Does the First House of Silk benefit from what I am doing? Running to save my life? Maybe even *your* life?

She doubted she would ever see her family again and in a fit of anger, decided she didn't much care. For them it had all surely been about status, not love. If the seers had warned against this, her family would have ignored the auguries. It had ever been her father's ridiculous dream to be a part of the imperial warp and weft...

But such thought wasted her energies and for this journey she needed to be alert. She patted the deep pocket of her jacket where lay the sharp silver paper knife she had pocketed from the Emperor's table, wondering if and how she might need it? She swore under her breath. The journey was fraught with ignorance, and it yawned in front of her like the chasm over which they had just crossed.

Only now there was no bridge.

They burst through cross-hatched branches of pine, brushing the fine needles free of their jackets as the river before them flowed in a swift but calm swathe, ever onward to the Raj. It seemed benign now, and for that, Lien thanked Chen Mo, the Great Mother. Pulled up between rocks and on the mud and pebbles, an aged grey punt glistened in the weak sun that wafted in and out of overhanging trees and gargantuan rocks. It looked as substantial as a matchstick and Lien heard Heng groan softly behind her.

'Heng, it must be sturdy, else why would Yue Lao have left it here for us? In addition, he did say we wouldn't die on the river, did he not?'

Heng walked to the vessel and looked inside. From under a seat, she pulled a stuffed bag, saying, 'There is no pole. Just another thing we cannot control.' She eased the hemp bag open. 'There is fruit, and a water bottle...' she shook it. 'Starvation won't be immediate. Or thirst.'

Her comments were flat and her face sullen, but Lien forgave her. At least she had some colour back, her cheeks faintly blushed and her lips a faded carmine. Her hair had begun to fall softly around her face and her eyes were brighter. *And me?* Lien thought. *Do I look the same? Careworn and faded?* She brushed strands of hair from her eyes and decided to rip up the hemp so they could bind their hair away from their faces.

She tipped the fruit out of the bag and pulled the paper knife from her pocket, slitting the hemp into two broad strips. She gave one to Heng and then began to drag her own hair back to bind it. Heng did the same and with another strip she took the remains of the bag from Lien, knotted it off and stuffed the fruit back in.

'We must stow everything tightly, in case it becomes rough, I think. Mistr...' she stopped, then smiled diffidently, 'Lien, do you think we should remove our jackets and stow those as well? They are quite heavy, and we can't move quickly if we have to.'

'Perhaps.' Lien shrugged hers off, passing it to Heng. She tucked the paper knife in her waistband as Heng shook off her own coat, folding it and pushing it under the seat. She began folding Lien's as Lien cast about the shore for a long branch that might serve as a pole.

Finding a branch of pine, she tested its strength, but as she walked back, her finger was shot through with slicing pain. She heard a shrill call from the forest. Dog-like, a howl, a hunting dog on a scent and her heart stopped beating. 'Quickly Heng, get in the punt. I will push!'

Heng had heard the animal call and jumped in with speed as Lien pushed the vessel. It slid easily into the shallows and Lien splashed through the cold water, pushing harder and then flinging herself in, shunting the boat with the branch until they were in deep dark water, watching behind as a flash of white sped down to the shore.

Gods! She has found us!

Kitsune reared on her fox legs, shape-changing to the majestic fur-swathed woman Lien remembered. She shouted after the two escapees, but they were too far away to hear and something about the way she stood, incandescent with obvious rage, made Lien think they were perhaps beyond her magick.

Was that possible?

'Lien, why did she not follow?' Heng looked back at the fast-reducing white shape on the distant riverbank. The river sped them away and they rounded a bend, the stone escarpments tinted in the morning sun.

'Perhaps she cannot travel on water. I don't know, nor do I care.' The pain in Lien's finger lessened but something hung about – a knowledge that they were far from safe, and on a course which was shrouded in darkness and fear. They may have fled from angry Han spirits but there were many more in other provinces. 'The river flows so fast we could be anywhere. Do you hear a sound?'

Above the river noise there was a gentle bass hum, like a prayer and looking up, they saw a rocky cast and atop, the white walls of a monastery.

'Oh listen, Lien. It's beautiful. Can you hear?' Heng's face for once was transported, alight and alive. 'They are praying. Who are they?'

'The monks and nuns from Jhokang Monastery. Then we are still in the Han. In which case I am sure Kitsune did not follow because we are on the water, and she is not a water-spirit. Blessings on this river.'

The reverberation shook the earth and water so subtly and for the briefest moment, as they floated past, Lien felt at peace. She sighed. If only it could be ongoing.

She turned her head slightly and could see that the escarpments were closing in again, forming steep, narrow ravines. In the far distance she heard another noise, a roar and about them, the river water swirled and small wavelets buffeted the low sides of the punt.

'It's getting rougher,' she said.

Heng gasped. 'By the Mother, I think we approach falls! We are gaining speed…'

Lien grabbed the branch to push them to the shore, but the water was too deep and she nearly tumbled. 'Yue Lao said we would be safe…'

'Mistress… Lien…' Heng's voice was shrill.

'My coat pocket, get the strips of paper, those charms…' Mist had begun to seep backward toward them and the river had begun to tumble into small rapids, the punt rocking and spinning so that she had to grab for the side.

Heng pulled Lien's coat out from under the seat and was scrabbling in the pockets. 'I have them. What do we do?' Her face was once again pale but there was a steeliness now and Lien was glad.

'Read! Shout it out! Oh by the stars, can you read?'

'Of course I can!'

'Then do it! The falls approach!' Lien tightened her hold on the side of the punt.

'Aiyah!' Heng screamed as the boat tipped, then looking at one of the flimsy strips, she called, her voice shaking,

'Gold does glimmer
in a sea wracked cave
a hidden sea secret…'

'Nothing's happening!' Lien shouted.

Heng took a deep breath and bellowed into the roaring mists of the angry river,

'Gold does glimmer
in a sea wracked cave
a hidden sea secret...'
... Cheng Mo, Mother of the Heavens, hear me!'

The boat flung fast into the ever-changing rapids, waves leaking over the blunt bow and the women tried valiantly not to scream as they held onto each other.

'The sound...' Heng almost sobbed.

Lien yelled above the river tumult. 'Yue Lao promised we will not die on this river...'

The crash and roar of the river had changed to a harsher sound, more rhythmic – crash and then a roaring break, then crash again. Like huge temple drums beating a ceremonial dirge. A funeral tympany, Lien thought, recalling the sound when the old Empress had died. Perhaps this *was* their end? But Yue Lao had promised, and they had to believe him. He was a God...

Lien had knowledge of nothing but calm lakes, small waterfalls and placid streams.

So what was this?

A wide angry swathe with a noise like a hundred thousand drums all thundering to the exact same immutable beat. The temple drums had been large square brass instruments with vast resonance, yellow-gold dragons curling around each corner. Furious dragons, indicative of the power of the reverberation. Such was the sound rolling back to Lien and Heng.

The mist parted and there was nothing but volatile grey

water, rolling up and down. Where had she seen this? One of her father's scrolls – a mountainous curl of water…

The sea?

'I think we are on a sea, Heng…'

'A sea?' Heng's face paled to ivory.

Lien's heart thundered in her chest, almost in time to that horrendous crashing that vibrated through the floor of the punt into their feet. She had no idea how to calm Heng because she was as afraid.

The sea!

What sea? She thought. Where did it end? Why did it make such an angry noise?

'The charm, Heng! Again!'

Heng took one hand from the seat and shook out the small scrap of paper in trembling hands.

'Mother of the World, Cheng Mo…' tears creeping down her cheeks.

'Heng! Do it!'

Heng's pallor rivalled any moon Lien had ever seen and she swallowed on her tears.

'Gold does glimmer…

Heng was weeping now, coughing as she sucked breath in and out rapidly.

'in a sea wracked cave
a hidden sea secret…'

They smashed up and down, gripping each other tightly, sinking into troughs and then rising to peaks. And then, from the top of an angry foaming wave, Lien could see why the pounding sea was so loud, why they could feel it through their bodies.

The sea crashed onto a shore, half sand, half rocks and she was sure without a shadow of doubt, that there was no way the punt could survive the impact.

Perhaps, neither would they…

CHAPTER NINE

Ming Xao

Home truths could oft take the wind out of one's sails,' Gallivant pushed harder. 'I shall say it again. You abused kindness and hospitality and stole from the very house that welcomed you. Did you not?'

Ming could think of nothing to say that would exonerate him from the charge of theft and hubris that Gallivant laid at his feet. His face burned. 'I did. And I regret it to this moment. Probably to my dying day.'

'Which may be sooner than you think,' Gallivant replied. 'If this is your bane – to die for your sin, then there is little I or anyone else can do to save you. To be honest, Ming, I am more interested in getting the map to Seraphina so that it may be destroyed and thereby potentially saving your world from a conflagration that could annihilate it.'

Ming grimaced as his heart skipped beat after beat. 'This Seraphina must be astonishing, surely!' He knew he sounded sarcastic and perhaps he was but every now and then, wild anger flooded through him. His better side knew it was anger at himself, but nevertheless, sometimes it burst out like muddy water from an unblocked drain.

'If there is one thing They will not stand for, it's humiliation,' Gallivant's eyes had slitted at Ming's tone. 'And that's what you have done by drawing your map. Anyway...' he stood, clapping his hands together. 'It's time for you to have a sleep of sorts. I will wake you when it is time, and we shall make haste. Come Maxi…'

The great dog levered himself up from the rug upon which he lay and shook himself. Fine silver skeins of dribble sailed off into the nether regions of the study.

'I bid you goodnight, Ming. Sleep well.' The hob walked backward through the study door, pulling it behind him.

Ming closed his eyes, rubbing his hands briskly over his face. He gazed around at the flickering candelabra, then at the shadowed shelves. The temptation was great, to take a candle and climb the ladder to examine the titles, but a prodigious yawn pulled the air from his body, and he longed for a pillow. So instead, he walked toward the chaise, surveying the titles of the books at waist height – herbals, histories, legends and sagas. He wished he was here in another time … before … when things had been simple, and he had been a foreign ingenue.

But there was no going back and so he shucked off his boots and pulled the ribbon from his hair, lay down and just stared at the glittering gold-leafed spines that surrounded him like a gilded cage. He pulled a woollen cover across his body, his thoughts running down like a clock that needs winding. He had memories of Lady Ibo, his previous betrothed and with whom he had escaped the Han when he thought he could no longer bear his fate. But then he had travelled, grown, observed and had returned to become the imperial future of the Han. As befitted an emperor, he had chosen a new bride, because the Lady Ibo, Isabella, had stayed in her rightful home. If the time had been different, he would have liked to question Gallivant on Isabella and what fate had dealt her. He had no doubt that it was fair, but he wanted to know.

But he was so very tired and he realised the hob had mesmered him to sleep and no amount of fight would stop the inevitable. Thus he sank into gentle oblivion, where no thought burst into dreams, no dreams fractured into nightmares.

It was dark when he felt a wetness drag across his cheek. Another slurp and he realised Max was licking him. He pushed at the dog's big head and the dog turned to recline on the floor, body facing away from Ming and toward Gallivant who held one candle.

'Good boy, Max,' the hob said and then gestured to the side table. 'Warm water, a linen towel, soap. Your comb and ribbon. I shall sit here while you conduct your ablutions and then, coat and boots on, and we shall go. No time to dally. It's the hour before dawn.'

The hob sat delicately on a balloon backed chair, flicking out the tails of his coat, crossing one leg over the other and swinging the foot back and forth in something close to impatience. If Ming had learned anything about the hob in the short time between yesterday and today, it was that *he* would dictate the day's progressions one way or another and Ming would have to follow. In this instance, passivity was all.

So he washed the sleep from his eyes, combed his hair and tied it back, pulled on the boots and black coat the hob had provided, removed the knife, purse and canister from his waistband to replace them in his pockets. 'I am ready,' he said.

'Then let us go while it is still dark. We need to pole across to the Ca' Specchio. Which I'm assuming you know.'

'Yes…'

'Then tell me how you knew it contained a gate. The whole story as we go.'

How I knew it contained a gate?

By happenstance was what it was…

Ming had departed Jasper's house all those years ago, leaving his friend Isabella to write a story the like of which sounded like legend but which was indeed true. A story about a *shifu* cloth bridge and about a goddess returning to the celestial heavens in the arms of a half-mortal. He knew the story had been written down because he had received a copy from a trader who returned from Trevallyn. He read it and hated the cruelty of Others anew.

After blind Chi Nü had been carried to her heavenly home across the bridge, her sight restoring, Ming never thought to see her again, however time proved differently. But that, he thought, was another story and one to be told at another, perhaps safer time.

'I observed,' he said now.

'Your memory is remarkable,' Gallivant opened the door of the palazzo and he, Ming and Maximilian slipped into a dark, fog-laden night. 'Good,' the hob added. 'Fog is good.' He wafted his arm in a balletic sweep, stirring the mist into swirls. 'But I shall make it thicker, just to be sure.' He walked to a heavy ring set in the wall on the edge of the canal in front of the palazzo and untied a rope, pulling a dainty gondola in close. The fog was deepening, winding around the travellers' legs. 'Hup, Max!'

Maximilian jumped in, the craft rocking precariously and then settling upon the silky-smooth water. The dog laid down and watched the two men as Gallivant hopped in next, holding onto the paved edging of the portico while Ming stepped aboard.

'Won't folk hear us?' he asked.

'The fog dulls sound, as it does sight. Besides, it's eldritch. Surely you realise that.'

Ming hadn't thought. But yes, how could it not be? That arm wave...

Settled, he watched Gallivant again waft his hand. The rope curled itself around the swan-like prow, the vessel reversed and swung gently into the vapour, and they lost sight of everything. The moist heaviness pressed on Ming's sensibilities and he took a breath.

'The boat knows where it must go, and we have time to talk. Please continue...' Gallivant's hand rested on Ming's sleeve and the light touch drew him back from the edge of anxiety.

'I left Jasper's through the Ymp Tree Orchard. I had seen Isabella and Nicolas come and go. Others too. There and then gone through the lines of Ymp Trees. I was sure it would take me beyond the Færan world in which I had found myself. I had no idea where I would be, but it didn't matter. I just wanted to move on. It had been such an emotive time.'

'And so you walked through the portal. How did it feel?'

'Like bursting through a bubble, but the colours, fragrances and textures became less crystalline, less perfect. I knew immediately I had left the mirror-image fey world and was in the mortal world in Trevallyn. And so I started walking northwest, the idea being that I would eventually, when I was ready, find the Han and my home.'

Gallivant nodded and signalled for Ming to continue.

'Gallivant, that is how mortals get themselves into trouble. They stumble into the Other world and by the time they get out, *if* they get out, the real world has moved on and everything they knew has aged, changed, even in some cases, vanished.'

Gallivant's mouth twisted and he frowned. ''Tis so...'

'Then if any of you had half a heart, you would realise that is why I mapped the portals. To give mortals a fighting chance.' Every muscle in Ming's body tightened with frustration that even this skinny, overly elegant Other spiriting him away from danger didn't seem to understand.

'But I do understand.' Gallivant grinned as Ming's head flew up. 'Yes, I can sometimes read thoughts. It's a skill I sharpened whilst with Adelina. If I hadn't, I shudder to think what might have happened in the end. Still, it's a story you know, so let us move on. The Veniche gate. Tell and be quick as I suspect we are almost there.'

Ming sighed. 'Once in Veniche, I visited many places. The islets and glassmakers, the mask-makers, the markets, the Museo, even the boatmakers and the Arsenale. I wrote single word references to jog my memory once I returned to the Han. As it was, I returned to my home with a pile of journals. I needed to remember things because I knew it would help my own province in the future. Of that I was sure.' He looked around but the fog seemed impenetrable, no shapes of other gondolas appearing out of the vapour, no buildings, just the lap of water against the side of their own craft and the sad sound of a muffled bell to their left. He continued. 'I went to the Ca' Specchio simply because it was a beautiful palace and I wanted to see it for myself. The doors were open, men preparing for another grand occasion, and I just wandered in. No one stopped me. I climbed the stair and entered the ballroom. By the Gods! Such a room – all faceted mirrors, sparkling glass and polished floors. It was like entering a diamond! I kept to the outside edge, out of the way as men and women worked – polishing, gilding, creating tall flower arrangements in urns the size of a man. I remember I was walking, looking up at the frescoed ceiling, a pastoral scene that transported me to things I had seen in Trevallyn and I stumbled against a rolled carpet. I began to fall sideways. I held out my hand as one does, and it collided with nothing. I kept falling and there was that burst bubble sensation again.'

Gallivant sat up straight. 'And…'

'I knew. Instantly I knew. The room I fell into was a mirror image, but clearer, brighter, even more beautiful if it were possible. The fragrance from the flowers was more intense and there was a small ensemble practising on a stage and the music was more melodic, more haunting and those

people moving about their duties were perfection personi-
fied. My heart leaped and crashed, and I backed away to the
mirror through which I had fallen, leaned against it and
passed back to the real world.'

The real world. A sane world…

'What did you do then?' asked Gallivant and Ming was
sure he detected a wry note in the question.

'I fled to the waterways. Hired a gondolier to paddle me
anywhere whilst I thought.'

Their own gondola touched something with a dull thud
and Gallivant wafted a hand so that the fog cleared a little.
They had arrived at their destination and the rope snaked
out, tied itself to a mooring pole on the edge of the grand
portico and the two men and the dog alighted. One of the
giant gold-limned doors opened silently with little pressure
from Gallivant's hand and they hurried inside.

'Is there no one here?'

'To my knowledge, no. Come quickly…'

Gallivant tapped up the stair with speed, Max leaping
beside him and Ming following. At the top, they entered
the darkened ballroom. With the seafog heavy outside the
windows and dawn still yet to birth, there was no sparkle,
glitter, nor even a glimmer of light and Ming was glad when
Gallivant mesmered a small candle whose flickering flame
allowed them to make haste to the mirrored panel that Ming
remembered so well.

So well that a bitter shiver coursed down his spine swiftly
and with such coldness that he gasped. Gallivant dropped
the candle and sucked in his own breath and Maxi whined.

'Sink me, no! No, no, no!' Gallivant muttered. He rubbed
at his forehead as if it had a prodigious ache.

'What?' asked Ming as the ice stayed pressed against his
spine. 'What ails you?' But something ailed him as well and
he had a feeling.

'Not me, dear man.' Gallivant turned a stricken face to
Ming. 'Not us. It's your bride.'

Ming grabbed at Gallivant's sleeve and Max growled. 'What do you mean, *my bride*?' But he knew.

Beloved Ancestors, please keep her safe...

Gallivant picked up the guttering candle and the flickers threw spectral shadows upon his face. 'She is in danger. She...'

'How? Where is she?' Ming thought of that lovely woman he had chosen as his consort. 'Gallivant, speak!'

'There has been a storm at sea...'

'It's Pymm! It's Pymm, isn't it?'

She has read the charms in the wrong order...

'Leave me!' Gallivant almost snarled this last, shoved the candle at Ming and hurried away to a mirror further down. Ming went to follow as the candle dripped hot wax upon his hand, but Max moved in front of him, a low rumble in his throat as Gallivant squatted down and lowered his head.

Moments passed with no sound but for Max's rumbles of warning and then Gallivant stood and walked back. If his face had been spectral before, it was now cadaver-pale and his eyes were as dark as a thunderstorm as he asked. 'Pymm, indeed. And how would she have got as far as Pymm, do you think?'

'It was a guess...'

'A guess. A wildly correct guess.' The hob's eyes closed to fierce slits. 'The vessel she was on is wrecked and she lies on the shore of a cave...perhaps you know of the cave...'

'Gods! Is she alive? How do you... Can you see?'

'I don't know if she lives. As to how, years of wretched experience. One day I might tell you. And you, mortal man, can return the favour.'

'We must go to Pymm! We must find her...'

Gallivant groaned then, holding a hand to his belly, subsiding onto the floor and vomiting. 'I'm sorry,' he panted between retches. 'The visions always make me ill...'

Ming kneeled beside the hob though the smell roiled his

own belly. 'What can I do?' But he knew he had nothing
to offer an Other except kindness and he placed a hand on
the fellow's shoulder. Through the tailored and padded silk,
he felt the bony unformed frame of an adolescent and he
wondered how such a young person could be so wise and let
it be said, mature.

I cannot let her die...

'Gallivant, tell me what I must do,' he begged.

'Give me a moment and some lemon tea with ginger. It
will settle.' He waved a limp hand, the vomit disappeared
and a mug of something steamily astringent manifested by
his side as Ming helped the hob stand.

'Gallivant, I must find her. In all conscience, I cannot
continue to the Ymp Tree Orchard when I know I'm the
reason she lies in a cave far from the Han.'

'You are right, of course. I would not expect you to do
otherwise. But even if we sail from here now, this instant, it
could take a sennight and then only if the winds are in our
favour.'

'You are eldritch, are you not? Can you not mesmer us
there?'

'Such a thing is beyond my magick, Ming.'

Ming knew he could do it himself, he knew the charms
by heart, knew they were invested with a power through
the ink with which he had written them. Invested with the
magick that he had indeed stolen from the house of old
Jasper. He knew that he could push through the mirror, that
portal so near to his shoulder, utter the right charm and he
would be on the Pymm Archipelago. But he dare not admit
it to Gallivant, because he trusted no one yet, not the hob,
nor the dog. Not even himself if the truth be known.

'Then I shall give the map to you,' he said, 'and you can
take it to Trevallyn to be destroyed and I shall find a ship
and search for Lien. She is an innocent in all of this, and it
is my duty.'

Gallivant finished the mug of tea and brushed his tailcoat down, running hands through his wispy hair. Beyond the windows, they could hear seabirds calling as the dawn light began to grow, the fog beginning to dissolve and the odd voice or two shouting from *calle* and *fondamenta*.

'I cannot do what you ask,' the hob replied. 'The map's destruction is something only you can resolve. Seraphina was quite specific.'

'Why, in the names of the Ancestors?' Anger seeped into Ming's question. 'Does it matter who delivers it? As long as it is destroyed?'

'Apparently it does. I know not why.'

Ming paced as a soft sheen of gold crept in a narrow bar from a full-length window, spreading across the parquet floor like tidings of great joy. 'I'm damned if I do or don't. Hell's blood!' Such a vast error of judgement at that moment in Jasper's study when he had seen the bottle of ink and held it to the light – watched the way the viscous liquid undulated so unusually as he held it, how small spangles of light appeared and then as quickly vanished inside the bottle. That monumental mistake when he had slipped it into the deep pocket of his coat, walked out from the study as innocently as he had walked in, and continued to the kitchen, taking some bread and cheese and then striding as if life was his for the taking, toward the Ymp Tree Orchard and an apocalyptic future.

I have no choice...

'I can get us there with speed,' he admitted. Lemons had tasted better on his tongue.

'Surely.' Gallivant's reply was grim.

'You know?'

'I know that you have more than a map, else how did Lady Lien get from the Han to Pymm? Whilst things don't quite add up just yet, there is something emerging and I am sure in time, you will explain.'

'I promise I will. But now we need the mirror and leave the rest to me.'

'Sink me! Leave it to a mortal,' Gallivant took Max by the collar. 'And since when has that ever ended well.'

'Show me a time when Others might have acted better,' Ming said as he spun toward the mirrored panel. 'I know the story of Adelina the embroiderer and how she left Jasper in horrified disgust. How she left even you. It's a story known all over Eirie. Many think it's a legend, but I know better. *She* was a mortal who took her destiny into her own hands and moulded it to her needs without your help, so no lectures please. I find I like her life's choices.'

As he went to pass through the eldritch mirror, Max growled. His fur stood in an angry ridge along his spine and his lips drew back from his teeth. His eyes were dilated and filled with volatility.

'Max?' Gallivant placed his hand on the dog's back. 'Sink me, Ming. They come!'

The hairs on Ming's neck stood and ice ran down his spine as it had when he had sensed the danger to Lien. But this was stronger, more terrifying. 'It's not Lien...'

'No,' Gallivant whispered. 'We are being followed by Others. At worst, they wait for us, like some evil trap on the other side of the mirror.'

'Then what do we do?'

Gallivant bent down. 'Maxi, where?'

The dog turned his head to the door at the end of the ballroom.

'Good dog! They're coming up the stairs. Quickly!'

Ming led off, his poem a whispered chant.

Gold does glimmer
in a sea wracked cave
a hidden sea secret...

Gallivant and Max raced on his heels as they pushed through the strange barrier. It stretched, almost resisting, and then suddenly gave way so that they burst into a dawn-lit copy of the room they had left; this one, so far, empty and echoing. Outside the long windows, gold light glistened as the sun rose and the mists burned off.

'Come on,' Gallivant urged, running across the ballroom floor toward a doorway. 'Run. Do what you must, Ming, or we will be caught!'

'Here, Gallivant. With me!' Ming stood in the gold beam that stretched along the room from the long window and the hob and dog joined him, the muscles along the dog's haunches and spine rippling, his teeth gleaming as spittle fell in streams to the floor, the growl puffing in and out from deep in his throat. As a foot and then a shoulder appeared through the mirror, Ming repeated softly, so the approaching insurgents wouldn't hear,

Gold does glimmer
in a sea wracked cave
a hidden sea secret...

Terrifying shouts sounded, men's voices filled with bloodlust and the thrill of the chase. A crowd of Others began to burst through the mirror, dressed in exotic silks, dark skinned and light, leather whips in their fists, hair swirling around their heads, faces snarling and eyes on fire. The Wild Hunt...

The gold surrounding Ming, the hob and the dog watered down as if by a damp brush. The harsh yells faded and echoed, echoed and faded, with the rhythm of something other than the vile chase. Above them, the frescoed ballroom ceiling blurred as though wafts of wispy muslin covered it.

'The sea!' Gallivant stared at waves washing onto shingle,

sucking and brushing, and then gazed up at the high roof of the seacave. 'Sink me, Ming. Exactly *what* magick do you possess! Even *I* could not have gotten us away. And to a seacave, by the stars! Will they follow?'

'You ask me? I'm mortal, Gallivant, remember? What would I know...' But relief softened Ming's reply and he looked for the steps he knew laced up from the cave to the ragged coastline that was Pymm.

CHAPTER TEN

Lien

Lien remembered nothing.

When she lifted her head from the gritty shore, such dizziness assailed her that she collapsed again, fading into a blackness that must surely be death. She thought she detected soft hands, like the beating of a moth's wing, and high-pitched whispers, but still she could not pull herself from the darkness.

She drifted. Carried by feathers floating on the wind and then sinking into a soft cloud which served to ease the punishing aches in her back and head, both of which alternately throbbed and shrieked with pain. She thought she swallowed a draught that tasted of nothing. Perhaps she did, as hands eased her to sit up and then laid her down again.

The next time she woke, a thought of her companion dashed through her mind at breakneck speed and she cried out 'Heng! Where are you?' But then the thought was gone, and her voice was nothing but whisper and croak.

She lost all sense of time. Days? Weeks? She had no idea until one morning, her eyes opened at a faint glow from a window.

Dawn?

She turned her head carefully because it still ached. The room was empty of all but the bed in which she lay, and a small table loaded with small jars and pots, a mortar and pestle and dried flowers. Three chairs were lined up along the wall. The chamber was whitewashed and simple, her covers light but as warm as a mother's womb. Had she been in the sea at some point? She frowned, trying to remember, but her face muscles ached and her fingers crept to her temple where she touched stitches of the finest silk.

Injured?

She grunted and closed her eyes again, drifting off as the faint glow moved across the floor to warm her legs in the cocoon of her bed.

The next time she woke, she stretched, her body more compliant. The glow had moved to the far wall and she saw the dimples and cracks of a surface that had been whitewashed many times, and a lavender fragrance drifted. Turning her head to the other side of her bed, she sucked in a breath as three small women sat in a neat row on the bentwood chairs. Their clothes were the colours of a wild garden, their hands folded on their laps and hair pulled to their crowns in blousy buns.

'You are awake, my dear,' said one. The voice was higher pitched than she would have expected with the age of the woman, and the others chimed in.

'Good to see.'

'At last, my sweet.'

She said nothing but then, 'Heng! Where is Heng?' A trickle of fear crept into her throat and she swallowed on it. 'My companion…'

'Heng?' The woman closest reached out and felt Lien's forehead. 'Calm yourself, my sweet. We shall help you sit up and wash, perhaps fetch some gruel for you and then, when you are fortified, we shall talk.'

Lien hadn't the strength to argue and found that her thoughts began but then drifted off, dissolving into a too-hard distance. She relished the warm water wash. Relished too, the unguents the women smoothed into her face and hands, over her shoulders and across her back. Some herbal cream she thought, which eased the tenderness of her obvious bruises and the muscle aches and pains. Savoured the feel of the finest lawn the women lifted over her head, the plumping of the massive soft pillows behind her and then the flavour of the oatmeal with honey, butter and cinnamon that they placed in front of her on a tray. Her hand trembled with weakness as she held the spoon, but she was hungry.

Although it exhausted her, the effort of washing and eating was not enough to push away the thread of concern that nestled in her breast, and she knew she must air it. She must find out…

'My friend, Heng…'

'Heng? We know no one of that name,' one of the women replied in a piping voice.

'But she was with me. You must have seen her…'

Lien examined the three and noted how small they were. Perhaps only to her shoulder or less, and in each case, lovely in a strangely wrought middle-years way.

Strangely wrought… enchanted? But I have eaten with them and they know my name!

Then, *I didn't offer my name so perhaps I'm safe…*

'Who are you? Where have you taken me?' she demanded. Despite her evident fragility, she recalled a boat and the vast sea and her loved companion. 'Tell me…'

'Ah. You are better than we thought if you need this discussion,' replied the woman dressed in lavender muslin, and who had five spikes of dried flowers through her bun.

'I remember a storm… my friend and I…'

'Yes, my dear. There was a terrible storm and your boat broke apart, some of it was thrown ashore. You were washed into a sea-cave and we found you on the shingle there as we collected dulse. The cave is a magick place and the best dulse is funnelled into the cave on currents…'

'My friend?' Lien interrupted. What did she care for dulse?

'You were alone.' The words dropped like boulders and Lien closed her eyes, tears creeping from the corners.

Heng, where are you? I need you by my side...

'Lien... yes, we know who you are and why you were on the sea.'

Then you know more than me, because I can't remember...

'Lien, we know too that you had a companion, but we must relay the awful fact to you that she was not with you when we found you.'

Lien looked at the faces of the three women. Their expressions were kind but ineffably sad and the one dressed in faded alizarin, the colour of berries, and whose hair was pale auburn threaded with grey, but whose eyes were bright hazel said,

'My dear Lien. We think your friend went missing at sea.'

'She could not swim...' Lien whispered.

'Ah...' all three chimed together.

Lien wept and the women stayed silent, allowing the tears to course freely. Every now and then, a hand would reach out and smooth her shoulder and she could not determine if she was grateful or repulsed. She was too tired to think on it.

Finally, the third woman who was dressed in the gold of a late summer's day and whose hair had the faded sheen of a middle-aged matron, held a mug for her and she drank. Elderflower. She'd had it once at a reception at the First House of Silk. Her mother had been pleased to show it off, having imported it from beyond the Wall. Then for a heart-beat, she thought of the Han and the damnable Emperor, her Would-be-Husband, her need to travel on a dangerous journey. But the thought ebbed like a tide, her eyes shuttered down, and she drifted into sleep.

Later, she heard agitated whispers from the three as she surfaced from a dark comforting space.

'There is something evil all about. The birds are quiet and the merrows cry.'

Another said, 'And have you noticed the moon has been absent this sennight with not a cloud to hide it? Just gone?'

'There is a mist each day,' said the third voice. 'It wafts back and forth and the sun struggles. Something evil comes.'

The first voice spoke again. 'It is connected. How can it not be? We must get her to safety.'

'But how?'

Lien struggled to sit up in the bed. 'Yes. How? And who are you?'

The lavender woman hurried over and plumped up Lien's pillows. 'Oh my dear. You are awake. More alert I think.'

Lien pushed the woman's hands away. 'Yes, alert.' She threw back the covers and swung her legs to the floor. 'I need to find Lady Heng and then we…'

But the world tipped up and she staggered.

'Lien, you hit your head badly. Just there,' the woman's dandelion-light fingers touched the stitching at Lien's temple. 'There was a profound gash which we stitched, and we've dressed it daily. It's healing well but that doesn't alter the fact that your head has had a knock that would send a big man senseless. Your body is also bruised all over. You were tumbled in the sea, against who knows what. To be honest, my dear, you are lucky to be alive. We think…' She stopped and looked toward her companions, who nodded. 'We think you were rescued by a selkie. She laid you on the shore in the cave and we found you the day after the storm.'

But not Heng. Heng is gone…

'How long have I been here?'

'A sennight.'

'Sennight?'

'Seven nights.'

'Seven! And there has been no sign of Heng in that time, none?' She took a faltering step from the bed, and another,

her anxiety and grief pushing her forward. She felt the reasons for her predicament rushing toward her like a terrible wind. She and Heng had been running away, looking for the Emperor. Because not only was his life in danger from the Celestials, but so was Lien's merely because she was his betrothed. He of course, carried some damnable map the Celestials, and all Others wanted.

She turned, holding onto the wall, leaning against it. The three women watched her. Maybe they wanted the map. Maybe they kept her prisoner. 'I want to know who you are and why you hold me here.'

'Goodness, Lien. We don't *hold* you here. We just needed to nurse you until you could leave. It is what we siofra do. Good things. We help mortals.'

'Siofra?'

'Siofra are spirits who help mortals whenever we can. In return for homes and clothes. You can see our little home is fine-built and our clothes are the best muslin. We have warm woollen cloaks and leather shoes with sturdy wooden pattens for the wet and winter days. It is what we are given for our kindness, because we would never hurt a mortal. I'm sure you have similar spirits in your own lands.'

Lien thought of Yue Lao, the God of Fate, a Terrestrial spirit, but she said nothing.

'We will help you on your way. But perhaps not till morning when you have had one more night's rest and some good food in your belly.'

Lien wanted to dress and go this instant but as her head thumped, the realisations that she could only rely on herself and that her dear friend Heng was gone, settled like a heavy net over her, trapping her tightly in knots and folds. She fell to the floor like a beached fish, almost gasping, and the three siofra rushed to her, taking her arms over their shoulders and shuffling back to the bed with her.

'Surely now, my dear,' said the lavender woman, 'you

can see that rest is vital. One or perhaps two more nights, good food and you will be more able to cope.' She wafted her hand in front of Lien and said, 'Sleep now and we will talk in detail at dinner.'

'Wait, wait,' Lien mumbled. 'What are your names?'

She knew she had been mesmered, that enchantment peculiar to Others. The Celestials and Terrestrials of the Han enchanted the luckless in similar ways. The mesmer took her in its embrace as she vaguely heard three piping voices reply to her question.

'Iolanthe...'

'Flavia...'

'Amaranthe...'

This time, when she woke, the curtain had been drawn back, the three women stood, staring out the window. Taut with tension and whispering further about mists and evil. She stretched, testing her body. It was stiff and there was a tenderness but surely it was less prevalent than yesterday. She pulled herself up as the three siofra turned at her movement, busying themselves. Water to wash in, a warming fire stoked in the hearth, a steaming bowl of oatmeal on the table, the honey golden, the cinnamon shaken across the repast like shimmers of deep amber.

'Good morning to you, Lien,' Iolanthe of the lavender muslin said.

'How are you feeling?' said, Flavia of the golden tints.

'You seem better today,' added Amaranthe of the crimson hues.

'Better than yesterday,' Lien replied as she placed one foot down on the smooth boards of the floor, and then the other. She took a step and her knees remained strong, and then another. With the confidence that her legs would carry her, she walked across to the window and looked out, trying to discern what so distressed the three Others.

A wood stretched below the cottage – half-hidden by the strange mist that wafted one way and then another. There was no sound of life – no birds, no breeze, no waves upon the coastal shore. Everything seemed in stasis, except for the movements behind her, where the siofra smoothed her bed and laid out clothing.

Lien walked round the room, her fingers grazing the whitewashed walls in case a wave of weakness should wash over her, but apart from a soreness across her back and a tightness where the stitches pulled her temple, there was nothing that could not be borne.

'Come, be seated,' said Iolanthe, 'and eat. Then when you are dressed, you might like to come downstairs and we can talk, plan.'

The warmed oatmeal was a gift from the Gods. It filled her stomach, and life flowed through her veins.

'See,' said Amaranthe to her sisters. 'That recipe is life incarnate. She heals before our very eyes.'

Lien nodded. 'Curious. I *can* feel an energy, and the pain is not as bad. Is it something you magicked?'

Flavia smiled and Iolanthe said, 'To a degree. There are florals which can enliven one, dull any sense of pain and loss so that one can function. We will give you a vial of the powders to take with you.'

Lien looked down at her fingers with their chipped nails and torn skin. 'I owe you much…'

'You owe us nothing more than continuing safely on your journey,' Iolanthe replied. 'Now we will leave you to wash and dress. If you can do that yourself, I think you are ready to join us down the stair.'

In a waft of floral air, they departed, closing the door so quietly it was as though they never were at all. The emptiness of the room echoed and re-echoed and Lien went once again to the window and looked down across the small garden to a wicker gate and the dark shape of the wood. Beyond that, the pearly mist obscured everything. Beneath the cliff, she presumed, was the sea cave. She wished she could see the horizon, its watery scope stretching for leagues one way and another and now housing the body of her beloved Heng. Surely her spirit was with the Ancestors. Lien touched her heart and looked to the grey and parchment skies, whispering, 'I am so sorry, Heng. Sorry for pushing you to make promises to accompany me. Sorry for testing you. Ineffably sorry for your death…'

Tears fell as she continued to gaze at the blurred scene beyond the windows. 'Please be free, Heng. And know that everything you did for me was appreciated and that there will be stories told of your bravery.'

Finally the tears eased and she wiped her face, returning to the table where a large white bowl steamed with perpetually warm water. There was a linen cloth and she washed, smoothing her face, easing around the stitches. There was a comb and she ran it through her hair, acutely aware that this had been Heng's delight. To brush and comb her mistress's hair until it shone like liquid ebony.

No more…

The clothes that lay on the bed were masculine but she didn't reject them, just pulled on breeches and boots that were alien after the free-fitting trousers of the Han. She slipped a snowy chemise over her head, tucking it in. One of her sleeves slipped up her arm and the red thread hung there, no worse for its terrible adventures in the sea. She wondered if Heng's still hung from her wrist as well, even in the Afterlife. Perhaps her fate was the storm and Yue Lao's thread around the maid's wrist had underlined what was to come.

But he had said we wouldn't drown and Heng did…

But no. He had said we wouldn't drown in the river, she thought. And they hadn't. It was the sea that had killed Heng. The sea and the Emperor and she would not forget.

She imagined Heng tumbling down through the sea water, down down and the red thread unknotting as Heng met her awful fate.

She sank onto the mattress, staring at nothing, just running her fingers back and forth over her own thread. Then sighing, she picked up a knitted woollen vest, buttoning it over the chemise and finally a knee length coat with pockets.

My coat! My pocket! The charms!

The memory of Heng pulling the jacket from under the seat, grabbing the charm-laden strips of paper and calling out the words.

She gasped at the memory. Gods! What was she to do now? No charms. Only her own devices and she had no confidence in those.

She thumped the bed, cursing Ming Xao and Kitsune and begging her Ancestors and Heng to see her safe. She thumped the bed again, walked the circumference of the room, realising that a pent-up flood fizzed through her – nervous energy which she could not dissipate. She flung open the door and clomped down the stair with ill grace, holding to the walls with the palms of her hands, not wanting to acknowledge any weakness at all, because if she did, she knew she would truly be adrift in every sense of the word.

'Ah there you are. Sit my dear, sit.' Iolanthe indicated a padded chair. 'You are feeling better?'

Lien grimaced. 'Not really…'

The siofra began to murmur.

'No, please. It is not your fault and indeed none of your potions and unguents can help.' She stood and began to walk back and forth. The room was what she expected – dried herbs and florals hanging from the rafters, large windows, worn floorboards, sparkling copper and brass. In the Han, some wood-wives had similar houses – the power of wild plants was well-known, even if the sliding doors were paper and the floors more highly polished, the roof-edges curving up like ducktails and good fortune chimes swinging in the trees. 'Quite simply…' she stopped. How much should she admit? She looked at the expectant faces. Grunting, she continued, 'I need to find an orchard, I think. I believe it's in Trevallyn?'

'Ah,' they all said. 'Not *an* orchard. *The* orchard.'

'You know? Well then, you see, I had charms to enable me to get to the place, but they sank…' she stopped, her voice choking, '…sank with Heng and our boat. They were left for me by Emperor Ming Xao with whom I am supposed to meet…'

'The man with the map,' said Flavia.

'As you say,' Lien replied. Gods but she could feel hate growing.

For a little while there was silence, broken only by a ticking clock in another room, counting the hours of life away for she and the Emperor.

Amaranthe stood and walked to one of the windows and looked out. 'The mist hangs about. It winds everywhere. But I don't think it's evil … just odd.' She watched a moment longer and then swung round, her face lit with excitement. 'Iolanthe! Flavia! The mist! It plays to our advantage! I believe it's here to protect Lady Lien. What do you think?'

Iolanthe slapped the table. 'Of course! How could we not realise! You are right indeed, sister. It came after the storm and shows no sign of abating. I think, my dear,' the lavender-clothed siofra said, 'that you have Others looking out for you, because as we have already said, something evil comes this way, but it seems the mist buffers us…'

'But how can a mist help me if there is evil there, as you say?'

'The miasma clothes the coast and countryside. It shows

no sign of relenting. Perhaps we can secret you into its midst all the way to Darlington where you can take ship for Trevallyn and the Orchard.'

'You mean I must take to the seas again?' Her voice peaked, and her palms began to sweat. The sea terrified her. The charms would have enabled her to avoid it again and Gods and Ancestors help her, they were now gone!

'I am afraid you must. Pymm is an archipelago you see. Made up of many little islands. But the journey from Darlington will take a day, sweet Lien. You will be safe.'

'You are so sure. *I* am not. I have seen the sea at its deathly worst. Waves as big as monsters, rearing up, swallowing you whole, the heartstopping coldness, the way you choke, sink, rise, choke again. Every breath may be your last...'

'Calm yourself, Lien,' said Iolanthe. 'Nothing is insurmountable. We have our ways, rest assured. But the mist waits, of that I am sure. So if you think you are strong enough then perhaps it is best you leave today. We will come with you as you know little to nothing of the evil that some Others might fling upon you.' She clapped her hands. 'Amaranthe, prepare the ponies. Flavia, a saddlebag for Lien, and pack a vial of our medic.'

Suddenly, the stillness that had pervaded the cottage became frenetic and as Amaranthe pulled open the door, the mist creeping in as Lien followed her. The siofra turned, looking up from her diminutive height. 'Lien, it is perhaps better if you wait indoors...'

'I can just sit here,' Lien indicated an elm tree at the door, heavy with dewy ribbons, and beneath which was a bench seat where the occasional drip fell. 'I need air, a private moment to grieve for my Heng...' She was surprised to find that a tear hung heavy on her lower lid and she blinked, knowing it would roll down her cheek, because she hurt. Deeply.

'Oh my poor lady. Then of course. Sit you there, it is not

so damp and wrap this around.' From her shoulders, she pulled a marled crimson wool shawl, reaching to lace the feather-light wrap around Lien's neck. 'I will be in the stable and will collect you after I have saddled our ponies.' She went to walk on. 'A word of warning though, Lien. Do not stray. We do not take what is behind that mist lightly.'

As Amaranthe hurried into the stone stable, Lien subsided, wondering why these eldritch women couldn't utter a charm and have her in the orchard in Trevallyn in no time.

She stared into the mist. Which way was the cliff and the path to the cave?

Perhaps the cave provided the answer – maybe there was some sort of conduit there. But with the world's sounds deadened, and no way to see through mist that had thickened like fog, she had no way of knowing. To her left, passing along the front of the cottage and then disappearing into the opalescent nethers, was a ground shell path. She thought beyond that would be the wicker gate which no doubt led to the cliff and the shore.

So…

Maybe I could follow the path, she thought.

From inside the cottage, she could hear Iolanthe and Flavia packing for a journey to Lien's imminent safety. Inside the stable, there was the muffled sound of hooves shifting, a nicker, and Amaranthe saying, 'Steady up, petal. There…'

Lien stood, lifting the shawl to cover her head and with caution, taking a step forward and then another, worried that the crunch of shells beneath her feet would betray her. A moment and she was wrapped in the dense seafog that muffled and concealed, almost carrying her forward until she reached the wicker gate.

Impressed with the eldritch nature of mist, relying on its security, she opened the gate, drawing in a breath as it stuck on the damp shellgrit. She sidled through and pulled it softly shut behind her, then began to walk as the mist parted with each step, allowing her to see the pathway, stunned as she turned back for a moment and saw it plaiting behind her, a tenuous veil of safety.

This is meant to be. I am doing the right thing…

Through a damp wood, walking up the dip and then further along the path.

The cliff dropped away in front of her, the path still there but cascading downward, around a large rock and then disappearing into a fissure just wide enough for her to squeeze through.

Her stomach writhed with nerves as she thought of what she had done, leaving the siofra, leaving security. She took a step forward.

The mist stayed at the entrance instead of proceeding with her and she paused. Why did it not waft in skeins through the fissure to surround her again in its delicate safety? She frowned. But then why would it? She was in an enchanted space after all, a location that few knew of. The cave filled with the mild suck of a swell, of the shift of grit as the waves, such as they were, stroked and cossetted.

Torches flared and flamed in comforting fashion from iron brackets fixed to the walls and the place glowed as golden as Flavia's silk-embroidered muslin gown.

Who lit the torches?

She glanced above and noticed that as she descended, so each torch snuffed behind her, leaving an indelible blackness and her heart jumped accordingly. She could see nothing but the torchlit progress below her and she could hear nothing but the gritty wavelets whispering, '*Come, come. Come to us…*'

She shook her head, pushing the fancies away, concentrating on not falling until she stood on the wide penultimate step.

Now what?

She tried to remember the charm, but it was a mess

of calligraphy in her mind, despite that Ming had written familiar Han characters. She stared at the water, amber and vermilion from the light of the torches arching over the sea. The cave soared into blackness now that most of the lights had dimmed. But there were sparkles, little glimmers of light illuminating flying buttresses. Little insects – gold fireflies. She had seen them in the garden of the First House…

She remembered the first line of a charm: *Gold does glimmer…,* but no, it referred to the cave, not where she wished to go and she sighed.

What were the words? She must remember. The charm was short and she knew it was there, right on the edge of her recall.

The water ruffled and from the sea entrance a breeze whiffled toward her, just a waft, but it spoke of chill and in the chill the ever-present danger of drowning.

'Ancestors,' she cried. 'Help me remember. Please! I have always revered you and paid my respects and now I beg you to help me, this poor daughter of your family.'

The water lapped and on the edge of the sound a moaning dirge whispered, and she chilled even further. This was not her Ancestors coming to her call.

The moan came closer and she cringed as the waves broke and ruffled and the breeze strengthened, the shadows on the walls jumping as they fought to stay alight.

Shadows!

Shadowy tree and leaf! That's it, surely!

She sweated in the cold, repeating the words over and over but the rest of the wordage refused to come and she felt tears gathering, her fists clenched.

She closed her eyes and tried again.

Shadowy tree and leaf

Dance…

But as she called out, a boat of the strangest kind drifted through the entrance to the cave on a shaft of pearly light.

Empty.

A craft made of bleached wood with graceful lines and an upturned prow carved into the head of a bird, a crane perhaps. Maybe a swan. Bird wings laced along the wales, to where a slightly less grand sternpost became an avian tail. The planks were scored, carved like feathers, and below the bird's head was script of some sort. Unknown to Lien but she was sure it was a charm. A whisper hung round the vessel like the mist – soft, kind, promising safety.

Step in, the whisper said. *Come aboard and we will see you safe...*

The boat glided to the shore, lightly beaching itself on the shingle as if it were as weightless as a feather. Everything in Lien pulled her away from the craft but the whisper continued.

We will take you close by the orchard.

Lien shivered, wondering who *we* was?

The bird carving reminded her of the imperial lake and of the Ice Dragon and she swallowed.

We can help...

The boat sat innocently immobile as the small wash broke and retreated, broke and retreated and Lien warred with her cautious self. Almost too perfect, too innocent...

But she so desperately wanted to find the man she hated and who owed her a life for her friend. The words of the charm would not come to her mind and the siofra had said it would be a few days at least to get to the orchard by pony and boat.

We can take you to the river that flows to the orchard, the whisper seduced.

Her scruples began to dissolve, and she took a step down, across the shingle and then her hand rested on the wale. She swung her leg up and over as if she were leaping aboard a horse and the vessel seemed to shuffle as she settled on the only seat.

But familiar voices shouted at the top of the steps and torches sprang into life, flames lighting the vaulted cave ceiling and the steps, fireflies dipping and flitting in agitation.

'No, Lien!'

'Jump!'

'A trap!'

Iolanthe, Flavia and Amaranthe sped down the stair as the bird boat drifted backward.

'Lien! It may be a malevolent spirit! Please, you must jump!' Iolanthe lifted an arm but whatever mesmer she tried to cast was blown on the chill breeze to the ceiling and a violent hiss filled the cavern, the torches dipping, many spluttering.

The siofra stared aghast at the boat. 'Lien, jump out!' cried Flavia. 'Oh my dear!'

Whatever confidence had propelled Lien into the boat vanished in a moment as she saw the desperation on the faces of the little siofra. She tried to stand but found herself irredeemably stuck to the seat – hands, bottom, feet, melded to the wood as if she and the wood were one.

The boat began to turn in the wider bowl of the cavern and with prow facing the entrance, its speed began to increase, and all Lien could do was weep and call to the three women, 'I'm sorry...'

CHAPTER ELEVEN
Ming Xao

The cliff path climbed upward from a rocky fissure to a grassy edge where a path of shell-grit laced inland between stunted pine trees angle-bent by fierce winds. The path slipped down into a small wood where beech and elm grew, protected from the salty winds by the dip. The sky was mottled grey and ivory – the last vestiges of a sea mist lying in hollow and shade.

Ahead, and watched over by a stately elm beneath which was a seat, a humble cottage sank into a garden filled with colour and scent. Gallivant opened the small wicker gate and the two men and the dog crunched past a stable and along the shell grit to the door of the dwelling.

'Shall I knock?' Gallivant asked. 'Or just call out?'

Ming reached over the hob's shoulder and rapped the door hard.

'Right,' muttered Gallivant. 'There you go then.'

Barely before he finished speaking, the door flew open and a vision in scarlet stared up at them. 'You are come too late!'

'Too late!' chimed a small woman in gold muslin.

'Far too late!' a woman in a violet gown pushed in front of the other two, petite like her companions but angry. 'Come in. We need to talk and swiftly with it!'

Ming needed no second bidding. Were the women talking of Lien? He had the feeling they were. He followed the apparent leader of the three and she indicated the table irritably. 'Sit, sit! You too, dog.'

Ming folded his height onto a chair, hands clasped tightly before him, Gallivant sliding into the seat next to him and Max collapsing to the floor and eyeing the women balefully. In truth, the dog could have knocked them flying in one leap, but as it was, the three women sat opposite like an inquisition.

'You are the mapmaker, are you not?' the violet-dressed one stated.

Ming sat back. 'Perhaps you should tell me who *you* are…'

The woman's eyes slitted and then she smiled tightly. 'Of course. You must be careful. I understand. I am Iolanthe and these are my siofra sisters, Amaranthe and Flavia. We know about you and we know you have come because of the Lady Lien. Sadly, you have come too late. The Lady Lien was here, we nursed her back to health and then she did a very stupid thing…'

'She was here?' Gallivant's voice rose an octave. 'And she is *gone*?'

'Indeed,' said the golden one called Flavia. 'Here and then gone…'

'Where?' Ming retorted, his temper flaring.

'We know not, sir. She climbed into a boat, unaware it was eldritch and dangerous, and was spirited away.'

'By the Gods!' Ming sensed things moving far from his command. Never in his life had he been so out of control – everything he had done, accomplished, – all planned and executed meticulously.

Until he had drawn the map…

'What sort of boat?' Gallivant asked. If he sensed his companion's enervation, he didn't show it, remaining calm, respectful of the siofra.

'Oh, Sir Gallivant!' said Flavia, her face filled with woe

as she dabbed at the corner of her eyes with a golden wool shawl. 'It was a bird boat, it was hard to see perfectly in the flickering shadows, but a crane's or swan's head was carved into the prow. There was no one aboard and the boat turned about and floated swiftly from the cave. Against an incoming tide! The Lady Lien tried to get away when we called to her, but she was as stuck to the seat as if she rode the Cabyll Ushtey.'

'I know of the Cabyll Ushtey,' murmured Ming. Gods! She could be carted into the deep sea, drowned and then torn apart to be eaten! By the stars, Yue Lao had said nothing of such cruel destiny.

'I don't think so,' said Gallivant. He stood and began to walk around the room, talking fast and Max watched him, his head sunk onto heavy paws. 'No, sink me! I think it's a swan boat. I think the Swan Maids have taken her away. Why I don't know, but if we can find just one swan and speak… *with* utter respect…' he turned gleaming eyes upon Ming, 'then we can find out more.'

'But Sir Gallivant,' said Amaranthe, her cheeks flushing almost the colour of her gown. 'There are no swans anywhere in Pymm. Not black ones nor white. But then I am sure you know this…'

Gallivant stopped his peregrinations. 'Well no, dammit. I didn't.'

'And hobs,' muttered Ming, 'are supposed to know everything.

'Respect is something you need to relearn, Ming. Which I alluded to earlier if you think on it. Along with hubris as I'm sure you've been told. Just remember if you please, that if you hadn't drawn that map, none of this would have happened.'

Ming made no excuses. He was mortified at what he had become – arrogant, angry, secretive – all of that, and he had never been known for that in his life. Except for that one moment of transgression. In his deep soul, he admitted he hated it, the recognition of a lesser person, one that should not and must not ever lead if he made such elemental mistakes.

'I am sorry,' he said to Gallivant and then, 'Ladies, the swan maids live only in Trevallyn, do they not? We shall search there but I would question how a swan boat came to be here. I... don't understand.' He clenched his fists, hating the fey more by the heartbeat, but then took a breath to calm himself. 'May I ask you to please tell me briefly how you came across Lien? She was to be my bride, you see...'

'Your bride! Is that so?' Iolanthe of the lavender muslin said. Of course she knew, she was Other, he thought, but why did the three smile so sadly?

'Is it that you love her and are fearing for her safety?' asked Flavia. 'Oh my poor dear man...'

'I have not known her long enough to love her. It was an arranged betrothal after I met her in a park in the imperial city. But I admired her spirit.'

'And her beauty surely. Her beauty is quite something,' offered Iolanthe.

Ming looked down at his tight fists. 'Yes. It is. But it was her spirit that drew me. Is she hurt at all?'

Iolanthe studied him and he squirmed like an ant under a boot. She was looking deep into his soul, he felt it, not just taking him at face value.

'Lord Ming,' she said. 'We know you are being hunted for a map that you drew. To be honest, the very birds of Eirie know and that is how we heard. But in any case, we knew there was an eldritch storm coming to Pymm's coast and that someone would be in danger. The two always go together and we have not had one of those in many years. As the storm died away, we searched our shore, of which the cliff and the cave are part.' She stopped as one of her sisters, the blushing Amaranthe, pushed a flagon of elderberry wine toward her, together with a heavy cut glass goblet. Iolanthe poured the wine and said, 'Thank you, sister. Perhaps a glass for everyone I think, and some of the warm bread. And bring some butter and that sharp cow's cheese with the thyme and rosemary through it.'

Amaranthe pushed back her chair and slipped off to the kitchen, followed by Flavia, but in moments, they had returned with trays of crusty bread smelling of a grain harvest, pats of golden butter and a slab of cheese that had green herbs laced through its fragrant texture. Horn-handled knives cluttered one tray and plates and glasses another.

'Please, help yourselves while I talk,' Iolanthe took a sip of her wine, watching as they began to eat, before continuing.

'We found her washed up on the shore of the cave. By this time, we knew her name was Lien and that she was connected to you and to the map. We were aware she was being hunted as a hostage and we wanted to help her. She was badly gashed on the forehead and bruised all over from the sea wreckage and rocks. To be frank, she is lucky to be alive. So we mended her cuts and bruises and fed her with our medics until she gained strength. Today was the first day she had been up and dressed.'

Iolanthe took another sip and so did Ming, surprised at the strength of the wine, feeling his body relax enough to listen intently to what the woman had to say. She was so pleasing of face, perhaps a matron, although he had the feeling that she and her sisters never aged, or if they did, in the style of the enchanted of Eirie, it was so slow as to be almost unnoticeable, which, he presumed, made the three women very old indeed. Stars and moons, he thought. What must they have seen!

'Indeed, Lord Ming. Much, I can tell you.' Iolanthe offered and he felt colour fill his face.

'She had night dreams where the sweat ran from her and she would cry out, "Heng! Heng!" We learned that she was accompanied by a woman friend called Heng who could not swim and was drowned at sea.'

Ming frowned. 'I do not know of Heng…'

'No. You may not. But she has been a companion of Lien's for many years, we believe.'

Ming thought back to the Park of Singing Birds, to the woman who walked behind Lien on that fateful day and who had chivvied her to move on. She was tall, with an ivory face, and pleasant enough features. 'I think she might have been Lien's companion-servant. A good and loyal woman I suspect, and I am sad at her apparent fate. Could she have survived, think you? Been washed onto a shore close by?'

'No. We searched and scried. There was nothing.'

Through all of this, Gallivant had remained quiet, eating and drinking. Now he wiped his mouth with a snowy linen kerchief and sat back. 'So she has lost her only friend and is now hostage to swan maids who are as like to lead a mortal astray as to help them. I am at a loss to understand why they captured her. Swan maids are immensely singular, rarely mixing with the enchanted of Eirie. They are a law unto themselves, and I cannot see what they have to gain.'

'Indeed, Sir Gallivant,' said Iolanthe. 'But let us go back a step. You have no doubt noticed a strange mist permeating everything around about and that the moon has disappeared. Gone. Every night is as dark as Hades. It is magick and we think the mist is buffering us from Evil. But I suspect that it may dissolve soon, especially now Lady Lien is gone. Thus evil will flow over us to seek her out. If I may say, as soon as we have told our story, you must leave, do what you must. Otherwise, the Others will have you and that,' she said, with thinly stretched lips, 'will be that!'

'Then is there nothing more to know?' Ming asked.

'No. Suffice to say we were packing to take her to Darlington, using the mist for protection. We had thought we could take ship for a short voyage to Trevallyn and the

Orchard which was her destination. Lien was sitting at the door on the bench. She'd been warned not to move for fear of what might be waiting beyond the mist but for some reason, some ill-thought idea, she *did* leave. Went to the sea cave and... then gone.' Iolanthe sat back, shadows beneath her eyes and her features tired and drawn.

'Ladies,' Ming said carefully. 'I am more than grateful for your care of my betrothed and I am sorry that you have been dragged into a problem that I accept is of my making. Please understand that I will do my best, give my life if I must, to right my wrong. I swear.'

Iolanthe smiled, a small glimmer of kindness. 'My lord Ming, everyone makes mistakes. You are not the first and you won't be the last. Now, it is time you departed. Amaranthe will pack some food and two costrels and you must get on your way.'

The men stood, accepted the provisions, and with Max, walked to the door with the three women behind.

At the door, Ming turned. 'Ladies, have you... did you... is there any way in your scrying that you might have found news of the Han, of any disaster...'

Iolanthe laid her hand on his arm, a featherlight touch. 'I wish we could tell you, but our scrying extends only to those within Pymm. As I said, news of your map came through other ways. I'm sure that if Others were angry enough to have laid waste to your province, we would have heard of that from bird or beast, but we have not. You must believe that your people are safe thus far.'

Ming was angry with himself for asking, for wearing weakness on his sleeve but he needed to know his people were not yet paying the terrible price for his misbegotten deed.

The men made their thanks, waving farewell to the diminutive siofra who stood at the door watching them. Strange, kind women, Ming thought. Like hens watching over hatchlings.

Thank you, Gods and Ancestors for protecting Lien. I beg that, if it please you, may it continue?

With Gallivant and Max by his side, he pushed on through the mist toward the sea cave. As their footsteps crunched on the shell grit path, Ming said, 'You were very quiet.'

'I was, wasn't I? I listened to what Iolanthe had to say and for the rest, I am constantly racking my brains to work out what swan maids would have to gain by spiriting Lien into their midst. Like I said, a law unto themselves. A puzzle…'

Ming forbore to comment. The enigmatic swan maids worried him, it was true. But they weren't as evil as some he could think of and thus Lien might have a fighting chance.

They sidled through the fissure into the sea cave, unsurprised to see the torches flaring, and as they descended the stair, Ming began to roll the charm through his mind, seeing the calligraphy on the strip of parchment that he had laid in the cabinet drawer for Lien.

If nothing else, he was proud of her assiduity, that she had found his clues and made it this far. But he was devastated at the loss of Heng. Of Heng's life. And all because of him. The words of the charm that would carry them away were pushed aside as he offered a prayer to Cheng Mo, the Mother of All.

Care for the soul of Lien's faithful friend, O Mother. Send her lightly on her path into the heavens of her Ancestors…

He realised they had walked down the stair and were almost at the fateful Pymm Gate.

Gallivant turned round. 'Well?'

Ming's hand felt for the red thread round his wrist and rubbed it back and forth as he called,

'*Shadowy tree and leaf*
Dance in a sweet blossom breeze
Home and safe at last…'

The walls of the cave brightened, vacillated, gold then soft green as if spring grew from the very creases in the stone. The light strengthened, a shaft of sun there, another here and the noise of the sea changed to the chuckling of a stream, a green canopy shielding them from peering eyes. A blue sky danced between the leaves, as innocent and clear as one could hope. The softest breeze, what people of Eirie called a welkin wind and which was most often filled with heady magick, laced round trunk and twig and Ming breathed in the scent of clover and grasses.

'Sink me,' sighed Gallivant as he held Max's collar. 'At last, we're almost home. Good job, sir, even if you aren't Other. Good job.' He looked around. 'But just in case you think to get above yourself, we have a long walk to the orchard and the house. If you remember, the orchard is leagues wide and long, so I expect you to tell me about the charms and how you managed to do what you have done. How you discovered the gates. For me, it is not enough that you drew a map. There is more to it than that.'

Ming ran fingers through his hair, dislodging the ribbon so that his shortened locks fell free. The welkin wind teased them and he shivered. 'Later, hob. I'm not going to the house yet. I must find Lien, make sure she is safe.'

'But… but the map.'

'Indeed. I *could* take the map to the house now and it could be destroyed. But Lien is still at the mercy of something dark. If I have the map in my pocket, I have something to bargain with.'

Gallivant sucked in a breath, rubbing the back of his neck, lips tightening. 'Ming, Seraphina waits…'

'No, Gallivant! I owe it to Lien to bring her here, to bring her to safety.'

If I do nothing else, he thought, to right my wrong, I will protect Lien from danger.

Gallivant squeezed his eyes shut, and growled, a young

pup prancing and pretending a fierceness he just didn't have. 'Aaarh! Then we shall have to go to the lake which is most often where the swan maids are, and that is *leagues* away from here! It would be so much safer if we had Seraphina with us and it would be faster on horseback but I *hate* riding!' He strode off. 'Damn you! Come *on*! There are horses close by.'

Ming paced after the dog and the narrow damask back, long wild grasses of henbane, coltsfoot, plantain and poppy grazing the top of his boots, and bees and butterflies bobbing drunkenly from flower to flower. The hob grumbled and muttered but Ming chose to ignore him.

They reached the farm – part of the late Jasper's estate and now Seraphina's. There was no one about and yet the horses were sleek, the barn swept, the hayracks filled with pale green and gold hay.

Of course…

'Pick your mount,' grumped the hob. 'I'm having this beast.' He tied a rope to a lumbering chestnut's halter and led it from its stall as big Max sat down and scratched at his neck. 'I swear, Ming. You are making things difficult to impossible. We might place ourselves in *awful* danger by not going to Seraphina immediately. The minute we move to the lake, we are open to foes of all kinds. My magick is not strong enough to protect us and I suspect you've used all that you had access to.' He carried a saddle to the horse, smoothing a blanket and flinging the gear on top, reaching under to grab the girth as Max sneezed violently. The gelding, conscious of bad moods and dogs and being cinched, reached round and nipped Gallivant in the side. 'Ouch! You *bastard* of a horse! *Damn* the beast and *damn* my life and *damn* you, Ming! I could be quite comfortable, listening to Adelina's stories or smoking a pipe with Phelim. And yet, here I am with *you*.'

Whilst Gallivant whinged, Ming had chosen a grey mare,

long of leg and with sleek lines. Her head was pure beauty, and she took Ming's breath away. She nuzzled him and he scratched her between the ears. She stood rock still as he saddled her, slipping a soft leather bridle over her ears, and she crunched the bit while he buckled the throatlatch.

'Then take Max and go to Adelina,' he said to Gallivant. 'I do not need you. I know where the lake is and can take responsibility for myself. To be honest, I would rather you did that. I need time to myself, Gallivant, and I say that humbly and with thanks for your kindness and company thus far. But the rest of this journey is mine to make, my error to mend. As you have said, you have little to no magick that can help me now and so I would be happier if you removed yourself from danger.' He mounted his mare, settled himself in the saddle and without waiting for a reply, trotted from the yard. Once through the five-barred gate, he touched the mare lightly with his heels and they began to canter, then gallop as he wound through the trees, leaving a skirl of emerald leaves in his wake.

He didn't look back. He suspected Gallivant would be standing watching him, swearing and trying to work his way out of a dilemma.

That was surely the hob's problem though. Not his.

He relished the freedom. How nice it might have been for an hour or two to forget what he had wrought and to ride in the slipstream of a welkin wind, letting the beauty of Trevallyn flash by, breathing its scent and being awed by its magnitude. Feeling the muscled grace beneath him as the mare snorted and extended her long legs, shaking her head, her ears pricked, head stretched. If Ming hadn't been aware of all that had gone before, and what might be approaching, he would have shouted with abandon and freedom. But apart from one egregious moment when he had drawn a map, he was a prescient man who took responsibility seriously and this was no time to shout with joy. It was time to put distance between he and the hob and to find Lien. And so the horse flew and Ming rode her easily – up slopes and down the other side, along left and right tracks, and hoping he was heading in the direction of the lake. Because in truth, he had no memory of the lake and how far from the orchard it was. He just had to trust to Fate.

The mare faltered slightly, and he wondered if she was tiring. He would hate to break her wind and so pulled gently on the reins, sitting down lower in the saddle. Almost as if the mare could read his mind, she shifted her pace down and began to canter, then trot. He spoke gently as he crested a rise to see the lake spread below in glistening glory.

'Whoa, my lady, whoa, see what is down there?'

Her ears twitched and her shoulders flicked as her muscles settled after the long gallop. She stamped and sidled with the excess energy, dark patches on her shoulder, and pulled the reins through Ming's hands, rubbing her nose against her knee. Another snort and she smelled the grass at her feet, shook herself, rattling Ming's bones, and then began to crop – the only sound the tearing of the grass and the jingle of the bit as she chewed.

Ming looked around. No bird sound.

And the welkin wind had gone.

Nothing…

And yet there was no sense of danger – the hairs did not stand on his neck and his skin did not prickle. The sky was fading, an apricot tint in the far distance but the air was clear. The saddle creaked as he dismounted to stare down at the lake. He let the mare graze and as he wiped her down with a twisted hank of long grasses, he wondered about his next step.

How did one call a swan maid? Were there any here? He squinted as he inspected all he could see of a huge lake that wound around tree and reed but there seemed to be no life, no waterfowl, nothing but a spread of water that shimmered like silver, wild grasses growing at its edge. He clicked the mare on, pulling gently on the reins and they walked together down the hill.

At the bottom, he wondered which way? Where was the sun?

There, in the languid sky, slightly to his left. So it was late afternoon and the sun headed west. He walked easterly – he had no idea why, but it seemed right. He and the mare brushed through the short grass with still no sign of bird life, nor frogs, crickets, butterflies or dragonflies.

As he rounded a spreading willow, a small grainy beach lay in a little curve, its edges clean and inviting. He looped the reins through the cheek-strap so the mare could graze at the edge of the shingle, running his stirrups up the leathers, loosening his girth slightly. Surely if there was anything eldritch, anything untoward, the mare would twitch, sidle, her eyes white with caution, her ears back, but this beautiful creature just snorted lightly, walked to the water's edge and drank, and then with drops falling from her mouth as she smacked her lips together, she walked back to the sweet grasses and continued grazing.

Ming watched her, amused at the way she ate her fill and then came to stand in the shade of the willow, her off-hind resting, her head drooping. He sat on the shingle near to her, his back against the trunk of the tree as he scrutinised the watery surrounds, wishing for a swan. Slowly, the softness of the day, and weight of expectations within his mind took their toll and he laid his head back against the grainy trunk. It wouldn't hurt to just close his eyes.

Just a moment…

'My lord, my lord...'

Gentle hands touched his shoulder and he stirred. The darkness of night had crept upon him and the beach was bathed in an ivory moonglow. The voice that spoke was mellow, a woman's tones and he squinted, rubbing the tiredness away. A lady stood before him, tall, willowy, her hair a waving mass of dark and light, black and grey. Her face was reminiscent of the Han, but there was something else there, some indefinable thing. Agelessness? Immortality? He pushed himself off the ground to stand but she said,

'No, stay where you are. I will sit and we will talk.'

Her gown was of silk organdie, a cloth he had tried to import into the Han but with little success. The Venichese weavers were protective of this beautiful fabric that waved in the breeze as if it had a life of its own. The gown's many folds intimated a midnight sky and here and there was a spark like a diamond or a star. Through her hair, there were sparkles of light as if she had twined an infinite galaxy. Something began to knock at his memory, and he was about to speak when he noticed a long, very fine silver chain around her neck, at the end of which hung a silver ball with little chips of diamonds scattered here and there. It reminded him of the moon...

'Moonlady,' he whispered.

She smiled. 'But you know me in the Han as Heng-O I think, the Moon Goddess. In the Raj, I am perhaps Rohini? In Trevallyn, Pymm, and Veniche, yes. I am the Moonlady.' She sat beside him, the folds of organdie crunching with delicacy as she pulled them closer in around her legs. 'You are in trouble, my friend.'

Ming frowned. The comment was nothing if not the truth and he could hardly deny it. She was an Other and knew everything. 'Yes...'

'A foolhardy act, I think.'

Again, unambiguous.

'Yes.'

'But you strive to do the right thing. You take the map to Seraphina.'

'I do. But first I must find Lady Lien. If necessary, I will bargain for her life.'

'Do you think you can bargain, Ming Xao? You, the man who is the cause of this misbegotten hunt? Don't you think they will just kill your betrothed as a lesson? Perhaps it is them with the upper hand, not you.'

He looked at this woman – something about her seemed familiar. 'Then I must find Lien and spirit her away to Seraphina where she might be safe.'

'It is a courageous thought.'

'I have nothing to lose,' Ming replied, 'and Lien's life to gain. I *have* to right the wrong I caused.'

'Yes.' Her reply was straightforward. 'Lien is a wonderful woman, Ming. She is owed a life. You made a good choice.'

'You speak as if you know her.'

'I do know her. I am a goddess, I know everyone.'

But no. There was more to this. For a moment, he scrutinised the oval face with the pale complexion and perfect skin. Her eyes were almond-shaped and she had elegant eyebrows but she wasn't perfect – not like Others he had seen. Not like Chi Nü.

For a moment, he had a memory of the Park of Singing Birds and Lien and then…

'You are Heng!' His mouth dropped open. 'Lien's servant! I remember you in the park…'

She laughed – a small arpeggio of notes. She took his hand and found the red thread on his wrist. 'Ah, mine has gone. Yue Lao gave Lady Lien and I one each.' There was the faintest note of regret in her voice. 'Yes. I am Heng. I *was* Heng. Now, I am Heng-O.'

'How?' He was dreaming surely. He looked around. It was night, the stars were in the heavens and the Moonlady sat beside him, lighting the willow, the dozing mare, the shoreline and the lake waters as if it were day.

She sighed. 'I have always felt as if I didn't belong anywhere. When I was sent from the serving halls to assist the Lady Lien, it seemed to me that this was a vocation that was meant. Service to someone who was exciting, intelligent, and who wanted to see more, do more. It is what *I* wanted, to see beyond the gates and the Wall. To see the world. The irony is that now I can – every evening.' She laughed again, a single sound. 'I realise now that Fate awaited me, and nothing could change it. Serving Lady Lien simply pushed me neatly onward.'

Ming was interested, more than interested, but idle chatter was surely holding him from his purpose.

'When we talk, Ming, moments and hours turn slowly. All is well.'

'You read my thoughts.'

'Yes.'

'Then you know I will ask how you *became* Heng-O. I don't understand. Surely the Moonlady is immortal…'

'Yes, but *you* surely know Others do eventually meet their banes. The Moonlady with whom you were familiar began to fade. Her light grew dimmer. It happens to us all – mortal and Other. As the Moonlady faded, Lien and I were on the high seas. We encountered a terrible sea storm off Pymm and were tossed into the ocean.' She stared across the lake as she told her story. 'I could not swim and began to sink. It would seem this was part of my Fate. I had no idea where dear Lien was and hoped to the stars she would survive, but for me, with my red thread on my wrist, I knew my days were done as I sank beneath the sea.'

Ming sat still – not entirely reassured that time *was* passing slowly.

'It is, I assure you.' She tapped his arm. 'Worry not.'

'But if you drowned…'

'Exactly. *If* I drowned…' Her lips tightened momentarily. 'I remember nothing beyond pitch black and deathly cold. Nothing at all until I felt myself soaring along a flickering pathway. *This is Heaven,* I thought. And it was. My soul was flying. I found myself in a shadow-light place. Little starlight, no moon. On a bed lay a woman dressed in the midnight navy and glister that you know well. I looked on her from above and thought she was asleep and after that, I knew nothing again except that it became intensely black, and I felt as lifeless as a spent dandelion. Of a sudden though, I took a breath and another and so the place, wherever I was, glowed a little lighter. I woke on that bed, dressed in the moon robes. The Moonlady that *I* knew was gone. I lay in her place and two red threads, mine and hers, lay on the floor entwined.'

'But why you? Heng-O, I don't mean to be disrespectful, but you are not Other…'

'That is what I thought. But it seems I *am*. I didn't know. No one guided me. I was just "left" as sometimes happens with careless Other parents. It's not unknown – an Other child is left in the mortal world if he or she is not wanted, and it seems I wasn't. Yue Lao suspected my Otherness but I had no idea, not at all. There were signs I suppose, like walking on the nightingale floor and making no sound, anticipating Lien's every thought and wish – but I was too ignorant to realise in those days. In any case, that,' she turned to face him, 'is the end of my story. It is as though something sown deep within is finally flowering and I can help those who need it, shine light in the darkest places.'

Ming could barely believe it. And yet, he had read religious texts from the monks at Jokhang Monastery that souls might migrate to new bodies in time. That it was pre-ordained. Fate again. But pre-ordained by whom? Others? Suddenly he was glad the monastics prayed and chanted in their eagle's nest. Theirs was a spiritual existence – praying for the world of the Han, for its peace and contentment. Their compassion surely balanced out the baselessness of the world because for sure, Others had no interest in peace, let alone contentment.

'Some do, some don't,' chided Heng-O and Ming's face flushed. 'But in respect of my story, this was ordained by the Great Mother, Cheng Mo, to whom those in Jhokang pray. For myself, Ming Xao, I am at peace and have absorbed the wisdom of ages by such reincarnation. Mostly it is a blessing but above all, Fate is what it is.' She stood up with a whisper of the beautiful organdie, the lights sparkling from deep in the weave, 'You must ready yourself. You came to the lake to seek swan maids, did you not? Then the time approaches. If I can give you any advice it is to treat whomever comes with the deepest respect. Swan maids can turn on the twist of a feather in the air, and ultimately, if they help you, they *will* demand payment at some point in your life. You must give it, or you will pay an awful price.'

'They would kill me?'

'They *could* contrive it, yes or the death of someone close to you. They are loyal to none but themselves.' She sat straighter. 'I must go, my lord. The night passes. Take care and heed me.' She took his hand and he felt the easy weight of something smooth. He did not see her leave as he looked down and found a miniature moon in his palm, glowing softly in the lunar light from the sky.

A pearl!

He ran a finger over its perfection and then looked to the heavens where the moon guided creatures of the night. He pushed the gem deep into his pocket alongside the map, and walked to the lakeside, unsure of anything.

The lake glistened pewter and steel, reflecting the glimmer of stars and the beautiful ivory sphere of the moon. He thought of Heng-O and her transformation from serving woman to the Moonlady. She made such a thing, such a final and dramatic moment, seem so easy.

But then death is never easy, what a stupid thought. She must have felt so afraid as she drowned, with no idea that Fate had other things in store. He glanced at the red thread round his own wrist and wished of a sudden, that Yue Lao had not tied it on. It spelled a grim finality.

Again, he asked himself why he had spent hour upon hour with just the white crane for company, drawing the map, mixing the animal fats with dark minerals and soot and setting them into their ceramic blocks for ink. Binding his own brushes with the finest animal hair. He liked black rabbit hair best and the handles were most often plain bamboo. He had been given many brushes – ivory, jade, even chaste silver – but he preferred humble tools. Everything that smacked of the common man and nothing of the noble. Everything of the hardworking artisan and not an aristocrat at play.

He remembered, as he now stood by the nightwaters of the swans' lake, that his great spirit friend, Chi Nü, had visited him in his island pavilion. He had made tea with the ceremony he had been taught as a student and the smell of the aromatic leaves steeping soon filled the library. Presently they sat, two friends who had been through much, one Other, one mortal, and she relayed a story she had heard amongst the Others recently.

'Apparently there was a peasant couple,' she said. 'Good honest people from the northern Han but very poor. They were young and their life might improve and they could have children if only they had some money to buy a small patch of land to farm. The husband, a good-looking man, broad of shoulder and with slick hair the wife brushed daily and plaited, said if the wife was brave enough, he would leave her for a little, journey to the imperial city and earn enough money to buy the small holding they so craved.'

Chi Nü took a sip of her tea and then placed her cup on the bamboo tray that lay before her. 'He said to his wife that he would return in three years and three years did indeed pass, and then some more and the wife knew her husband would have returned if he had not fallen foul of something evil. She set out to look for him and after walking many leagues, chanced upon an old hag by a river. She knew the river was an enchanted place, one that folk avoided because of those who haunted it. But the wife was desperate and so she begged the hag to tell her if she had seen the husband.

The hag burst out laughing, shape-changing into the most beautiful woman the wife had ever seen – all ivory and silk and with almond eyes. The Other, for of course it was, said she had met the husband and seduced him, the stupid man had lusted for her until she became bored with his love and when he pestered her, what could she do but change him into stone? The Other asked the woman who was weeping, did she want to see him, and the poor woman said yes. And sure enough, a little further along the river which ran dark and deep, there was a cave and at its entrance, was a tall, well-turned stone and touching it, the wife knew it was indeed her husband.

She turned on the Other, scratching her face, dragging her nails across the woman's throat but to no avail, because the Other just turned the wife to stone. It is a horrible story Ming.'

Ming placed his cup down and agreed that yes, terrible that a pair of innocents should be treated so carelessly by Others.

'And,' he growled. '*My* people. Hard working, honest folk who just wanted to live a simple life, farming and raising children.'

Gods he was angry! There were so many of these stories, right across the world of Eirie, horror stories where Others played and killed wantonly on a whim.

Chi Nü had gone, and he had lain in his bedroll that night in the pavilion, swearing that somehow things must change – that mortals should be able to even the score, correct the imbalance. Slowly, as he thought of all the dread entrances to the world of Others that he had seen on his travels, so many and varied – a seventh wave here, an Ymp tree orchard there, a cave, a lake – so many – and he could name them by the simple expedient of having been vigilant and possessing a profound memory.

The next day, he had gathered brush, inkstone, water and parchment and had begun to make a map that he hoped would change everything.

It had.

For the worst…

CHAPTER TWELVE

Lien

'Sorry!' she cried, watching the three siofra waving their arms, calling helplessly. They had been so kind, so caring.

So sorry and so stupid, she thought as tears rolled down her cheeks. Who had done this to her? Why? Her heart pounded. That she was now in the power of Others was undeniable, that they had trapped her, were spiriting her away, that her life was forfeit from this moment – all facts.

The quaint craft with its upturned prow floated swiftly from the cave and into a grim, foggy light. For all she knew, there may even have been no sea beneath the vessel as there was no sound, no slapping of wave against the strakes, no veil of spray as the bow must have broken through the swell. All she could hear was the whistling of wind in the stays as the craft swept on through the fog, an eery high pitched sound – any louder and she would think it was death spirits singing her to a terrible end.

She wept for the loss of Heng, for her own precarious position, for the home she missed, for the fact her grandmother had told her the Emperor was a good man.

Was he?

He had created something disastrous for which her life, his life and the existence of the Han could be held at ransom. As she tugged angrily at the seat to which her hands were stuck, she hated him with a passion.

If she had been left to sit in the Small Garden of the First

House of Silk, embroidering carp or lotus, blossom or leaf, perhaps she would have settled to contentment and Heng would still be alive.

But what of the Han?

Indeed. What *of* the Han? Whilst she stitched her beautiful work, around her the province would succumb to some terrible punishment with disease and death and a never-ending grey sky from the funeral pyres that would be lit all around the Great Wall.

And in truth, as galling as it was, she knew she would not have been happy in the Small Garden, stitching her life away. Hadn't she told Heng that she craved adventure, that she wanted to see beyond the Wall?

The wind dried her tears upon her cheeks, and she began to shiver with cold, wishing this journey would end. Better to know what would happen than to imagine, to anticipate.

Tiredness enveloped her, as thick and cloying as the enchanted fog, and she fought against it, blinking hard, shaking her head. But with each breath of the damp air, her muscles loosened and there was a roaring in her ears – her heartbeat as the blood coursed round her body. The energy to fight back faded, becoming nothing but a vague idea and then something soft encircled her shoulders and with the warmth, she slept.

She had no idea how much time had passed when she woke. It could have been a day, a month, or years. Beyond her, a stretch of calm water was lit silver by a sliver of moon, a subtle light. The water rippled in a breeze that raised the hairs on her arms, a magick breath for sure. She shivered underneath the cloak and then realised that someone, *some thing*, had laid it round her shoulders as she slept the sleep of the enchanted. She knew everything that was happening to her was no accident and that she was being controlled as if she were a puppet. Her neck ached from sleeping upright and she longed to rub it but still her hands remained stuck.

'By the stars!' she yelled. 'How long do I have to sit here? Do what you must! I don't care anymore.'

Didn't she? To have her life snuffed out? It was what happened to Heng after all. Why did Yue Lao encourage them both on this dangerous path if he knew they would both die?

There was no answer to her call, but her hands loosened and she sucked in a breath, looking round, rubbing the back of her neck. Her fingers ached and she huffed on them, clapping them together, wriggling the taut bones. Feeling her knotted body slacken as the morning light grew stronger. She pushed herself to stand, but found she was still glued to the seat, her feet to the floor.

'*Still* a prisoner,' she shouted, grabbing at the cloak which had begun to slide off one shoulder. It was cool to the touch, silky soft, and a glossy ebony. Where the moonlight struck, it almost gleamed turquoise.

She ran her fingers over it.

Feathers!

Inside the cloak, the finest down cossetted her body, small fur-like plumage. She had seen similar feathers in the Small Garden beneath nests where fledglings had shaken themselves when learning to fly.

Small Garden… The carp pool, the elm, the singing birds, the sound of the First House of Silk going about its daily business.

Her heart hurt.

I am bereft, she thought as an image of Old One flashed through her mind – that precious, wrinkled woman who had taught her to embroider when her mother had been too busy running First House. Old One who had been so phlegmatic about life. What would she think of her granddaughter now?

'Have some strength, dear child. Remember from whom you are descended and what your future will be. You will be an empress…'

An empress! She hated the Emperor with a passion now. It filled every part of her body, fuelling her. She would not be cowed by his indiscretion. If she had to kill him to right a wrong and save the Han, save her family, save Old One … avenge Heng, then she would.

He had been weighed and measured. By the stars, there was *nothing* of greatness in him.

'Thy face is criss-crossed with hate.'

Lien gasped and she twisted to see who spoke. 'How would you know *what* my face is like? You are behind me.'

'Swan maid knows all, silly child.'

Swan maid?

'Then free me and let me stand before you, if you think I am a child.' Lien knew nothing of swan maids. Enchanted beings of course, else she wouldn't be trapped like a spider in a web but were they good or bad? She pushed against the seat and found she could move, her invisible bonds dissolving as if they had never been.

'Lien of the Han may step over the wale of the boat to shore.'

Still Lien had not seen the speaker, so she took a step over the boat's side, sliding down to the shingle. She turned first one way and then another, finally confronting a black swan standing a few paces away.

All around was silence.

No birdcall. No breeze. The grasses, reeds and wildflowers did not shift and sway. A frozen stillness. Lien's heartbeat lifted, and her eyes twitched – something that would often happen when she was tired from close stitchery. She would know to put her work down, to close her eyes and surrender to the small waft of air through the elm and which rattled the delicate windchimes as the singing birds and the ambience eased the strain to her neck and shoulders.

But here?

Nothing. A ghostly silence, wrapped in vague moonlight and with a majestic swan which took one step toward her.

It was as though the woman stepped out of the swan's feathers, growing gracefully taller, her skin as white as the snow in the Long Ma mountains, her lips blood red, her hair the colour of pitch, her eyebrows a perfect arc, her eyes – oh by the stars, her eyes! Mesmeric, sparkling green and they stared at Lien with cool fascination.

'So,' the woman said, holding her luscious-feathered cape close about her shoulders as she walked around Lien, coming to stand directly in front of her. 'Lien of the Han. Thy fame spreads.'

'My fame?' Lien grimaced at the woman's strange way of speaking.

'Indeed. All Others know thee to be betrothed to the hunted man.'

Careful...

'Hunted by you?'

The woman hooted, her eyes ever watchful, her mouth a slightly amused smirk. 'Not by Maeve Swan Maid. Although there might be other swan maids who would seek him to hand him over.'

'Hand him over to whom? Who is chasing us to the death?'

'Who indeed? Many or most, it appears. It is like Wild Hunt. Thy life hangs by a short thread, Lien. Did'st thou not have *any* idea what damage thy betrothed caused? Did he not realise that gateways are secret for a reason?'

'What reason? If it is good enough for Others to enter *our* world through those entrances, then surely it is only fair for mortals to enter your world the same way.'

Maeve Swan Maid hissed as she advanced upon Lien. 'Idiot mortal! Hast though never heard what happens to those who stumble across the Other world by accident?

Premature ageing, insanity, loss of place, death. If mortals seek to enter at will, then such intrusion in a secret world will cause mayhem. Accidental intrusion Others cope with, wholescale intrusion not so.'

'Unbalanced and unfair...' Lien muttered.

'So thou sayest,' growled Maeve. 'But it perpetuates a peace.'

'Huh, of a kind,' said Lien.

'By the stars, thou art an insolent bitch! Maeve wonders why she bothered to try and save thee.'

'Then tell me, Maeve Swan Maid, why did you? What do you have to gain?'

Maeve's mouth had tightened, her eyes hardening from glittering emerald to malachite. 'Maeve Swan Maid has a ... friend. Friend asked for help. Maeve thought on it long and hard and finally agreed.'

'What friend? And help in what way?' If holding her prisoner and spiriting her away was help when she had already been in the gentle care of the three siofra sisters, she had reason to doubt the swan maid's words.

'Do not be hasty in thy judgement. Siofra were generous, but their way of getting thee to the orchard was fraught. Maeve's way was quick. Thou art now close to Seraphina's home.'

'Ah...' Lien remembered this almost holy name bandied about. 'The all-powerful Seraphina who might, I gather, be able to destroy the map.'

Maeve nodded. 'Just so.'

'Then surely you should be seeking my betrothed and not me. He is the one with the map.'

'Emperor of the Han is not far from here.'

'You say?' Something ugly surged through Lien and she took a hard hold of herself. 'Then, Maeve Swan Maid, I thank you. Please take me to this Seraphina, so that I may finally meet my betrothed.'

Maeve looked at Lien quizzically. 'Thou hast never met him?'

Lien frowned. 'This was an arranged betrothal. I did not ask for it.'

Maeve snorted, a soft mocking exhale of breath.

'I had no wish to marry,' Lien defended herself. 'It was nothing but business. My family would gain imperial status and the Emperor would gain breeding loins. 'Tis nothing more.'

One of Maeve's beautifully sculpted eyebrows rose, and she replied with chill arrogance. 'Maeve cares not why or how. She must protect thee on her honour. Come. 'Tis time to leave...'

But as she turned, an arrow rushed past Lien's ear, the feathers flicking her cheek. She cried out and dived forward, pushing the swan maid to the ground in a cloud of ebony plumage.

'Go!' Maeve yelled from beneath Lien's cloak.

Lien ran, bending double. She launched herself into the deep undergrowth, breath heaving, peeking through the thick acid green leaf and prickle of hawthorn, the thorns hooking her clothes and hair, scratching at her hands.

Maeve had shape-changed and even now was in the sky, climbing beyond the reach of more arrows and circling, then heading away from Lien.

She lay deep in leaf fall, hearing footsteps. How many? She listened. One, perhaps two? She counted the times she had heard arrows thumping into the ground. Three, four?

She was too afraid to move in case there were more hunters, that this was merely a feint to draw her out. Listening all the time until the silence was so deep it surely spoke of no one nearby.

In truth, could the siofras' way have been any more dangerous? A tightrope came to mind right now. If only she could get to the orchard, to this infamous woman they called Seraphina.

And then what?

Indeed, she thought. What is my plan? Do I take my revenge on the Emperor? Or let the Others do what they must because for sure they won't let him live.

The moonlight had become stronger – the colour of pearls. It afforded her cheer when she knew there was precious little to feel. At least now, she could see one foot in front of the other.

She crawled as carefully as she could, scratched and bruised but nursing such a hatred of Ming as each insult to her own being began to pile up. She knew she would carry those hurts until he paid in some way and by the stars, she hoped it would be soon.

She had crawled far enough to edge out from the hedgerow and stand, and so she pulled herself to her feet, brushing her body down, flipping torn hands through mussed hair. A mist had drifted down again – loose, floating ribbons and she sighed at the dampness. One deep scratch on her face dripped blood and she dragged a sleeve across it, grimacing at the stain on the fabric.

She kept Maeve's flightpath behind her and took a step forward.

A strong hand grasped her upper arm and a voice that sent shivers through to her very marrow broke the silence. 'Ah, 'tis the Lady Lien, for sure...'

She turned, looking up at the tall man who held her easily with one hand. The moonlight illuminated a perfectly defined face – etched cheekbones, an aquiline nose, eyes and hair as dark as sin and which lay easily upon the collar of a glistening white shirt. She noted he carried a bow, white-fletched arrows stuck through his leather belt. She shivered, aware of his beauty, his height and wondering if she should be afraid of the bow and arrows. Such perfection must be Other, surely.

To meet two immortals in such a short space of time

could only mean that one was not to be trusted. She thought of Maeve's sneering, of her mockery. Dangerous? And yet it was she who had spirited Lien to the edge of the Ymp Tree Orchard with such speed and as the arrows launched upon them, it was she who urged Lien to run.

This man looked right into her very soul and she could barely turn away as he smiled and said, 'Don't be afraid. I am here to help you. You're almost home...'

Home? So far away. A tear slipped down her scratched cheek, and she scuffed it off. 'Then I thank you,' her voice shook, and she cursed it. 'May I ask who you are? You know my name after all.'

'True. I *do* know.' He gently plucked leaves from her hair, and her skin tingled as his fingers brushed the bark and moss from her back. 'Are you thirsty?' He held out a costrel and she shook her head. ''Tis only water, lady. It will not hurt.'

She bit her lip. By the Ancestors she *was* thirsty. Maybe just one or two sips. 'Perhaps,' she replied, taking the costrel. 'And while I drink, you can tell me your name.'

She effected an insouciance and courage she did not feel right at that moment. There was something extraordinary about this man and the air about him rippled across her skin. The mist twined around them both, as fine and elegant as a spider's web.

'Actually,' she said, her tongue almost cleaving to the dry roof of her mouth. 'I'm not thirsty. But thank you for the offer.'

'As you wish.' He took the costrel back and smiled down at her. 'But when we get home...' How that word stung her. 'Then you might like apricot juice from the Orchard's very own fruit. I would be lying if I said it wasn't magick.' He laughed, a deep warming sound that she loved. Almost as much as she loved his voice which was like velvet – soft, beguiling and so very rich. 'Tell me,' he prompted. 'What happened to Maeve Swan Maid?'

'You know her?'

'Indeed.'

'Oh, she was so very kind. She found me in a cave in Pymm and literally spirited me away…' She knew she sounded like a silly girl, all gush and lack-a-care, but it was as if she had known this man all her life. 'What did you say your name was?'

'I haven't yet but rest easy. I *am* worried about Maeve though…'

'We were attacked by bow and arrow – it seemed they were shooting at her, although why, I don't know. We did not see our attacker and she sent me this way and she flew off.'

'Bow and arrow you say? I might know who endeavoured to hurt her.'

'You do?'

'Lady Lien, I will tell you all when we get you home. In the meantime, you must trust me to do what is best for you. Can you do that, do you think?'

He smiled at her again. A charmingly honest smile that set butterflies flitting in her belly – beautiful butterflies, turquoise and aqua and spreading a warmth all over. She acquiesced. 'Yes…'

'Then follow me. We haven't far to go…'

He set off, she at his heels like a puppy, knowing without doubt that she was at last safe, that soon she would see Seraphina. Her limbs felt soft, as if bathed in warm honey and milk and she looked at the way his hair waved along the collar edge and at the breadth of his shoulders, tapering into narrow hips. She had never felt like this in the company of a man and so she followed him, two steps of hers to one of his as they skirted a slope where horses grazed and where in the far distance was a wooden building.

She thought she saw a movement in the far sky, a bird perhaps, but kept her eyes firmly on the man in front, almost as if he was a lifeline.

Did she hear a cry, a rasping birdcall?

Her rescuer swung around, grabbed her and shoved her behind him so that he faced whatever came from the far-off distance.

She couldn't see anything. Just felt the breadth and warmth of this man who promised she would be safe.

And she believed it…

CHAPTER THIRTEEN

Ming

The night was black but in the high heavens, a crescent moon shone like a shaving of alabaster in the sky.

He needed full moonlight, not half shadows. He fingered the pearl and then heard it.

A whisper. A slithering of sound across the late night. 'Here…'

Further away an echo. 'Here…'

A chilling murmur. 'Here. Come…'

A grunting hiss. 'S'here!'

Different voices lacing together to form a torment that sucked at him, and he knew he was surrounded. He began to edge backward into the lake until the cold, dark waters reached his ankles.

They were ghouls of the night, nightghasts, creatures of nightmare. He knew of them – wretched beings that prowled on frightened souls. When alive, rejected by their villages for their oddity, their madness, their strange shapes, they were unburied on death, left to fester and rot. Thus their humiliated souls wandered for evermore, preying on the unwary and anxious. Shambling, grey, foetid breath and matted skeins of thin hair, bloodshot eyes and rotten teeth – their language a whispered moan. They advanced in an ugly line of sibilant sound.

'S' him. The mapman…' Excitement swelled along the rank and a nauseating body odour filled the shoreline.

The mare started, throwing her head up, snorting with fear. She reared high, spun around and with reins trailing, galloped away from the oncoming monstrosities.

Ming's heart raced as he backed till the water licked his knees, knowing full well that an equally deathly creature might lie in wait in the depths. Facing the nightghasts, he felt for his dagger, wishing it was silver, aware that this iron weapon could kill nothing enchanted. As insurance against harm, he might as well have been armed with a feather.

He thought he heard a distant splash and glanced back. What was in the deeps? But no; nothing in the half moonlight, just the advancing hideous mob.

They drew closer like a net trapping fish, but he backed away further and the waters were now to his groin. One of the ghouls reached out for his arm and he hacked with his weapon but they laughed – a wretched madman's cackle on the air. Another grab and he slashed again, making contact, and the ghoul howled, eyes reddening with fury.

'Ming! Ming!' He glanced behind. A dinghy rowed toward him at pace, positioning itself between he and the nightghasts. 'Hurry! Get in, man!' the rower yelled, and Ming threw himself over the wale as a ghoul grabbed at him, the slimy fingers sliding down his sleeve and onto the skin of his right hand. He lay on the strakes gasping, looking up at his rescuer who shouted at the horrors on the shore. '*Leáigh, créatúir bharúla bréan. Leáigh!*'

Ming knew the words, he had learned many languages beyond the Han. 'Melt, you barrow creatures! Melt…'

The ghouls howled as first one, then another melted from the feet, their legs dissolving and then their torsos, their arms, shoulders, until their awful heads sat on a wet gruesome mass and then only eyeballs, until those melted as well.

'It won't last. Nothing can kill those already dead,' the man pulled at the oars, rowing hard, sending the boat rushing over the shallows of the lake before the vessel turned and began to move swiftly across the gleaming pewter waters.

'Mother of the Universe!' Ming stared at the rower.

He had not aged an iota in the few years since Ming Xao had last seen him. That fateful night, Ming and his companions, Poli and Isabella, had slept the sleep of the enchanted around a table in the Ymp Tree Orchard as the blind Goddess of Weaving, his forever Other friend, Chi Nü, was carried by this man from the world of mortals to her rightful place amongst the Gods of the Han. He knew that in that moment, Chi had regained her sight and Nicholas, cursed halftime mortal that he was, had regained his lost voice.

It was an eldritch story and Ming recalled the night, remembered the terrible dilemma and how he had spoken to the goddess, outraged at the malicious trial Celestial Others had placed before her. Ah yes, it flashed through his mind in a blink, as fresh as if it happened moments before…

'But it is not so simple, is it, my lady?' Ming Xao took off his spectacles and polished them. 'For I know what they have said.'

Chi Nü closed her eyes, her shoulders shifting with a mighty sigh.

'They offer you trial by the Bridge of Celestials, don't they? I have scrolls in my library that tell this story.' Ming Xao began to pace, filled with ire. 'And being a trial, they didn't offer your sight back, did they, unless you can cross that bridge?'

The Celestial nodded, her eyes sparkling with tears.

'Then how can you cross when you are blind!'

When the three mortals had woken, Nico and Chi had vanished and all that remained was a pile of paper and the folds of sunrise-sunset silk – what had been the fateful *shifu* cloth. The papers had hinted at a story, and it led Isabella to a great telling. But for Ming, that awful moment when

Chi learned what her fellow Gods offered her, was one more prick of his soul, driving him ever closer to revenge and redress.

'Nico?' he croaked, sucking in a breath as pain spiked up and down the bones of his fingers. They felt crushed, withered, the nerves shattered, yet sending such unutterable messages to his brain. 'We thought you were banished to the celestial world, never to return…'

'I was. I am… But Chi has a way, and she contrived for me to return when she saw what was happening. My presence here is moments long. There may be an awful price to pay if we don't hurry.'

Ming closed his eyes. 'A price. Of course,' his tone was graceless and derisory. 'There is always a price, isn't there? What this time? My life? I think you will find that is already forfeit. And if it *is* my life, why did you bother to save me?'

'We, Chi and I, bothered because we care for you. And yes, there is always a price.' Nico shifted on the seat, his dark clothes and handsomely carved face thrown into the light of the new moon, but as quickly sinking to shadow again. 'I don't know what your price shall be, Ming. That is between you and Fate. Right now, I must take you to Lien…'

'Lien!' Ming tried to move his hand and cursed at the awful pain.

'Is your hand injured?'

'A nightghast's fingers slid down to my own…'

'Ah.' Nico's face creased.

Ming held out his right hand where violent blue and ochre-tinged bruising had stained the skin. 'And?' he prompted as Nico continued to row with powerful sweeps of the oars.

'A ghoul's touch can mean many things.'

'Ambiguous,' Ming said, slipping his hand into the buttoned vest of his clothes, sitting with knees hunched. 'Nico, I *must* help Lien. She is an innocent in all of this. And then I must…'

'We know what you must do,' Nicholas broke in. He reached out and squeezed Ming's shoulder and the touch was warm. 'Nothing is easy, is it my friend? I don't forget our past journey and thus you will always be my friend, despite your troublesome map. Maybe even more *because* of it. I find part of me agreeing with what you have done. I confess I am unsure why you couldn't just hand it over to Chi and yet, that was not to be. It's almost as if Fate wants you to pursue a great trial. It is the way of it, Chi says, and she is an Other and must be listened to.'

'But Lien,' Ming broke in. 'This is not her fault. Why should she be threatened? If she weren't my betrothed, she may have been safer, but she is and may pay a terrible price. She knows nothing of life beyond the Han and has no idea of the ugliness that lurks amongst Others.'

'I can do nothing for her, Ming.' Nico eased the oars as the boat's stem ground on shingle. 'And this is where I am forced to leave you. I can come no further …'

Ming grabbed at Nico's arm with his uninjured hand, feeling muscle and strength beneath the shadowy velvet sleeve. 'Thank you, but I beg you, please ask Chi Nü to protect Lien if she can. I owe Lien this. I have wronged her, I've wronged the Han and I've wronged Others I care about. I beg you – argue on my behalf. I will do whatever it takes to right this wrong.'

'Even the giving of your own life?'

Ming answered swiftly. 'Yes. On my word. Even that.'

'Then you are brave. And I'll pray that it does not come to that. Take heart, my friend…'

As Ming climbed from the boat, he gasped at the pain in his hand and saw it had turned as pale as death. 'Thank you…' He turned but Nico had gone. Vanished as quickly as a breath in and out. Ming was left with the pattering of the smallest shore wave and a feeling of such deep melancholy that he could barely move his limbs.

It was as grim as the Afterlife and he felt as if he were already dead.

Dawn cast a pearled light from the far eastern hills and a light mist wound around his legs. Better than night perhaps, but the dampness was leeching. He longed to bask in the sun's warmth for just a moment. He wondered where Gallivant and Max were, but most importantly, as the light strengthened, he wondered how he would find Lien, because for as much as Nico had saved his life, he had given no clues and this lake seemed to stretch forever. She might not even be here.

Maybe an Other had found her and even now was hauling her away to be used in a game of threat. Threat was the only game Others played – feint and counter-feint, bargain and counter-bargain. Take and take and never give...

Somewhere the hoarse piping of a swan sounded, shredded and wispy like a *habbān* he had heard playing in the Raj. Again the bird shrieked. Louder and filled with anger.

He turned as the call echoed and re-echoed. Again and again with such piercing fury that he began to run. The cry sent thrills of dread down his spine because Lien had disappeared in a swan maid's vessel and swan maids were a dangerous unknown.

He ran over uneven ground, rough pebbles that turned his booted feet this way and that. He jumped over fallen logs and smashed through osiers and reeds.

Ahead, a black feathered swan arced in the sky, turning, diving down, wings spread, neck and body in a fierce arrow-like trajectory. The red beak would be like a steel bodkin as it hit its prey.

Lien!

He crouched in the osiers, dragging out the dagger in his good hand, ready to spring forward.

A tall man stood on the lake track, beribboned by mist trailing across his broad shoulders. Behind the man, Ming saw Lien looking up into the sky. The man attempted to pull an arrow from his belt to nock it into a hunting bow but the swan, faster than light had almost reached the couple.

'Lien,' Ming shouted. 'Lien, drop down!' He leapt from the shield of the osiers and Lien, for it was she, crashed to her knees. As the man attempted to pull her up, the black swan swooped, smashing his head with the sharp red beak, causing blood to run down the man's forehead. He tried to thrust the bird away, but it rose swiftly to the sky, banked and returned to hit him again.

Ming ran forward, grabbed Lien's arm, and dragged her across the rocky track to where he could guard her as the fight between swan and man played out.

But there was nothing for the swan to attack beyond a little man, handsome and well-turned out for sure, but with malevolent glinting black eyes below the trickling blood. He yelled at the swan.

'I ought to stick your damned gizzards and pull them out of your arse!'

The swan swooped in to land and then walked toward the man, shape-changing into a sinuous black column of a woman with rippling ebony hair and a pale visage that was as cold as the winter snows.

'Foul lecher! Leave this woman! She is not thy prey this day.'

Black eyes met ebony, like watching two thunderclouds, but then the little man stepped back and bowed.

'As always, Maeve, you make such questionable partnerships with mortals, do you not? But one day, pretty feathered one, you will meet your bane and swan pie will be served.'

Maeve Swan Maid spat at him, as good as any swan hiss but he laughed, turning away, the mist trailing off his shoulders – a comely little man with none of the height and breadth of his alter-ego. He vanished into the pearlised grey air and the swan maid turned to Lien.

'Thy life was nearly done, Lady Lien. Thou needs protection here in Trevallyn – thou knows little of the dangers.'

'I've survived thus far!' Lien clambered up, pushing at Ming Xao's hand. 'Leave me! Look at what you've done to my knees. How dare you!'

'Thy betrothed helped thee because he cares for thee.' Maeve shouldered her fine feathered cloak.

'My betroth…' Lien flung and then stared at Ming Xao.

She could be forgiven for not knowing, he thought. They had only met once, and she hadn't known he was the Emperor at the time, and he had no doubt that with his shorter hair and the tattoo of the crane peering from the top of his chemise, he looked anything *but* Han, let alone imperial.

'Art thou unaware of the illustrious company thou keeps?' Maeve's cloak was now settled on her shoulders, and she tossed her magnificent waterfall hair back.

Lien didn't answer.

'If Maeve had not stayed close by, thou would have been doomed, fair Lien. That man with whom thou walked, he is called the Ganconer and he shape-changes into a tall, handsome man, beguiles women such as thee, kisses them and on that kiss, thy Fate is sealed. If he had kissed thee, thou would have pined – neither eating nor sleeping, and walking thyself to death as thou searched for him.'

'By the Ancestors! Did he kiss you?' Ming asked.

Lien's fist bunched and she punched him hard on the chest. '*What* do you think I am that I must fall for the first man I meet? I followed him because he promised to take me to safety.' She bent and rubbed at her knee which was bleeding through her breeches. 'But I thank *you,* Maeve Swan Maid, for seeing me safe from the Ganconer. Perhaps you can see me safe from this imposter as well.'

'He is no imposter, Lien of the Han. He is thy Emperor.'

'She speaks the truth, Lien. I am Ming Xao and I *am* the Emperor.'

Lien's jaw set and she hissed at him as if she too, were a swan maid. 'Ah, our illustrious Emperor!' She folded her hands and bowed over them. 'So. Finally I get to see the man who has condemned himself and the whole of the Han to death by a thousand cuts because he chose to draw a *map*! Gods save me from the company of fools.'

The *habbān* sounded again and both Lien and Ming glanced to the lake. Maeve, now a black swan, was swimming away. Her head turned, imperious, condescending, calling her thready cry and then with a clatter-flack of her massive wings, she lifted to the sky.

'Even she thinks we are fools,' Lien muttered, and Ming could feel his anger and frustration building – thick and black and oozing with contempt. Anger that he had tamped down since he had been forced to leave the Han, fury at himself. Hatred of Others. And now, with this confrontation, spleen at this self-important woman in front of him. Gods, he was done with it!

'Yes, I drew a map.' Ming said through clenched teeth. 'I did it for reasons I thought were right at the time. But I made a mistake. I am attempting to right the wrong. *Cease* speaking and let me *finish*!' he shouted as Lien tried to break in with accusations. 'Perhaps you are unable to understand the idea of mistakes, given that you are evidently so perfect!'

'Oh, we all make mistakes, *Excellence*,' she replied. 'Mine was to allow myself to be betrothed to an emperor.' Tears began to fall. 'My friend *died* because of you!'

'Nothing I can do will make that right,' he tried to soften the moment. 'I wish with all my heart that you could speak once more with her.'

'Speak with her? By the stars! She's dead! Dead! Does that not mean anything to you?'

Lien had pulled up the leg of her breeches and was wiping the blood away from the grazes. The knee was ripped and ragged from where Ming had dragged her away from the Ganconer.

'Here,' Ming bent down, taking her kerchief from her, padding it and swabbing the cuts. His fingers hurt – as if they were filleted and mere bone remained. 'You need a salve. Perhaps Seraphina can help.' He took out his own clean kerchief and folded it, tying it round the wound.

'Ah yes. The enchanted Seraphina who will save the world.'

Ming looked up. 'I hadn't realised that you have the taste of acid upon your tongue.'

Lien's eyes opened wide, and she pushed at his hand and ripped the leg of her breeches down. 'And you have a blight upon your foolish brain.'

She reminded Ming of a flighty horse – one move and she would shy and gallop off. He kept his voice low, attempting to defuse her anger and by consequence his own. 'Then perhaps you might follow this fool to safety. After that, I care not what you do.' He strode off. To where he was unsure as the lake was so big, an inland sea, and nothing seemed familiar.

He didn't look back but sensed that Lien followed. Occasionally there was the crisp crack of leaf and twig and he was content she followed for no other reason than the intention of not being left behind.

It was obvious she hadn't recognised him. Why would she? He had disguised himself in the Park of Singing Birds and like most First House daughters in the Han, she led a circumscribed existence. And now she trailed him like a ribbon of regret.

CHAPTER FOURTEEN

Ming and Lien

I'll make you pay. I will avenge Heng and I will avenge the Han... Lien followed behind her *emperor*, every step coloured with fury.

His soul for Heng's. At the very least. Right and just.

I hate you. I hate you more than you could ever imagine!

He was taller than she had expected, and broader than the man she had seen at the First House of Merchants when the Lady Ibo had become his first betrothed. Ah, where was *that* lady now? She had left in secret with the Emperor, and he had been gone for almost three turnings of the year wheel.

Probably dead. Maybe it is what he does. Like some foul night creature.

His hair was cut roughly, grazing his neck and was threaded here and there with silver which made him look wise, maybe even compassionate. And yet! He drew a map of the most forbidden places in the world and his people would pay for his audacious vanity.

He remained silent and it allowed her to think.

Would she have the courage or the moral fortitude to right wrongs? How would she do it? He was bigger, stronger than she'd anticipated and may best her physically. Although, *there* was a curious thing – he cradled his right hand, she'd seen the bruising when he swabbed her knee.

He'd been gentle, not wishing to hurt her.

Stop it!

His stride was long and determined and he held his head high, almost an arrogant pose, until she noticed him scanning the surrounds, looking for something – Others? The Orchard? Seraphina's house?

Poison.

The awful thought exploded into her mind as she limped behind him. All colours of the rainbow, like skyfire. Illuminating a thought with purpose. Poison … it made sense. But which? How?

Seraphina.

She felt as if she were two people as ideas galloped through her mind. The witch that they called Seraphina, she would surely have a library of books, a still room, shelves of dangerous plants.

It could be possible…

Gods and Ancestors, she thought. At what point did I become so vile that I would commit murder? And not just anyone. My Emperor … my betrothed…

But then she recalled Heng and the maidservant's shy wish as she brushed Lien's hair before the long walk to the imperial palace. She wanted to see more of life beyond the Wall.

More? She died! And because of him!

If her glance was a dagger, then the sharpness of it would have killed him a hundred times over. But no – poison was quieter, less obvious.

Then what of me, she thought?

What of you? You were nothing before and will be less than nothing after.

She thought of Old One, her grandmother, and Sun Sen, First Minister, and knew that after Ming's Xao's death, she must return to the Han. She would tell Sun Sen that the Emperor had died as he destroyed the map…

And there was a thing. She must delay the poisoning until after Ming had done what ever Seraphina deemed necessary for the map to be destroyed.

So yes, she would return to the Han, make her obeisance to the First Minister, and as befitted the betrothed of a deceased emperor, she would enter the Jhokang Monastery where she would sit with the nuns in their prayer hall, the monks in theirs, and she would reflect on her crime and pray for forgiveness. For who would know that she was the Emperor's assassin?

The more sensible part of her just hoped that the map's destruction would be enough for the Others. That the Han would be left alone. But who knew? Others might, in their treacherous way, decide the Han was forever an enemy.

She recalled those she had met – Kitsune the Fox Lady, Chi Nü, the siofra, the swan maid. How many had wished her true ill will? For sure Kitsune had been frightening in her luminous beauty but she had never said she would kill Lien if she hadn't got her way. No, she merely *implied* threat. Would she have protected Lien and Heng against the worst the Gods might have done?

As for Chi Nü, gentle Goddess of Weaving – she had tried to guide, not harm. And Yue Lao – a wise Ancient – another mentor. The siofra and the swan maid – they had done their best to protect her. It deserved some thought…

'You say little,' she said as they walked along.

'There would hardly be any point,' he answered with a sigh, 'in speaking to you, because you would only repudiate anything I had to say.' His voice was deep. In any other man she might have found it enticing.

'You are right,' she replied. 'Why listen to the ramblings of a fool because you are definitely that? *And* a murderer…'

His stride checked momentarily but then he shook his head and walked on, bigger strides, covering more ground and she had to hurry to stay in his shadow.

The sun had finally burst free of its shackles, coating

the countryside in a soft sheen. The mists dissolved and blades of grass, cobwebs and leaves glistened. They entered a shaded wood, walking beneath oaks, ashes and elms and here and there shafts of brilliant morning light pooled on green mosses and over ferny growth. It seemed enchanted and perhaps it was. Lien looked around, her eyes ever wide, searching for danger. Birds chirruped, fluttering between the branches, but nothing untoward sounded and she felt no enchanted *frisson* on her skin.

They walked up a slope, bursting free of the shaded wood, and continuing over thick grass until they crested the rise. Beside them, an old stone fort crumbled into the rocky ground from whence it had come – grey stone pockmarked with lichen and smoothed with aeons of weather.

'How far have we walked? Where are we?'

He turned and for a moment she could see shadows beneath his eyes, lines of exhaustion from nose to mouth. He pushed his hair back from his face impatiently and said, 'I don't know.'

'You don't know? Where is the orchard? I thought I was in your care...'

'Lady Lien,' there was little warmth as he spoke. 'I will protect you until we reach Seraphina's. You are safe.'

'I hardly think so. We are in the middle of nowhere. No trees, nothing to shelter or shield us and you don't know where we are!'

'I suspect we have somehow moved away from the orchard and house rather than toward it.'

'Gods and Ancestors! How far?'

'I suspect too far to walk before the sun sets. We must stay the night in those ruins.' He pointed at the fallen folly with its tumbled masonry. 'It's at least a shelter of sorts.'

'We have no weapons, no food, no directions. Tell me, my lord, are you always so helpless?'

But he had walked up to the ruins and was surveying the

old arch that was once the entrance. He walked beneath it and she hurried after him, afraid to be left alone. The wall was circular, and whilst there was no roof, nor apertures of any sort, it was a kind of shelter, and she liked the rounded nature. No corners for spirits to hide. They would follow the wall around and disappear out the door again. Good fortune.

Ming had been walking back and forth over the floor, pulling at fallen timbers, stacking them up. 'We can make a fire…'

'And you have the skill to light it?'

'I have a knife as I'm sure do you. With some dry grasses, we might start a flame.'

She snorted.

'And there is always this…' he grunted, bending to pull on a rusty iron ring. A door opened in the ground, with steps leading down into a black hole, a stone stair leading into heart-stopping darkness.

'I'm not going down there. We have no flame, nothing to light the dark.'

'Then we shall light a fire and stay here, shall we not?'

'Can we not make more distance before it grows dark?'

'We could, but if I can see the night sky, I can plot our direction by the stars. A safer option, I think, is to stay here, rest, make a fire and see what we can find to eat.'

'You jest of course…'

'No. Over the low wall beyond the arch, can you see? A blackberry vine and there, a little down the hill, an old apple tree.'

'But it is not autumn – there will be no fruit.'

'There is always fruit in Færan.'

'We are in the Other world?'

'Yes.'

'When?'

'For me, when I arrived near the orchard.'

'You have already been within the orchard?'

'*Near* the orchard.'

'Then why are you *here*? Why did you not stay, give the cursed map to Seraphina and finish this once and for all.'

'Because you were in danger, Lady Lien. I wanted to find you and protect you. You are an innocent player in this and whilst I can do nothing for Heng, I can honour her love of you by seeing you safe.'

Lien leant back against the circular wall. Pretty words for sure. She closed her eyes and said nothing. Words were just that and easy to say. It was too late now.

She pushed herself off the wall and climbed over tumbled stone and old timbers to the blackberry vine and sure enough, there were berries. Some lettuce-green, some palest pink and some rich black and juicy. She picked those, piling them onto a stone.

'Here…' his voice broke the silence, and he passed her a kerchief which he had knotted to form a container.

'You have a surfeit of kerchiefs,' she noted.

'I have no idea what is in my pockets.' He patted the capacious welted pockets of his tailcoat. 'Huh…' he withdrew a metal pommel from a broken knife. 'And parchment.'

'A broken knife and parchment,' she said dismissively. 'But then perhaps you plan to write a letter.'

His grey fingers unfolded the parchment and even she could detect the irony in his voice. 'It is a map.'

'A map,' she snapped. 'Of course there would be a map.'

'This is not mine, Lady.'

'Then whose? she asked. 'And of what?'

'Trevallyn,' he replied and pointed with his damaged hand. Gods it was a mess – it looked dead. She wondered what had happened but forbore to ask.

'There, you see,' he said, 'the lake, the orchard, there are other places too, but they have no relevance to us.'

'What do you mean when you say you have no idea what is in your pockets?'

'The clothes were given to me on the journey.'

'By whom?'

'My friend, Gallivant. You'll meet him at Seraphina's.'

'Are we close by?' She leaned forward.

'I think this is Fort Belvedere. See?' His finger traced the rounded shape of the fortress. It looked like the tower from a chess game. 'I am sure it is this place.' He sucked in his breath. 'Gods!'

'What?'

'We are on the wrong side of the lake. Look, there is the orchard.'

'Well, that won't take long. If we started now, we would surely be around the lake by dark.'

'The lake, Lady Lien, is ten leagues wide.'

'Ten leagues!' Suddenly she was tired beyond belief and her skull ached, hammer on anvil. She had run from life into chaos the minute Heng had dressed her in the yellow silk robe, and she hadn't stopped running and for one moment, only a dot in the passage of time, she wanted to sit, hold her head in her hands and weep.

But she was Lady Lien and had no time for such weakness.

'I think we must rest, Lady. You and I have been running for days and nights.'

She looked at him, shocked at his words, as if he read her mind.

'We need to gather ourselves to get back to the orchard,' he continued. 'It is after midday now and the evening will fall before we know it. On the morrow at dawn, we will follow this map and I hope we can be close to the orchard by mid-afternoon.'

Gods! With only blackberries and apples to sustain us, Lien thought. She sighed and walked to the apple tree, twisting softly striated fruit until her pockets bulged. Ming picked fruit from the higher branches and then together they climbed back to Fort Belvedere.

She wondered if the fort would be safe after dark. The place had the unholy feel of somewhere left alone for a reason and that reason, the evil and undead. She shivered.

'Are you cold?'

She shook her head as she found a spot against the wall of the fort that gathered the sunbeams through the tumbled ruins. Ming offered her some blackberries and she took a handful and an apple and proceeded to eat alone, not engaging, turning a little to the side to avoid him. But he walked to the edge of the tumbled stone and stared into the distance. She didn't want to speak with him at all, nursing her hatred like a babe in arms, cossetting it so that it could grow into a fearsome companion.

Her thoughts were like maggots – writhing, grey and foul. She wondered if it was some malign spirit from this Other world that had entered her soul, but she didn't care. Loyal Heng had been so trusting of Lien, so innocent, and to think that her life had ended so brutally, so unjustly because of loyalty and love.

It had to be avenged.

Ming slipped his hand into the deep right pocket of his coat. The pain rang louder than the most clamorous tocsin. It felt as if the nails been ripped off, that the fingers had been filleted like a fish from the bones, and that the bones were being ground to dust before his eyes. He, a grown man, could have howled with the agony of it and all the while, the colours circulated like some hideous colour wheel – blue and yellow, then deathly-white and finally, corpse-grey. He learned to hate the white because he knew that then the grey would come and drag him to screaming point and he was sure maggots would then slide from the corpse of his hand.

But he hid this from Lien. He bit down on the torture, pushing himself into a death-deep silence, gritting his teeth and thinking of anything but the torment. The awful injury was a nightghast wound, one which he was sure would have some terrible result and he had been through a hundred of them in his head.

Worst was the thought of death or more particularly the timing. He didn't mind dying. It happened to everyone and if it was his Fate then he could hardly gainsay it. But he needed to stay alive until the map had been dealt with. He owed it to his people, to Chi Nü, and to Heng and even to the shrewish Lady Lien.

The truth of it was that whilst he could still use his hand, it was marginal, the pain grotesque. If he had to defend Lien, it would need to be with his left hand, at best clumsy, at worst, useless. His defencelessness was worrisome, but even more so, the Lady Lien's fury. He had expected some degree of anger for her position, but not the hate.

The map canister sat in his coat, and he felt for it now, digging his healthy hand deep into the left pocket in which it lay. He fingered the smooth wax seal and wished again, as he had so many times before, that he'd listened to Chi Nü and that he had not been so arrogant. But wishing wasted his energy and he could only hope that Seraphina could help him.

He hoped to the depth of his heart that the siofra had been right, that as long as the winds and birds had carried no news of a decimation in the Han that there had been none. A small measure of comfort if one excluded Heng. But Heng's life – that was something else entirely.

If she had stayed in the First House of Silk, what then? Would she still have moved inexorably forward to her destiny?

So often he had read of the immutability of Fate. That it was written at birth and nothing, no Gods and no enchantment could change it. Destiny, as he had been told so often by the monks, seers, even Chi Nü, was everything.

Heng had said she was always destined to become Heng-O, even though she had been ignorant of the fact. But the red thread on her wrist confirmed it – the way it plied itself together with the former Moonlady's as if the threads had been joined in another life. Yue Lao, the God of Fate, had merely been a messenger, tying on the thread, tethering her to her destiny.

Ming looked at the red thread round his own battered right wrist. The discoloration stopped at his wrist bone, his right arm healthy and pulsing with life above the thread. What did this thread say of his own Fate? He would like to have talked with Lien about this but how did he tell her that Heng lived? That she was a goddess?

He cast a surreptitious look at the lady, but she sat with her coat tight around and her head lying back against the roughened wall of the fort. Her eyes were closed, and he thought how tired she appeared, how sad. But then also, as he saw the lines ploughed across her forehead and between her sculpted eyebrows, how angry.

And there was no way he could ameliorate it and so he kept his distance.

The day drifted on, the sun in the perfect sky sinking to a flawless dusk of pink, of gold and a deeper blue that spoke of the approach of a clear, diamond-studded night sky. As was the case in the Other world, everything was perfection and this night would prove to be no different. Except, he thought, for the barrow creatures, the fell creatures who wandered the nights throughout immortal and mortal worlds, and they were the ones he feared.

He felt again in his pocket, drawing out the broken pommel. He would swear it was silver and that must surely be a bonus, broken or not, but in his pocket? Who had placed it there? And the map? If that was not a turn of the wheel of destiny, then what was?

The haft was cool in his grasp, and he held it in his good hand, weighing it, then ran his fingers over the engraving along the metal. A needle-like blade shot out with the speed of light and he gasped, almost dropping the weapon. By the Gods it was a cruel dagger – a stiletto like the *misericordes* he had seen in Veniche.

The haft was crafted superbly – a story etched into the silver from the tip of the pommel to the blade. He looked closer – a legend of some sort perhaps, fine engraving by an artist who understood the metal. It told of the blade's fame. How it had bested a dark monster, slaying it and then as the hero held the blade to the sky, light pouring forth from its tip. A truth? Was this dagger magick? He played with it, turning it over, trying to discover the join where it had hinged to release the blade, but so perfect was the craftsmanship it was invisible.

There must be some point to press ...

He turned it over and over and then ran a finger across the engraving of the stream of light and the killing blade withdrew. He ran his finger over it again and the blade slid out with eldritch smoothness – silent and deadly. He pressed the engraved light-stream a little harder and a sliver of the whitest light shot out, illuminating the crumbled and fallen fort as if the sun shone directly above. He pressed the engraving again, the light withdrew and the blade slipped back into the haft.

He sat back.

In his hand he held something eldritch, something silver and something that might conceivably save their lives.

For the first time in an age, he felt some degree of confidence and it propelled him to pile up dry grasses. He searched the debris, pulling up small pieces of rock to see if there was flint. With a good shard, he began to stroke his mortal knife against the rock edge, sparks flying into the air, more and more until some fell onto his tinder and began to smoke. He bent to blow on the fledgling glow and a flame began to burn and so he placed twigs on the nest of burning grass, blowing it again and the flames became more energetic. More twigs and more until the fire was burning readily, and then very carefully because he didn't want to smother it, he fed it with fuel, old branches, broken planks, until the flames were roaring.

Lien had watched him, he knew, but she remained silent, so he said, 'If you are chilled, Lady, come to the fire. I'll fetch more fuel for later. I would keep it burning through the night – it can protect us.'

'Will it not just let evil beings know we are here?' She stayed where she was.

'They can smell us if they want us. They don't need to see flame. But at least we can stay warm and arm ourselves with burning brands if we need to. Also, to allay your concerns, you should know that the broken pommel in my pocket is actually a retractable dagger made of silver. Silver is every enchanted being's universal bane.'

'So we are safe.' She sounded unimpressed.

'As safe as we can be when we are mortals within the world of immortals.'

'Huh,' she muttered, but gathered her coat around her and moved closer to the fire. There was no gratitude for the flame, merely a surliness that did her no favours.

He moved away to give her space. In truth, he didn't want to speak with her at all. As she was now, Lien was not the woman he had met in the Park of Singing Birds. *That* woman had been alight with curiosity and verve, brightness and beauty sparkling from her eyes and from the few words she uttered. This woman who sat huddled like misery within her black coat, was smothered in a bitterness which drifted around her like a sea fret.

He looked out at the dusking. Night moved in an elegant swathe from the east – clear dark blue with a promise of the glister of stars. The moon though was shy, remaining an infant crescent and there was part of him that wanted to drag Lien to look at it, to explain…

But she was unapproachable. Perhaps there would be more appropriate times. Who knew?

The countryside flowed down the hill toward the lake – a lake that they would have to cross or go around and he worried because the worst of Færan came from underneath. Underneath the water, underneath the fields, underneath the mountains. But even now, in the dusky shadow it had a flowing softness, as if nothing could be awry. In the distance he could hear a lark singing the day to bed – and closer, perhaps in the apple tree, the hoot of an early and ambitious owl.

When he had first seen the world of the Færan so many years ago, he had been in awe, astonished at the magnificence. And the Færan folk themselves – so beautiful as to be unbelievable. But ineffably boring in their surfeit. And thus They ventured into the mortal world, into Ming's or Lien's world – playing games. Lethal games that enticed mortals into their company and which inevitably involved heartache for the unfortunate whose life they sought to ruin.

Was it any wonder he sought to ameliorate such things?

He sighed, positioning himself where he could watch the entrance to the fort and also the tumbled rear wall. He pulled out his steel knife, the one he had purchased in the Raj. It was nasty enough – and he slipped it into his waistband where he could grab it swiftly. His hand had returned to the yellow-blue bruising again and was more pliable, less painful, even though he knew it would last momentarily. Whilst so, he pulled out the stiletto, flicked it open, weighing it with his left hand, practicing a feint, a slash, a drive. Not a proficient action but it would do as there was little else. He walked back to the fire to feed the hungry flames, piling on broken timber and then retreating to watch it roar briefly before it settled into an even flame broken only by the occasional spit of cinders, when the fiery specks would drift upward, golden against the black of the sky until he couldn't tell the difference between spark and star.

Heng-O, Lien needs your wise words. May you visit her and dispense your compassion – she is dissolving in bitterness, and it is a waste...

But a waste of what?

He would free her from her obligation to marry him. He would lose his life over the map. It was a given. And why should she be tainted with an association that she did not ask for?

She sat huddled asleep in her coat, her arms by her sides, her palms open and relaxed and he hoped to the Gods that such sleep rested her, eased her grief and even her anger – just a little. He noticed that a small knife lay across her open palm, and he recognised it from his worktable in the imperial library.

His face stretched into something of a smile. So, prescient enough to grab a knife.

Good woman.

His hand skimmed over the stiletto that he had once again placed on his right thigh, and he looked around the soft darkness of the fort to the outer shadow beyond the tumbled walls.

He heard it then... the sound of a distant scraping footfall amongst the choke of rocks that lay down the hill. Not just one set of footsteps but many and there was a spreading chill, the flames flaring up and down as if in fear of being dowsed.

He pushed the stiletto into his waistband and moved softly to Lien to clamp a hand over her mouth...

CHAPTER FIFTEEN
Lien and Ming

A hand sealed her mouth and she struggled, clasping her knife in a clenched fist.

In the light of the flames, Ming lifted one of his decaying and palsied fingers to his lips – a gesture of silence. He jerked his eyes to the arc and shook his head, an indication of impending danger, and pulled her with him toward the trapdoor. Heart pounding, she let him take her, even though every part of her screamed at the idea she must descend into terrifying blackness, let alone with this man even the Gods had forsaken.

He lifted the door and was guiding her down steps that were vaguely lit by the flames above, but she dragged on his arm, looking back and sensing, if not seeing, something malevolent flowing into the fort. Then the fire went out and Ming quietly pulled the trapdoor shut over their heads and pushed home the two bolts on either side.

Utter darkness, as suffocating and thick as heavy cloth. Cloying and confining.

Panic seized her, thoughts unwieldy, heart pounding, sweats and chills, and the idea that if she ran she would be safe. 'I can't see…'

'Ssh, hold on to me…'

She grasped the back of his coat because she had no option and they made slow progress down steps that aeons of time and footfall had worn into unstable troughs.

What if there is something waiting below?

She sucked in a fearful breath.

'We are on the floor at the bottom,' Ming whispered.

'So black...' she murmured to herself as the fear squeezed her breath. 'I can't ... I cannot...' She turned to run back up the steps to the world above, but he grabbed her.

'Listen to me,' he shook her hard, hissing. 'Be quiet, Lien! Every fearful move you make, every panicked thought you have is like life's blood to the malevolence above. Do you hear me? Breathe. In. Out. Good, that's better. Again...' he breathed with her. 'I have light. If I let you go, can I trust you?'

She whimpered. 'Yes...'

And then there was a shaft of the whitest light pointing along a narrow corridor of neatly crafted stone. 'How...'

'Enchantment.'

Enchantment?

They spoke in whispers and then moved forward with speed until they had rounded three or four bends, going ever on.

'Where...' she asked.

'Onward.'

'What is this path?'

'Maybe a lych-way,' he said. 'But then perhaps not. More a secret lovers' way, I suspect. The fort would have been a meeting place. Lovers could perhaps come and go in secret.'

Lien said nothing. There was much she wanted to say, all disparaging. How Others probably trapped unwary mortals and sought to imprison them here – playing with them, raping them and worse. 'What is a lych-way?'

He shone his light over the arched tunnel walls. 'A corpse-way. A path along which bodies are carried for burial.'

'Oh,' she whispered.

Lovers' Way is better.

He shone the light along the tunnel, but then it vanished, sinking them into the suffocating blackness again.

'What?' she hissed.

'Ssh.'

Oh Gods!

But the malevolence seeped along the tunnel – a noxious mist dragging hope from Lien's heart and replacing it again with panic.

'Stay behind me,' Ming whispered. 'Arm yourself with anything. A rock or that nasty little knife.'

She held hard to the knife, but she knew nothing would best an Other. Nothing but silver.

Silver... my betrothal ring!

Beautiful white jade set in silver and wrought in the shape of a dragon, something she had given no thought to since Heng had slipped it back onto her finger as she readied for her journey to the palace.

She held her ringed finger to her lips and kissed the jade, begging Cheng Mo to assist her children in their hour of need. Every beat of her heart dragged the horror closer, and her breath became shallower and swifter until she thought she would faint.

Ming's left hand reached for hers and he squeezed her fingers. 'Breath slowly,' he said. 'You are strong.'

Am I? she thought. *Mother of the Heavens, help me...*

They stood in the stultifying darkness as a malevolent chill drifted over them.

Ming let go of Lien's hand and reached for the stiletto. *I can vanquish just one, surely.* In the dark, he stroked the haft, the blade shooting out and then he pressed the hilt and the pure white beam burst from the tip of the blade, blinding the *nightghast* that shambled toward them. As the creature stood dazzled, Ming leapt with the silver blade, struck and the creature howled as if the world had come to an end. It folded over itself, and Ming shouted, '*Leáigh! Leáigh!*'

In the illumination from the lightbeam the *nightghast* began to melt until its eyes sat atop a pool of black ooze, then the eyes dissolved, and Ming grabbed Lien's arm, forcing her to run.

'Quickly. The enchantment will not last. The Undead can never die.'

As a young lady, Lien had always walked sedately. Even as a child, she had been chided if her steps had been more than a swift walk. Now she was glad for breeches and boots, and she ran as if the *nightghast* was even now reaching to touch her shoulder. Round corners, along the damp narrow corridor. Forever, it seemed.

Flinging around a bend, she and Ming came to the end of the tunnel, almost blocked by a ruckle of boulders and they clambered over them, bursting into fresh night air. There were no sounds behind or ahead and the sickle moon shone a shy light across the tips of trees.

The stiletto's beam disappeared but Lien had no intention of letting go her knife and when she asked, 'Where now?', the words puffed out in tired exhalations.

'I suspect we have come out the other side of a chain of hills.' He pulled out the parchment and unfolded it, using night light to assess their location. 'There,' he said. 'The lake. Not far. If we can find our way there…'

'Then what? Fly? Can you magick a boat from your pocket as easily as your stiletto?' She knew she was angry but by the Gods she was exhausted. 'I have little strength left,' she added. 'So thirsty…' she muttered.

'Of course you have strength, Lady Lien; you do not deceive me. When I first met you…'

She shook her head, realising that he had taken her by the arm and was hurrying her along a narrow defile.

'It is a track made by wildlife.'

She looked back to check behind. 'How do you know they won't follow?'

'Speed is not their strength,' he said. 'They shamble and more often take folk by accident than design.'

'You are sure we head for the lake?' Gods she had a stitch in her side. She stopped, leaning over her knees. They felt as if they would dissolve, that she would collapse onto the path and never get up again. 'I cannot sustain this pace…' She was a lady, an embroiderer and noble from the First House of Silk. When would she have ever run to save her life?

He bent to help her stand straight. 'I am sorry, Lady, but we must make haste. Speed is all we have.'

'Along with your eldtritch stiletto,' she growled.

They ran, jumping over fallen logs and pushing aside ferny foliage. The moon led them, always a little ahead, and they followed its delicate ivory path until the lake stretched before them and over the lake, a reflected beam of moonlight paved a path from one shore into an unseen distance.

'There, I think, is our answer. The Moonlady in her generosity, has given us a road across the water. We are, quite simply blessed.' Ming sucked in deep breaths.

'I have heard of moonbridges in legend,' Lien croaked as she once again bent over the needle-sharp pain in her side. 'They aren't easy to cross and that one is so narrow…'

Ming surveyed the surface of the lake but said nothing.

'Please can we rest,' Lien begged, breath huffing in and out. 'I'm so thirsty and I need to breathe.'

'A moment only. We need to cross the bridge before dawn, and we have little time.'

Little time?

'How much?'

Ming looked up at the night sky. 'The moon has passed its zenith. We will be lucky to make the distance.'

Her heart sank. 'Then would we be better to walk around the lake and live than risk the moonbridge dissolving beneath our feet?'

But Ming didn't answer. 'Are you ready?'

No. Nor will I ever be.

But she sighed and followed him as he stepped from the shore onto the shoulder-width alabaster path. There was one heartbeat moment when she took stock – walking on a reflection which felt as solid as the rock path within the tunnel. It stretched for leagues in front of her and she picked up her pace as Ming's long legs covered more and more distance. She looked back and already in the night dark, the shoreline had vanished, no sign of the shadow-bulk of the trees. Her tongue cleaved the roof of her mouth, and she licked her lips.

So thirsty... all that water...

She slowed down, stopped, and looked into the dark, cool lake. It was like seeing a bowl of steaming dumplings when one is hungry, or a platter of crispy rolls. But it was just water, and she was so desperate.

She bent down and cupped her hand, the better to scoop a cool, refreshing mouthful.

Her hand dipped below the silken surface and she almost salivated. She thought she saw the flash of a sinuous pale shape but decided it was just the moonlight scattered on the water here and there and she held her hand in the water so it would fill.

'Lien! No...' Ming shouted.

Chilling fingers grabbed her wrist and a ghostly water creature, a woman with undulating hair, bitter eyes and a snarling smile, began to pull her off her knees.

She screamed...

Ming ran back toward Lien, his heart in his mouth. She was tipping forward, the grasp of the water sprite cruelly tight. Any moment and she would be dragged off the moonbridge and down into the dark, unlit depths, fighting for air and kicking with fear but held by the unrelenting grasp of the succubus until Lien's heart stopped. Only then would the water demon let go, all fun gone, and Lien would sink to the muddy darks to lie there and rot. The water demon, meanwhile, would swim on, looking for more prey.

Ming grasped the stiletto and reaching Lien, grabbed her shoulder, yanking her back hard and slashing down with his ugly right hand. The needlepoint found its mark and the creature shrieked, a high-pitched howl that echoed and re-echoed into the inky heavens. The evil hand slid away from Lien, and Ming pulled her up, holding her tight against him as she trembled.

'I hate this place!' she cried. 'I hate it!'

She pushed past him on the narrow moonbridge and began to run, and he loped after her, knowing it was impossible to talk and so they ran with just their footsteps and their breaths filling the air – all the while the moon moving a little further in the other direction to the western sky.

Lien's pace was steady for a long while, no doubt, Ming thought, because of the fear that drove her on and he wondered how much further before they reached the other side. He searched the distance and there! There, he was sure, a line of shadowy shore, and above the trees a vaguely lighter sky – opalescent, pearly, presaging sunrise and danger for them if they couldn't reach the edge of the lake in time.

He looked back and what he saw was terrifying, but he dared not tell Lien. As the moon sank lower, so the bridge dissolved behind, revealing a lake that began to glow with the dawn light.

'Come on!' he pushed Lien's back. 'Faster!'

Her heart was bursting, her throat on fire, the pain in her side like a knife. How could she run any faster? She dared a glance over her shoulder and saw the bridge disappearing and yelped, picking up her pace, seeing the shore, feeling the bridge become flimsy, soft, and with one last burst when she was sure her heart would stop beating, she leapt for the lake's edge, her toes dragging in the water. She crashed to hard ground, shoulder biting into the grit, sucking air in and out. Ming grabbed her and pulled her from the waterside, but she pushed him off and stood, walking in circles as she sucked in air and then puffed it out. In, out and her chest burned as if it were alight. She couldn't say a word.

Speech? What is that?

Ming was bent over, hands on knees. He glanced at her, but she invited no words and thankfully he left her to walk off the dreadful pains in her legs, in her chest, until she could walk no more. Sinking down onto a mossy bank, she laid her head back against the trunk of a beech tree – closing her eyes against the image of the lake and of the man who had caused her such terror. If it was possible to hate him any more, then she had reached that point.

He let her to sit alone.

What was there to say? She had faced such alarm in such a short space of time – how could he ever explain? His relationship with this beautiful young woman was forever sundered and it was entirely his fault. He walked a little, glancing back at the lake to see a dimpled surface, rippled by a welkin wind. The sky lightened – passing from opalescence to peach laced with gold shards as the sun rose above the trees.

As Ming's and Lien's breath slowed, the shore filled with the sounds of forest birds and waterfowl and a small dove grey rabbit skittered past.

'I'm thirsty...' her voice cracked, split with effort and so he withdrew a small costrel from his deep pocket and went to the lake edge, dipping it in, filling it with water that was silver and gold in the light of a newborn day. He passed it to her, and she drank greedily.

'Slowly, Lien, or you will vomit.'

'Just another high point…' she coughed and continued to sip, swilling the water around her mouth and then swallowing. Finally, she handed the costrel back. 'Thank you,' she said, and he was surprised.

She settled her back against the tree and he took a draught of the water himself, walking away from her to stare out over the lake.

Moonlady, thank you for what you did. I am in your debt. In your debt in so many ways. Your life was forever altered because of what I did. If you and Lien had stayed in the Han…

But of course, it wasn't true. Fate had other ideas. So he left the thoughts to disperse and instead began to think on the Han.

He wondered if First Minister had assumed governance of the province. He knew Sun Sen would be earnest and diligent, but he was an old man, and such responsibility would inevitably wear the First Minister down. *Don't be another casualty in this reprehensible debacle…*

'And now?'

He jumped. 'I'm sorry?'

'Where to now?' Lien's voice was split and worn with exhaustion, and she had deep shadows pooling beneath her eyes. Her clothes were creased and torn – nothing of the slim elegance in silk that he had seen in the Park of Singing Birds. His heart twisted just a little. So much potential for the ideal partner. All gone…

'The hill behind us,' he indicated the grassy slope that stretched up beyond the shaded lake side. 'From the top, you will see the orchard. Not far to safety.'

'So you say.' She levered herself up, feeling every joint and muscle stretch and groan like Old One's. How many times had she heard her blessed grandmother complain of the vicissitudes of age. She headed for the slope. 'Come on then. Before I collapse and die I would find safety in the glorious Seraphina's fine home.'

She heard the sourness in her comment but didn't care. She cared nothing at all for what she said to this intolerable man who accompanied her, nor how she said it. She wanted whatever needed doing done, and then she would ask for safe passage back to the Han.

They climbed the hill slowly. It rose gently and easily but she was so tired that every part of her legs screamed in angry protest until what spread before her made her suck in a breath. Never ever had she seen anything like it. A veritable inland sea of blossom and green leaf. Chartreuse, shell-pink and ivory and the thrilling call of hundreds of songbirds. The fragrance – floral and woody but laced with the scent of fruited apricot and peach. Above it all, the sky sparkled with a clarity that must surely be stuff of the imagination. Blue to infinity and not a cloud in sight.

'The Ymp Tree Orchard,' Ming said unnecessarily, and she didn't bother to reply.

And then noise – a frustrated, excited voice. 'Ming! Ming!' Followed by hoofbeats as a chestnut gelding puffed up the hill from the orchard.

Ming Xao sighed as the gelding, huffing wildly in and out, stumbled to a halt in front of them. 'Gallivant,' he acknowledged, as Maximilian reached the crest, huge tongue hanging out. He collapsed to sit on his haunches, panting in the early sun.

'Sink me! I could murder you, you fool. How dare you gallop off! And then your mare arrived back at the stable in such a lather and scared out of her wits! What happened? I thought you dead but Seraphina said no...' He scrutinised Lien and bowed. 'The Lady Lien? I am Gallivant, the hob.'

Hob? A quaint man-boy who chatters incessantly and is dressed in fine silks?

She knew nothing about hobs, had no idea about anything. Out of her depth completely in this foreign land. If only Heng was beside her, she would have had strength and support. She folded her hands tightly behind her back and remembered she knew one thing for sure, and it was all that mattered. Revenge is a small word, she thought, for such an overwhelming action.

Gallivant frowned, a slight crease between his brows as he straightened from his most perfect bow and studied her.

'Yes, I am the Lady Lien,' she acknowledged, thinking it best to say or think nothing else.

'Trouble?' Gallivant asked, his intent gaze sliding from Lien to Ming.

'In a manner of speaking,' the Emperor answered. 'But someone whom I never thought to see again came to my aid.'

'Oooh. We must talk…' the hob said excitely as he held tight to his reins. The horse nodded its head up and down furiously, rattling the bit and pulling at the hob's arms.

'Maybe so but not now. The lady has had her own narrow escape and is in need of care.'

'Then you must mount my horse, Lady Lien.' Gallivant said, holding out cupped hands for Lien to mount. 'Let it carry you to safety.'

She nodded and pushed past Ming, giving her leg to Gallivant to boost her into the saddle and then she let the two men do what they must to get her to safety.

Gallivant tried his best to draw her out but she was too tired to reply with more than the occasional word. She let his words fall over her like a soft woollen wrap and could almost have fallen asleep in the gentle air in which they travelled.

Ming was grateful for one thing only and that was that Lady Lien had once again subsided into silence. Pity then, that Gallivant didn't follow suit. Instead, he chattered to the lady, telling her of the orchard, asking about her knowledge of the Other world, about her health and welfare, about the Han. She answered with just a word here and there in between Gallivant's ceaseless babble and Ming thought that perhaps it was comforting for the woman, helping her relax. For sure, Gallivant was friendly and kind and it must make her feel safer.

They entered the foaming landscape that was the orchard, a thing of strange and eldritch beauty and at one of the gates with which Ming was familiar. His head flew up.

One *of the gates*…

I only know of four, he thought and yet already, he had experienced others. The way he and Gallivant had arrived in Trevallyn elsewhere than the orchard. The way he had arrived in Veniche elsewhere than the ballroom. So even though he had drawn a map, the truth was that there were myriad entries and exits to the Other world. Traps for a mortal whichever way they turned. He knew of the popular hearsay of portals to the Other world, the superstitions, but he wanted to shout, 'No! They are truths.'

Which begged the obvious thought – why in the Gods' names did his paltry map of four entrances and exits matter?

Was this an *excuse* for a deadly game for Immortals to play?

With possession of his map the task for the winner?

What then would be the prize? His death?

Surely Yue Lao would have known that it was a mere game. And Chi Nü. Was Heng even now just a dreadful casualty as they were all moved about the board?

They moved easily amongst the soft shade of the orchard where lush spring-green leaves and golden fruit hung in abundance. Soon they crossed a wide velvety swathe of grass, passing over a timber bridge laid across a ha-ha, and where the horse's hoofbeats echoed in the midday peace. Ahead of them, up a small rise, was a cleverly woven garden gate, and a hedge of privet that had been clipped and smoothed to a thickness that invited no prying eyes.

'I shall leave you here,' Gallivant pulled the gelding to a halt. 'If you would dismount, Lady Lien, I'll take the horse to the stables, and you can make your way to Seraphina.'

'But we don't know where to go,' Lien said as she dismounted, holding on to the horse's thick mane.

'Ming knows this place well, he'll take you. I shall see you anon.'

He clicked the horse onward, and Ming suffered Lien's angry glare.

'You know this place well? But of course. A pity then, if you were here before, that you didn't stay here.' She brushed past him and opened the withy gate. 'Just think of what could have been avoided. At the very least, my friend's life.'

A dagger mindfully thrown, and Ming felt the blade enter and turn. Why wouldn't he?

CHAPTER SIXTEEN

Ming and Lien

So he has been here before, she thought. She meant it when she had snarled back at him. What a pity indeed that he had not stayed here. So much to be avoided.

But inside the withy gate was a garden of such perfection that she stilled in her tracks. A sweep of thick green lawn cushioned her feet and led up to central steps which she assumed led further to a paved area, because the house behind, an elegant structure, had open double doors made with glass. She had never seen glass in buildings, but she had drunk from glass goblets imported from Veniche, so she was aware of its transparent nature. Even now, the early morning sun caught upon the windowpanes, reflecting tree canopies and sparkling with flashes of gold.

She heard a sharp intake of breath behind and turned around to glimpse the Emperor cradling his hand, his eyes shut and his expression one of intense pain.

'What happened to your hand?' She wasn't sure she cared, but there was something in his face...

'I... it was injured...'

'How?'

But as he went to answer, a woman's voice interrupted. An elderly lady stepped through the doors, homely looking, pleasing of face, of indeterminate age and with pale grey hair twisted into a bun at her nape. Small tendrils curled round her cheeks as she smiled.

'Finally, you are here,' she said. 'Come come. You must be in need of sustenance and care...'

So Lien and the Emperor climbed the wide stone steps, crossed the paving stones that were interspersed with sweet-smelling thyme and stepped into a spacious drawing room. Their feet tapped on polished boards as they passed a cedar table piled with books and deep chaises that looked as if one could be lost in the upholstery. The room smelled of beeswax and cedar oil and Lien took in every detail. Despite pervasive exhaustion, just observing this room cast a feeling of safety and well-being over her, like a warm wrap or a quilted robe.

'You must both need to eat, I think. Follow me to the kitchen...'

'May we wash?' Ming asked. His voice was strung tight, and he still cradled his hand.

'You can wash in the sink, eat and drink and then I will take you to your rooms where I have had baths filled for you.'

'Seraphina?' Ming asked as they followed the woman down a hall and into a wide kitchen where the smell of food made Lien's belly burble.

'She is elsewhere just now,' the woman replied. 'Wash yourselves in the kitchen trough.'

'But...' Ming chivvied.

'Madame Seraphina said not to concern yourselves. All will be well.' And such was the strong persuasive nature of the woman's words that Lien at least, was content to let things lie. She washed her hands with lavender scented soap in warm water and then she dashed water on her face, taking a linen towel from the woman to wipe herself dry. 'Thank you,' she said as she handed the towel back. 'You are very kind.'

'Not at all. And by the way, my name is Hester. I will leave you to eat in peace. You have only to say my name. I am always within reach...'

And with a sweep of the folds of her ankle length grey dress and calico apron, she left them, the kitchen door hushing shut behind.

Lien sat down, fatigue once again like a heavy weight on her head and shoulders. Her legs folded like a piece of paper, and she realised that they ached with stiffness. Everything hurt as she subsided at the table. As the air of this house wrapped around her and safety seemed implicit, every part of her body whispered and snarked to remind her of what she had been through. Her appetite began to fade but then the fragrance of the creamy white soup in front of her took hold. She picked up a spoon, as Ming was doing, and ladled a spoonful to her mouth, swallowing as she broke a chunk of steaming bread. The soup warmed her belly, and she swore it was magick as her aches diminished enough for her to eat more soup and to even sip at a goblet of ruby red wine. She glanced at Ming, realising he was having difficulty tearing at the bread with one hand and she broke off a piece and passed it to him. He looked up, surprise at the gesture written large on his face.

'Thank you…'

'No matter. You were going to tell me what happened to your hand…' She sat back, the goblet of wine in her hand.

'Was I?' He scrutinised her closely. He had the deepest brown eyes, but there was such an air in their depths. Sadness? Loneliness?

She squirmed under his gaze and said in a sharp voice, 'Well?'

'I was attacked by a nightghast. This…' he held up the hand, the claw of a cadaver, 'is an enchanted injury.'

'Then Seraphina will fix it, will she not? Enchantment is her strength as we would not be here otherwise.' She was well aware of the arrogance in her voice, no compassion for an injury that was obviously excruciating. She suspected he was a courageous man so to suck in his breath when it pained, he surely deserved a little sympathy?

But… dear Heng was dead and it was his fault. What is an injury compared to death?

He watched emotions flying across her face. She was so easy to read. It was something he had found charming in the Park of Singing Birds. He had seen interest then, wistfulness, courage even, because to flout the laws of etiquette and talk to a peasant about life was surely courageous in the Han. Such a pity that he had ruined it all, because he was so sure they could have lived a well-matched life.

'Perhaps,' he replied and continued to eat and drink. By the Gods – he was hungry despite his pain. Or perhaps it was Hester's food. He remembered that from when he had been here before. All food tasted excellent, and loss of appetite was unheard of. Hester was obviously an enchantress with food – it was most likely for anyone living in the house of the late, great Jasper of the Færan.

He pushed his bowl away, took the last of his bread and walked to the large window above the kitchen trough. A provender and medic garden stretched within a complicated pattern of interweaving hedges and he could almost smell the fragrance of herbs and vegetables from where he stood. Trevallyn was so perfect, and sometimes he wished he had been born to the simple life of a workman in the Han because then he could have left and made his home here, even in Other Trevallyn if the privilege had been allowed.

But as the Emperor, he had responsibilities. He was doomed to live the imperial life in the imperial palace in the imperial city until his death. His body would then be placed on a high rocky cast and left for the vultures and eagles to consume. Such a lonely life before death, which was why choosing someone of Lien's ilk to be his consort had been so right, so good. She would have made it all bearable.

He looked back at her. She had pushed her bowl away

and was sipping the red wine with her eyes closed. She was so beautiful – the three siofra were right. He'd not noticed it so much in the park. He was so entrapped by her manner, her voice, her enthusiasm for life that her comeliness had been of little consequence. In any case, it mattered little now because her antipathy toward him was clear. In addition, his life was as short as the thread around his wrist, so she would never have the chance to learn for herself that he might be a better person.

She sensed him turning away and opened her eyes.

Some part of her recognised the loneliness in his posture and there was a brief moment where she felt sadness for him, but she quickly quashed it. He had so much to answer for and by the Ancestors she would make him pay.

The door opened as she chewed the last of her bread and a woman of indeterminate age and great presence entered. She was the same height as Lien and had wild dark grey hair streaked with pale strands that looked like light-beams in a mist. The woman's hair had a life of its own, sweeping around her shoulders as she scrutinised Lien. Lien squirmed, so intense were the woman's almost-black eyes. Her blue linen gown was as pale as a wren's egg and over the top, she wore a linen apron the colour of a summer night. She smiled.

'Lady Lien, good day to you.' She took Lien's hand in her own, and turned it palm up to stroke the lines with a long index finger. 'So,' she added. 'You are she…' She fingered the red thread, rolling it back and forth.

'She what?' Lien asked dragging her hand from the woman. Her fingers sizzled and she crushed them into her other hand.

'Lady Lien, betrothed of the Emperor of the Han. A lady of great strength and strong opinion. Perhaps dare I say, misguided thought.'

Fury built and Lien flushed. 'No you dare not say, whoever you are. My thoughts are my own and not for anyone to consume and pass comment upon.'

'Ho,' the woman replied, unperturbed. 'I can see you and I may have a battle of wills. So be it...'

Ming walked from the window and bowed his head to the woman. 'Lady Seraphina. I am glad to meet you at last.'

Lien's eyes widened at the name as the enchantress took his good hand and gazed at the lines on his palm. 'Interesting,' she murmured before smiling again. 'Lord Ming Xao, it is good to finally meet you. We have difficult times, do we not?'

'Indeed madame. I can only apologise and beg for your help. I have already cost one loyal subject her life. Perhaps even more in my realm. I need your assistance and wisdom before worse happens.'

Seraphina pulled out a chair and sat at the table and Lien shivered. There was a swirling aura – nothing visual, more like a welkin wind, and it set the hairs standing on Lien's neck. That the woman could see into Lien's soul was possible and she knew she must erase her thoughts when in Seraphina's presence.

'Let me set your mind at ease for the moment,' Seraphina replied to Ming. 'Your people are safe. Your friend, Chi Nü, has worked diligently and hard to make sure the Han is momentarily protected from any wilful damage.'

Ming subsided onto a spare seat. 'Thank the Gods...'

'But,' Seraphina held up her hand. 'Others search for you, Lord Ming. The Hunt is bigger, more aggressive than they have ever been. Even if I can help destroy the map, I'm not sure that I can save *you*.'

Lien could barely stop her lips curving and Seraphina threw her a glance.

Gods, does she know?

'I know many things,' Seraphina said quietly, looking

at neither Lien nor Ming, 'but stopping Death requires the greatest magick. I am as yet untried...'

'I do not expect to be spared, Lady Seraphina. I merely want to right a grievous wrong. If my life is forfeit, then so be it.'

Seraphina gazed at him unblinking and said, 'We shall see,' as she reached out for his damaged hand.

Lien noted that the colours were still at the morbid stage, deathly, spectral and he winced as Seraphina prodded the bones. 'You have been touched by a nightghast.'

'Yes,' he replied, and a small nuisance part of Lien's heart contracted at the evident pain in his tone. Gods, how bad *was* his injury?

'I can help you with the pain, although what I dispense may cloud your judgment, but I doubt I can save your hand, Ming.'

Lien watched the exchange with horrified interest.

'I am aware,' he said. 'It is as it must be.'

At that, Lien sat straighter. He was so accepting, so phlegmatic...

'Lady,' he continued to Seraphina. 'Will you excuse me? I would walk through your garden.'

'Of course,' she replied. 'When you return, you must bathe and rest.'

He bowed his head and left quietly through the door, leaving an air of exhaustion and desolation behind. Outside, a pair of white doves flicked-flacked up from the paving stones and then floated down behind him as he walked to the small fountain in the centre of the potager.

Seraphina spoke into the peace of the kitchen. 'He is a good man who meant well. He recognises what he has done. A lesser man would not.'

'Perhaps,' Lien replied. 'But because of him, my friend is dead.' She felt the woman who sat with her hands clasped loosely in her lap would appreciate a truth. 'I find that difficult to forgive.'

'Time is what you need. And rest. Come with me now to your room. After you've slept, you will feel less like a taut wire and more like the woman Lord Ming believed could be his empress.'

Lien followed the enchantress along a hall to a wide staircase and then up to the first floor where a passage striped in sunshine traversed the entire width of the house. 'But then, I had no say in my betrothal and nor did I know him beforehand. Which makes this whole mess even worse.'

'Like I said, taut as a wire.' Seraphina swept her hand in front of her. 'This is your room. It has a view across the front lawns, quite beautiful really. And Hester has made sure your bath is filled and warm. There are clothes laid on the bed and if you want to sleep, do. You have been through great trauma, Lady Lien, and you need to resume your equilibrium. By the side of your bed, Hester has placed a jug of good wine and a goblet. It will help unlock your muscles. I shall leave you now and see you anon. Don't forget that you merely have to say Hester's name for her to be at your service.'

With that, Seraphina left the room like a wisp of mist, her linen gown and apron folding softly around her and her hair floating in some breeze of her making. Such an enigma, thought Lien, unable to determine if the woman was a seer, a magician, or just an eccentric woman who was playing both she and Ming like harp strings.

Ming wandered through the gardens, allowing the fragrance of mint, rosemary and thyme to lift his jaded spirits. He ran his fingers through the feathery foliage of a huge fennel, the aroma momentarily waking him. He tried to think of nothing, but every inch of him ached with an exhaustion that threatened to pull him to the ground. He spotted two benches at the corner of one of the clipped knots and shaded by a vast oak which was filled with birds twittering at his approach. They were not songbirds and for a moment, he longed to be in the Park of Singing Birds, opening just one more bamboo cage and allowing another linnet to find its freedom. He fingered the red thread – but not even the idea that Fate had marked him could pierce his utter exhaustion and so the little wrens and finches sang to him and presently, his eyes grew heavy.

Somewhere deep in his mind, he knew he dreamed but whatever, he felt sucked into an inevitable vortex, the one he'd been running from for days and which had now caught up with him as he slept. He had unfolded the map and was holding it out in his poisoned hand. To whom he could not see but there was laughter and the flash of something and then the map was gone.

But there was much blood and he cried out, becoming soaked in gore and knowing that he would die because there was no one to help him. He shifted and groaned with pain and then there was a touch.

'Lord Ming, wake.' A gentle voice. 'Lord Ming, I am here…'

He opened his eyes, sweat pouring down his face.

'You dream. You are safe.' Seraphina sat next to him.

'But I am not,' his voice croaked in reply. 'Truth be told, I am not safe and have little time left.'

Seraphina's face, remarkably unlined except for a fan of lines at her eyes, twisted and she replied, taking his good hand and stroking it, rolling the red thread back and forth. 'Perhaps. Perhaps not. I am not sure. But things will reveal themselves. One thing I do know is that there will be a price to pay.'

'It is what the Pymm ladies said.'

'Ah, the siofra – you met Iolanthe, Flavia and Amaranthe.'

'Yes. They cared for Lien…'

'They are good women. Ming,' Seraphina shifted to face him more directly. 'Have you dreamed before?'

'In the context of the map? No. I have not slept much at all, since leaving the Han. It was too dangerous. Except in Veniche when Gallivant drugged me. This,' he gestured at the garden, 'is the first time since then.'

'So you dropped your defences. My dear, you are very tired,' she said. 'I would that you went to your room, bathed and slept. In this house you will revive, I assure you. Ah, I think I hear busy feet...'

As she spoke, Gallivant and Max emerged from a clipped archway in the privet hedge. 'Sink me, there you are! I've been twiddling my thumbs for an age, waiting. Is he hale, Seraphina?'

'As hale as we can hope for, Gallivant, except for a *night-ghast* injury.'

Gallivant's face fell open. 'No! When? I thought I managed to get you here unscath...'

'It was when I left you. My fault. My hand...' Ming held out his right hand which was again drifting through the primary phase – bruised, yellow and swollen with fluid.

'But it gets worse, it is what happens!' Gallivant exclaimed. 'By the stars, Ming, I know it does...'

'Yes.' What else could he say?

Seraphina broke in. 'I have told him I can give him something for the pain, Gallivant, but more than anything, he needs to bathe and sleep, so I would that you took him upstairs to his room. It is the one he slept in during his last visit.'

If Seraphina was admonishing Ming in that last comment, he didn't feel it. Besides, it was true. He wanted a bath, and then to sleep the sleep of the Dead. Well, perhaps not the Dead. Not yet.

'Lord Ming,' Seraphina stood. 'You will find some medic on a tray by your bed. It will help ease the pain and when you wake, you will feel a little better. One thing...' She held a finger to her lips and then frowned. 'The map. May I have it?'

Ming started. The map? How did he know he could trust someone he had just met?

'You can, believe me.' Her voice was soft.

His eyes opened wide and he flushed, feeling into his pocket for the small sealed canister. He held it out with his injured hand which had changed to shroud-white.

Seraphina reached to pluck it from him but a shock coursed up his arm and his fingers closed involuntarily. 'Madame, I am *not* doing that! I swear! Take the map, please!'

She tried to pluck it from him again and again his fingers closed hard. He looked aghast at Seraphina. 'What is happening? Please help me.' His arm burned with the shock that had run for a second time from his fingers to his armpit as his ugly, poisoned fingers once again uncurled.

'Calm yourself, Ming. It would appear you and only you can hold this map. I was not expecting this, and I am unsure why it is so.' She stared at his trembling fingers, puzzled and concerned. 'Put it back in your pocket, Ming Xao. There is no point trying again. I see now that you and only you can destroy this map but how it is to happen, I have no idea. Please excuse me. I now have much work to do to find out what is to occur. And you, dear man, have a body to rest and regird. I shall see you on the morrow.'

She walked away, a determined stride but gracefully upright, her hair waving and her shades-of-blue linens moving around her body.

'Well!' Gallivant jumped up from the opposite bench, fizzing with his customary energy. 'That was a strange turnabout. Come on, let's get you sorted.'

They walked together around the paths between the knot gardens and through the open kitchen door.

'I really don't need to show you where to go, do I?' Gallivant asked.

'Not really,' Ming had done talking and allowed the hob to chatter away.

'By the stars, dear man, Lien's beauty is symphonic. I swear I could hear some heavenly orchestra playing. Entrancing! I can see why you wished to become betrothed to her. Ah, here we are…' He pushed the bedroom door ajar and they went in. 'Hester's done her work I see. There's the bath,' he pointed toward a small room from which lacy steam emerged. 'And there is the medic – it's a liquid. Follow the syrup with some wine, it won't hurt. But perhaps when you get *out* of the bath. We don't want you insensible and like to drown now that you've come this far.' He turned and looked at Ming. 'You're beyond listening, aren't you? Have your bath. I shall return when you are done to make sure you need nothing else.'

'I don't…'

'No arguments. Go.' And like Hester and Seraphina, the hob and Max disappeared out the bedroom door, quietly for a change. Ming took a deep breath, soughed it out and went to the bathroom to bathe.

Lien thought she slept without dreams. But when she stirred much later, after strips of gold had stitched themselves down the sides of the curtains at the windows, she had a vestige of something in her memory. Something chilling. But it was so faint – as if she looked at it through muslin, and so she let it drift away, stretching in the bed and realising that her aching muscles were now butter-soft.

She stepped to the windows, opening each pair of curtains to reveal a green landscape, a sweeping carriageway, avenues of oaks and elms. Birds singing. Somewhere a dog barked. A deep throaty sound for sure and then she heard a male voice and a laugh. The voice was a pleasant tenor. Ah, the hob-man. Gallivant? He seemed pleasant enough and he *had* been trying to put her at her ease. But he had looked at her curiously, as if he had discovered something secret that upset him.

Do these folk read minds?

The woman, Seraphina, had examined Lien deeply.

Do they know?

The forgotten dream flooded through her memory, and she felt a surge of fear, but then exultation, righteousness. She had seen racks of dried herbs, bottles of liquids with labels. Her hand had reached for one…

Somehow, she must banish the thoughts from her mind, else she had no chance of avenging Heng. Good Heng who had been her maidservant for three years. Kind, quiet, efficient, anticipating every need. She was Lien's right hand and tears pricked Lien's eyes. My friend, she thought. My companion. She shared my dreams – we could have done so much together when I became Empress. Instead, she drowned. Her greatest fear – water travel – because the poor peasant girl could not swim. And all because we had to run for our lives…

Footsteps tapped along the corridor and there was a slight knock at the door – genteel and soft. 'Lady Lien? It is Gallivant.'

She grabbed a woollen wrap from a chair and flung it round her shoulders. 'Come in…'

The door opened and the giant dog pushed in, his tail wagging. Gallivant followed as Lien bobbed down to greet the dog. 'I saw your curtains open. Did you sleep well?'

'I did. I gather I slept right through half of yesterday and all last night.'

'You did. So did the Emperor.'

She ignored this and took the dog's big face in her hands. 'He's a beautiful dog. What is his name?'

'Oh, I didn't tell you yesterday, did I? Maximilian, Max, Maxi. Whatever you like on any given day. He's a good man and if you keep playing with his ears like that, he'll be your servant forever.'

She laughed. 'I could do worse. If I dress and have

something to eat, would Max take me for a walk?' Max tilted his head as she spoke, and his tail swept back and forth.

'He says yes,' Gallivant said.

'He does?'

'The tail. Get dressed and come to the kitchen. Hester has made a porridge that is creamy lightness, and it will fill you with energy.'

'Porridge?'

'A milk-dish made with oats. You will like it. Come Max. We shall see you anon, Lady.'

He walked to the door, the dog pushing past him and as the door closed, she began to wash and dress. All she wanted was food and to feel the weight of grief lifting, just for a moment. She knew it was grief – the sadness, the furious anger, the exhaustion. She grieved for Heng, it was a given, but she also grieved for the Han and for Old One. For her parents she had but one moment, but they were so infrequently a part of her life, lost in the interminable business and social demands of a First House, that Old One had been her mainstay. Teller of stories, wiper of tears, kissing her on the forehead and telling her she was Old One's little love. Her hands were the ones that had taught her to stitch with such excellence and it was her words, not her parents', that had encouraged her to believe that she *could* be a consort. And now, what were the chances of her ever seeing Old One again? So slim…

These thoughts, as she buttoned the clothes that had been left for her, were to be buried, concealed from all in this household and so she pushed them to a farflung shelf in her mind. She brushed her hair into a high, swinging tail, glancing at the cursed red thread that was revealed as her sleeve fell back.

She fingered it, tugged at it to try and break it as she had done so often, but it didn't yield – as fresh as the day Yue Lao had tied it round her wrist. What Fate awaited her?

She thought this so often when the thread caught her eye. It hung on her wrist, reminding her that Fate is everything. Inexorable…

She tugged her sleeve down angrily and pulled on short leather boots that sat by the door, and then slammed the door behind her with no good grace.

CHAPTER SEVENTEEN
Lien and Ming

She was sure the whole Other world was bewitching her in the most evil way. Old One had taught her love and respect, to never hurt living things.

'My darling child, there is a way the Universe has of turning upon those who seek to injure others. The Gods sit and watch. So do your Ancestors. It is worth remembering.'

Lien had never seen Old One harm or hurt. Even when she was wronged by a servant, she merely inclined her head, smiled gently and said softly, 'Never mind…' Once, her dog, an old bitch-dog with a flat nose and copious hair, had bitten Old One badly when she had attempted to lift the animal.

'She is sore with age. I understand her pain, poor little thing. We shall not chide her. I will have the apothecary make up a pain tincture to drop in her food.' She hadn't asked the apothecary for something to treat the painful bite but he had made a paste of garlic, mustard oil and plantain leaves anyway and it healed without damage or complaint.

If she knew Lien planned to avenge Heng, what would Old One say?

The look of probable disappointment in Old One's eyes haunted Lien's dreams and yet her fury at Ming Xao was greater than any hurt her grandmother might feel. But by the stars, the pull and tug on her soul made her head ache.

'You look unhappy, Lady Lien,' Hester was waiting at the bottom of the stair – tall as a beanpole, upright, aware

– always sharply aware. 'Is aught wrong? Was the chamber not to your liking?'

'I have rarely been so comfortable, thank you.' Lien knew they had drugged her, but she had been too tired to care, and it had been such a reprieve to feel nothing – no fear, pain, grief or anger. 'In fact I am grateful beyond belief. The wine...' she frowned as she searched for the right words. 'The wine was perhaps just what I needed.'

Hester's glance lingered, causing a flush to spread across Lien's cheeks, and then she nodded. 'Good. Then follow me and we shall feed you. Gallivant said that after you have eaten, to go to the garden and he will send you and Max off on your little walk around the grounds. Seraphina is busy momentarily.'

'She works on Ming Xao's behalf?'

Hester dipped her head. 'These are trying times and she is seeking answers. She said that time is of the essence.'

Something in her tone made Lien's stomach turn over. 'Hester, are They close?'

'Ah...'

'Please,' Lien reached for the woman's sleeve. The knitted cloth was warm under her fingers and felt as soft as baby's down. 'I have been running for an age. I need to know that the enemy is not close by...'

Hester's eyes hooded and she rubbed her forehead. 'There is news on the wind that the Hunt is coming. The skies rumble in the far northeast as They set out from Veniche. But Lady Lien, I promise you are safe here. Seraphina's land is unassailable.'

'Even by the Hunt? Does *Their* magick not counter hers?'

'She is as strong as we need her to be. Now, eat, Lady, for I have warmed porridge for you and there is honey and cinnamon. And if you like toast, I have apricot and almond confit to spread upon it.'

Lien had no idea what confit was and despite that the

Hunt might be here any day or any hour, she found she *was* hungry and so sat at an oak table as Hester placed a bowl of creamy porridge before her. She laid a silver spice shaker on the table and a small silver dish of honey with a spoon whose bowl was moulded in the shape of a beehive. Such implements would have been strange to anyone but a First House resident, where goods from outside the walls of the Han were imported, used with curiosity, and then marvelled about.

She sweetened the bowl of creaminess, then added some cinnamon and spooned the porridge into her mouth. It was like eating a soft cloud and it warmed her very soul. Perhaps it too was enchanted as she found herself focusing on nothing but the food, until a thought struck her.

'Hester, where is the Emperor?'

'He still sleeps, Lady Lien. He suffers great pain and so Seraphina treated him with milk of the poppy. He carries a great weight and needs to rest so that he can do what must be done.'

'The map?'

Hester nodded. 'It will not be easy. And his life will be at stake.'

'So *he* says,' Lien said tartly.

'You do not believe him?' Hester frowned at Lien's manner.

'I'm not sure what I believe anymore.' She knew she sounded wistful, and she sighed. 'This journey has been so hurtful and even now I do not understand how this threat can matter to Others who can change an entrance or an exit with the click of their fingers. And yet, *They* seem to want vicious revenge. I feel overwhelmed by the magnitude…'

She spoke the truth as half of her, the good half, warred with the half that was angry and vicious.

'Do not be,' said Hester kindly, her hand smoothing Lien's shoulder. 'Seraphina has a way about her. You will see.'

She turned to the door as a voice called her. Seraphina's call, thought Lien. 'Now I will leave you to enjoy what is left of your meal. If you need anything, just call my name. When you are done, make your way to the knot garden and you will find Gallivant and Max under the oak.'

There was a fleeting moment when Lien wondered if Hester had meant for her not be angry or vicious, or even overwhelmed, but the housekeeper was gone in the blink of an eye and Lien spooned the comforting porridge into her mouth, feeling splintered edges sanded away and breathing a little easier.

Ming woke briefly, his mouth tacky and he reached for the mug of cool water that had been left by the bed. His head pained him, and his limbs ached prodigiously, heavy with uneasy lassitude, his skin touchy. He shivered and pulled at the heavy quilt, laid his head back on the down pillow and lapsed into an erratic doze.

Sweaty then cold, hot again and a cool hand against his forehead. A woman's voice.

'He has a fever.'

'Is it his wound?' Another woman's voice.

'I believe it might be. But I think not *yet* badly enough to presage any danger.' Cool fingers held his damaged hand, the voice wondering. 'There, so curious. That red thread. It's almost as if it prevents the poisoning from spreading further. See? It's like a dam beyond which no flood can spread.'

'What is the red thread? Do you know?' A man's tenor voice. Ming tried to open his eyes but they were weighted with lead. Gallivant. Gallivant's voice…

'I have heard the odd tale, nothing more.' The women's voices became difficult to separate and Ming was limp and confused.

'Can you help him?' Gallivant's tones seeped into the tangled thoughts in his head.

'I must get some herbs. In between times, you must keep him cool when he is sweating and warm when he shivers. Hester, you must make sure he takes a little water. Not too much. He may purge.'

The voices faded and Ming's dreams lurched from wispy memory to awful nightmare and at times he thrashed his arms.

A woman, Hester perhaps, would take his good hand and hold it and rub cooling cloths across it and across his forehead. But for the most time he lurched between Heaven and Hell and wished they would drug him again so that he didn't have to think or feel at all.

Time passed and there was the pressure of a goblet against his lips. He didn't care what it tasted like, just that it was cool.

'What do you give him?' Hester's voice?

'Elixir of sweet wormwood.' This more authoritative voice must be the healer. Ming tried to recall her name but it wouldn't come through the haze. 'It will ease his fever. I also have a potion of elderflower, yarrow and white willow bark. But I would try the wormwood first.'

Vaguely he swallowed, the wormwood trickling down his throat. The cold liquid was like snow and ice and he thanked the Gods.

'But what then?' Hester again – her lovely mellow tones deeper with concern.

'When the fever has settled, I would give him a little poppy. He needs to sleep. He has a gargantuan task ahead and needs all his strength to manage it.'

'By the stars! You know, don't you?' Gallivant's voice.

'Yes.'

'What?' Hester's and Gallivant's voices together, but Ming felt himself falling as Seraphina replied.

'For his ears only, my friends.'

Lien made her way along a white pebbled path – small, crushed stones that crunched as she walked. Around her the garden lived its own life – butterflies fluttered here and there, bees worked with purpose from flower to flower until heavy with pollen they made their way back to withy hives that were lined up against a far-off hedge. The birds, from paunch-bellied doves to tiny finches and wrens, from hens who clucked across the potager pulling at worms to sky larks high above, filled the surroundings with morning song and there was a moment when Lien felt such an ache for the Park of Singing Birds and for the chirrup of the linnets that the old men had in cages which they hung from the trees.

In a moment, she had an image of a young man with a straw *dǒulì* on his head and a cage with a pure-toned linnet. She remembered him opening the door and letting the linnet jump upon his finger and then holding her breath as he carefully withdrew the bird. There was a moment when the bird looked around, bright eyes looking at her, tilting its head, and then the peasant who held his hand aloft. The bird took wing and Lien recalled her breath releasing in a gush of pure envy for the bird and its freedom.

She envied the bird even more now, constrained as she was by the evil circumstance that surrounded her. She looked around. Even this beautiful garden was as walled as the Middle and Small Gardens of the First House of Silk. She was destined to forever be a prisoner, for sure.

And when she had fulfilled her plan, any likely freedom would be done. Religious walls would close around her and her living and sleeping hours would be defined by the holy framework of prayer and service. And guilt.

A part of her wondered if she deserved to retreat to the monastery. Somewhere the words '*You Shall Not Kill a Living Being…*' whispered on the light breeze that shifted the young oak leaves so they rustled like silk.

She would have broken the Divine Law. No matter that

she had tried to protect a realm from future harm. In truth, her life should have been forfeit. Perhaps it still would be.

Was she scared?

Only as scared as Heng must have been. So she would be brave and honest for Heng's sake.

And besides, had not the Emperor broken the Divine Law when Heng had been killed? He had done it…

A throaty bark dragged her from the heaviness of her thoughts, and she looked up to see Max raising himself from a sunbask, stretching his massive forelegs and then shaking himself so that shining tendrils of drool flew across the garden like dew-bedecked spiders' webs. He nuzzled her hand.

'Good morning, Maximilian.' She fondled his ears and he leaned hard against her, almost knocking her down. 'And where is your master?' She looked around but there was neither sight nor sound of the hob and so she added, 'Then you shall have to be my escort around the grounds. Shall we begin?' He looked up at her as she placed her hand on his back and they walked, he with an air of purpose and authority.

They passed beneath an arch cut into the hedge, a mirror of the one that had led into the garden from the Ymp Tree Orchard. She tried to find that place as she and the dog walked but it was as though everything had shifted in order to confuse, and if that was the case, and she was sure it must be, why did Ming's map matter at all? Surely Others could waft their magick and move all entrances and exits on a daily basis.

She must ask someone. Hester? Possibly. Gallivant? If she could get a word in edgewise. Seraphina? If and when the wise woman ever put in another appearance.

They were now walking across a square of dense lawn, surrounded on all sides by buildings. She ventured into one and there was a herringbone paved floor, giant struts holding up the roof – big flying buttresses amongst which pigeons perched and cooed. The building housed a plethora of garden tools and nothing more. Another with the same arching roof was filled with barrels, sacks and bins filled with barley and oats, with loose hay piled along the wall and a pitchfork lying in front as if someone had just stepped outside for a moment. From the third side of the lawn she could hear snorts, the scraping of hooves and paving and when she and Max entered, three heads turned from stalls to observe. Ears flicked back and forth and one, an elegant grey horse, nickered. There was a bucket of apples at the door and Lien picked up three, offering one each to the horses. They dripped juices and crunched in pleasure as she and Max walked out the door.

Such an odd place – no one around anywhere. Where was everyone?

'Max, where are the retainers? Who does the work here?'

Max sat and scratched at his ear with a jingle of his collar. His face wore the somewhat aloof expression Lien associated with owls. He shook himself, more drool flying so that she had to step back and then he pushed under her hand to move her on. He obviously had no answers.

The final building was filled with carriages and carts and a wall was lined with trusses holding saddles and collars; hooks hung with bridles and harness and there was a heady aroma of oiled and polished leather. Such an enigma. Who polishes the harness? Who cares for the horses? Who harvests the grain, the hay?

Together, she and the dog walked under an archway which housed a dovecote and the doves burbled in a sonorous way. So much of this place slept, Lien thought. The birds were soft in tone and flight, the flowers waved gently in the mild breeze, the horses were quiet and relaxed, even her own footsteps could barely be heard and Max's, not at all. It was enchanted, without doubt. Enchanting? She hoped not, she needed her wits sharp and at the forefront.

They followed a path and above them, the sun had moved to its highest point, cloaking the surrounds in a golden glow. When they approached a bend with a seat, she and the dog stopped for a moment as she had thought to rest and think, for there was surely a lot to digest. Seraphina's domain seemed like a ghost-house and she would love to ask so many questions if there had been someone to accompany her. As it was, she felt ill at ease, as if she were watched from somewhere, and yet by whom? And why?

On the far edge of the park, she noticed a wooden building – edged on two sides by wide windows and a door. Its roofline echoed the high-pitched roofs of the outbuildings and atop the pitched front was a finial fashioned in bronze with verdigris spreading in a viridian tide.

She set off without Max who watched her for a moment before thumping up beside her and nudging his nose under her hand. She laughed at him and let her hand slide along to his shoulder, but he swung in front of her and pushed her with his head, once, twice.

'Max! Are you turning me away? I want to see what is in that building. Stop it!' She spoke sternly and shook her finger at him, but he growled and pushed at her again. 'Leave it, Maximilian. You can come with me nicely or not at all. Bad dog!'

She skirted round him and ran the last few steps to the small house and Max, defeated, trailed behind her. But she didn't care. This was a place of mystery and by his very actions, Max had told her it was forbidden to her. All the more reason to investigate.

She looked through the sparkling windows. The ceilings were hung with plants – rack after rope after string. Against the far wall she could see bookshelves almost bending under the weight of tomes big and small. Long tables stretched the length of the windows, with neat arrangements of glass vials, mortars and pestles, knives, cutting boards stacked on top of each other and baskets filled with stoppered bottles, flasks and jugs.

Lien sucked in a breath.

Her dream...

Her dream indeed, promising mayhem, lay before her.

It required merely a hand on the doorlatch, a little push.

As she took a step, Max barked. But she ignored him and put her weight against the door. He growled, a deep rumble in his throat and when she turned to him, there was nothing of the gentle giant. His teeth were bared, and the drool fell in sheets, his hackles stood and his massive head was lowered, eyes cold and menacing. He advanced and grabbed at her, but she stepped quickly inside and slammed the door on him, leaning against it as he barked loudly. Then his bark became fainter, and she saw him galloping over the park and round the bend where the seat stood underneath the oak, still lit gold and promising peace.

He's gone to get someone, I know it! I have only a moment...

She raced to the books, inhaling the air of dried plants and crushed herbs, knowing the written Trevallyn script would mean nothing to her and wondering how she would decipher what she needed. There were hundreds of books.

She spun round and saw shelves with ground plants in jars, other jars with tinctures and potions and all with labels, none of which she could read. She groaned, running her fingers along the shelves looking for something, anything. Each jar was numbered and everything in meticulous order.

Numbers...

She knew numbers from foreign lands – had learned them from her father's invoices within the First House of Silk.

There must be a ledger or a catalogue. At the very least a notebook – something that indicated what each of the jars contained. She scanned the space, desperate now, and anger, resentment, hatred of Ming Xao built in her heart like some noxious poison. If only she could bottle it and drip it into his wine.

She hit the edge of the table in animal frustration and pages jumped next to her – a thick notebook bound in red leather. She grabbed it and there written in a black-as-night ink – Number One. There were words next to it – she had no idea what, and a number of stars, perhaps something indicating its efficacy. The next and the next after that, three stars, five stars. Until a number of pages further on, Number Twenty with a red circle with a line through it.

She flicked a few more pages, and there, another red circle with a line. No stars. Something told her this symbol meant danger, perhaps death. She noted the number fifty five and flew to the shelves, running along them, looking for the corresponding numbers.

It sat on its own – a tiny bottle with a cork pushed deep into the neck. She grabbed it and held it to the light as she heard Max barking again – getting closer. The viscous brown liquid inside slid back and forth and she had a feeling this was a powerful poison. Lethal even…

She shoved it into the waist of her trousers and then grabbed a book of flowers and subsided to the floor as Max's paws thumped against the door. It flew open as Gallivant's voice spoke sternly.

'Cease Max! Cease!' The dog, obedient, became quiet and shook himself. He sat and eyed Lien. He had been her friend and now it was almost as though he could see inside her mind and his opinion of her had changed momentously. No more tender ear rubs.

'Lady Lien, what are you doing here?' Gallivant's voice dripped ice.

'I saw the building and it's so charming, I wanted to see what it contained.'

'Then may I say that is rather rude of you to do so without permission. This place is Seraphina's workroom and none of us has ever dared come inside.'

Lien pushed the botanical encyclopaedia back amongst the others, making sure it was neat. 'There was nothing to indicate I shouldn't enter, Gallivant,' she added as she pushed past him to breathe the park air. 'No signs, no locks.'

'Seraphina has never had need of locks. Till now.'

'Oh by the stars, I have done nothing wrong! I sat on the floor reading a book on flowers!' She snapped at him – tired of the subterfuges that leaked from the very air of this place like the sparking air before a thunderstorm.

Gallivant pulled the door behind him, slamming it hard. She wondered how often he displayed anger. 'You trespassed against the woman who is trying her best to help you and to save the life of your Emperor.'

'My *Emperor* shouldn't have done what he did and then he wouldn't need saving.' Gods, but she sounded hard. Was it h*er* voice that answered so caustically? What had happened to the person Old One loved?

'Perhaps you are right, but in any case, right now he is desperately ill. I don't put too fine a point on it when I say Seraphina is concerned.'

Lien's heart stopped and then raced again as her fingers grazed the waistband of her trousers. 'You say?'

'Indeed. But then you obviously care little.'

She stopped for a moment and pushed errant strands of hair from her face. 'But I do, Gallivant,' she replied with feigned empathy. 'I care very much.'

Gallivant grabbed her hand, pulling her closer to his fine face. 'But about what, I ask, Lady Lien? And tell me,' he fingered the red thread on her wrist, 'where did you get this? The Emperor has one the same.'

'They were tied on our wrists by Yue Lao, the God of Fate. It is impossible to remove them. They fall off when one meets one's Fate.'

'Huh,' Gallivant examined the thread and then let her hand go, brushing his hands together as if they had been tainted by touching her. 'Then perhaps the Emperor will live a while yet as his is still intact. For myself I am glad. I suspect you might be less so.'

A rush of fury coursed around her body – hot and blood red so that she was sure her face flushed bright. 'What I think and feel is mine to think and feel, Gallivant.' She left him then, quickening her pace, feeling the poison at her waist chafing at her skin and when she reached the house, she stormed inside, meeting no one thank the stars, before running up to her room swiftly and slamming the door. She looked for a key to lock it but there was none – it seemed this house was considered enchanted enough to protect anyone, even her.

And yet she had been able to enter Seraphina's work room at will and find something she knew would avenge Heng and speed the Emperor on his journey to the Ancestors.

Seraphina obviously trusted those on her domain far too much.

CHAPTER EIGHTEEN
Ming and Lien

Ming lay still, too afraid to move for fear the pain and sweats would launch across his body once more.

It was obviously night as the curtains were drawn across the windows and flickering lamps cast a subtle glow around the room. He turned his head a little and saw the hob seated at a table, a book open, but his head lay on the pages and his hand dangled down by his side.

The huge dog, Maximilian lay facing Ming, eyes open and staring at him.

Ming moved his hand from under the quilt – the injured hand, the one that was obviously set to kill him eventually. He let it flop, and the dog pushed himself up and padded over, as silent as a shade. Ming had thought to pat him, pain or no, as the dog was a wondrous beast, loyal and gentle and…

But Max had smelled Ming's hand and backed away, sneezing, great exhalations of drool and air as he shook his head.

'Sssh, Max, shhh…' Gallivant jerked up his head. 'Oh. You are awake.' He ran fingers through his fine wispy hair as he walked to Ming's bedside. 'How do you fare?'

'Weak as a newborn kitten.'

'You have been very ill, Ming Xao. I suspect without Seraphina's potions, by now, the nightghast poison might have spread. Although Seraphina says that your quaint red thread is warding off evil.'

Ming lifted his injured hand. It felt as heavy as an anvil and whilst there was a shadow of an ache, it was true, something was fighting to hold it at bay. The red thread lay where it had been since the moment he had met Yue Lao and even to his exhausted eyes, it was obvious that above the thread, his arm was healthy whereas below, it looked like exhumed flesh.

'Do you think my hand rots?' he asked, knowing he didn't care for the answer.

'Um, that is the sort of question,' Gallivant answered with caution, 'you would need to ask Seraphina. I'm just a hob, not a healer.'

Ming smiled, his head cradled by pillows covered in fine linen and thick with down. 'And a very fine hob too. I owe you for your care of me.'

'Not so good really.' Gallivant poured water into a mug. 'Else you would not now be fighting for your l…' he stopped and placed the water flask back on the table. 'Fighting this illness that has halted you temporarily. Here,' he held the mug to Ming's lips. 'Seraphina's instructions – you must drink plenty of water and when the clock strikes midnight, you must have some more of this medic that she has made for you.'

'Where is she?' Gods, the icy water felt wonderful as it slid down Ming's parched throat.

'She sleeps. She has been working hard with all manner of potions to find what she can to make things easier for you. Do you *feel* easier?'

'I feel very little pain so whatever she has concocted is a miracle. And I'm still alive…' He fingered the red thread.

'The Lady Lien has a thread too.'

'Yes…'

'Is it true they can't be removed? That they will fall away when you meet your Fate?'

Ming frowned, the effort costing him much. His weakness did not bode well for whatever he needed to do to placate those who hunted him. 'So the legend says.'

Gallivant humphed and busied himself pouring liquid from a small jar into a mug of wine.

'Is the Lady Lien well?' Ming asked.

'Oh yes!' Gallivant scoffed and then as a whisper, 'Sink me! Too well, if you ask me.'

'I heard you,' Ming said.

'Then I'm sorry if I offend, but she is wilful and rude and shows no respect to someone like Seraphina.'

'You say?' But Ming knew Gallivant was right. The woman he had delivered to Seraphina's door was a very different woman to the one he had known in the Han.

'Why on earth did you betroth yourself to someone so wayward?'

Why indeed, Ming thought. But he told Gallivant about the wonderfully alert, excited woman he had met in the Park of Singing Birds and how they shared ideals of freedom. He made no mention of her beauty because for him, that was mere skin-deep. It had been the other side, the curiosity in and a desire for an alternate life to the one she lived at the time. He related so well to that.

'Yes, well!' Gallivant tidied the table. 'Sharing ideals is all very well but I think you should have examined her manner a little more before committing yourself.'

'What do you mean?' Whatever strength Ming had was ebbing fast and it was all he could do to keep his eyes open. Somewhere down the stair a case clock chimed the midnight hour and Gallivant approached him with the next dose of medic. But Ming held up a hand, the injured one, and Gallivant shuddered at the sight. It was in its cyclic third stage – the rotting corpse moment which normally created such pain but which, thanks to whatever drugs he had been given, at that moment seemed inconsequential. 'What?'

'Here, drink this.' Gallivant held the mug to Ming's lips as he said, 'She has no scruples, Ming. There is something not quite right. Even Max senses it.'

'Not quite right?'

'She hides something.'

Of course she did. She's grieving the loss of her only friend and she has been forced to leave her home. Ming tried to get the words out but he fell backward onto a cloud and drifted away and the words dissolved as he slept.

Lien had refused food and had allowed no one to enter her room by the simple expedient of pushing a chair under the door handle. Gallivant had remonstrated, becoming more waspish by the moment until Lien finally raised her voice.

'Leave me alone, hob! I want peace and you are not allowing it. Go away!' She shouted this last and when no answer came and she could hear his quick steps down the stair, she heaved a sigh of relief.

A short while later there was a gentle knock and Hester's comforting voice said, 'Lady Lien, there is a tray outside your room. If you are hungry, avail yourself. We will leave you alone.'

Lien waited until she heard the footsteps moving away and then removed the chair, opened the door and examined the tray. There was a pot of hot tea, tendrils escaping from the spout, a fine white porcelain cup and saucer and under a lawn napkin, neat triangles of bread with creamy butter spread across. There was also a small ceramic pot of honey with a beehive spoon.

She lifted the tray inside and ate and drank. The tea was fragrant and reminded her of her home with its cleansing, grassy flavour. Tears sprang to her eyes and she dashed them away. She would not succumb, no matter that she felt as if a great wave broke over her and threatened to drown her. She ate the bread and honey and then poured another cup of the fragrant tea and walked to the window, gazing at the gilt-edged light as the sun slid down from its apogee. She saw none of the perpetual beauty of her surrounds though. Her thoughts lay with potions and lives lost. When she was done, she found she was yawning as she placed the tray outside the door and pushed the chair under the latch again.

She laid on the bed, covering herself with a woollen shawl, grateful that this deliberate seclusion allowed her a measure of thought. She wondered *why* Seraphina had barely spoken to her since she had arrived. Was she, Lien, so inconsequential in the scheme of things? Her apparent inconsequence galled her. Not so inconsequential that she could not have remained in the Han with those she loved. Nor so inconsequential that the Emperor did not need, or *want,* to find her.

The Emperor! Was he so ill that he required constant nursing?

What if he died before the map could be dealt with? What price the Han then?

Someone would have to hand the map over surely, and as his consort, would that not be her? But then, she wasn't really his consort, was she? They had not yet been married. She was merely his betrothed. Would that suffice?

But why should *she* be held accountable for the Emperor's foolish mistake?

No! She would make that very clear when she handed the map over.

She thought of Heng. If the Emperor died before she could avenge her dear friend and servant, she, Lien, would feel such an acute sense of failure.

She reached into her pocket and eased the small bottle out. Holding it up to the light, she rocked the bottle and the brown-black liquid as thick as tar oozed back and forth. There was something grim in its colour and in the menacing way the liquid moved. Predatory.

Yes, it means death, she thought. Whatever is within this bottle is designed to end life, she had no doubt. She walked to the table where lay all manner of writing materials, including a knife to trim quills and she slipped the blade under the black wax coating over the cork. Small pieces cracked and fell to the floor until eventually the cork was free to be manoeuvred back and forth. She was careful, she didn't want the cork to break. A little pull here, a small twist there.

With a faint pop, it came free.

A dark vapour drifted out of the neck, foul-smelling and cauterising her nose as she held the bottle at arm's length. The vapour moved like a murmuration, back and forth, shape-shifting, entrancing her as it formed into a terrifying image. She almost dropped the bottle as a skull with dark cavities for eye-sockets stared at her and a ridge of teeth top and bottom of the jaw stretched into a macabre grin.

Some part of her knew that if she dropped the bottle, all the sins of the world would break forth and so she jammed the cork back on, twisting it tightly. She thrust the bottle into her pocket and opened the window – the vapour thinned, eddying back and forth until the nightmarish murmuration drifted outside and vanished.

She stood panting, staring at her hands, her heart thumping and the green tea rising into her throat until she could hold it in no longer, retching into an empty bowl on the chest of drawers. She puked until just bright yellow bile emerged and then she took the fine linen towel from the chest and wiped her mouth, tears running down her cheeks.

There was no going back.

She had surely taken the step to the dark side, and she felt nothing but nausea.

She decided to bargain with herself: *if I can avenge Heng, then I shall, willingly, be held accountable for the imperial error.* She would beg for leniency for the Han, on the grounds that *she* had enacted vengeance upon the Emperor for his mistake. To save the people of the Han. Surely the Gods and Others would listen.

She shut the window and walked back to the bed, laid down, exhausted, and refusing to listen as Old One's voice whispered from a faraway past. *'Before you embark on a journey of revenge, dig two graves.'*

Of course she knew she'd been drugged. As soon as she heard the hammering on the door, she realised that she had slept for hours, that the fragrant green tea, so redolent of the First House of Silk, had been some sort of herb that sent her to the dream world. But there was a thing, she had not dreamed. She had hovered in some sort of soft nothing-state until hands shook the door latch and Gallivant shouted, 'Lady Lien, Lady Lien! You must come!'

She stepped from the bed and pulled the chair away, wrenching the door open with ill grace. 'What!' she demanded. 'What is it that has you breaking down my door as if the Hunt is coming.'

'Because, Lady Lien, it is. Listen...'

She stood for a moment and then heard in the very far-off distance, the rumble of thunder.

''Tis but a thunderstorm. Not unusual, I think.'

'In Færan it is, my lady. We only have fine weather...' Gallivant's voice dwindled as another rumble could be heard in the far hills. This time the sky lightened perceptibly and then darkened quickly after. 'Lightning,' he whispered. 'They get closer.'

'And so They get closer. We give them the map and all is well, surely.' And I must get to the Emperor and give him the potion, she thought. He must be dead by the time the Others arrive.

'You must come with me, Lady Lien. The Emperor needs to see you.'

And I him. 'He is getting better?'

'We wish that were so...' Gallivant guided her along the hall, his hand at her back, gently pushing her.

She felt in her pocket. Still there... 'Seraphina?' she asked.

'She is with him. She has doctored him as much as she is able. The rest is in the Heavens' hands. But you should know – she has found the way to stop all this madness.'

Lien halted. 'She has? How?'

'I have not been told. She has told Ming Xao and he is at peace with it.'

'He is to give up his life, yes?' *Not before I take* his *life...*

'I do not know. I hope that is not the case because he is a very kind and good man.'

She would have laughed at this if they had not reached a door and Gallivant had not knocked and then opened it.

The chamber was large with huge windows that reached the ceiling and which flashed yellow as the lightning in the hills moved closer. A candle flickered as the door opened and another dowsed but the woman in the black gown, the one with wild greying hair and dancing eyes whom they called Seraphina, pointed her finger at the candle and it sprang into bright life again. Thunder rolled ever closer and the windows rattled.

'Lien,' the Emperor pushed himself from a chair by the fire. He was pale but his cheeks were feverishly flushed. His eyes were illness-bright and his hair was brushed and pulled back into a narrow ribbon. He had on riding pants like Lien's and a dark knitted sweater that clung to his wide shoulders. He leaned heavily on the carved arm of the chair and smiled.

She bowed her head. 'Excellence,' she said. 'I hope you improve.'

'As well as I can.' Thunder crashed and a horse shrieked from the stables. 'Lien, we haven't much time and I need to talk with you.'

'Ming, we shall be downstairs while you speak with Lady

Lien.' Seraphina gathered Gallivant before her. 'Remember that time is no longer your friend.' She shut the door behind, leaving the faint fragrance of honeysuckle.

'Time has never been our friend,' Lien said acidly. 'Not since I went to the palace for a wedding that never eventuated.'

'Lien, I have no time to offer platitudes, but I would ask that you hear what I have to say. Seraphina has told me what must be done, and I will do it. Will you come with me?'

'Me? Why? It is you who must hand over the map. What role would I play?'

'Seraphina has administered just enough medic to halt pain and fever, but if I am…' he stopped and clenched his good fist into a knot where the bones shone bright, then gritted his teeth. 'I ask for you to accompany me because you are my betrothed, and also because you are from the Han and will be able to relay to those in our province, that despite all, the Emperor remedied what he had made wrong.'

'You don't need me, Ming Xao. If what everyone says to be true,' she let acid drip, 'then the very birds will carry the message.'

He walked back and forth, holding onto furniture, so weak that Lien thought he would collapse at her feet. He pressed the fingers of his good hand against his eyes.

'What I must do, what payment… is …' He took a breath and turned away from her looking at the distant yellow flashes. 'Simply Lien, I'm afraid. As frightened as a little boy. The consequence of my ill-thought action is no more than I deserve and I will do it, but I *need* your courage.' He turned a fevered face to her. 'I have *seen* your courage. I have seen what you can do and I'm in awe. I listen to you and think that not once have you been cowed in this journey you have had to undertake. You are immeasurably brave and I would ask you to lend me your strength to me. Just this once. I'm as weak as a newborn babe, as you see.' He held on to the chair near him. 'What I must do will not be pretty but I need you near, to lend me your strength if you think you can.'

He was close. Close enough for her to smell lemons and cloves and for her to see the sweat beads on his forehead and to note that his hands, both the good and the bad, trembled like a child in a nightmare. 'By the Gods,' she said. What must be given? A *shi* of flesh?' She felt the smallest pity for this pitiable man, but then she wanted her *shi* of flesh too.

'In a word? Yes…' he replied. 'Please will you help me?'

She took a step back from him and slipped her hands into her pockets, feeling the potion against her fingers.

'When?' she asked.

'Now. We must leave now. They wait in the hills – it's impossible for Them to approach through the Ymp Tree Orchard. Seraphina has contrived it so with warding off spells.'

'But the Orchard is one of the gates. Can they not just come through a gate?'

'Seraphina has moved the gate…'

'But I don't understand,' said Lien as Ming put his good hand under her elbow and guided her to the door. 'If a gate-way can be moved, why then are Others so aflame with your map? The solution is simple…'

'It's to teach me and anyone else a lesson. This will become a story across the world of Eirie and mortals will tremble at the power of Others.'

Like his hand, thought Lien, as his fingers trembled on her arm.

How I hate this place. How I hate him…

He pushed her on gently and she walked ahead of him down the stair. Waiting at the bottom were Hester, Gallivant and Max.

'I have saddled the grey for you, Ming,' said Gallivant.

'I have placed wine and food in your saddlebags and the medic you need,' said Hester.

'Thank you. I owe you…'

'You owe us nothing,' Hester replied. 'But I would say, come back to us safe.'

'Dear Hester,' he reached for her arm and touched it. 'I think we know that is unlikely.' He walked through the front door to the circular gravel forecourt, where a grey horse was tied to a wrought hitching rail.

Ming's knees folded a little and he sucked in a breath to avoid a faint.

Just give me a while longer. Just enough time…

But who he was asking? The Great Mother? Chi Nü? Perhaps Yue Lao.

Seraphina glanced at him as he burned with fever. 'Ming Xao, you cannot go alone. You are very ill.'

'The drugs are in my saddlebags, are they not?'

'Yes, but…'

'In any case, I do not go alone,' he answered as he reached to the horse's girth.

But a hand pushed him aside and the Lady Lien grasped the leather strap and re-buckled it, the horse shifting slightly. 'He does not go alone, Madame. I go with him. It is only right. I *am* his betrothed.'

Her voice was cool and uncompromising, and no one could see her face as she bent to check the girth strap was not twisted and then she stood.

'Well, I did not foresee that. Strange…' Seraphina examined Lien's face and then Ming's.

She doesn't trust her, Ming thought. Why?

'Ming Xao, you are fading rapidly,' said Seraphina. 'Lady Lien will need to administer drugs in perhaps an hour. Gallivant!' she called this last. 'Fetch my chestnut for the lady and be quick!'

Gallivant ran back through the house and Seraphina led

the grey to a mounting block for which Ming thanked the Gods. He hadn't the strength to haul himself into the saddle.

'Ming Xao,' she said, as she wrapped a cloak around his shoulders and fastened it with a bone pin, 'you will have to ride through the day and night to make it to the hills by dawn. This is more than you are fit to handle but it is as it must be. Have you told the lady what you must do?'

'She knows that They will have their *shi* of flesh.'

He could not bring himself to say what They actually *would* have and knew that before he and Lien reached the hills, he must tell her. Explain the likely outcome.'

'Lady Lien, then it is up to you if you want to save the Han from future pain and destruction. You must make sure your emperor arrives at the appointed place safely. If he does not, nothing that you do will be worth a thing in the annals of history. This is a mistake that only the Emperor can fix. Despite the cost.'

Ming shivered beneath his cloak, unsure if it was the fever or anxiety. Either way, he knew his life was measured by the time it took to reach the hills.

Gallivant came trotting round the corner of the house with a chestnut gelding of stocky build and impressive hocks and rump.

'My horse is called Rufus,' said Seraphina as she held the horse still after Gallivant had slid off. 'He is calm and very surefooted on the hills. Give him his head and he will carry you safely.'

Ming watched Lien climb into the saddle from the mounting block and then bend down for a cloak held by Hester. She flung it round her shoulders and fastened a wooden brooch to the shoulder. He caught her eye, but she didn't smile, her expression intent. He realised that he could not read her at all, not like he did in the Park of Singing Birds. That day, he thought he had found a kindred spirit. But now, she hid herself behind a façade as thick as the grey woollen cloak that surrounded her and stretched over Rufus' rump.

He knew she was angry, that she was hurt to her soul and that she had no respect at all for her emperor and he could not blame her. He resolved to speak with her as they rode. To set her mind at rest in some way. It was the least he could do for someone who was already scarred and who after the next day, would be scarred even more.

Seraphina stood with her household as Ming and Lien turned their horses down the drive. No one said a word and Ming had the feeling that they grieved for someone who had a death sentence. So be it, he thought.

It is what it is…

CHAPTER NINETEEN

Lien and Ming

They wound through the blossoms of the Ymp trees and when they cleared them, Ming clicked his horse into an easy lope. His head pounded with each hoof strike but he knew they must reach the foot of the hills before dark. After that, he must surely be able to rely on moonlight…

'For how long do you think They will beat their drums?' Lien asked as Rufus edged beside Ming's horse.

'Drums? Ah, the thunder? I don't know. They know I'm coming. Perhaps it will stop.'

They reached the foothills in good time and Lien said she must administer Seraphina's potions, as instructed. He agreed but stayed mounted, convinced that if he slid down, he would fall and not get up again. He had reached a point of craven longing for the drugs that Seraphina had made for him. For sure there was wormwood and slippery elm, willow even, but it was the poppy he wanted. He had passed the gate of no return there and thought of the opium dens in the Han where men wasted to nothing in pursuit of the drug's pleasures. For him it didn't matter. He needed to be pain free for the next few hours because to be pain free meant he could speak with Lien and that he could carry out what was required of him. After that…

She passed up the costrel and a small tumbler of liquid the colour of honey. He swallowed the medic and then followed it with a gulp of wine from the costrel before handing both back to Lien. Their hands touched and he felt a jolt of such ecstasy shoot up his arm that he gasped. Had she felt it? He looked at her but all he saw was a frown as she jammed the top into the costrel's neck and then stashed it and the tumbler into his saddle bag.

She swung herself back in the saddle, clicked Rufus on and they began to climb the first of the hills they must cross to arrive at the meeting point.

'What is your horse called?' Lien asked.

Surprised that she even spoke, he did not answer.

'Excellence?'

'Moonstriker,' he said, reaching to smooth the grey's mane.

'A good name for a horse the colour of moonlight,' she replied.

'Yes…'

They rode on, up to the top of the first hill beneath oaks and elms. And then down the other side, following a narrow defile between the trees. The birds had quieted, and daylight was muted by the lacy leaves and branches. Of sunlight there was none, just a leaden grey sky with hefty rolling thunderclouds. But he had been right – the thunder and lightning had stopped.

'Lien,' he began. How did he put into words what must be said? They rode side by side now, the track widening and every now and then, their knees touched, and he felt that strange thrilling excitement. He found it odd – smacking of something, if only he knew what it was. 'I wish that we could resolve what sits between us before tomorrow.'

For a moment she rocked with Rufus' easy stride and then, 'But Excellence. It is unlikely. To be bald, I blame you for the death of someone I held very dear and no amount of talking will change that.'

Ming wished he could tell her that Heng lived on, that she had indeed met the Fate that was her destiny and that nothing could have changed that. But such a thing was for Heng, or Heng-O, to reveal when the time was right.

How then would he bridge the chasm that sat between them, threatening to engulf this beautiful woman in lifelong bitterness?

'Lien, I am so sorry. I mourn for her and for you…'

She pulled her horse to a stop and her voice cut through the air like a knife through butter. 'Do you? Why would *you* mourn her? You didn't know her. She was just one lowly servant within the Han. She meant nothing to you.'

'But she meant something, everything, to you it seems, and your pain is evident. You bleed from it, and I would ease that if I were at all able. But I cannot. In time, I hope you will forgive what happened.'

But I will not see that moment when it comes, he thought. How he would like to have said that to her, but it was not to be until he could exchange a little more than vitriol. Instead,

'Tell me about her.'

He could see her confusion at such a question, and he hoped it would take the frost from her heart just for a moment.

She said nothing as Rufus walked along but he could see by her face that she had drifted into memory and he allowed silence to exist, hoping that in time, she would open up.

Lien was shocked when the Emperor had asked about Heng. What insidious game did the man play? And yet, such a simple statement – *Tell me about her* – had caused a flood of memories, and she found she could not stop that flood and then the memories articulated into words and she cared not that she spoke to the man she hated. It was such a release to speak the memories at all.

'When she joined our house, not long after you vanished from the Han with the lady Ibo, she was a mere brown sparrow. Plain, always terribly thin no matter that cook filled her with buns and dumplings. She was assigned to me because she was quiet and biddable, and I liked that. She became my shadow, almost uncanny with her ability to be there when I needed her and even before I called her name. She anticipated my every wish. There were times where I would swear she *was* uncanny, an Other. But then she would brush my hair and catch a knot or bring me the wrong tea leaves and I would realise she was as normal as the rest of us.'

Lien settled to the telling, savouring the warmth that flooded her as she recalled moments with her servant. 'She always wore the indigo robes of a servant until I decided that I wanted her to wear different colours and so I bade her sort through my old robes, and I decided that she could wear anything that was turquoise, azure, aqua, lapiz, mint or celadon. It lifted the pale colour of her skin and brightened her eyes. But when I asked her to wear her hair in a horsetail, she declined the order, explaining it wouldn't be right and so it was the one time I allowed her to have her say. My father and mother were angry that she dressed in my cast-offs, but Old One, prescient as she was, could see that Heng was the consummate servant and companion and that it was something that could make me happy. Old One knew what a lonely life I led and perhaps knew that my future life would be even lonelier. Because dear Heng never acted above her station, my parents allowed Old One to have the last word.' Lien gave a small, sad laugh. 'Old One is my ancient grandmother – more of a mother to me than my own. It breaks my heart to think that I am breaking hers by my failure to fulfil my destiny. In short, Excellence, I am bringing shame upon the First House of Silk by being absent, by not marrying you, by any number of things that can never and will never be remedied.'

'Lady Lien,' replied the Emperor, his voice stronger now that the medicine had been absorbed. 'I assure you, that when you return to the Han, you will be exalted. Your family will have every reason to be proud.'

Lien studied him. He was a fine-looking man beneath his evident pallor. He had grown much taller since she first saw him with the Lady Ibo so long ago. Gone were the spectacles and the cowed appearance. The man who rode next to her had wide shoulders, enough to carry the weight of his position. That he was thin and ill was obvious, especially in the clothing that Seraphina had supplied, but his short hair had grown a little and it sat neatly in its ribbon. He caught her looking at him and smiled – an expression of genuine warmth. She pinched herself hard and then replied to him. 'And how would they know, Excellence?'

'I have left a document which Seraphina has promised to deliver to the First Minister. It says all that needs to be said. When you return to the Han, you will be asked questions to corroborate what I have recorded. Rest assured that your family's reputation, and your own, will be intact. But enough of that, tell me more of Heng.'

She felt disarmed by his forethought, let alone by his interest in Heng, but because she mourned and no one had asked her till now, she now found that talk of Heng eased the insidious pain that squashed her heart like a boulder.

'She was gentle and had an earthy wisdom that I often appreciated. I am very headstrong, you see...'

'No,' the Emperor laughed. 'Really?'

She found she laughed back, not loudly but perhaps ruefully, and then wondered how either of them could laugh in such dangerous times. 'Yes. Really. She had the knack of quietly reeling me back from any wayward behaviour and in time I would see the rightness of her action. The day of my ... our wedding ... I knew I would be unable to continue without her and contrived for her to attend me...' She stopped speaking, remembering that fateful conversation as she was prepared for the long journey to the Palace. 'She told me once that she could dream through me and it seemed to connect us by a thread almost as fateful as a red thread.' She looked down at her wrist and then at the Emperor's. 'When you look at your thread, do you ever wonder what will happen?'

'No longer. I know what will happen and to be frank, I would rather talk of Heng. She is a wondrous being, Lien.'

'A wondrous being,' Lien agreed. 'Strange words, but yes. Courageous, wise, a strength that I had not realised until it was too late. Do you know, she said to me that she dreamed of *Life beyond* … and I said to her, *Beyond the First House of Silk?* But I should have known that she meant something far greater, and it took some heartbeats for me to realise and then I said *Beyond the Wall! You too! … You see things my way.* And that, Excellence,' she said, her voice trembling, 'was the beginning of the end for the most faithful Heng.'

She told him of the journey across the lake, of the Ice Dragon, of Chi Nü, of the Bridge that Never Was, of Yue Lao and the river. And then she told him slowly as the tears began to fall, of the ocean and the storm. 'So you see, Excellence, if she and I had not had the same ideals and if I had not dragged her along in my perilous wake as I proceeded to your palace and your misdirected life, Heng, most faithful and brave servant would still be alive…'

She started when his hand, the strong one, reached across and covered her own as it grasped the pommel of her saddle, and his touch was a taper. She sobbed. For the contact, for the empathy and because for an age now, she had just wanted someone to listen and understand.

Gradually her tears lessened, and she was glad when Rufus stumbled over a root and the Emperor's touch was broken. Her hand tingled, as it had when their hands had touched before and as it had when their knees had touched as they rode. It almost felt as if he was Other to contrive such a feeling because there could be no other reason. She took up Rufus' reins, glad that she knew how to ride, and clicked him on along the wider path.

The day was settling into a gloomy afternoon and Lien said to the Emperor, 'If we are to ride at night, would it not be best to stop now, rest the horses because the hills become steeper and perhaps eat a little ourselves? Besides, you will be due your medic in less than an hour…'

He agreed, too willingly she felt, and then realised that whatever poison was making him ill was becoming stronger than Seraphina's drugs. She wondered if they would arrive at the meeting place at all and whether all this would be for nought. She was also concerned that she rode into a situation that had not been explained – she felt as if she were blind, and it served to reignite her antagonism. She halted Rufus, and dismounted and stood watching the Emperor as he slid down from Moonstriker, staggering slightly as his feet hit the ground so that he had to grab at the stirrup leather with his damaged hand. He sucked in an agonised breath and grunted but for the rest, she believed that it was a playact as he turned to her, his face wiped clean of agony and with an appearance of strength, if not health.

'We have food, Lady Lien, in my other saddlebag. Can you…' he held up his toxic hand and she walked around the horse and took out bread wrapped in linen and some cheese wrapped in muslin. There were apricots and peaches and of course the costrel of wine. And lying there, the little bottle of honey-coloured medic that would keep the Emperor painfree until what had to be done was done. She felt in her pocket for the death-potion and realised that if she were to do what *she* wished, there would perhaps be no other opportunity.

She heard a sound, thinking that the Emperor had walked behind her, but there was nothing, so she looked around Moonstriker's rump and saw the Emperor lying in a pool of grey cloak folds.

'Excellence, Excellence!' She ran to him. *Not yet, not yet! I must...*

'He has fainted, Lady Lien. He is under great duress, so cushion his head and he will sleep.' The voice that spoke was familiar and she tried to place it, pulling off her own cloak and wadding it under his head. He was as loose as a newborn babe and as she held his head in her hands, there was again that fizzing feeling along her arms, as if he was Other. She pulled his cloak around him for warmth and then looked for the voice that had spoken to her.

'Who are you, show yourself,' she tried to inject some vehemence into her words but then stepped back as a woman walked toward her along the path. The woman's hair had a life of its own, black with strands of silver like Seraphina's and there were fine threads of pearls laced through as she walked forward with grace. Her gown flowed like organdie or lawn, layer upon layer of shades of grey that matched the sky above and all across were stitched stars and moons in filaments of silver and silky white – a whole universe that if it had been night, would have glinted and sparkled. The woman was close now and Lien looked at her face, such a familiar face and she whispered,

'But I dream. It is because we were talking...' and everything faded into roaring tunnels of black until she felt the ground catch her and then she knew nothing.

Ming had watched her walk to the saddlebag as Moonstriker rested his hind hoof, hip lopsided. Both horses chewed their bits and snorted and then settled to rest. He thought they must find water for them before they began the next ascent. He felt so weak and prayed to the Great Mother to give him strength enough to do what must be done. He was so afraid of the pain that would occur but reasoned that in that bottle filled with opium, wormwood and willow, there would be enough to dull the cruelty to nothing and then after, he knew he would collapse. Relief incarnate that it was over and that the Han and perhaps Eirie had been saved from Other wrath. He no longer castigated himself for drawing the map. It was a waste of his energies and he needed everything left to him to get him over the hideous oncoming line.

Moonstriker shifted slightly, dislodging Ming's grasp on the stirrup leather and there was a buzzing sound in his ears and then a roaring as if he coursed down a long tunnel and then he folded like a cloth upon the ground and knew nothing else.

Hands patted Lien's face and then she heard the voice again.

'You do not dream, Lady Lien.'

'Heng...' Lien opened her eyes and stared. 'Heng!' Her voice broke and tears welled. 'You live!'

'I live, Mistress. But there is much to tell. Here,' Heng-O held the costrel of wine to Lien's lips and Lien sucked back a mouthful and then coughed. 'Sit and listen and do not say anything until I have finished.'

Thus the tale of the two red threads was revealed – Heng's and the Moonlady's. That it was in fact, indeed had always been, Heng's fate to meet Heng-O and to become the Moonlady in time. 'No one killed me, Lien. I did not die. Not as you would think. And now I can see the whole world whenever I want. Just as we talked about when I said to you, I wanted to see beyond the Wall. It is within my power as well, to help those I choose to help and even foil those who disturb me. And on that point, I would ask you, what do you have in your pocket?'

The question hit Lien as if she had been pinioned by a boar spear and she gasped.

'You cannot deny it, Lien, because the Moonlady sees all. Show me.'

Lien sucked in a breath as Heng-O scrutinised her. Her tentative grasp went to her pocket, and she pulled out the tiny bottle with its black-brown contents so that it lay in the palm of her hand.

'Tell me what it is,' Heng-O ordered.

Lien, hating the feelings of guilt and shame that coursed through her, said, 'There is no point.'

Heng-O's voice lifted. 'Tell me!'

Lien shivered. Swallowing the lump in her throat she whispered, 'I do not know. But when I opened it, a vapour drifted out and massed to form a skull. In the notebook it had a red circle next to the number with a red line through it. But I do not read the language of Trevallyn.'

'But you assumed?'

'Yes. That it is…'

'Yes?'

'Deadly.' She whispered the awful word and kept her eyes cast down.

'And what, Lien of the First House of Silk, Betrothed of the Emperor, did you plan to do with it?'

Lien was shivering now.

'Tell me, Lien!' Heng-O's voice was raised and as hard as a bed of nails, each one driving into Lien, front and back.

'Kill him,' she said, closing her eyes, willing the tears not to fall.

'*Kill* him? In the name of the Ancestors, Lien, why would you?'

'Because of what he has done. Condemning all of us to Heaven's knows what agonies from Others. And because of him, your life was ended!' Lien regained some spine and raised her voice but could barely look at immortal Heng-O. She remembered a saying from her home in the Han – a colloquialism oft used in argument: *You are weighed in the balances and are found wanting.* Everything about Heng-O, her cold eyes, her grim mouth, the way her hair waved in a welkin wind, indeed the way her organdie gown flew back against her slim body – she exuded ire and disgust and she had indeed found Lien to be wanting. 'You are not the woman I knew, Lien of the First House of Silk. The woman I loved as my sister and who was my mentor and friend and whom, once, I would have died to protect.' Heng-O grabbed the poison and threw it into the air where it somersaulted once and vanished.

As Lien gasped, the Moonlady continued. 'Listen to me and listen hard if you want to redeem yourself in my eyes. No! Do not speak. Let me be very clear. If you desire to see the Emperor die for his sins, then you will most likely get your wish. Seraphina did not tell you what is to happen? The Emperor did not tell you? Ask yourself why? Why everyone seems to be trying to protect your sensibilities, how every-one is kind, thinking of *you* while *you* planned to murder the Emperor.'

Lien could say nothing, but tears ran down her cheeks as Heng-O continued.

'In asking you to talk about Heng the servant, the Emperor was trying to break through your manner toward him, to create some sort of civility that he could take in his heart to his destiny. He is a lonely man, afraid of what is to come, but he obviously felt that you were the only one who would understand, having trod in his footsteps this far. He has tried to protect you, bringing you to Seraphina.' Heng-O sat on the ground next to Lien and Lien swiped at the tears that dripped onto her knees. She dared look into Heng-O's eyes – Heng's eyes, those gentle, almond-shaped eyes that had softened every time the servant did something for her mistress. Even now, she could not believe that Heng was alive and that she was the Moonlady, legendary Other.

'I am as you see me,' Heng-O's hand reached for Lien's

and she clasped it in her own, the other hand wiping Lien's tears. 'I will not pretend the Emperor did not precipitate all of this. But perhaps it sets in train a series of events that are shaping us all for the better – you, the Emperor and I.'

Lien snorted. 'How so, Lady Heng-O? The Emperor's life will be cut short, you will never be by my side ever again and I will be moonstruck after all of this…'

'You catastrophise. Allow me to continue,' Heng-O said.

Lien wondered at Heng-O's calmness. Beyond, in a few hours, one life would be shattered, maybe more. Lien knew that just like the sea storm, she would carry that with her for the rest of her life, probably for the worst. Her mind stretched into distorted shapes and her heartbeat quickened.

'Lien,' Heng-O's voice broke into her galloping thoughts. 'Breathe, dear friend. You must trust me when I say all will be well. Have I not returned to you, do you not see that forever now, we can talk often if you need me?'

It was true. Lien had been broken by Heng's apparent drowning at sea. She knew it had turned her into a monster and she glanced at the still loose form of the Emperor. His face was easy in repose, with none of the draw and pleat of pain and responsibility. Was she prepared to admit that he suffered for his foolhardiness? That he wanted to right a terrible wrong? Perhaps with his life?

'Are you?' asked Heng-O. 'Prepared to admit that he feels such sadness and pain at what he did?'

Lien looked at the man who would be her husband and for one heartbeat of a moment, wondered if they might have been a kindred partnership.

'Yes. You would.'

'But too late,' murmured Lien. In a few hours, it will all be too late.

'Perhaps so, but let me tell you more…'

CHAPTER TWENTY

Ming and Lien

Ming lay still, eyes closed, fighting against the pain, listening to everything.

Heng-O had come! Thank the stars! But to hear that his betrothed would have killed him? His heart sank at how much she evidently hated him. And yet, in many ways he wished she had been successful in his demise. At least the pain and guilt would be done, and he wouldn't have to fight the wretched fear of what was to come. That terror racketed through him in waves for what man would not be afraid?

He hoped they couldn't see that he was awake – he knew they would talk more, and he so desperately wanted to hear, wanted to know that Lien was indeed the woman that he had chosen in the Park of Singing Birds. That her violent thoughts had been temporary anguish. He needed to take that with him. Something to cling to, for doesn't everyone need kind memories to dwell amongst at the last fateful moment?

Gods, he needed some poppy! But no, he must pace himself because the effects were wearing off with speed now and he needed them to be strong at the right time.

He wished he had not coerced Lien to accompany him. But there was a thing. Had she really been forced? Surely she only agreed because she had thought it would be her one chance to rid herself and the Han of their pathetic Emperor.

Ah, whatever the case, it was a chance to make good

something that was rotten and for that he was grateful. The women were talking again, and he bit down on his pain, kept his eyes closed and his breathing as regular as he was able.

He was listening with a kind of desperation, if truth be told…

'Are you aware that when the Emperor tried to pass the map to Seraphina, his hand would not release it, a thing not within the Emperor's control?'

Lien was confused and shook her head. 'No one has told me anything beyond what you have said today and what the Emperor himself said which was that he was afraid and that I needed to observe what he will do so that I can answer any questions that come from his court and his ministers, if he doesn't survive.'

'I see.' Heng-O frowned. 'Mortals *do* make things worse for themselves, as if this isn't already a dire situation. A little bit of honesty very early on wouldn't have gone astray.'

Hearing Heng-O say the word *mortals* made Lien realise beyond a shadow of a doubt that whilst her beloved Heng was alive, she and her former maidservant were now separated by much more than class and status. In truth, Lien was far below Heng-O, for mortals were always base beings compared to immortal folk.

'It should not matter,' Heng-O reached and touched Lien's cheek so that once again Lien knew her thoughts were not her own. 'Think of Chi Nü and the Emperor. Of the Emperor and Nico. Of Gallivant and Adelina the Stitcher. You have heard of these friendships, have you not? Then it will be no different for you and I. But right now, I must inform you of all that I know so that you may take up your own thread in this tapestry.' She squeezed Lien's shoulder again, but Lien could not bring herself to smile in return. She felt winded every time Heng-O opened her mouth.

'It seems that the map is more enchanted than anyone thought,' Heng-O said. 'Whatever ink he used has connected it to him in ways that no one, not even Chi Nü or Yue Lao foresaw. Seraphina went to her library, but even amongst her vast resources, she could find *nothing* that would break the enchantment between the map and Ming Xao. Finally, she sat at her scrying ball and after long hours, she saw the dreadful thing that must happen, and she told him. He was calm. Afraid, for sure, but very calm. All along he knew his life would be at stake and Seraphina merely confirmed it. He is brave enough to accept that his life is forfeit and to not fight against it. Do you understand, Lien? He does this for you, for your family, for the sake of the Han and for all of Eirie.'

Lien remained silent. What could she say? That he deserved what was coming? That hubris is every man's downfall? That this was his nemesis? All of that she supposed, and yet as she looked at him lying still, barely breathing, a small iota of compassion crept into her soul. 'I accept that he is brave,' she said. 'Stupid, of course, to bring this about, but honest and brave to accept the consequence. But Heng-O, I don't understand why I need be with him...'

But Heng-O was looking at the folded and cloaked body on the ground. 'Ah, Ming Xao, you wake. Are you well?'

He injected as much strength as he was able into his reply. 'Well enough.' He pushed himself onto his knees and wished himself to stand. Perhaps Heng-O knew what effort it cost him, but he stood upright, tall, trying not to let Lien see how frail he was. 'Perhaps I needed rest more than I thought. For that I apologise.'

'You need not apologise,' Heng-O said kindly. 'You must take rest when you can. I'm sure the Lady Lien agrees.' The Moonlady turned to Lien, and Ming watched the shadows fly across the face of his betrothed.

'Indeed, Excellence. If you need to rest, you have only to say.' Lien bowed her head, somewhat chastened, perhaps. But he knew that it was just the thought of a desperate and lonely man...

'Ming Xao, is it not time to explain to Lady Lien what Seraphina determined from her scrying?' Heng-O asked. 'At least then, the Lady can decide for herself whether she wants to continue on or whether she wishes to turn back.'

The Moonlady knows how much I fear to confront my final moments alone...

'Ming Xao, you will never be entirely alone,' Heng-O offered. 'I'm sure Seraphina told you that and I corroborate it fully. You will have friends...'

But not someone from the Han, he thought. Someone who has indeed trodden my path. Someone who might have been my wife, my partner in life. Someone who might have been the Dowager Empress if we had married – an empress of great strength and even wisdom with First Minister to advise her.

Heng-O said nothing, although he knew she had read his thoughts.

'You are right of course, Lady Heng-O. It is time to explain...' He walked across to Lien with as much fortitude as he could and took her hand in his uninjured fingers. 'Lien, I am sorry for what this has come to. I am sorry I coerced you into attending me from Seraphina's...'

'Excellence, you did not coerce me. I came willingly...'

'I think not. I think you felt coerced,' Ming said, looking straight into Lien's beautiful eyes. 'By any number of reasons.'

He knows, thought Lien, as her fingers rested in his. There was that curious jolt that gave her butterflies in the belly and sent a blush of guilt coursing across her cheeks. He knows I wanted to kill him. She glanced at Heng-O, but the

Moonlady stood by, gleaming in her ivory and grey subtlety, totally inscrutable.

'Excellence,' said Lien. 'Whatever those reasons may have been, they were ill-considered and so very wrong. It is I who should apologise. I was mad with grief, insane with it. But all has been revealed by Lady Heng-O and I am much soothed by her words.'

She was, there was no doubt. Her shameful behaviour had faded. Granted, she was still angry with him for the damned map, but the violent being that she had become as her mind slipped with loss had eased. She would not shame her old friend Heng, or her beloved Old One…

Gods, but she was lovely, thought Ming, as she cast her glance downward and the blush spread across her face. He tightened his grip on her hand a little and she looked up at him from beneath a fan of black lashes. 'Your anger was justified but now that you know your Heng is alive and that she has an exalted position in the world of Eirie, I hope you can forgive me just a little.'

'But…'

'Not forgive me for the map. I can't forgive myself so why would I expect you to forgive me. But perhaps just see it in your heart to look at me a little more kindly.'

She found his deep voice soothing and she found she listened to what he had to say, *wanted* to hear what he had to say. His face was pale and drawn but it was so much stronger than she remembered. Now, she thought, *any* maid might simper before him. As it was, she was the one who stood in front of him, she was the one whose hand he held and she was his betrothed. 'Excellence, in time, I will…'

'Lien,' he said tiredly. 'We don't have time. We have till dawn. No longer.' He shook her hand a little and she frowned.

Now. Tell her now.

'Let me speak if you will. I would deliver this and have done.' Their eyes were still upon each other and hers were curious, although he felt there was the faintest shadow of doubt. She seemed like one of the linnets from the bamboo cages in the Han – that she might take flight at the slightest thing. He swallowed. 'At dawn tomorrow, overlooking the lake from the high hills, I will meet all those Immortals, those Others who hunted me.' He took a deep breath. 'I will take the map in its canister from my pocket, and I will walk to the ceremonial stone that They will have in position, and I will lay my hand with the map upon it. Nothing will be said by me because nothing I can say will make any difference. They will then proceed to sever...' She gasped and tried to pull away from him by he held onto her hand grimly. 'They will sever my hand from my arm and the map with it.'

She twisted her hand from his and stared at him, her colour drained white with horror. 'I said a *shi* of flesh, but I did not mean it ... not like that.' Revulsion raced through every vein in Lien's body. 'And *this* is how they teach mortals a lesson? Despite that they can move the gates to wherever they choose, whenever? Why? By the stars, they are such sick monsters!' She howled her fury, her voice sharp and loud. 'For the first time I can see why you drew the map – to give mortals a fighting chance against Them. They, all of them, are barbaric! *This* is barbaric!'

She wrapped her arms around her waist as she walked swiftly round the horses whose ears laid back and whose tails twitched uneasily. All the while, her beloved Heng, Heng-O, watched her, probably assessing her, she thought.

She stopped directly in front of the Emperor. 'Excellence, you will bleed to your death!'

'Most like,' he said, with a horrible acceptance. 'But as you have oft said, it is *my* mistake and thus I must accept my punishment.'

'But how do you know it will be enough for Them? How do you know They won't continue to make mortals pay? By the Gods, I hate Them!'

'In answer to your question, I don't know if They can be trusted. I have to rely on people like Chi Nü, on Yue Lao, on Nico and Gallivant, on Seraphina, Maeve Swan Maid, on the siofra. And on our own dear Heng-O. On all those who have been good and kind and who protect us as much as they are able.'

'But you will die...' her voice became impassioned and curse it, she thought, tears rolled down her cheeks.

'Do you *care*, Lien,' he said quietly. 'Do you really care?'

She stared at him, at this tall, slim man who seemed to be begging her to care, begging her to forgive and her heart twisted. It surprised her – her heart had been such a cold stone in her chest for so long. *Did* she care? How deep did she have to dig into her soul to find out?

She had been through a kind of Hell, for sure – dragged on a terrifying journey, losing Heng, wanting to take the worst revenge...

'If you can forgive me, Excellence, I can forgive you...'

'Lien, there's nothing to forgive you for and to not put too fine a point on it, life is too short.' He walked to her and with his good hand, pulled her gently toward him. He placed a soft kiss on her forehead and her heartbeat lifted. She wanted him to hold her close and such a thought shocked her.

Ming wanted to hold her for longer.

It reminded him of what might have been and he would

have liked so much to have taken such touch and feel to the block when he went. Something that his mind could escape into in that final moment. He turned to Heng-O. He had been conscious of her quiet watchfulness as he and Lien began to speak with each other to build a bridge of sorts. He had a feeling that this, above all else, was what she desired. 'Lady,' he said. 'It is done. It just remains now for Lien to decide if she wants to ride on with me or whether she wishes to cut her losses and ride back to Seraphina. I am at peace if that is what she decides.' He grasped the Moonlady's white hands. 'I am beyond grateful for your timely arrival, and I thank you from the depths of my heart. It is pitch dark and I think we must ride on if we are to get to the top of the High Hills by dawn.' He bowed his head, let go of the Moonlady and took the reins of Moonstriker, leading the grey to a log to mount up. Gods but he would love some of the poppy now as the agony pulled him into twisted pieces. But he must be sparing. Maybe in an hour…

Lien took up Rufus' reins, feeling such sorrow that she must leave someone of great import to her. 'Heng, I know I should no longer call you that, but you will ever be Heng to me. I cannot explain the warmth and relief I feel in my heart. To know that every night I shall see you… oh Gods, I cry *again*!' She dashed a hand against her cheek. 'I tremble for what is to come but I will try to be as strong as I can. For you and for Old one.

'My dearest Lien, your decision must be for you and for the Emperor, and for no one else. Destiny decrees it.' said Heng-O.

Lien hugged the Moonlady, feeling the enigmatic insubstantiality of the woman as she began to fade in Lien's arms. Soon, all that lit the glade was a moonbeam and by that light, she mounted the chestnut, her cheeks damp, and moved in behind Ming, as sure a sign as any that she intended to follow him.

For the moment.

As Moonstriker put a strong shoulder into the rise of the hills, Ming closed his eyes with relief. She was coming and he felt like an untried boy that it should matter so. But loneliness had been implicit in his life. He had little relationship with his imperial parents. His teachers had been his mentors in his early life, his servants had been his friends. Later, when he had reached young adulthood, it was First Minister who became his father-figure, and he loved the man. But it was not a hard decision to depart the Han with the Lady Ibo on the eve of their marriage. His parents ruled the Han, First Minister and the ministerial forum aiding them. He felt he would not be missed, and he needed desperately to see beyond the suffocating Wall – to see how the rest of the world existed. He had a small number of scrolls from those slavers and traders who trekked beyond, and he was tantalised.

When he met his first betrothed, a slave woman from far away, he could see the yearning in her eyes, her desperation to return to her home, and he knew he could deliver her freedom to her, thereby freeing himself for a time. He had no plans to remain absent. He knew he would return to the Han eventually, armed with vital knowledge and experience.

And so it was.

But he was filled with pain when he found that his parents had become ill with heartbreak for their lost son. And when he eventually took his seat on the throne, he determined beyond everything, that the Han would break down its secretive life, that people would live freely and prosperously, that the Han would become famous for its silks, its spices, its cultural traditions. That there was much it could offer the wider world, whilst the rest of Eirie offered even more in return.

There had been just the flies in the ointment.

Others.

How they entrapped mortals with their wretched gates and then damaged folk, often beyond repair.

While he travelled, he made notes, drawings – things which would ultimately enable him to draw a map of great importance. Or so he believed.

But then, of course, the rest was awful history.

He looked behind him and met the intent gaze of the Lady Lien as she rocked with each stride of her horse, holding onto the pommel of the saddle as they continued up the steep incline of the High Hills.

He wondered why she had decided to accompany him? Did she feel something *for* him after all? Because Gods Above, he could now acknowledge that he felt something for her and had done since the day in the Park of Singing Birds. He recalled the feel of her soft skin as he had bent, less than an hour before, and kissed her forehead and a surge of love and lust spread from his groin to his heart.

Too little too late…

Lien's gaze had been fixed on the Emperor since they began the ascent. Gods! What was happening? She had thought it was impossible for such feelings to emerge after the journey she had just endured. And yet, the touch of this man's hand upon her, his gaze, and when he had kissed her forehead… It was as though an impenetrable wall had been breached. Was she some naïve girl experiencing her first longing to behave in such a way? How could hate turn to love so swiftly? Well, she reasoned, perhaps *not* love – but understanding and a willingness to broach chasms. He was measured, unambiguous, even kind. Old One had said so the day she readied her granddaughter for her wedding and Lien had not believed her.

Knowing Heng lived, albeit as an Immortal had a twofold effect. The one eased her bitter heartbreak, knowing that her one and only friend still existed. The other was the thought that all through her life with Heng, she had never known Heng was fey. How she longed for another conversation when all this was done.

This what? The death of the Emperor?

She sighed and shook her head as thoughts twisted back and forth through her mind, creating bigger and more tangled enigmas.

'You sigh, Lady,' Ming said, staying his big grey so that Rufus could walk alongside.

'I do. I think on Heng-O. She has been Other all her life and I didn't know.'

'Neither did she, to be fair,' he said and told her of his meeting with Heng-O. 'She said, *'I didn't know. No one guided me. I was just "left" as sometimes happens with careless Other parents. It's not unknown – an Other child is left in the mortal world, almost as if he or she has been forgotten about or is not wanted, and it seems I wasn't.'''*

'Oh but she was,' said Lien. 'Wanted I mean. Our family put complete faith in her as my companion-servant. But I remember the day she told me that her parents, her mortal parents I presume, told her that her skin was the colour of moonlight.' She smoothed Rufus' mane. 'I wonder where they found her? And did *they* suspect she was Other?' Lien clicked her tongue and sighed again. 'I was always too engaged with my own life, my own day, that I took her for granted and never asked anything about her life, her thoughts until the day of the betrothal and my journey to the palace. I regret my behaviour deeply.' But then she turned to Ming and smiled. 'I do remember that once I told her I would call her Heng-O because her face was as pale as the moon. Many a true word, it seems, is spoken when jesting.'

Ming smiled in return, saying, 'Yue Lao suspected, I think, that Heng was not what she appeared to be.'

'Oh, yes, I recall! He seemed surprised. He said as much as he tied on her red thread. Now I see that he was sealing her Fate...' She looked down at her own red thread, tied neatly, sitting there almost as an admonishment for glibness and ignorance. 'Now I look at mine and my heart turns over as I wonder what will happen.'

Ming looked at his, fingering it. Odd, thought Lien, that it was tied on to the wrist of the beleaguered hand. 'I know what my thread means,' he said without rancour or sadness. 'How could I not?'

Lien wondered at his courage. 'You have said you are afraid, and yet you seem so calm.'

'What else can I be? I'm afraid of the excruciating torture of course, of the fact that my blood vessels will drain and no one will stop it and that I will die. No amount of fret and fear will make it any better and so I must be sanguine.'

'It is admirable, Excellence.'

'Not really. I have brought about my own demise, as you and many others have told me, by hubris.'

Lien could not gainsay that. She had been forthright and could not take the words back. They rode on in silence for a little and Lien had to admit to herself that she was terrified of seeing what would happen to Ming Xao. She had no stomach for bloody violence and this...

'You can turn back, you know.'

'Pardon?'

'You can turn back. It is unkind of me to pressure you to attend me. There will be observers who can relay the truth of it to the Han...'

Lien rode on for a little more before she answered. 'I could return, but I will not.'

'Tell me why.'

He wanted to know. He so badly wanted to know that his choice had been the right one, that Lien of the First House of Silk was as he had thought. He had made one bad choice by drawing the map and surely everyone needs to know they have done something right as they go to their deaths.

Lien did not look up from flipping segments of the chestnut's mane back and forth over the horse's neck. 'Because I think you are a brave man, and that the Han should know. And I would not have you face such a terrible thing alone. Yes, there will be plenty of observers if what you say is true. But they will all be Other and Others have no heart. I would that you had a friend close by...' she blushed as she said this.

'Friend?' he laughed. 'You wanted to kill me, Lien. You have changed swiftly.'

Her mouth stretched to a grimace. 'I cannot change what I thought to do and I cannot explain my madness succinctly. It's done and you know of it. That Heng-O is still a part of my life means I'm finding some peace. I'm disgusted with my insane heartlessness and being with you now is the only way I can make reparation.'

Ming could push her no more. He had his answer. She had realised her error and for that he must be thankful. 'Lien, I free you from your obligations as my betrothed. I am more grateful than you'll ever know for attending me to the stone, but I would that you turn your back when it happens. I would not have you see...'

She cried out at that. 'Have me see? Gods, Excellence, I don't *want* to see but I will pay you the respect of observing! First Minister shall hear of your courage in unmitigated detail.'

He had nothing to say in reply and they rode on through the darkling hours, a moonbeam guiding them all the way.

CHAPTER
TWENTY ONE
Lien and Ming

The forest had settled to a haunting quietness.

An owl brushed past Lien's shoulder, its grey-white shape like a spectre's shadow. She had started but did not call out as there was something in the bird's flight that was calming. It flew to a tree branch ahead of them and observed them intently.

'One could be forgiven for thinking he knows something we don't,' said Ming. 'If it is indeed a he.' Gods but he wanted to stop and rest. His hand felt as if it were filled with shards of white-hot metal twisting, turning, slicing every tendon and muscle, carving through bone. He did not look at it. He knew by the crescendo of torment that he was in the horrendous third stage. There were times where if he had a sharp enough blade, he could almost have sheared it off himself. Take it, he wanted to scream, take it!

Then it would fade back to the first stage again. It was like an oft-breaking ocean wave crashing him repeatedly onto razor sharp rocks. But some poppy, just a little to alleviate the next hour or so. Enough to get him to the stone and those Others who wished to procure a map that meant nothing.

Absolutely nothing!

Because all of this had been a hunt for fun. They could just have moved the gates. By the stars and Gods above, if he'd known They moved gates often, he would never have drawn it.

But he had made that mistake and Others wanted to make an example of him. Their minds were ever facile.

So be it.

'Lien, I think I must stop for a little. I need to drink some water and the horses need to rest. It's been a steep climb.'

'Of course, Excellence...'

'Don't call me Excellence!' He answered testily and then added more gently, 'Can you not just call me Ming?'

She laughed softly, thank the stars, unoffended with his tone, and he held the sound tight in his memory. 'Ming...' She was almost shy, he was sure.

Ah, they could have got on so well. But he must not think on that. The owl sat watching them from above, looking down its crescent moon beak. Its eyes were tawny, almost molten gold and its feathers, white patterned with palest grey. If he didn't know better, he would say the bird was another embodiment of Heng-O, but it wasn't likely. She was no shapeshifter. He swung his leg over the saddle and slid down. Unmanfully he was sure and was pleased to see Lien had swung down away from him, so she hadn't seen his ungainly dismount and the way he hung onto the stirrup leather for dear life with his good hand.

She approached him with the costrel and the tiny flask of honey-coloured medic that he had grown to love like his closest friend. He took it from her, clasping it as she eased the cork out and then he tipped it up. By the Ancestors, he could have drunk it all, but he must save it. Not long now.

'How much further?' Lien asked as she screwed the top back on. The moon now hung full and benevolent, and the forest was lit as if by day.

'Another half an hour and then we just wait.'

'How far away is dawn?'

I don't know and I don't care, he thought. Preferably hours. 'Not long. Maybe an hour at the most.'

'Oh...' she passed him the costrel uncorked and he took a swig of cold water, feeling the poppy loosening his limbs a little.

As he returned the costrel, he said, 'Try not to be afraid. We can be brave for each other.' But she turned back to the bag that hung from Rufus' saddle and he could not see her face.

Brave for each other? She dashed a tear away. She had nothing to say to him then and so they sat resting on the moonlit moss whilst the owl twisted its head this way, that way, inspecting the surroundings. Of a sudden, it sat immobile, its eyes on a far distance and then she heard it.

A howl, a drawn-out bay to the skies – powerful and strong and which sent claws scraping down the nubs of her spine.

'Did you hear?' she turned to Ming, her hands gripping the reins.

'Yes,' he replied. And then another howl came from closer, and another and another, leaving no doubt that they were encircled. Albeit far off but encircled.

'Gods!' she cried. 'How many?'

'It's the Hunt. They're close.'

Rufus pulled at his reins, sidling around her. Moonstriker too began to dance on the spot, and she grabbed at his reins as the Emperor tried to mount.

'Thank you,' he said as he heaved himself into the saddle with no mounting block and she thought to herself that he was getting ineffably weaker. She jumped astride her chestnut and noted that the owl was swooping silently back and forth and that the moonlight had become pallid. She looked to the skies and heavy cloud had begun to spread across the sky, moonbeams struggling to shine through.

It becomes dark and intimidating, she thought, grasping

at whatever courage she had left. Her jaw set tight as she gritted her teeth. 'How will we find our way? What if we are not there by dawn?' She looked again at the sky where the moon had almost completely vanished. Gods, she was trying so hard to be brave, but she thought she would puke with fear. What will they do to me, she wanted to cry out?

Heng-O, where are you? Are you fighting for us? Please help us!

Ming looked up at the moon. They begin to harass us, he thought. They want us to shake and tremble, to be so filled with fear that we can barely stand upright. More of their hideous games. He had heard tales of the Hunt shrieking down upon an innocent – ghoulish, terrifying and forcing the hunted to run, heedless of danger – over the edge of cliffs, into bogs, falling into deathly traps...

In front of Moonstriker, the owl swooped back and forth and even in the darkling forest, its pale colours flashed through the branches. 'The owl, Lien. See? The owl is our guide. Follow the bird. Don't worry about the moon!'

Where did the owl come from? From whom? Chi Nü perhaps? Or Yue Lao? He pushed his horse in the wake of the bird, Moonstriker skittish, snorting at the baying from around the forest. Next to him, Rufus had gathered himself tight, and it would take little for the horse to spin around and take flight, but Lien did her best to rein him in. She though, was terrified. He could see it in the set of her jaw and her shoulders, and the horse would sense this. 'Deep breaths, Lien,' he said.

I don't want you to faint and fall, he thought. I cannot leave you here alone. Gods but he wished he had left her with Seraphina, cursing his own insecurities that he thought he needed her with him. It had been wrong. He had subjected her to so much already and *still* he hadn't learned his lesson...

'I *am* trying to breathe!' she snapped, and he shifted in his saddle, relieved that she could be angry for in anger there was spine and with spine she could accomplish anything. But anxiety drifted on the air along with the scent of resinous pine and the owl kept flying forward and then returning urgently to scoop them up in its trail. The horses shied and sidled over twigs and branches, aware only of the haunting bay of the wolf pack.

'Perhaps the wolves will kill us first,' she said.

'They are designed to scare, that is all. Remember that – this is merely a game. Everything They do is to heighten our fear, to try and make us flee so They can give chase. If you can see everything from now on as mere artifice and nothing more, then we will be safe. Remember that when all is said and done, They want me alive at the stone, not dead.'

'Good for you,' she answered as Rufus stepped sideways off the path and she cursed. 'But what about me? Do They care whether *I'm* alive or dead at the appointed time?'

'Yes. I believe They care very much.'

'Why? What does it matter?' She kicked Rufus up next to Moonstriker and her knees rubbed against Ming's own. There was that sizzle of nerves along his legs, and he wanted more of it. He hauled the feisty grey to a halt and then reached out and slowed Rufus to a stop. Both horses snatched at their bits, but each rider stroked necks up to polls and back, trying to calm them a little.

'Lien, in as much as I had hoped you would be able to tell Han folk that in the end, their Emperor had done what he could to protect them, I think in a perverse way, Others want you to also tell Their story – about Their power, Their anger if They are crossed. They want all of Eirie to know this story and you will be the teller.'

'Huh,' she snorted. 'I'm no teller of tales.'

'But you can relay the facts to someone who is. Isabella perhaps.'

'The Lady Ibo? Your first betrothed?'

Yes, he thought. The one who indirectly set this whole sorry tale in motion when she made the shifu cloth. 'The same. She is a tale teller. Her stories fire the world.'

'And this story, your story, as filled with sorrow as it will be, will fire Eirie?'

'I think so. A tale of ego, of hubris. It will be like any morality story – a cautionary tale...'

'Excellence...' she turned to him, and even in the darkness he could see her eyes glistening. 'Ming Xao, you may not believe my words after my behaviour, but a cautionary tale is not worth your life. Can we not fight for you?'

Gods, this was why she had so impressed him in the Park of Singing Birds! She had this spirit beneath the surface and was barely aware of it. 'You can never fight Others and win, Lien. I know this now. I have no magick, I have no power. It is what it is. If I can give in with grace and courage, then is not that something to be proud of? Is it not something special to know that in the end, I will have taught Eirie the importance of diffidence, care and humility?'

Lien looked down as she took the reins into her hands again. 'Special yes, but such a waste. I can see now that you would have had so much to give.' She sucked in a shaking breath, and he could hear the tears even if he couldn't see them clearly. 'Such a waste...' she repeated.

Her voice dwindled as a fresh round of wolf cry began and together, they clicked their fractious horses on in the wake of the ever-present owl as it swooped forward and back, a guiding light on a dark and dangerous journey.

A waste, he thought, that I was stupid enough not to listen to a friend who warned me that I played with fire. A waste that I do not get to spend a good life with you.

Such a waste...

Old One had been right. This man beside her *was* a good man. Honest, thinking only of his province, of the whole world of Eirie if she thought on it. How awful it was that she had allowed grief to flip her into madness. That she almost committed the worst sin of all. This man could have been her husband and now she could see that it would have been a good pairing. He was an articulate and compassionate mind that balanced out her spontaneous fervour. She knew in an instant that the Han would have prospered and now it would sink once more into ennui, just as it had when he went missing with the Lady Ibo. Isabella, who had written of the shifu cloth. She would read it. There was learning to be had, but so sad that it would all be too little too late.

Such a waste...

She looked up at the sky. Half of an hour must surely have passed. Perhaps it was her overactive mind, but she would swear that the sky was lighter – but patchworked with heavy black storm cloud and was there not a faint rumble of thunder? Around them a breeze had begun to strengthen, soughing through pine needles. She recalled a scholar named Liu Chi from the Han who said that nothing is better suited to windsong than the pine. That the sound could relieve anxiety and humiliation, wash away confusion and impurity, expand the spirit and lighten the heart, make one feel peaceful and contemplative, cause one to wander free and easy through the skies and travel along with the force of Creation.

Ha, thought Lien – all those qualities of the kind we need at this moment. Here she was, riding through pines to the Gods knew what kind of torture and punishment and she felt no easing of her spirit. By the moment and with each heartbeat, her fears increased until she could hardly breathe. If she felt like this – on the edge of white-hot panic, what did the Emperor feel?

And there was a thing. Try as she might, she could no more think of him as Ming or Ming Xao. She *still* found difficulty seeing him as her betrothed, despite that he freed her from the obligation. No, she could not see him as Ming. He was Excellence. He was the Emperor, her Emperor. No amount of strange feelings as he touched her, of female thoughts when she scanned his broad shoulders and finely cut face would change any of that.

In any case, a tiny treacherous voice whispered, what does it matter? In two hours, maybe three, the Emperor of the Han, Ming Xao, His Most Radiant Excellence, would be no more.

Holy Mother, Cheng Mo, help me. Help us. Feelings emerged from deep in her heart and soul as she thought, *Help* him...

As she took in a shallow breath, Rufus leaped forward almost unseating her and there was a ragged wet growl as she hauled on her reins yelling, 'Steady, Rufus, steady!' But then she heard another snarl and another, not just one but many. She turned and saw amber eyes in the darkness of the trees and screamed as the black-as-hell wolves, a semicircle of them, prowled behind and to the side of her, teeth bared.

The owl swept round her, screeching loud, pushing at the wild pack, giving her time to urge Rufus up hard against Ming and Moonstriker. The pack of wolves bayed and snapped at the owl, but it turned, unafraid, and flew past the semicircle of predators again and each time they stopped, almost cowed, giving Lien and Ming time to ride on to the top of the hill.

Lien's heart almost froze, iced over like the moment on the imperial lake, but she kept on, knee hard against the emperor's, horse pressed against horse as they stepped onto a plateau denuded of trees but with a large stone block sitting on the ground.

'Holy Ancestors!' Lien cried when she saw it. 'No, oh no…'

'Listen to me! They are almost here and we have little time!' Ming fought to get the words out so gritted were his teeth. The wind had picked up and the horses laid back their ears, spinning to turn away from the predatory gusts. The wolves had formed a snapping circle round the edge of the plateau and the smell of spoiled meat and stinking canine breath filled the air. The owl swept round the circle of wolves and screeched long at them, back and forth, until they cowered and whined and then the bird swooped to land on the awful stone.

Every breath, every word hastened him to an end that he could never have imagined when he first picked up a bamboo brush with finely shaped rabbit hair and began to draw the map. 'I release you from your obligations to me, Lien. You are free. Follow your dreams for me. I thank you for having the courage to attend me this far and will plead that you might turn your back on the punishment. I would not have you see. Hush! Say nothing!' His good hand brushed hers as he dismounted, the *nightghast* pain ferocious, the fever burning through every inch of his body. He let his reins drop and Moonstriker swept in a fractious circle, 'Quickly Lien, grab the bag and get off!' He knew instantly that Moonstriker and Rufus were moments away from bolting. Their bulging eyes were white-rimmed. 'Gods! Throw yourself *off*!'

He held tight to the chestnut who tried to rear as Lien pulled the saddlebag free and jumped off. Thunder rattled overhead as dark quilted cloud filled the sky, dawn a mere suggestion of the light it might have thrown across the world. The wind smashed and pummelled and screaming cries could be heard in the distance. Ming let Rufus' reins go and both horses spun away from him as one, galloping toward the wolf circle and leaping, as if the wolves had been a five-barred gate. The wolves snapped but the owl swooped again and they subsided as if hit by a magick force, crouching and whining.

As the horses bolted, it was tantamount to a sign. Everything was final, no escape. 'Quickly. The poppy...'

She pulled at the strap of the saddlebag and ripped the medic out. Without asking, she unscrewed the lid, passed it over and they locked eyes.

She knew. She knew that he wanted to be drugged to the point of least resistance. 'Don't judge me,' he said and upended the bottle, sucking it all away, feeling the power of the poppy strike his muscles almost instantly.

'I don't judge you at all. I applaud you.'

'Applaud?'

'To have the courage to admit your mistake, to readily present yourself for the punishment and to drink the poppy to escape the pain. Withstanding pain is not the measure of a man. Having the courage to fight for mortal freedoms, to admit you are at fault despite that it is clearly centuries of *Their* behaviour that caused this – *that* is the measure of a man.'

His knees buckled slightly, and she came under his shoulder. 'Lean on me, Excellence. I shall be your support.'

'My support?' His mind was slowing, but he could still think clearly enough to answer her. 'My strength, I think...'

The owl screeched loudly from the stone, the sound presaging a whooping call as one after another of the foul Hunt alighted on the plateau, manifesting from the skies. Chimei, cruel God of the Mountains, Huapigui – murderous shapeshifter and Vetala from the Raj, desperate for blood. All three were clad in sumptuous silks, with curved scimitars by their sides. Swathed in white furs, lithe and beautiful Kitsune, the Fox Lady, stood apart from the Others, a haunting glint in her eyes. There were lesser Immortals whose faces shone with lust for what was to come and who jeered at Ming and Lien.

Ming Xao held his head high, even though he wanted to subside to the ground and dissolve into the mosses. Behind him, there was a vague noise, a murmur that grew on the wind. The Hunt hissed as Chi Nü, Goddess of Weaving, and her partner Nicholas, whom they called the Halftime Mortal arrived. There was Yue Lao, God of Fate, leaning on his ancient staff with his white beard waving in the wind. Maeve Swan Maid, clad in her sumptuous cloak of black feathers, and the three siofra – Iolanthe, Flavia and Amaranthe.

Gallivant stood holding the collar of Maximilian who slavered and growled at the wolves. Gallivant's mouth set in a grim line as he met Ming Xao's eyes and Ming was sad that they had been so often ill-met.

But he uttered a small laugh when he saw who stood in front of the stone, leading those who had been so kind to he and Lien.

Clad in an oyster grey gown over which flowed a white feathered cloak, was Seraphina.

His heart filled with warmth, or perhaps it was the poppy. He ignored those who were his bane and with Lien's arm supporting him around the waist, he walked toward the Healer from Trevallyn. 'You are a shapeshifter…'

'Yes.'

'I did not know.'

'Neither did I until I became so filled with ire on your behalf that the change to a white owl just happened.'

'Enough!' Chimei roared and Lien jumped. The God's robes reminded her of the time she had walked along the palace corridors with Sun Sen, First Minister, and so many dragons had been crafted around the pillars. Chimei wore a blood red coat, embroidered with one gold and black dragon writhing front to back. The coat was slit at the sides to reveal a black silk undertunic, his slippers were as red as gore, and he wore his black hair loose so that it swirled in the wind. His eyes were as cold as his robe was hotly red and he pinioned both Ming Xao and Lien with his glare. His long-nailed hand clasped and released his sword hilt and Lien's bowels twisted as the God spoke.

'Paltry Emperor of the Han,' He jeered. 'It is said that the map cannot be separated from your hand and that therefore *you* must be separated from your hand. Show me!' He towered over Ming Xao as Ming pulled the map from the depths of his pocket and held it out flat. Chimei grabbed at it but it stuck to Ming Xao's palm as if it grew from him. The God roared, pushing Ming by the shoulder to his knees so that he almost kowtowed, his head hanging. Gods, he has had too much poppy, thought Lien. *Nothing* seems to matter to him at all!

'We would chop off the map and be done!' Chimei's voice dripped menace and Lien felt sick. The crowd of dark Immortals surrounding him hissed, stamped their feet and hammered haft upon haft.

Lien swept the plateau until her glance settled on the white beauty of Kitsune. The Goddess raised her eyebrow at Lien and Lien wondered what the insouciant look meant. She expected her pricked finger to pain her and yet there was nothing – as if the realm of Trevallyn had its own way of protecting the innocent. She neither smiled nor frowned at the Fox Lady, trying to maintain a mask of inscrutability whilst everything inside her wanted to scream and run.

Huapigui shapeshifted into a dragon and with the speed of light, slid toward Ming Xao and Lien, its stiletto-sharp teeth glittering, but Maximilian, magnificently wild, leaped in front of the pair and crouched, his teeth bared, slaver slick and dripping upon the ground, his snarl enough to halt Huapigui in her tracks. In a breath, she shapeshifted to a snake and slithered around the pair but Max roared and grabbed the snake behind the head, shaking it and throwing it through the air, until it lay at Chimei's feet, shifting back to the evil goddess that she was. She stood, wicked and beautiful, her chest heaving, snarling in fury.

Lien held her breath, her hand daring to creep to Max's head in a gesture of thanks. In truth, she wanted to hold onto him for dear life but he crouched again, another rumble deep in his throat as Chimei shouted at the surrounding Immortals.

'The time has come. Ming Xao, so-called Emperor of the Han, has transgressed against the Other world enough. He must be punished so that his sin is never repeated.' He signalled to his minions, 'Take him to the stone!'

Ming was pulled roughly away from Lien's side but his knees buckled and she quickly moved with him. 'The Emperor is ill. I will support him,' she said, conscious that her voice lacked courage and conviction.

Chimei surveyed the pair. 'Ah... the little betrothed who ran after the Emperor.' He was close enough now to put one of his long twisting fingernails under her chin to lift her head so that she had to look up into his pitch-black eyes. Gods, the cruelty she recognized within seemed boundless, a bottomless pit of barbarism.

'Lien of the First House of Silk,' He said, his voice dripping life-stealing acid onto her skin. 'We have no care for you and would be happy to put you to the sword today, but one or two have argued your case. You will be our messenger. Truss him!' He ordered the two gargoyles who held Ming Xao. 'Tie he and his hand to the stone!'

Fire and acid filled Lien as Ming was tied like a goat for slaughter. 'I will *not* be anyone's messenger!' She stood tall, feeling her blood roar around her veins as she shouted at the God, her face hot. 'Unless it is to tell how Your gates are oft moved and that Your lives are nothing but childish fantasies of chase, hunt, and kill. I will say to all that You are self-serving and care nothing for this world and that You are a scourge that Eirie could do without!'

Chimei weighed her words and then he burst out laughing, his peers sneering and hollering along with him.

'Well yes', He grinned, his startling white teeth splitting his face into a rictus of evil. 'We care nothing for *any* mortal. It is well known. You are prey – it's what we live to do. Hunt and in time, destroy.'

Lien vaguely heard a whisper behind – she thought it was Gallivant. 'Speak for yourself, you whoreson.' It was enough to give her strength.

'Be warned, Chimei!' she said. 'For when anyone discovers one of Your gates, its location will be spread far and wide. Every time you move it, so be it, but the next and the next will be found, and knowledge will be imparted.'

'You seek to warn *me*?' Chimei shouted at her, spittle hitting her cheek as He drew himself up to His impressive height. 'Then let *your* hand be tied with your betrothed's! Make what you want of *that* loss.' He snapped his fingers. 'Take her!'

She was grabbed roughly and her arms twisted by a gargoyle, pulled to the stone and kneed in the back of her legs so that she collapsed to kneel. When looked at Ming Xao, she knew the poppy had him so much in its embrace that he was barely cogniscent of her presence next to him. His arm was grabbed and tied to the stone, red thread gleaming, the awful hand holding the map canister.

As They had done to the Emperor, so They tied her feet together and tethered her to iron posts set by the sides of the stone. On the rock itself, there was one iron ring to which they had lashed Ming's arm and now they knotted her right arm to the same ring.

She had never felt such raging anger, wishing she could explode with wrath but suddenly she couldn't breathe and her heart stopped, breath choking. She tried to twist around, to find Seraphina, but one of Chimei's acolytes hit her in the temple and she stilled, head hanging, ears ringing, longing for anyone at all to intercede.

CHAPTER
TWENTY TWO
Ming and Lien

Ming Xao's eyes were closed and he felt nothing but softness
– a dandelion soft heartbeat, the blood drifting delicately
around his body, thoughts floating like feathers through his
mind but so gently that he couldn't grasp them. Nor did he
try. He felt as loose as a newborn babe. In one brief moment,
a feather-thought landed, and he wondered if he were dead
already and being reborn into a new infant body.

But then there was a curious sensation, so alien to the
pain that had been his constant, cruel and capricious enemy
for days now, and he endeavoured to open his eyes. Another
hand had slid over his – a delicate hand with elegant fingers
and a red thread tied around the wrist. Those fingers locked
into his and he opened his eyes wider and saw Lien on the
other side of the rock, trussed like a bird and a cold wave
of anxiety washed some of the poppy aside. Lien's hand
squeezed his and what should have hurt did not – a sensation of softness, of intimate caring. He met her gaze and she
smiled – tremulously to be sure, but a smile nevertheless.

'Ming Xao,' she said, voice low and shaking. 'We are to be
punished together. There will be no tale-telling from me. We
must rely on the birds, on our friends who stand behind us.'

He could barely think of a word to say and turned his
head as far as he was able and there were the Others who

had guided and helped. The poppy began to leave his veins like a fast-ebbing tide and he was glad. *So be it, I will be strong for her as she is for me. She* is *courage.*

There was a concerted intake of breath from everyone on the plateau – kind and cruel alike as Vetala, lover of blood, approached. The storm clouds had thinned to a pewter sky and a pallid light glinted on a massive axe blade.

Lien whimpered but Ming whispered to her, 'Have faith, we will be brave for each other. It will be over quickly.'

But he did not tell her that the pain after, as severed nerve endings shrieked and blood gushed, would be so shattering that her heart, that stalwart young heart, might stop with shock and that she would die. That they would become corpses to be burned and their story so much dust...

No! He shook the feathers and dandelions from his head and lifted it to stare at the axeman.

Vetala stood at the stone, laid the blade just above their joined wrists, measuring his line, then lifted the fearsome weapon. Its shadow fell on Lien's face as the pallid sun rose higher, kites and eagles screaming in the skies and a clamour of baying came from the wolves who encircled the plateau.

Ming sucked in a breath and shouted, 'You, Vetala, and You, Chimei, are making the most profound mistake! You may think to frighten mortals with Your actions, but by killing us, You are creating martyrs, and martyrs have almost immortal strength. With our death, mortals across Eirie will rise against You!'

Chimei laughed. 'We have magick,' he called to the crowd. 'All of us! What do you have? You will never win against the likes of Us.'

But a well-spoken woman's voice broke across the guffaws and howls. 'The likes of *some* of You, Chimei. There are Others who live in peace, who help rather than horrify.'

Vetala lowered the prodigious weight of his axe by his side and turned to Chimei, who sneered at the woman. 'The lovely Seraphina, newfound Other. And yet You could not save these pathetic mortals, could You? And You think that Your little band will be enough to protect the world against Us?' He chuckled, and then roared with sharp laughter that cut the air like a dagger through skin.

'My little band, as You so patronisingly put it, is the tip of a very big iceberg, my friend. Do you know of icebergs?' It was her turn to laugh. 'Oh but of course! What would *You* know of the ice wastes of Oighear Dubh?'

In that moment, Ming thought that Seraphina was legendary, and he cast a quick look at Lien, who still trembled and whose eyes were wide.

Chimei's face flushed, his eyes blackening like an ink stain. 'Enough, woman! Vetala! Do it!'

Vetala raised the axe swiftly and brought it swishing down toward Ming's and Lien's hands and Lien screamed. But Ming returned her grip, shouting, 'Keep looking at me, Lien. Me! Only me!'

The axe sped down from its high point and Vetala let out a loud roar with the anticipated force of the blow.

But the blade hit something just above Ming's and Lien's wrists and there was an horrendous ringing sound, Vetala yelling as the axe rebounded. He let the haft go and jumped back as it bounced end over end to lie on the ground in front of Chimei.

'Lien, look!' Ming whispered.

The red thread on their individual wrists was unbinding, re-joining and re-knotting, tying them together.

Chimei picked up the axe, hefted it high and advanced on the two, his ghastly robe and black hair flying in a welkin wind. But again, the blade jumped and the agony of the crash against the unseen barrier saw the haft dropped, the axe again bouncing away.

'It is no good, Chimei,' Seraphina said. 'Your power and strength cannot win against the power of a Fate as strong as this. Tell Him, Yue Lao.'

The old man hobbled forward, leaning on his carved staff. His gait and long white hair were signs of venerable age. The oatmeal-coloured robe and crook, the signs of a revered wiseman. 'It is true, Chimei. This time, You threaten two innocents who are protected by the Great Mother, Cheng Mo. And even *You* should know that Her power transcends us all.'

Chimei looked around. 'So where *is* She? That was a mere magick barrier, that is all. We can untie the two, cast Our own spells and in moments the job will be done.'

'I think not,' said Yue Lao. 'You see the knotted red thread? That came from the Great Mother herself. Both Lady Lien and Emperor Ming Xao were a predestined partnership, ordained by the most Holy Cheng Mo and when such a thing is decided by Her, not You nor I nor Seraphina nor anyone can change that. She is the final arbiter of Fate, Chimei. Is it not better that You untie the mortals and allow them to live whatever life Fate has in store? Would You really dispute the Great Mother's wishes?'

Chimei stood, pride and arrogance warring with Yue Lao's words. His face was puce with anger, his eyes mere slits as He snarled. He bent to pick up the axe again, standing tall and lifting it over Ming's and Lien's red bound wrists.

In that moment, the dark grey skies released a crack of thunder that rocked every tree and stone in Trevallyn and a bolt of yellow lightning burst from the heavens, hitting the axe blade.

It blasted into myriad splinters of iron and timber. Chimei screamed an unholy cry that sent His Immortal band stepping many paces back from the site of desecration. He lit up like a burning tree – flames of red and black rising high, his body a roaring silhouette. And then it began to curl on itself like a dried, dessicated leaf and quickly, thank the Gods, the Immortal was but grey ash on top of hot coals.

Ming's and Lien's hands clasped, the map in its canister

held between their palms as Yue Lao touched the binding ropes with the tip of His staff. They unwound – first their arms, their feet, and then Seraphina bent to help each to stand.

'The map, Ming Xao!' the Ancient God urged. 'Throw the canister into the coals! You *must* do it.'

Ming uncurled his palm and tied by the red thread to Lien of the First House of Silk, together they dropped the canister into the coals.

The fire exploded into life again, the canister melting, the map unfurling, and for one brief moment, the whole of Eirie glowed, images there and gone, and then, like Chimei, the parchment curled on itself, burning to dust. As a welkin wind began to blow the detritus toward the forest of pines, still their hands remained yoked by the red thread. But, thought Ming, they were yoked by more than that and he turned an unsmiling but calm face to the woman who had once been his betrothed.

Lien doubted she would ever forget what had seared itself in her mind. How it began, the awful conflagration, the hissing sound of the Immortals as they turned their backs on the flaming carcass that was Chimei. The story of the way he had met his bane would be a legend for the telling, of that there was no doubt.

But what of their own story?

The red thread had slowly untied, witnessed by those kind Others who were their friends. It unwound with no sound from anyone, no welkin wind. Only the birds in the pines – swallows, nuthatches, jays, sparrows – all trilling their melodies. A song, thought Lien, that would spread across Eirie and soon be sung to the linnets in the Park of the Singing Birds in the Han.

Ming's hand was a normal colour, his touch warm and

she welcomed it as he held tight to her, bending to pick up the red thread. 'I will keep this forever, Lien. As a reminder of your courage.'

She wished she could smile but she was empty of feeling and words. It was as though fear and then relief had wiped her mind clean and she had to learn again how to enunciate joy.

'It will come,' Seraphina said from behind them both. 'Give yourself time, Lien. This has been a shock. Gallivant, why don't you and Max take the lady to her horse and ride with her back to the house. I would walk with Ming for a little.'

Lien looked around. The plateau was empty of threat, the only folk left those she trusted. She took Gallivant's arm when he offered it, and Maximilian shoved his massive head under her hand. She smiled at that, relieved that some warmth was re-entering her heart. As she and the hob walked toward the pines where she could see Rufus standing with Moonstriker, she looked back.

The stone was gone, the grasses velvet soft and thick with mosses. But she would swear that in that encroaching clump of pines on the other side, she saw a flash of white and heard a small yip.

Max nudged her and in a moment she walked on.

Ming watched her go and it felt as if an invisible tether between she and he was stretched tight.

'It will not break, you know,' Seraphina stood beside him, the owl feathers of her cloak ruffling in the welkin wind. 'Yue Lao's red thread made sure of it.'

He shoved his hands into his pockets, the wind nibbling at his coat and lifting Seraphina's hair. Her smile was open and her eyes crinkled at the edges. She was older than he thought, he hadn't noticed before. Perhaps it was the way with great folk, that age was inexorably bound with wisdom.

'Not always…' she said.

He laughed. 'I'll never get used to my mind being an open book. I *must* learn to control my thoughts!' He rubbed at his wrist. 'Was it the red thread that halted the blade?' In his mind's eye, he saw the glinting edge of the axe blade dropping again, remorseless in its hideous progress.

'No. Something far greater, I think. Show me your hand.' He lifted his hand and Seraphina studied the normality of it, rolling it over, testing the fingers and then lifting an eyebrow. 'Like I say, something far greater. How do you feel?'

'Grateful. Filled with gratitude to *You*, to all those Others who choose to be kind to we mortals. But more than anything, and with respect to You, gratitude that is immeasurable to the Great Mother.'

'As it should be. She whom you call Cheng Mo and whom we call Aine and who protects us all, even we Others, when we need succour.'

They walked on down the hill. The skies were melting to a clear blue, unsullied by cloud, and as they entered the pine forest, the trill of the forest birds surrounded them. Further on, Ming could hear the chatter of his companions of the last few weeks. Even the dulcet swan maid to whom he owed much. And then in a clearing, stood a posse of horses and a cart and the little siofra were climbing aboard whilst Gallivant mounted a fat bay pony and Lien upon Rufus. Moonstriker stood square while Ming mounted, and Seraphina slid onto a perfectly white gelding with an arching poll and high-held tail. Of Chi Nü, Nico and Yue Lao there was no sign and he suspected they had melted into the ether and were even now, hastening back to the Heavens of the Han.

Maeve Swan Maid turned her long black elegance to Ming. 'Thou hast bested the worst, Ming Xao of the Han. Maeve doubts she will meet thee again and thanks thee for such an … interesting spectacle. Life can become humdrum, as Maeve is sure Ming Xao knows.' Ming was surprised at her faint levity, she who was always so severe, and he nodded.

'Indeed, Maeve Swan Maid, and I thank you for assisting us as you did…'

But before he had finished speaking, she had eased her black feathered cloak more firmly onto her shoulder and transformed into the beautiful black bird that she was. Her wings spread wide, shimmering with opalescent greens and blues as she shook them, and then with an echoing swan cry, she took a few steps on bright red webbed feet, the great wings spread wide and she launched into the skies, rising above the trees and flying away.

'Go safe and go well, Maeve.' Ming watched until she was a spot in the distance and then turned Moonstriker after the others, walking slowly, lost in introspection.

'Too much time in one's head is not a healthy thing, Ming Xao.' Seraphina had ridden back to him. 'I am thinking that you and Lien need to find your feet again. Perhaps a sennight at my house, just existing, letting the wounds of the last weeks lessen and pale. And then? Well, then it will be time to return to your home and to take up the reins of your position. Only this time with your bride.'

'We are no longer betrothed, Seraphina. I freed her.' He could see Lien's black-clad back far ahead as she and Gallivant rode together, with the cart and Max rumbling alongside.

'Ha,' Seraphina laughed. 'It means nothing. Did I not say that Yue Lao's thread means everything? You must learn to trust Others again.' She gathered up her reins. 'Trust, Ming, is everything.'

Her white stallion flicked its banner of a tail, danced on its toes and cantered away.

'As is Fate,' whispered Ming sitting down in the saddle and urging Moonstriker into a gallop after her.

THE EPILOGUE

Lien sat close to Old One, holding her parchment dry hand and relishing the love and attention that the old woman paid her. Her parents had been less welcoming despite the tale that had begun to spread across the Han. They admonished her for her disappearance on her wedding day and it seemed they cared only that their connection with the imperial house remained unaffected.

The news of Ming's and Lien's journey had reached the Han swiftly but then so it had been foretold so perhaps she should not be surprised. Old One cared not for gossip, just that Lien was safe and that her fear of the Emperor was assuaged.

'You see, he is a good man, little flower,' Old One's voice quavered and Lien worried that every day that passed meant Old One moved closer to the Heavenly fields of the Ancestors.

'He is, Grandmother and I have respect for him…'

'Will your respect grow to love?' Old One asked with a smile in her voice.

'That,' Lien said, as she tapped her grandmother's hand, 'is in the laps of the Gods.'

Many a true word she thought, as other thoughts of Fate and a red thread sped through her mind.

She looked up at Old One from where she sat at the woman's feet and could see that she slept, her chin dropped onto her grey silk robe, gentle snores puffing in and out in a sweet rhythm. Lien laid the lined hand on the grey covered lap and stood quietly, before heading along the path to the Small Garden, her favourite place in the First House of Silk compound. The elm was filled with small birdcages and linnets sang as she subsided on the bench by the carp pool. There was only one thing missing – the calm quiet presence of Heng. There was an emptiness in her life now that she doubted would ever be filled.

The carp pool lay so still – occasionally a flash of gold or vermilion, but then it would settle again into reflective calm and it soothed her mood. Her image looked back at her.

Her black hair was pulled into a neat tail and her robes, celadon green with watermelon peonies embroidered over the surface, folded around her feet as she sat. She could even see her sash embroidered with her life story – ah, so much more to stitch there, she thought. A whole tale…

'So much to stitch indeed,' said a voice that sent ice rattling down her spine.

She did not turn. She wouldn't give this spirit the satisfaction.

So instead, Kitsune sat on the bench beside her – white silk and furs rubbing against Lien so that Lien shrank further to the side of the seat.

'You are returned safely,' the Fox Lady said.

'No thanks to those such as You,' Lien snapped. Perhaps she should have had a care but there was a light in her now that would not be dimmed.

'Lien, I will speak in My defence. You should know that I tried to protect you.'

'Ha!' Lien growled. 'Hurt me. Gave me pain!' She held up her finger which had a white scar upon it. 'Remember this? Was that supposed to have bound me to you so that I did your bidding? What a failure! As soon as I left the Han it healed, and you could do nothing to me!'

Kitsune reached for Lien's hand, but Lien jerked it out of the way. 'You weren't meant to leave the Han,' the spirit said. 'I had hoped that you would have found the map and given it to me, that I could pass it to Chimei and that you would be safe.'

Lien sprang up. 'Lies, Kitsune. Chimei was intent on Ming Xao's death. Terrible events proved that. Whether You had passed the map over or not, the Emperor's fate was sealed. I was to be collateral damage. Gods! No wonder Ming Xao did what he did.'

Kitsune stood too, face to face with Lien, angry lines pulling at her beautiful visage. Lien realised that she felt nothing, no fear at all of this spirit, just a righteous zeal and she realised that such righteousness had been what led the Emperor to his flight in the first place and so she tempered her manner.

'Kitsune, it is all over. The map is destroyed, Others are at liberty to reposition gates to their world anywhere they like whenever they like. The story of the Emperor's trials will be told, and all will learn that they must fear Others just as before. Whilst the Emperor and I may have changed, nothing much else does. Now, if you don't mind, I would that you left this garden and allowed me just a small moment of peace to offer thanks to the Great Mother for returning me to my home.'

Kitsune seemed to shrink at Lien's lack of fear, but she pulled her furs around and answered back. 'I am not lying. I did wish to protect you. Perhaps Chi Nü will vouchsafe me, and you will see. I am sorry that you have been through so much, sorrier still that you lost your beloved Heng. But We in the Other world gained the steady and calm Heng-O and We can only benefit. I hope in time, you will learn that I can be as good a friend to you as to the Lady Ibo. Fare you well, Empress-to-be. Perhaps anon?'

She faded then, until there was nothing but a welkin

wind in the branches, the carp pool rippling and then settling, and the linnets beginning to sing again.

Lien offered a prayer to Cheng Mo and then realised she
had no gift for the Great Mother and hearing the linnets and
thinking back to her betrothed of so long ago, she went from
one bamboo cage to another, letting each linnet fly free, carrying tales in their song that would spread far and wide.

'Excellence,' First Minister bowed before Ming Xao as the
Emperor sat on the little pavilion overlooking the lake.
He knew it was from here that Lien had begun her voyage
into the unknown and once again, he was in awe that she
intended to take up her place by his side.

'It is good to have you back,' said Sun Sen. 'Everything
begins to return to its routine and the people are content. I
think the Han was concerned that the country would sink
into isolation again with your absence. There are people who
remember when you went missing with the Lady Ibo and to
see you vanish again with another betrothed, they began to
see it as a blight upon our province.'

'Sun Sen,' Ming indicated that his First Minister sit. 'I'm
sorry you have had to carry such weights on your shoulders.'

'Excellence, it is my job and my honour. I have heard
much...'

'Did you believe what you heard?'

'I didn't, Excellence, in truth. It sounded like some sort
of Tale of the Unexpected. Until this arrived.' He held up a
linen-wrapped package and passed it to Ming who carefully
unfolded the creamy linen to reveal a book written in the
Trevallyn language.

'You can read this?'

'I cannot. But I had one of our traders read it to me
yesternight. It took all night, and I am exhausted on your
behalf.'

Ming turned the book to the spine and noted the title embossed in gold, *The Red Thread*, and the author's name. Isabella! Teller of tales. 'Do you know who wrote this?'

'Yes, the Lady Ibo. Did you see her in your travels with Lady Lien?'

'No, but I left notes for her of what occurred. I was informed that she is a writer. I'm astonished that this has arrived so swiftly.'

'True, Excellence, but then from what you say there are Others who may have helped.' Sun Sen looked at the book and then smiled. 'Perhaps with special ink or magick? Who knows?'

'Indeed, who knows?' He laid the book down carefully. 'Tell me, the villagers in Sie…'

'Ah. I sent guards to see what should be done and they found nothing wrong at all. No plague, no burnings. Just a peaceful little village high in the mountains that had no idea it was purportedly caught in some Other lie.'

'Artifice…'

'Eh?' said First Minister, straightening his newly acquired spectacles.

'Artifice. It is a game that Others play to frighten and deceive. We're lambs to the slaughter.'

'I do not necessarily approve of your words, Excellence.'

'No. Of course not. Suffice to say that this book, as you saw for yourself, allows us to put hope in the Great Mother and to believe that there are Others in our lives who would move Heaven and Earth to be our friends.'

'It is a good message, Excellence.'

'It is…'

At that moment, a flock of free-wheeling linnets flew over their heads, singing their heavenly song and Ming looked up, remembering back to a moment in time.

He remembered the beautiful Lady Lien – young, innocent, spontaneous and how she had attracted him like a bee to honey. Things hadn't changed – he was still charmed by her but knew that like those linnets above his head, she must be given freedom to fly. In such freedom, he knew she would be by his side when he needed her.

'Sun Sen, I would make a new law, I think. People are still at liberty to have linnets in cages for there is no doubt that the birdsong in the trees of the Park of Singing Birds is a wonderful thing. However, it will be law now to always have the doors of the cages open so that the birds may come and go. If I have learned one thing, it is that freedom is not just a gift but a right.'

'Excellence, the bird owners may not much like it…'

'Then, on the day we are wed, Lady Lien and I will take our linnets to the Park, and let the populace see that the birds *will* come back. Upon my word they will reward such love and care from their owners. You will see…'

Sun Sen left to draw up the necessary papers and Ming Xao bent forward to pick up the book. He opened it to the first page:

"She weds him tonight,' said Chimei of the Han, 'She will be in the palace and will be able to find the map.'

Kitsune looked the God over – a man with cruel eyes and a swagger when he walked. 'Or else?' she asked, knowing full well that this time, it was no idle thing the Spirits toyed with …"

Fin.

AUTHOR'S
ACKNOWLEDGEMENTS

To John Hudpsith who has been my editor for all of my writing life. He is my coach, cutting and honing my words until he feels they have the polish necessary for a market of demanding readers.

To Jane Dixon Smith for not just formatting for both print and e-book, but most particularly for designing the cover of the book. Knowing I hoped that this latest novel could take its place in the series called *The Chronicles of Eirie*, she cleverly linked it back to the original four books from nearly ten years ago and which were designed by Floating Studio. I'm so immensely grateful to her as she's captured the absolute essence of the story.

To my online friends and followers whose kind words and support I value so much. You really are the best people!

To friends who have been immensely patient when I've gone MIA.

To my family for always keeping me grounded.

To my Terrier for being demanding…

And finally, to my beloved husband who is always there and without whom I would be so much the lesser person.